For Heather Osborn,

Malachi Wolfe's biggest fan.

the Indigo Spell

A *Bloodlines* NOVEL

RICHELLE MEAD

PENGUIN BOOKS

PENGUIN BOOKS

Published by the Penguin Group
Penguin Books Ltd, 80 Strand, London WC2R ORL, England
Penguin Group (USA) Inc., 375 Hudson Street, New York, New York 10014, USA
Penguin Group (Canada), 90 Eglinton Avenue East, Suite 700, Toronto,
Ontario, Canada M4P 2Y3 (a division of Pearson Penguin Canada Inc.)
Penguin Ireland, 25 St Stephen's Green, Dublin 2, Ireland (a division of Penguin Books Ltd)
Penguin Group (Australia), 707 Collins Street, Melbourne, Victoria 3008, Australia
(a division of Pearson Australia Group Pty Ltd)
Penguin Books India Pvt Ltd, 11 Community Centre, Panchsheel Park,
New Delhi – 110 017, India
Penguin Group (NZ), 67 Apollo Drive, Rosedale, Auckland 0632, New Zealand
(a division of Pearson New Zealand Ltd)
Penguin Books (South Africa) (Pty) Ltd, Block D, Rosebank Office Park, 181 Jan Smuts
Avenue, Parktown North, Gauteng 2193, South Africa

Penguin Books Ltd, Registered Offices: 80 Strand, London WC2R ORL, England

penguin.com

First published in the USA in Razorbill, a division of Penguin Group (USA) Inc., 2013
Published simultaneously in Great Britain in Razorbill,
an imprint of Penguin Books Ltd, 2013

001

Set in Fairfield LH Medium
Printed in Great Britain by Clays Ltd, St Ives plc

British Library Cataloguing in Publication Data
A CIP catalogue record for this book is available from the British Library

ISBN 978-0-141-33716-6

www.greenpenguin.co.uk

MIX
Paper from
responsible sources
FSC C018179

Penguin Books is committed to a sustainable
future for our business, our readers and our planet.
This book is made from Forest Stewardship
Council™ certified paper.

ALWAYS LEARNING   **PEARSON**

CHAPTER 1

THIS WASN'T THE FIRST TIME I'd been pulled out of bed for a crucial mission. It was, however, the first time I'd been subjected to such a personal line of questioning.

"Are you a virgin?"

"Huh?" I rubbed my sleepy eyes, just in case this was all some sort of bizarre dream that would disappear. An urgent phone call had dragged me out of bed five minutes ago, and I was having a little trouble adjusting.

My history teacher, Ms. Terwilliger, leaned closer and repeated the question in a stage whisper: "I said, are you a virgin?"

"Um, yes. . ."

I was fully awake now and glanced uneasily around my dorm's lobby, making sure no one was around to witness this crazy exchange. I didn't have to worry. Aside from a bored-looking desk attendant on the far side of the room, the lobby was empty, probably because no sane person would be up at

1

this time of night. When Ms. Terwilliger's call had woken me, she'd demanded I meet her here for a "life-or-death" matter. Getting interrogated about my personal life wasn't quite what I'd expected.

She stepped back and sighed in relief. "Yes, of course. Of course you're a virgin."

I narrowed my eyes, unsure if I should be offended or not. "Of course? What's that supposed to mean? What's going on?"

She immediately snapped back to attention and pushed her wire-rimmed glasses up the bridge of her nose. They were always slipping down. "No time to explain. We have to go." She grabbed hold of my arm, but I resisted and stayed where I was.

"Ma'am, it's three in the morning!" And then, just so she'd understand the severity of the situation: "On a school night."

"Never mind that." She turned in the direction of the desk attendant and called across the room, "I'm taking Sydney Melrose with me. Mrs. Weathers can argue with me about the curfew tomorrow."

The attendant looked startled, but she was just some college student who'd been hired to sit there overnight. She was no match for the formidable Ms. Terwilliger, with her tall, gangly stature and birdlike face. The real authority keeping girls in my dorm was the security guard outside, but he simply nodded in a friendly way when Ms. Terwilliger dragged me past. It made me wonder just how many girls she'd abducted in the middle of the night.

"I'm in my pajamas," I told her. It was the last protest I could offer as we reached her car, which was parked in a fire lane. She drove a red Volkswagen Beetle with flowers painted on the sides. Somehow, this didn't surprise me in the least.

"You'll be fine," she said, fishing car keys out of her massive velvet purse.

Around us, the desert night was cool and silent. Tall palm trees created dark, spiderlike shapes against the sky. Beyond them, a full moon and smattering of stars glittered. I wrapped my arms around myself, touching the soft fabric of my microfleece robe. Underneath it, I had on full-length striped pajamas paired with fluffy beige slippers. The ensemble worked well in my cozy dorm room but wasn't exactly practical for a Palm Springs night. But then, going out in pajamas wasn't really practical in any place.

She unlocked the car, and I stepped gingerly inside, having to dodge empty paper coffee cups and old issues of *Utne Reader*. My neat sensibilities cringed at that kind of mess, but it was the least of my worries right now.

"Ms. Terwilliger," I said, once we were driving through the suburban streets. "What's going on?" Now that we were out of the dorm, I hoped she'd start talking sense. I hadn't forgotten her "life-or-death" comment and was beginning to grow nervous.

Her eyes were on the road ahead of us, and lines of worry marked her angular face. "I need you to cast a spell."

I froze as I tried to process her words. Not long ago, this proclamation would've sent me into protests and fits of revulsion. Not that I was comfortable with it now. Magic still freaked me out. Ms. Terwilliger taught at my private high school, Amberwood Prep, by day and was a witch at night. She said I, too, possessed a natural affinity for magic and had managed to teach me some spells, despite my best efforts to resist. I actually had a few good reasons for wanting to avoid anything arcane.

Aside from inborn beliefs about magic being wrong, I simply didn't want to get caught up in any more supernatural affairs than I had to. I already spent my days as part of a secret society that kept vampires secret from the human world. That and my schoolwork were enough to keep anyone busy.

Nonetheless, her magical training had gotten me out of some dangerous situations recently, and I was no longer so quick to dismiss it. So, her suggesting I perform magic wasn't the weirdest thing going on here.

"Why would you need me for that?" I asked. There were few cars out, but occasionally, passing headlights would cast a ghostly light over us. "You're a million times more powerful. I can't cast a fraction of the things you can."

"Power is one thing," she admitted. "But there are other limitations and factors at work here. I can't cast this particular spell."

I crossed my arms and slouched back in the seat. If I kept focusing on the practical aspects, I could ignore how worried I was growing. "And it couldn't have waited until morning?"

"No," she said gravely. "It could not."

Something about the tone of her voice sent chills down my spine, and I fell silent as we continued our drive. We were headed outside of the city and suburbs, into the wilds of the true desert. The farther we drove from civilization, the darker it became. Once we were off the freeway, there were no street-lights or houses in sight. Spiky desert shrubs created dark shapes along the side of the road that put me in mind of crouching animals, ready to pounce. *There's no one out here*, I thought. *And no one back at Amberwood knows you're here either.*

I shifted uneasily as I recalled her virgin question. Was I

going to be a sacrifice in some unholy ritual? I wished that I'd thought to bring my cell phone—not that I could have told my organization, the Alchemists, that I was spending so much time with a magic user. And not just any magic user—one who was teaching *me* to become one too. Better to risk being sacrificed than face the Alchemists' wrath.

Twenty minutes later, Ms. Terwilliger finally pulled to a stop along the side of a dusty one-lane road that seemed to be a direct route to nowhere. She got out of the car and motioned for me to do the same. It was colder here than it had been back at Amberwood. Looking up into the night sky, I caught my breath. Free of the city lights, the stars were now out in full force. I could see the Milky Way and a dozen constellations usually hidden to the naked eye.

"Stargaze later," she said curtly. "We need to hurry, before the moon progresses much further."

A moonlight ritual, a barren desert, virgin sacrifice . . . what had I just foolishly walked into? The way Ms. Terwilliger pushed me into magic always annoyed me, but I never thought she posed a threat. Now I berated myself for being so naive.

She tossed a duffel bag over one shoulder and headed off into a desolate stretch of land, dotted with rocks and scraggly vegetation. Even with the brilliant celestial display there wasn't much light out here, yet she walked purposefully, as though she knew exactly where she was going. I dutifully followed, wincing as I crossed the rocky ground. My fuzzy slippers had never been intended for this sort of terrain.

"Here," she said when we reached a small clearing. She carefully set down the duffel bag and knelt to rifle through it. "This'll do."

The desert that was so mercilessly hot in the day became cold at night, but I was still sweating. Probably my own anxiety had more to do with that than the temperature or heavy pajamas. I retied my robe more tightly, making a perfect knot. I found that kind of detail and routine soothing.

Ms. Terwilliger produced a large oval mirror with a scalloped silver frame. She set it down in the middle of the clearing, glanced up at the sky, and then shifted the mirror over a little. "Come here, Miss Melbourne." She pointed to a spot opposite her, on the other side of the mirror. "Sit there and make yourself comfortable."

At Amberwood, I went by the name of Sydney Melrose, rather than my true one, Sydney Sage. Ms. Terwilliger had gotten my made-up name wrong on the first day of class, and it, unfortunately, stuck. I followed her directions, not that I could really get all that comfortable out here. I was pretty sure I could hear some large animal scuffling out in the brush and added "coyotes" to my mental list of dangers I faced out here, right below "magic use" and "lack of coffee."

"Now then. Let's get started." Ms. Terwilliger peered at me with eyes that were dark and frightening in the desert night. "Are you wearing anything metal? You need to take it off."

"No, I—oh. Wait."

I reached around my neck and unfastened a delicate gold chain that held a small cross. I'd had the necklace for years but had recently given it to someone else, for comfort. He'd given it back to me recently, by way of our mutual friend Jill Mastrano Dragomir. Even now, I could picture the angry look on her face as she'd stormed up to me at school and thrust the cross into my hand without a word.

I stared at the cross now as it gleamed in the moonlight. A queasy feeling welled up in the pit of my stomach as I thought about Adrian, the guy I'd given it to. I'd done so before he professed his love for me, something that had caught me totally off guard a few weeks ago. But maybe I shouldn't have been so surprised. The more I looked back—and I did so all the time—the more I began to recall telltale signs that should have tipped me off to his feelings. I'd just been too blind to notice at the time.

Of course, it wouldn't have mattered if I'd seen it coming or not. Adrian was totally unsuitable for me, and it had nothing to do with his many vices or potential descent into insanity. Adrian was a vampire. True, he was a Moroi—one of the good, living vampires—but it made no difference. Humans and vampires couldn't be together. This was one point the Moroi and Alchemists stood firmly together on. It was still amazing to me that Adrian had voiced those feelings to me. It was amazing that he could even have them or that he'd had the nerve to kiss me, even if it was a kiss that had left me dizzy and breathless.

I'd had to reject him, of course. My training would allow nothing less. Our situation here in Palm Springs forced the two of us to constantly be together in social situations, and it had been rough since his declaration. For me, it wasn't just the awkwardness of our new relationship. I . . . well, I missed him. Before this debacle, he and I had been friends and spent a lot of time together. I'd gotten used to his smirky smile and the quick banter that always flowed between us. Until those things were gone, I hadn't realized how much I relied on them. How much I needed them. I felt empty inside . . . which was ridiculous, of course. Why should I care so much about one vampire?

Sometimes it made me angry. Why had he ruined such a

good thing between us? Why had he made me miss him so much? And what had he expected me to do? He had to have known it was impossible for us to be together. I couldn't have feelings for him. I *couldn't*. If we'd lived among the Keepers—a group of uncivilized vampires, humans, and dhampirs—maybe he and I could have . . . no. Even if I had feelings for him—and I firmly told myself I didn't—it was wrong for us to even consider such a relationship.

Now Adrian spoke to me as little as possible. And always, always, he watched me with a haunted look in his green eyes, one that made my heart ache and—

"Ah! What is that?"

I squirmed as Ms. Terwilliger dumped a bowl full of dried leaves and flowers over my head. I'd been so fixated on the cross and my memories that I hadn't seen her coming.

"Rosemary," she said matter-of-factly. "Hyssop. Anise. Don't do that." I'd reached up to pull some of the leaves out of my hair. "You need that for the spell."

"Right," I said, getting back to business. I set the cross carefully on the ground, trying to clear my mind of green, green eyes. "The spell that only I can do. Why is that again?"

"Because it has to be done by a virgin," she explained. I tried not to grimace. Her words implied that she was not a virgin, and even if that made sense for a forty-year-old woman, it still wasn't a thought I wanted to spend a lot of time on. "That, and the person we're looking for has shielded herself from me. But you? You she won't expect."

I looked down at the shining mirror and understood. "This is a scrying spell. Why aren't we doing the one I did before?"

Not that I was eager to repeat that spell. I'd used it to find someone, and it had involved me staring into a bowl of water for hours. Still, now that I knew how to do it, I knew I could perform it again. Besides, I didn't like the idea of walking into a spell I knew nothing about. Words and herbs were one thing, but what else might she ask of me? Endanger my soul? Give up my blood?

"That spell only works for someone you know," she explained. "This one will help you find someone you've never met before."

I frowned. As much as I didn't like magic, I did like problem solving—and the puzzles magic often presented intrigued me. "How will I know who to look for, then?"

Ms. Terwilliger handed me a photograph. My eyes had adjusted to the darkness, and I looked into the face of a pretty young woman. There was a striking resemblance between her and my teacher, though it wasn't initially obvious. Rather than Ms. Terwilliger's dull brown hair, this woman's was dark, nearly black. She was also much more glamorous, dressed in a black satin evening gown that was a far cry from Ms. Terwilliger's usual hippie attire. Despite those ostensible differences, the two women shared the same high cheekbones and aquiline eyes.

I glanced back up. "She's related to you."

"She's my older sister," Ms. Terwilliger confirmed, her voice remarkably flat. Older? I would've guessed this woman was at least ten years younger.

"Is she missing?" I asked. When I'd scried before, it had been to find a kidnapped friend.

Ms. Terwilliger's lips twitched. "Not in the way you're thinking." From the never-ending duffel bag, she produced a small leather book and opened it to a marked page. Squinting at where she indicated, I could make out handwritten Latin words describing the mirror and herbal concoction she'd dumped on me. Following that were directions on how to use the spell. No bloodletting, thankfully.

"It sounds too simple," I said suspiciously. I'd learned that spells that only had a few steps and components usually required a lot of mental energy. I'd passed out from the other scrying spell.

She nodded, guessing my thoughts. "It takes a lot of focus—more than the last one. But, as much as you don't want to hear this, your strength has grown enough that you'll probably have an easier time than before."

I scowled. She was right. I didn't want to hear that.

Or did I?

Part of me knew I should refuse to go along with this madness. Another part of me worried she'd abandon me in the desert if I didn't help. And still another part was insanely curious to see how this would all work.

Taking a deep breath, I recited the book's incantation and then set the picture in the middle of the mirror. I repeated the incantation and removed the picture. Leaning forward, I stared into the shining surface, trying to clear my mind and let myself become one with the darkness and moonlight. A hum of energy coursed through me, much more quickly than I expected. Nothing changed in the mirror right away, though. Only my reflection peered back at me, the poor lighting dulling my blond hair, which looked terrible both from sleeping on it and having a bunch of dried plants hanging in its strands.

The energy continued to build in me, growing surprisingly warm and exhilarating. I closed my eyes and sank into it. I felt like I was floating in the moonlight, like I *was* the moonlight. I could've stayed that way forever.

"Do you see anything?"

Ms. Terwilliger's voice was an unwelcome interruption to my blissful state, but I obediently opened my eyes and looked into the mirror. My reflection was gone. A silvery gray mist hung in front of a building, but I knew the mist wasn't physical. It was magically produced, a mental barrier to keep me from seeing the image that lay beyond it. Strengthening my will, I pushed my mind passed that barrier, and after a few moments, the mist shattered.

"I see a building." My voice echoed oddly in the night. "An old Victorian house. Dark red, with a traditional covered porch. There are hydrangea bushes in front of it. There's a sign too, but I can't read it."

"Can you tell where the house is?" My teacher's voice seemed very far away. "Look around it."

I tried to pull back, to extend my vision beyond the house. It took a few moments, but slowly, the image panned out as though I were watching a movie, revealing a neighborhood of similar houses, all Victorian with wide porches and creeping vines. They were a beautiful, perfect piece of history set in the modern world.

"Nothing exact," I told her. "Just some quaint residential street."

"Go back further. See the larger picture."

I did, and it was like I drifted up into the sky, looking down upon the neighborhood the way some soaring bird would. The houses extended into more neighborhoods, which eventually gave way to industrial and commercial areas. I continued moving back. The businesses became more and more densely packed. More streets crisscrossed between them. The buildings grew taller and taller, eventually materializing into a familiar skyline.

"Los Angeles," I said. "The house is on the outskirts of Los Angeles."

I heard a sharp intake of breath, followed by: "Thank you, Miss Melbourne. That will be all."

A hand suddenly waved across my field of vision, shattering the city image. Also shattered was that state of euphoria. I was no longer floating, no longer made of light. I came crashing down to reality, down to the rocky desert landscape and my stuffy pajamas. I felt exhausted and shaky, like I might faint. Ms. Terwilliger handed me a thermos full of orange juice, which I drank greedily. As the nutrients hit my system and strengthened me, I began to feel a little better. Intense magic use depleted blood sugar.

"Does that help?" I asked, once I'd downed the thermos. A nagging voice inside me started to chastise about how many calories were in orange juice, but I ignored it. "Was that what you wanted to know?"

Ms. Terwilliger gave me a smile that didn't extend to her eyes. "It helps, yes. Was it what I wanted?" She stared off into the distance. "No, not exactly. I was hoping you'd name some other city. Some city far, far away."

I picked up my cross and refastened it around my neck. The familiar object brought on a sense of normality after what I'd just done. It also made me feel guilty, looking back on the euphoric high the magic had given me. Humans weren't supposed to wield magic—and they certainly weren't supposed to enjoy it. Running my fingers over the cross's surface, I found myself thinking of Adrian again. Had he ever worn it? Or had he just kept it around for luck? Had his fingers traced the cross's shape like mine often did?

Ms. Terwilliger began gathering her things. When she stood up, I followed suit. "What does it mean exactly, ma'am?" I asked. "That I saw Los Angeles?"

I followed her back toward the car, and she didn't answer right away. When she did, her voice was uncharacteristically grim. "It means that she's much closer than I would like. It also means, whether you want to or not, you're going to have to work on improving your magical skills very, very quickly."

I came to a halt. Suddenly, I felt angry. Enough was enough. I was exhausted and ached all over. She'd dragged me out here in the middle of the night and now had the presumption to make a statement like that when she knew how I felt about magic? Worse, her words frightened me. What did I have to do with this? This was her spell, her cause. Yet, she'd given the directive with such force, such certainty, that it almost seemed as though I was the reason we'd come out here to this wasteland.

"Ma'am—" I began.

Ms. Terwilliger spun around and leaned toward me so that there were only a few inches between us. I gulped, swallowing whatever outraged words I'd been about to utter. I'd never seen her look like this. She wasn't scary, not exactly, but there was an intensity I'd never seen before, far different from the usual scattered teacher I knew. She also looked . . . frightened. *Life or death.*

"Sydney," she said, in a rare use of my first name. "Let me assure you that this is not some trick on my part. You will improve upon your skills, whether you like it or not. And it's not because I'm cruel, not because I'm trying to fulfill some selfish desire. It's not even because I hate seeing you waste your ability."

"Then why?" I asked in a small voice. "Why do I need to learn more?"

The wind whispered around us, blowing some of the dried leaves and flowers from my hair. The shadows we cast took on an ominous feel, and the moonlight and starlight that had seemed so divine earlier now felt cold and harsh.

"Because," Ms. Terwilliger said. "It's for your own protection."

CHAPTER 2

MS. TERWILLIGER REFUSED to say much more after that. She drove us back to Amberwood and hardly seemed to know I was there. She just kept muttering things to herself like, "Not enough time" and "Need more proof." When she finally dropped me off, I tried pressing her for more information.

"What was all that about protecting myself?" I asked. "Protection from what?"

We were parked in the fire lane again, and she still wore that distracted look. "I'll explain later, in our session tomorrow."

"I can't," I reminded her. "I'm leaving right after my regular classes. Remember? I have a flight to catch. I told you about it last week. And yesterday. And earlier today."

That brought her back to attention. "Did you? Well, then. I suppose we'll make do with what we must. I'll see what I can have for you in the morning."

I left her for my bed after that, not that I could get much sleep. And when I showed up to her history class the next morning, she was true to her word. Before the bell rang, she walked up to my desk and handed me an old book with a cracked red leather cover. The title was in Latin and translated to *Elements of Battle*, which sent a chill down my spine. Spells to create light and invisibility were one thing. There was a practicality to them that I could almost rationalize. But battle spells? Something told me I might have a little trouble with those.

"Reading material for the plane," she said. She spoke in her usual, addled scholar voice, but I could see a glint of that anxiety from last night in her eyes. "Focus only on the first section. I trust you'll do your usual thorough job—and then some."

None of the other arriving students paid any attention to us. My last class of the day was an independent study session on late-antique history, which she served as my mentor for. More often than not, she used the session as a passive-aggressive way to teach me magic. So, her giving me books like this was nothing out of the ordinary.

"And," she added, "if you could find out where that neighborhood is, it would be extremely useful."

I was speechless for a few moments. Locate one neighborhood in the greater Los Angeles metropolitan area? "That's . . . a very large area to cover," I said at last, choosing my words carefully with witnesses around.

She nodded and pushed her glasses up her nose. "I know. Most people probably couldn't do it." And on that semi-complimentary note, she returned to her desk at the front of the classroom.

"What neighborhood?" asked a new voice.

Eddie Castile had just arrived and slid into a neighboring desk. Eddie was a dhampir—possessing a mix of human and vampire DNA that had been passed down from days when the two races mixed. For all intents and purposes, though, he was indistinguishable from an ordinary human. With his sandy-colored hair and brown eyes, he also bore enough resemblance to me to support our cover story that we were twins. In reality, Eddie was here at Amberwood as a bodyguard for Jill. Dissidents among her own kind, the Moroi, were hunting her, and even though we'd seen no sign of them since coming to Palm Springs, Eddie was always vigilant and ready to pounce.

I slipped the red leather book into my messenger bag. "Don't ask. Another of her wacky assignments." None of my friends—save Adrian—knew about my involvement with Ms. Terwilliger's magic use. Well, and Jill by default. All Moroi possessed some sort of elemental magic. Adrian's was a rare and powerful one called spirit, which could work miracles of healing. He'd used that magic to bring Jill back from the dead when assassins had killed her. Doing so had made Jill "shadow-kissed"—that is, it created a psychic bond between them, one that allowed Jill to feel his emotions and sometimes see through his eyes. As a result, Jill knew more about what went on between Adrian and me than I liked.

I took my car keys out of my bag and reluctantly handed them over to Eddie. He was the only one I trusted to drive my car, and I always let him borrow it when I left town, in case he needed to run errands for our group. "Here you go. I better get it back in one piece. Do *not* let Angeline near the driver's seat."

He grinned. "Do I look suicidal? I probably won't even use it. Are you sure you don't want me to drive you to the airport later?"

"You'd miss class," I said. The only reason I was able to cut school early was because of the unusual nature of my independent study.

"I wouldn't mind, believe me. I've got a science test." He grimaced and lowered his voice. "I hated physics the first time, you know."

I couldn't help a smile. Both Eddie and I were eighteen and had graduated high school, me through homeschooling and him through an elite Moroi and dhampir academy. We couldn't pose as students without going through the motions of class, however. While I didn't mind the extra work, Eddie wasn't as taken with a love of learning as I was.

"No thanks," I told him. "A cab will be fine."

The bell rang, and Eddie straightened up in his desk. As Ms. Terwilliger called the class to order, he whispered to me, "Jill's really bummed she can't go."

"I know," I murmured back. "But we all know why she can't."

"Yeah," he agreed. "What I don't know is why she's mad at you."

I turned toward the front of the classroom and pointedly ignored him. Jill was the only one who knew about Adrian's declaration of love, thanks to that bond. It was another one of those things I wished hadn't been shared, but Adrian couldn't help it. Although Jill knew vampire-human romances were wrong, she couldn't forgive me for hurting Adrian so badly. To make things worse, she was probably personally experiencing some of his pain.

Even if our other friends didn't know what had occurred, it was obvious that something wasn't right with Jill and me. Eddie had picked up on it right away and immediately interrogated me. I'd given him a vague excuse about Jill not liking some rules I'd instated for her here at school. Eddie hadn't bought that, but Jill had been just as close-mouthed on the matter, leaving him clueless and frustrated.

The school day zipped by, and before long, I was in a taxi and on my way to the airport. I'd packed light and only had one small suitcase and my messenger bag, both of which could be carried on. For what seemed like the hundredth time, I took out a small silver and white gift bag and examined its contents. Inside was an expensive crystal sun catcher, the kind meant to be hung on a porch or in a window. It depicted two doves in flight, facing each other. Wrapping it back in its tissue paper, I returned it to its gift bag and then my own bag. I hoped it would be an acceptable gift for the upcoming event.

I was going to a vampire wedding.

I'd never been to one before. Probably no Alchemist had. Although we worked with the Moroi to protect their existence, the Alchemists made it clear they wanted no involvement that went beyond business contact. After recent events, however, both groups had decided it would be good to improve our professional relations. Since this wedding was a big deal, a few other Alchemists and I had been invited.

I knew the couple, and in theory, I was excited to see them married. It was the rest of the event that made me nervous: a huge social gathering of Moroi and dhampirs. Even with other Alchemists there, we'd be hopelessly outnumbered. Being in Palm Springs with Eddie, Jill, and the others had gone a long way in improving my feelings toward their kind. I got along with that little group well and now considered them friends. But even as liberal as I was in such matters, I still possessed a lot of the anxiety other Alchemists had inside the vampiric world. Maybe Moroi and dhampirs weren't creatures of evil, like I'd once believed, but they certainly weren't human.

I kind of wished my Palm Springs friends were coming with me, but that had been out of the question. The whole point of Jill and the rest of us being in Palm Springs was to hide her away and keep her safe from those trying to kill her. Both Moroi and Strigoi tended to avoid sunny, desert regions. If she suddenly showed up at a major Moroi function, it would defeat the whole purpose. Eddie and Angeline, another dhampir protecting her at Amberwood, had to stay behind as well. Only Adrian and I had been invited to the wedding, and we were thankfully on separate flights. If anyone had noticed that he and I were traveling together, it could attract attention back in Palm Springs, which could then expose Jill. Adrian's flight wasn't even leaving from Palm Springs. He was flying out by way of Los Angeles, two hours west, just to make sure we weren't linked together.

I had to connect through a different flight in Los Angeles, which reminded me of Ms. Terwilliger's task. Find one neighborhood in all of Los Angeles's greater metropolitan area. Sure, no problem. The only thing I had going for me was that the Victorian houses were so distinct. If I could find some historical society, there was a good chance they could direct me toward areas matching that description. It would narrow my search considerably.

I reached my gate at LAX an hour before the scheduled flight. I'd just gotten cozy with Ms. Terwilliger's book when an overhead announcement declared, "Paging passenger Melrose. Please come see a customer service agent."

I felt a sinking feeling in the pit of my stomach. Gathering up my things, I approached the desk and was greeted by a cheery airline representative.

"I'm sad to tell you this flight has been overbooked," she said. From her peppy voice and big smile, she didn't seem sad at all.

"What's that mean for me, exactly?" I asked, my dread growing. "I have a confirmed seat." I dealt with bureaucracy and red tape all the time, but overbooking flights was something I'd never understood. How did that even happen? It wasn't like the number of seats was a surprise to them.

"It means that you're no longer on the flight," she explained. "You and a couple other volunteers gave up your seats to accommodate that family. Otherwise, they would've had to be split up."

"Volunteers?" I repeated, following her gesture. Off to the side of the seating area, a family with seven children smiled back at me. The children were tiny and adorable, with big eyes and the kind of cuteness you saw in musicals about orphans finding new homes. Outraged, I turned back toward the agent. "How can you do that? I checked in way ahead of time! I have a wedding to get to. I can't miss it."

The woman produced a boarding pass. "We've more than made up for it. We've booked you on another flight, to Philadelphia—one that's leaving sooner. And you've even been upgraded to first class for your inconvenience."

"That's something," I said. I was still annoyed at this, simply out of principle. I liked order and procedure. Altering those threw off my world. I looked down at the boarding pass and then did a double take. "It's leaving now!"

She nodded. "Like I said, sooner. I'd hurry up if I were you."

Then, on cue, I heard a last-call announcement for my new flight, saying all passengers need to be on board now, as they were about to shut the cabin doors. I wasn't the swearing type, but I almost was then—especially when I saw that my new gate was on the opposite side of the terminal. Without another word, I grabbed my things and sprinted toward the gate as quickly as I could, making a mental note to write a letter of complaint to the airline. Through some miracle, I made it just before my new flight was closed to passengers, though the agent working that gate sternly told me that next time, I should plan ahead and allow more time.

I ignored her and headed into the airplane, where I was greeted by a much nicer flight attendant—especially when she saw my first class ticket. "You're right here, Miss Melrose," she said, pointing to the third row of the cabin. "We're so glad you could join us."

She helped me put my suitcase in the overhead bin, which proved to be pretty difficult since other, earlier passengers had taken up most of the space. It required some creative knowledge of spatial relations, and when we finally managed it, I practically passed out into my seat, exhausted from this unexpected flurry of excitement. So much for a relaxing trip. I had just enough time to fasten my seat belt before the plane began backing up. Feeling a little steadier, I plucked the safety card from its pocket so that I could follow along with the attendant's presentation. No matter how many times I flew, I always thought it was important to be up to speed on procedures. I was watching the attendant fasten an oxygen mask when a familiar and intoxicating scent washed over me. In all of the chaos of making this flight, I hadn't even bothered to pay attention to my seatmate.

Adrian.

I stared in disbelief. He was watching me with amusement and had no doubt been waiting to see how long it would take me to notice him. I didn't even bother asking what he was doing here. I'd known he was flying out of LAX, and through some wacky twist of happenstance, I'd been bumped to his flight.

"This is impossible," I exclaimed. The scientist in me was too amazed to fully realize the uncomfortable nature of the situation I now found myself in. "It's one thing for me to get moved to a new flight. But to end up next to you? Do you know what the odds of that are? It's incredible."

"Some might call it fate," he said. "Or maybe there just aren't that many flights to Philadelphia." He raised a glass of clear liquid to me in a toast. Since I'd never seen Adrian drink water, I had to assume it was vodka. "Nice to see you, by the way."

"Um, you too."

The engines roared to life around us, momentarily sparing me from conversation. Reality began sinking in. I was trapped on a five-hour flight with Adrian Ivashkov. *Five hours*. Five hours sitting only a few inches from him, smelling his overpriced cologne and looking into those knowing eyes. What was I going to do? Nothing, of course. There was nowhere to go, nowhere to escape since even first-class passengers weren't allowed parachutes. My heart began to race as I frantically groped for something to say. He was watching me in silence, still with that small smirk, waiting for me to lead the conversation.

"So," I said at last, staring at my hands. "How's, uh, your car?"

"I left it out on the street. Figured it'll be fine there while I'm gone."

I jerked my head up, jaw dropping. "You did *what*? They'll tow it if it's left there overnight!"

Adrian was laughing before I even finished. "So that's what it takes to get a passionate reaction, huh?" He shook his head. "Don't worry, Sage. I was just kidding. It's tucked away safely in my building's parking lot."

I felt my cheeks burn. I hated that I'd fallen into his joke and was even a little embarrassed that I'd just flipped out over a car. Admittedly, it wasn't just any car. It was a beautiful, classic Mustang that Adrian had recently purchased. In fact, he'd bought it to impress me, pretending he couldn't drive manual transmission in order to spend more time with me while I taught him. I thought the car was amazing, but it still astonished me that he would have gone to that much trouble for us to be together.

We reached our cruising altitude, and the flight attendant returned to get Adrian another drink. "Anything for you, miss?" she asked.

"Diet Coke," I said automatically.

Adrian tsked once she was gone. "You could've gotten that for free back in coach."

I rolled my eyes. "Do I have to spend the next five hours being harassed? If so, I'll go back in coach and let some lucky person 'upgrade' to my seat."

Adrian held up his hands in a placating gesture. "No, no. Carry on. I'll entertain myself."

Entertaining himself turned out to be doing a crossword puzzle in one of the in-flight magazines. I took out Ms. Terwilliger's book and tried to read, but it was hard to focus with him beside me. I kept sneaking glances out of the corner of my eye, partly to see if he was looking at me and partly just to study his features. He was the same Adrian as ever, annoyingly good looking with his tousled brown hair and sculpted face. I vowed I wouldn't speak to him, but when I noticed he hadn't written anything in a while and was tapping his pen loudly on the tray, I couldn't help myself.

"What is it?" I asked.

"Seven-letter word for 'cotton gin pioneer.'"

"*Whitney,*" I replied.

He leaned over and wrote in the letters. "'Dominates the Mohs' scale.' Also seven letters."

"*Diamond.*"

Five words later, I realized what was happening. "Hey," I told him. "I am *not* doing this."

He looked up at me with angelic eyes. "Doing what?"

"You know what. You're luring me in. You know I can't resist—"

"Me?" he suggested.

I pointed at the magazine. "Random trivia." I angled my body away from him and made a big show of opening my book. "I have work to do."

I felt Adrian look over my shoulder, and I tried to ignore how aware of his proximity I was. "Looks like Jackie's still got you working hard in her class." Adrian had met Ms. Terwilliger recently and had somehow charmed his way into a first-name basis.

"This one's more like an extracurricular activity," I explained.

"Really? I thought you were pretty against doing any more with this stuff than you had to."

I shut the book in frustration. "I am! But then she said—" I bit off the words, reminding myself that I shouldn't engage with Adrian any more than I had to. It was just too easy to slip back into old, friendly behaviors with him. It felt right when, obviously, it was wrong.

"Then what?" he prompted, voice gentle.

I looked up at him and saw no smugness or mockery. I didn't even see any of the burning hurt that had plagued me these last few weeks. He actually looked concerned, which momentarily distracted me from Ms. Terwilliger's task. Seeing him this way contrasted drastically with what had followed in the wake of our kiss. I'd been so nervous at the thought of sitting with him on this flight, and yet, here he was, ready to support me. Why the change?

I hesitated, unsure what to do. Since last night, I'd been turning her words and the vision over and over in my head, trying to figure out what they meant. Adrian was the only person who knew about my involvement with her and magic (aside from Jill), and until this moment, I hadn't realized how badly I was dying to discuss this with someone. So, I cracked and told him the whole story of my desert adventure.

When I finished, I was surprised to see how dark his expression had become. "It's one thing for her to try to get you to learn spells here and there. But it's a totally different thing for her to drag you into something dangerous."

His ardent concern surprised me a little—but maybe it shouldn't have. "From the way she talked, though, it wasn't like it was her doing. She seemed pretty upset about . . . well, whatever all this means."

Adrian pointed at the book. "And that'll help somehow?"

"I guess." I ran my fingers over the cover and embossed Latin words. "It has protection and attack spells—things that are a bit more hard core than what I've ever done. I don't like it, and these aren't even the really advanced ones. She told me to skip those."

"You don't like magic, period," he reminded me. "But if these can keep you safe, then maybe you shouldn't ignore them."

I hated admitting when he was right. It only encouraged him. "Yeah, but I just wish I knew what I was trying to stay safe from—no. No. We can't do this."

Without even realizing it, I'd slipped into the way things used to be, talking to Adrian in that easy, comfortable way we had. In fact, I'd even been confiding in him. He looked startled.

"Do what? I stopped asking you for crossword help, didn't I?"

I took a deep breath, bracing myself. I'd known this moment was coming, no matter how much I wanted to put it off. I just hadn't expected it to come while on a plane ride.

"Adrian, we have to talk about what happened. Between you and me," I declared.

He took a moment to consider my words. "Well . . . last I knew, *nothing* was happening between you and me."

I dared a look at him. "Exactly. I'm sorry for what happened . . . what I said, but it was all true. We have to move past this and go on with our lives in a normal way. It's for the good of our group in Palm Springs."

"Funny, I *have* moved past it," he said. "*You're* the one bringing it up."

I blushed again. "But it's because of you! You've spent the last few weeks all moody and sulking, hardly ever talking to me.

And when you do, there's usually some nasty barb in it." While recently having dinner at Clarence Donahue's, I'd seen one of the most terrifying spiders ever come crawling into the living room. Mustering all my courage, I'd caught the creepy little beast and set him free. Adrian's comment on my brave act had been, "Wow, I didn't know you actually faced down things that scared you. I thought your normal response was to run kicking and screaming from them and pretend they don't exist."

"You're right about the attitude," he said now, nodding along with my words. Once again, he looked remarkably serious. "And I'm sorry."

"You . . . are?" I could only stare. "So . . . you're done with all of that . . . stuff? Done with, uh, feeling that way?" I couldn't bring myself to elaborate. *Done with being in love with me.*

"Oh, no," he said cheerfully. "Not at all."

"But you just said—"

"I'm done with the pouting," he said. "Done with being moody—well, I mean, I'm always a little moody. That's what Adrian Ivashkov's all about. But I'm done with the excessive stuff. That didn't get me anywhere with Rose. It won't get me anywhere with you."

"*Nothing* will get you anywhere with me," I exclaimed.

"I don't know about that." He put on an introspective look that was both unexpected and intriguing. "You're not as much of a lost cause as she was. I mean, with her, I had to overcome her deep, epic love with a Russian warlord. You and I just have to overcome hundreds of years' worth of deeply ingrained prejudice and taboo between our two races. Easy."

"Adrian!" I felt my temper beginning to flare. "This isn't a joke."

"I know. It's certainly not to me. And that's why I'm not going to give you a hard time." He paused dramatically. "I'll just love you whether you want me to or not."

The attendant came by with hot towels, putting our conversation on hold and allowing his slightly disturbing words to hang in the air between us. I was dumbfounded and couldn't muster a response until after she came back to collect the cloths.

"Whether I want you to or not? What on earth does that mean?"

Adrian grimaced. "Sorry. That came off creepier than I intended. I just mean, I don't care if you say we can't be together. I don't care if you think I'm the most evil, unnatural creature walking the earth."

For the briefest of moments, his choice of words threw me back in time, to when he'd told me I was the most beautiful creature walking the earth. Those words haunted me now, just as they had then. We'd been sitting in a dark, candlelit room, and he'd looked at me in a way that no one ever had—

Stop it, Sydney. Focus.

"You can think whatever you want, do whatever you want," Adrian continued, unaware of my traitorous thoughts. There was a remarkable calm about him. "I'm going to just go on loving you, even if it's hopeless."

I don't know why that shocked me as much as it did. I glanced around to make sure no one was listening. "I . . . what? No. You can't!"

He tilted his head to the side as he regarded me carefully. "Why? It doesn't hurt you or anything. I told you I won't bother you if you don't want me to. And if you do, well, I'm all about that. So what's it matter if I just love you from afar?"

I didn't entirely know. "Because . . . because you can't!"

"Why not?"

"You . . . you need to move on," I managed. Yes, that was a sound reason. "You need to find someone else. You know I don't—that I can't. Well, you know. You're wasting your time with me."

He remained firm. "It's my time to waste."

"But it's crazy! Why would you do that?"

"Because I can't help doing it," he said with a shrug. "And hey, if I keep loving you, maybe you'll eventually crack and love me too. Hell, I'm pretty sure you're already half in love with me."

"I am not! And everything you just said is ridiculous. That's terrible logic."

Adrian returned to his crossword puzzle. "Well, you can think what you want, so long as you remember—no matter how ordinary things seem between us—I'm still here, still in love with you, and care about you more than any other guy, evil or otherwise, ever will."

"I don't think you're evil."

"See? Things are already looking promising." He tapped the magazine with his pen again. "'Romantic Victorian poetess.' Eight letters."

I didn't answer. I had been rendered speechless. Adrian never mentioned that dangerous topic again for the rest of the flight. Most of the time, he kept to himself, and when he did speak, it was about perfectly safe topics, like our dinner and the upcoming wedding. Anyone sitting with us would never have known there was anything weird between us.

But *I* knew.

That knowledge ate me up. It was all consuming. And as the flight progressed, and eventually landed, I could no longer look at Adrian the same way. Each time we made eye contact, I just kept thinking of his words: *I'm still here, still in love with you, and care about you more than any other guy ever will.* Part of me felt offended. How dare he? How dare he love me whether I wanted him to or not? I had told him not to! He had no right to.

And the rest of me? The rest of me was scared.

If I keep loving you, maybe you'll eventually crack and love me too.

It was ludicrous. You couldn't make someone love you just by loving them. It didn't matter how charming he was, how good looking, or how funny. An Alchemist and a Moroi could never be together. It was impossible.

I'm pretty sure you're already half in love with me.

Very impossible.

CHAPTER 3

TRUE TO HIS WORD, Adrian made no other mention of the relationship—or lack thereof—between us. Every once in a while, though, I could swear I saw something in his eyes, something that brought back an echo of his proclamation about continuing to love me. Or maybe it was just his typical impertinence.

A connecting flight and an hour-long car ride later, it was night by the time we finally reached the small resort town in the Pocono Mountains. Getting out of the car was a shock. December in Pennsylvania was very, very different from December in Palm Springs. Crisp, frigid air hit me, the kind that freezes your mouth and nose. A layer of fresh snow covered everything, glittering in the light of the same full moon that Ms. Terwilliger and I had worked magic by. The stars were out here in just as much force as the stark desert, though the cold air made them glitter in a sharper way.

Adrian stayed in our hired car but leaned out as the driver

handed me my small suitcase. "Need any help with that?" Adrian asked. His breath made a frosty cloud in the air.

It was an uncharacteristic offer from him. "I'll be fine. Thanks, though. I take it you aren't staying here?" I nodded toward the bed-and-breakfast the car had stopped at.

Adrian pointed down the road, toward a large, lit-up hotel perched on a hill. "Up there. That's where all the parties will be, if you're interested. They're probably just getting started."

I shivered, and it had nothing to do with the cold. Moroi normally ran on a nocturnal schedule, starting their days around sunset. Those living among humans—like Adrian—had to adapt to a daytime schedule. But here, in a small town that must be bursting with Moroi guests, he'd have the chance to return to what was for him a more natural schedule.

"Noted," I said. A moment of awkwardness followed, but the temperature gave me an excuse for escape. "Well. I'd better get in where it's warm. Nice, uh, traveling with you."

He smiled. "You too, Sage. See you tomorrow."

The car door closed, and I suddenly felt lonely without him. They drove off toward the towering hotel. My bed-and-breakfast seemed tiny by comparison, but it was cute and in good shape. The Alchemists had booked me here precisely because they knew the Moroi guests would have other accommodations. Well, most of them.

"Are you here for the wedding, dear?" asked the innkeeper as she checked me in. "We have some other guests staying with us as well."

I nodded as I signed my credit card slip. It was no surprise that there'd be overflow to this inn, but there'd be a lot less here than the other hotel. I'd make sure to lock my door. I trusted my friends in Palm Springs, but all other Moroi and dhampirs were questionable.

Towns like this, and the inns within them, always seemed intended for couples on romantic getaways. My room was no exception. It had a California-king-size bed draped in a gauzy canopy, along with a heart-shaped Jacuzzi by the fireplace. It screamed love and romance, which brought Adrian back to my mind. I ignored it all as best I could and jotted out a quick text to Donna Stanton, a higher-ranking Alchemist who oversaw my assignment in Palm Springs.

Arrived in Pocono Hollow. Checked into inn.

Her response came quickly: *Excellent. See you tomorrow.* A second text followed a moment later: *Lock your door.*

Stanton and one other Alchemist were invited to the wedding as well. But they were already on the East Coast and could simply travel here tomorrow. I envied them.

Despite my uneasiness, I slept surprisingly well and dared to emerge for breakfast in the morning. I had no need to worry about Moroi, though. I was the only person eating in the sun-drenched dining room.

"How strange," remarked the innkeeper as she delivered my coffee and eggs. "I know many of the guests were out late, but I thought at least a few might be here to eat." Then, to emphasize the oddness of it all, she added, "After all, breakfast is complimentary."

The nocturnal Moroi, who were all still in bed, emboldened me to explore the town a little that day. Even though I'd prepared with boots and a heavy coat, the weather change was still a bit shocking. Palm Springs had made me soft. I soon called it an early day and spent the rest of the afternoon reading Ms.

Terwilliger's book by the fire. I flew through the first section and even went on to the advanced one she'd told me to skip. Maybe it was the fact that it was forbidden, but I couldn't stop reading. The scope of what the book described was so gripping and consuming that I nearly jumped a foot in the air when I heard a knock at the door. I froze, wondering if some confused Moroi had mistaken my room for a friend's. Or, worse, for a feeder's.

My phone suddenly chimed with a text message from Stanton: *We're at your door.*

Sure enough, when I opened it, I found Stanton standing there—with Ian Jansen, an Alchemist the same age as me. His presence was a surprise. I hadn't seen Ian since he, Stanton, and I had been detained by Moroi for questioning in the escape of a dhampir fugitive. Back then, Ian had had an unwelcome crush on me. Judging from the dopey smile on his face when he saw me, things hadn't changed. I gestured them inside, making sure to lock the door when I closed it. Like me, both Alchemists had golden lily tattoos on their left cheeks. It was the sign of our order, tattoos infused with vampire blood that gave us quick healing and were magically designed to stop us from discussing Alchemist affairs with those who didn't know about them.

Stanton arched an eyebrow at the heart-shaped tub and then settled into a chair by the fire. "No trouble getting here?"

Aside from traveling with a good-looking vampire who thinks he's in love with me?

"None," I replied. I regarded Ian with a frown. "I didn't expect you to be here. I mean, I'm glad you are, but after last time . . ." I paused as something hit me. I looked around. "It's all of us. All of us that were, uh, under house arrest."

Stanton nodded. "It was decided that if we're going to foster good relations between our groups, the Moroi would start by making amends to the three of us specifically."

Ian scowled and crossed his arms, leaning against a wall. He had brown eyes, with matching brown hair that he wore in a neat haircut. "I don't want any 'amends' from those monsters after what they did to us this summer. I can't even believe we're here! This place is crawling with them. Who knows what'll happen if one of them drinks too much champagne tonight and goes looking for a snack? Here we are, fresh humans."

I wanted to tell him that was ridiculous, but by Alchemist reasoning, it was a very legitimate concern. And, reminding myself that I didn't know most of the Moroi here, I realized perhaps his fears weren't that unfounded.

"I guess we'll have to stick together," I said. That was the wrong word choice, judging from Ian's happy smile.

The Alchemists rarely had social time, and this was no exception. Stanton soon got us down to business, going over our plans for the wedding and what our purpose was here. A file folder provided background on Sonya and Mikhail, as though I knew nothing about them. My mission and history with Sonya were secret from other Alchemists, so, for Ian's sake, I had to nod along with everything as if it was as new to me as it was to him.

"Festivities will probably last until almost sunrise," said Stanton, gathering up her papers once she'd finished the briefing. "Ian and I will be departing then and will drop you off at the airport on our way out. You won't have to spend another night here."

Ian's face grew darkly protective. "You shouldn't have stayed here alone last night. You should have had someone to look after you."

"I can look after myself," I snapped, a bit more harshly than I intended. Whether I liked it or not, Ms. Terwilliger's training had empowered me—literally and figuratively. That, and recent self-defense classes had taught me how to watch out for myself and my surroundings. Maybe Ian meant well, but I didn't like the idea of him—or anyone—thinking I needed coddling.

"Miss Sage is quite well as you can see," said Stanton dryly. Ian's crush had to be obvious to her, and it was equally obvious to me she had no use for such frivolity. Her gaze drifted to the window, which was glowing orange and red with the setting sun. "Well, then. It's nearly time. Shouldn't you be getting ready?"

They had arrived in their dress clothes, but I still needed to prepare. They talked together while I got ready in the bathroom, but each time I emerged—to get a hairbrush or earrings or something else—I'd see Ian watching me with that sappy look. Great. This was not what I needed.

The wedding was being held in the town's claim to fame: a huge, indoor garden that defied the wintry conditions outside. Sonya was a huge lover of plants and flowers, and this was pretty much her dream location for a wedding. The glass walls that composed the building were steamed from the drastic difference between inner and outer temperatures. The three of us stepped inside, into an entry area that was used to sell tickets during the greenhouse's normal operating hours. Here, at last, we found the Moroi that had been hidden to me in daylight.

There were about two dozen of them milling around in this entryway, dressed in rich clothing and eerily beautiful with their slim, pale features. Some were ushers and other attendants, helping organize the event and guide guests into the atrium farther into the building. Most Moroi were simply ordinary guests stopping to sign the guest book or chat with friends and family they hadn't seen in a long time. Around the sides, dhampirs in neat black and white suits stood sentry, watchful for any sign of danger. Their presence reminded me of a far, far greater threat than some drunken Moroi mistaking us for feeders.

Holding the event at night meant exposing us to attack by Strigoi. Strigoi were a very different type of vampire—so different, in fact, that I almost felt foolish being unnerved in this group. Strigoi were undead, made immortal by killing their victims, unlike the Moroi, who simply drank enough blood from human volunteers to sustain themselves. Strigoi were vicious, fast, and strong—and only came out at night. The sunlight that Moroi found simply uncomfortable was lethal to Strigoi. Strigoi made most of their kills on unwitting humans, but Moroi and dhampirs were their preferred food. An event like this—Moroi and dhampirs crammed into a small space—was practically like offering up a Strigoi buffet.

Eyeing the guardian dhampirs, however, I knew any Strigoi would have a difficult task breaking into this event. Guardians trained hard their entire lives, honing skills to fight Strigoi. Seeing as the Moroi queen was attending this event, I suspected the security I'd seen so far didn't even begin to scratch the surface.

A number of those gathered here stopped talking when they saw us. Not all Moroi knew about Alchemists or how we worked with their people. So, the attendance of three non-feeder humans was a bit of an oddity. Even those who knew about Alchemists were probably surprised to see us, given the formality of our relationship. Stanton was too experienced to let her unease show, but Ian openly made the Alchemist sign against evil as Moroi and dhampir eyes studied us. I did a pretty good job of keeping my cool but wished there was at least one familiar face in this crowd.

"Miss Stanton?"

A round-cheeked Moroi hurried forward. "I'm Colleen, the wedding coordinator. We spoke on the phone?" She extended a hand, and even tough Stanton hesitated before shaking it.

"Yes, of course," said Stanton, voice cool and proper. "Thank you for inviting us." She introduced Ian and me.

Colleen waved us toward the atrium's entry. "Come, come. We have your seats reserved. I'll take you there myself."

She swept us past the curious onlookers. As we entered the atrium, I stopped and momentarily forgot the vampires around us. The main greenhouse was magnificent. The ceiling was high and vaulted, made of that same steamed glass. A central area had been cleared and set with seats draped in flowers, very much like what you'd see at a human wedding. A dais at the front of the seating area was covered in more flowers and was obviously where the couple would take their vows.

But it was the rest of the room that took my breath away. It was like we'd stepped into some tropical jungle. Trees and other plants heavy with brightly colored flowers lined the sides, filling the humid air with a perfume that was almost dizzying. Since there was no sunlight to light up the greenhouse, torches and candles had been cleverly placed throughout the greenery, casting a mysterious—yet still romantic—light on everything. I felt as though I'd stepped into some secret Amazonian ritual space.

And of course, nearly hidden among the trees and bushes, black-clad guardians paced and kept watch on everything.

Colleen led us to three seats on the right side of the seating area, marked with a RESERVED sign. They were about halfway back—not as esteemed a spot as family would get, of course, but enough to show that the Moroi thought highly of us and really were trying to undo the strained relationship caused by our detainment.

"Can I get you anything?" Colleen asked. I realized now her exuberant energy was partially nervousness. We made her almost—but certainly not quite—as uneasy as she and the others made us. "Anything at all?"

"We're fine," said Stanton, speaking for all of us. "Thank you."

Colleen nodded eagerly. "Well, if you need anything—no matter how small—don't hesitate to ask. Simply grab one of the ushers, and they'll find me immediately." She stood there a moment longer, wringing her hands. "I'd best check on the others. Remember—call if you need anything."

"What I need is to get out of here," muttered Ian once she was gone. I said nothing, not trusting any response. If I reassured him we were safe, I'd be regarded with suspicion. Yet if I acted like our lives were in danger, I'd be lying. My views were somewhere in the middle of those extremes.

Someone handed me a program, and Ian leaned a bit more closely than I would've liked in order to read over my shoulder. The program detailed a list of songs and readings as well as the members of the wedding party. I could tell from Ian's face that he was expecting to see "Unholy Bloodletting" right after the Corinthians reading. His next words affirmed as much.

"They do a good job making it seem so normal, huh?" he asked, not bothering to hide the disgust in his voice. I was a bit surprised at how vicious his attitude was. I didn't remember him being quite this extreme last summer. "Like it's a real wedding or something."

He also wasn't regulating his volume, and I glanced around anxiously, making sure no one overheard. "So you're saying it's not a real wedding?" I whispered back.

Ian shrugged but at least took the hint and lowered his voice. "With them? It doesn't matter. They don't have real families or real love. They're monsters."

It was ironic that he mentioned "real love" just then because at that moment, Adrian and his father were ushered to the opposite side of the atrium. Adrian was always a nice dresser, but I'd never seen him in anything so formal. I hated to admit it, but the look was great on him: a navy suit and vest that was nearly black paired with a pale blue shirt and blue-and-white-striped tie. It stood out from the more somber black and gray suits most men here were wearing, but not in an outlandish or tacky way. As I was studying him, Adrian glanced up and caught my eye. He smiled and gave me a small nod. I almost smiled back, but Stanton snapped me back to reality. I allowed him one last, lingering look, and then I turned away.

"Mr. Jansen," Stanton said in a stern voice. "Please keep your opinions to yourself. Regardless of their validity, we are guests here and will behave in a civilized way."

Ian nodded grudgingly, flushing slightly as he glanced in my direction—as if being so openly chastised might ruin his chances with me. He didn't have to worry, seeing as he didn't have any chance to begin with.

Colleen sent an usher to check on us, and while he spoke to Stanton, Ian leaned toward me. "Am I the only one who thinks it's crazy that we're here?" He nodded toward Stanton. "She thinks this is okay, but come on. *They held us captive.* It's unforgivable. Doesn't that make you mad?"

I certainly hadn't liked it at the time, but I'd come to understand why it had happened. "I hate that they did that," I lied, hoping it sounded convincing. "I'm angry every time I think of it."

Ian actually looked relieved enough to drop the topic.

We sat in blessed silence as the atrium continued to fill up. By the time the ceremony was about ready to start, there must have been close to two hundred people in the room. I kept looking for familiar faces, but Adrian and his father were the only ones I knew. Then, at the last minute, a brightly clad figure came scurrying in. I groaned at the same time Stanton tsked with disapproval. Abe Mazur had just arrived.

Whereas Adrian had made color work with formal wear in a stylish way, Abe used color to offend the sensibilities. To be fair, this was one of the more subdued ensembles I'd ever seen Abe don: a white suit with a bright, kiwi green shirt and paisley ascot. He wore his usual gold earrings, and the sheen of his black hair made me think he'd been hitting some hair oil pretty voraciously. Abe was a dubiously moral Moroi and also the father of my friend—and Adrian's former dhampir love— Rose Hathaway. Abe made me nervous because I'd had some secret dealings with him in the past. He made Stanton nervous because he was a Moroi the Alchemists would never be able to control. Abe seated himself in the front row, earning a horrified look from Colleen the coordinator, who was supervising everything from the side of the room. My guess was that wasn't part of her seating chart.

I heard a trumpet sound, and those sitting in the back suddenly fell to their knees. Like a wave, those seated in the rest of the rows began following suit. Stanton, Ian, and I all exchanged confused looks. Then I understood.

"The queen," I whispered. "The queen is coming."

I could see from Stanton's face that was not something she had considered. She had a split second to decide on protocol for this situation and how to maintain our "civilized" guest status.

"We don't kneel," she whispered back. "Stay where you are."

It was a valid call, seeing as we owed no fealty to the Moroi queen. Still, I felt flustered and conspicuous at being one of the only people in the room not kneeling. A moment later, a ringing voice declared, "Her Royal Majesty, Queen Vasilisa, first of her name."

Even Ian caught his breath in admiration as she entered. Vasilisa—or Lissa, as Adrian and Rose continually insisted I call her—was a picture of ethereal beauty. It was hard to believe she was the same age as me. She carried herself with a poise and regality that seemed ageless. Her tall, willowy body was graceful even among Moroi, and her platinum blond hair fell around her pale face like some otherworldly veil. Although dressed in a very modern lavender cocktail dress, she managed to wear it as though it were some grand Victorian ball gown. A black-haired guy with piercing blue eyes walked at her side. Her boyfriend, Christian Ozera, was always easy to spot, providing a dark contrast that worked perfectly with her lightness.

Once the royal couple was seated in the front row—seeming very surprised to find Abe waiting for them there—the throng returned to their seats. An unseen cellist began to play, and everyone released a collective breath as we fell into the comfortable ritual of a wedding.

"Amazing, isn't it?" Ian murmured in my ear. "How fragile her throne is. One slip, and they'd fall into chaos."

It was true, and it was why Jill's safety was so important. An old Moroi law said that a monarch had to possess one living family member in order to hold the throne. Jill was the only one left in Lissa's line. Those who opposed Lissa because of her age and beliefs had realized killing Jill would be easier than going after a queen. Many opposed the law and were trying to change it. In the meantime, the political fallout from Jill's assassination would be monumental. The Alchemists, whose job it was to keep the Moroi world hidden and protected , needed to prevent their society from falling into chaos. And on a slightly more personal level, I needed to prevent Jill's death because against all odds, I'd grown to care about her in the short time we'd been together.

I shifted my mind from those grim thoughts and focused on the next stage of the wedding. Bridesmaids in deep green satin led the procession, and I wondered if Abe had been attempting to match them with his suit. If so, he'd failed.

And there, I spotted my first friendly face, aside from Adrian. Rose Hathaway. It was no surprise she'd be a bridesmaid, seeing as she'd been responsible for the happy couple getting together. She'd inherited her father's dark hair and eyes and was the only dhampir among the bridesmaids. I didn't need to see the surprised looks of some of the guests to know that was pretty unorthodox. If Rose noticed or cared, she didn't show it. She walked proudly on, head held high and face glowing with happiness. With that humanlike dhampir appearance, she was shorter than her Moroi companions and had a more athletic build than the slender, small-chested Moroi.

Rose had what was a very normal, very healthy body among humans. Yet when I compared myself to Moroi, I felt enormous. I knew it was ridiculous—especially since I wore a smaller size than Rose—but it was a hard feeling to shake. Adrian had recently had an unwelcome intervention with me, going so far as to claim I was on the verge of an eating disorder. I'd been outraged and told him to mind his own business . . . but ever since then, I'd taken a hard look at my behaviors. I now tried to eat more and had gained exactly one pound, something that had felt torturous and wrong until my friend Trey had recently commented that I was "looking pretty good these days." It had reinforced the idea that a few more pounds wouldn't kill me and *might* actually be good for me. Not that I'd admit any of that to Adrian.

We all stood when Sonya entered. She was glorious in ivory silk, with tiny white roses adorning her fiery hair. The queen had been magnificent, but there was a glow about Sonya that dwarfed even Lissa's beauty. Maybe it was just something inherent to brides. There was an air of love around Sonya that made her shine. I was surprised to feel a pang in my chest.

Ian was probably disappointed when no bloodletting followed, but the ceremony was sweet and filled with emotion. I couldn't believe how stone-faced my Alchemist companions looked—I was on the verge of tears as the couple recited their vows. Even if Sonya and Mikhail hadn't been through hell to be together, this was the kind of ceremony that couldn't help but pull at the heartstrings. As I listened to them swear they'd love each other forever, I found my gaze drifting to Adrian. He didn't see me looking at him, but I could tell the ceremony was having the same effect on him. He was enraptured.

It was a rare and sweet look for him, reminding me of the tortured artist that lived beneath the sarcasm. I liked that about Adrian—not the tortured part, but the way he could feel so deeply and then transform those emotions into art. I had feelings, just like anyone else, but that ability to express them into something creative was an area I would never, ever have expertise in. It wasn't in my nature. I sometimes gave him a hard time about his art, especially his more abstract pieces. Secretly, I regarded his skills with awe and loved the many facets of his personality.

Meanwhile, I had to fight to keep my face blank, to look as though I was a normal Alchemist with no concern for unholy vampire events. Neither of my companions questioned me, so apparently I pulled it off. Maybe I had a future in poker.

Sonya and Mikhail kissed, and the crowd erupted into cheers. They only got louder when he brazenly kissed her a second time—and then a third. The next stage of the festivities, the reception, was being held in the hotel where Adrian and most of the other Moroi were staying. Sonya and Mikhail left first, followed by the queen and other high-ranking royals. Stanton, Ian, and I waited patiently for our row to be dismissed so that we could line up for the limos that were ferrying guests the half mile to the hotel. It normally wouldn't have been that bad of a walk, even in heels, if not for the freezing temperature.

Our turn came, and the three of us got into the back of a limo. "Now we just have to get through the reception," said Ian as the driver shut our door. "At least we've got our own car."

Suddenly, the door opened, and Abe slid in beside me. "Room for one more?" He beamed at Stanton and me. "So nice to see you lovely ladies again. And you must be Ian. A pleasure." Abe extended his hand. At first, it looked as though Ian wouldn't shake it, but a sharp look from Stanton dictated otherwise. Afterward, Ian kept looking at his hand as though he expected it to start smoking.

The drive only took about five minutes, but I could tell from the other Alchemists' faces that it felt like five hours for them.

"I think it's wonderful that you three were invited," said Abe, perfectly at ease. "Considering how much we work together, we should have more of these pleasant interactions, don't you think? Perhaps you'll invite us to one of your weddings someday." He winked at me. "I'm sure you have young men lining up for you."

Even Stanton couldn't keep a straight face. The look of horror in her expression said there were few things more profane than a vampire coming to a human wedding. She looked visibly relieved when we reached the hotel, but we weren't free of Abe yet. Some thoughtful person—probably Colleen—had put us at his table, probably thinking it would be nice to be seated with a Moroi we knew. Abe seemed to take great delight in the awkwardness his presence provided, but I had to admit, it was kind of refreshing to have someone who openly acknowledged the strained relations between us rather than pretending everything was okay.

"There's no blood in that," Abe told us when dinner was served. The three of us were hesitating over cutting into our chicken marsala, even me. "The only blood is in the drinks, and you have to actually ask for those at the bar. No one's going to sneak you something, and the feeders are being kept in another room."

Ian and Stanton still looked unconvinced. I decided I would be the brave one and began eating without any more hesitation. Maybe vampires were unnatural creatures, but they certainly had excellent taste in caterers. A moment later, the other Alchemists joined me, and even they had to admit the food was pretty good.

When the plates were cleared, Ian bravely left for the bathroom, giving Stanton a brief opportunity to lean toward me for a hushed status report. "Everything was okay when you left?" Strained relationship or not, our mission to keep the Moroi stable hadn't changed.

"Fine," I said. "It's all quiet back there. No sign of trouble." She didn't need to know about my own interpersonal drama. Keeping my tone casual, I asked, "Any news about the Warriors? Or Marcus Finch?"

Stanton shook her head. "None. But I'll certainly let you know if we uncover anything."

I answered with a polite smile, seriously doubting her words. I hadn't always liked my Alchemist missions, but I'd spent most of my life following orders without question because I believed my superiors knew what was best and were acting for the greater good. Recent events now made me wonder about that. In thwarting some crazed vampire hunters who called themselves the Warriors of Light, Stanton had withheld information from me, citing that we were on a need-to-know basis. She had brushed it off, praising me for being a good Alchemist who understood such policy, but the incident had made me seethe with anger. I didn't want to be anyone's pawn. I could accept that fighting for a greater cause meant tough decisions, but I refused to be used or endangered because of "important" lies. I'd given my life over to the Alchemists, always believing what they did and told me was right. I'd thought I was important, that they would always look out for me. Now I didn't know.

And yet . . . what could I do? I was sworn and sealed to the Alchemists. Whether I liked what they'd done to me or not, there was no way out, no way to question them. . . .

At least, I'd thought that until I learned about Marcus Finch.

I'd only found about him recently, after discovering he'd once crossed the Warriors of Light by helping a Moroi named Clarence. Although the Warriors usually only went after Strigoi, a rebel group had once decided to target Clarence. Marcus had stepped up and defended Clarence against the Warriors, convincing them to leave him alone. I'd almost believed Clarence was making up the story until I saw a picture of Marcus.

And that was where things got *really* weird. Marcus seemed to have also crossed the Alchemists. In fact, Clarence and one of the Warriors had hinted that Marcus had at one time been an Alchemist—but was no longer. I hadn't believed it until I saw his picture. He didn't have a golden lily—but a large tribal-looking tattoo done in blue ink that was large enough to cover the golden one, if you were trying to hide it.

Seeing that was life changing. I'd had no idea it was possible to tattoo over something so powerful. I certainly hadn't thought anyone could leave the Alchemists or that anyone would even want to, not with the way our purpose was drilled into us practically from birth. How could someone consider abandoning our missions? How could someone go rogue and just walk away from the Alchemists? What had happened that would make him want to do that? Had he had experiences similar to mine?

And would they let him go?

When I'd asked about him, Stanton claimed the Alchemists had no knowledge of Marcus, but I knew that was a lie. She didn't know I had his picture. His blue tattoo was big enough to cover a lily, and I'd seen metallic hints of one underneath, proving he had indeed once been one of us. And if he'd had the Alchemist mark, then they most certainly knew about him. They were covering him up, and that just intrigued me further. In fact, I was a little obsessed with him. Some instinct told me he was the key to my problems, that he could help me uncover the secrets and lies the Alchemists were telling me. Unfortunately, I had no clue how to find him.

"It's important no one here knows what you're doing, so remember to be discreet," Stanton added, like I needed to be reminded. A small crease appeared between her eyebrows. "I was particularly worried about that Ivashkov boy coming to this wedding. We can't let anyone know you two have more than a passing acquaintance. Little things like that could compromise our mission."

"Oh, no," I said quickly. "You don't need to worry about Adrian. He understands how important our work is. He'd never do anything to compromise it."

Ian returned, and our discussion ended there. Dinner soon gave way to dancing. With the atmosphere more relaxed, a number of Moroi came over to introduce themselves to us. I felt nearly as popular as the bride and groom. Ian shook so many hands that he eventually became immune to it. And as uncomfortable as it was for my companions, I could tell this event was actually accomplishing its goal of smoothing relations between

Alchemists and Moroi. Stanton and Ian were by no means
ready to be best friends with any of them, but it was clear they
were pleasantly surprised at how friendly and benign most of
the guests seemed.

"I'm glad we got this chance to be together," Ian told me
during a lull in our public relations. "It's so hard with our jobs,
you know? I'm in St. Louis now, in the facility archives. Where
do they have you?"

Secrecy was key in Jill's protection. "I'm in the field, but I
can't say where. You know how it is."

"Right, right. But you know, if you ever wanted to visit . . .
I'd show you around."

His desperation was almost cute. "Like for a vacation?"

"Well, yeah. Er, no." He knew as well as I did that Alchemists
didn't get vacations easily. "But, I mean, they're doing all the
holiday services, you know. If you decide to come to one, well,
let me know."

Alchemist priests always conducted special services around
Christmas in our main facilities. Some Alchemist families made
a point of going to them every year. I hadn't been to any in a
while, not with the way my missions kept jumping around.

"I'll keep that in mind."

There was a long pause, and his next words came haltingly.
"I'd ask you to dance, you know. Except it wouldn't be right in
this kind of unholy setting."

I gave him a stiff smile. "Of course. That, and we're here
on business. We've got to focus on building good relationships
with them."

Ian had started to respond when a familiar voice interrupted
us. "Miss Sage?"

We looked up and found Adrian standing above us, dashing in his shades of blue. His face was the picture of perfect politeness and restraint, meaning something disastrous was probably about to happen.

"It's so nice to see you again," he said. He spoke as though it had been a while, and I nodded in agreement. As I'd assured Stanton, Adrian knew too much familiarity between us might create a trail back to Jill. "Did I just hear you two talking about building good relationships?"

I was tongue-tied, so Ian answered. "That's right. We're here to make things friendlier between our people." His voice, however, was most decidedly unfriendly.

Adrian nodded with all seriousness, like he hadn't noticed Ian's hostility. "I think it's a great idea. And I thought of something that would be an excellent gesture of our future together." Adrian's expression was innocent, but there was a mischievous sparkle in his eye that I knew all too well. He held out his hand to me. "Would you like to dance?"

CHAPTER 4

I FROZE. I didn't trust myself to respond.

What was Adrian thinking? Putting aside all the drama between us, it was absolutely unforgivable to ask this here, in front of other Moroi and Alchemists. Maybe in Palm Springs, where things were a little more casual with my friends, it might not be that crazy a request. But here? He risked exposing that we knew each other, which in turn risked Jill. Almost as bad, it could be a tip-off of his feelings for me. Even if I insisted that I had no matching feelings, the fact that things had progressed this far could get me in serious trouble with the Alchemists.

As all these thoughts raced through my mind, a more concerning one suddenly popped up. A good Alchemist shouldn't be worried about any of those things. A good Alchemist would have simply been horrified at the immediate problem: dancing with a Moroi. *Touching* a vampire. Realizing this, I quickly mustered an outraged expression, hoping I looked convincing.

Fortunately, everyone else was too shocked to pay much attention to me. Good relations only went so far. Stanton and Ian wore legitimate looks of disgust. The Moroi nearby, while not appalled, were astonished at the breach of etiquette. And yet . . . I also saw a couple exchange looks that said they weren't entirely surprised Adrian Ivashkov would suggest something so outrageous. This was an attitude I'd seen a lot with him. People often shrugged off his behavior with, "Well, that's Adrian."

Ian found his voice first. "She . . . no! She absolutely can't!"

"Why not?" Adrian glanced between all our faces, his expression still sunny and unassuming. "We *are* all friends, right?"

Abe, who was rarely shocked by anything, managed to shake off some of his surprise. "I'm sure it's not that big a deal." His tone was uncertain. He knew that Adrian wasn't a total stranger to me but undoubtedly assumed I had the usual Alchemist hang-ups. As tonight had demonstrated, most Alchemists still struggled with handshakes.

Stanton seemed to be waging a mental war. I knew she thought it was an outlandish request . . . yet she was still conscious of the need to keep things pleasant. She swallowed. "Perhaps . . . perhaps it would be a nice gesture." She shot me a sympathetic look that seemed to say, *Sometimes you have to take one for the team.*

Ian jerked his head toward her. "Are you crazy?"

"Mr. Jansen," she snapped, conveying a stern warning in just his name.

All eyes turned toward me as everyone realized that ultimately, it was my decision. At this point, I didn't know if I should be shocked or scared—and the thought of dancing with Adrian made me feel both. I met Stanton's eyes again and slowly gave a nod. "Sure. Okay. Good relations, right?"

Ian's face turned bright red, but another sharp look from Stanton kept him silent. As Adrian led me to the dance floor, I heard a few whispered comments from curious Moroi mentioning "that poor Alchemist girl" and "there's no predicting what he does sometimes."

Adrian put his arm around my waist, perfectly proper and distant. I tried not to think about the last time I'd been in his arms. Even with appropriate spacing between us, our hands were still clasped, our stances still intimate. I was hyperaware of every single place his fingers rested on my body. His touch was light and delicate but seemed to carry an extraordinary heat and intensity.

"What were you thinking?" I demanded once we were moving to the music. I was trying to ignore his hands. "Do you know how much trouble you may have gotten me in?"

Adrian grinned. "Nah. They all feel bad for you. You'll achieve martyrdom after dancing with a mean, wicked vampire. Job security with the Alchemists."

"I thought you weren't going to pressure me about . . . you know . . . that stuff. . . ."

The look of innocence returned. "Have I said a word about that? I just asked you to dance as a political gesture, that's all." He paused for impact. "Seems like *you're* the one who can't get 'that stuff' off your mind."

"Stop turning my words against me! That's not—no—that's not right at all."

"You should see that Stanton woman watching us," he remarked with amusement, glancing behind me.

"Everyone's watching us," I grumbled. It wasn't like the entire room had come to a standstill, but there were certainly a number of curious onlookers, gawking at the unlikely sight of a Moroi and a human—an Alchemist, at that—dancing.

He nodded and swept me into a turn. He was a good dancer, which wasn't entirely a surprise. Adrian might be brash and impertinent, but he knew how to move. Maybe dance lessons had been part of growing up in an elite tier of Moroi society. Or maybe he was just naturally skilled at using his body. That kiss had certainly show a fair amount of talent. . . .

Ugh. Adrian was right. I *was* the one who couldn't get over "that stuff."

Unaware of my thoughts, he glanced over at Stanton again. "She's got the look of a general who just sent her army on a suicide mission."

"Nice to know she cares," I said. For a moment, I forgot my dance floor woes as I thought angrily back to Stanton's "need to know" attitude.

"I can pull you closer, if you want," he said. "Just to see how much she cares. I'm always willing to help like that, you know."

"You're a real team player," I said. "If putting me in danger is for the greater good, then Stanton probably wouldn't do anything about you moving in on me."

Adrian's self-satisfied smirk faded. "Did she ever come clean about that guy you were trying to find? Martin?"

"Marcus," I corrected. I frowned. Her denial still bothered me. "She keeps claiming she doesn't know him, and I can't push too hard if I don't want her to get suspicious."

"I thought of a way you might find him," said Adrian. I would've thought he was joking if his face wasn't so serious.

"*You* did?" I asked. The Alchemists had vast information at our disposal, with hands in all sorts of agencies and organizations. I'd been scouring them these last few weeks and found it unlikely that Adrian would have access to something I didn't.

"Yup. You've got his picture, right? Couldn't you just do the same spell you did the other night? Locate him that way?"

I was so surprised, I nearly tripped. Adrian tightened his grip to keep me from falling. I shivered as that small gesture brought us closer. The tension between us kicked up a notch, and I realized that along with our bodies being nearer, so were our lips.

I had a little difficulty speaking, both because of how it felt to be so close to him and because I was still stunned by what he'd said. "That's . . . wow . . . that's not a bad idea. . . ."

"I know," he said. "I'm kind of amazed myself."

Really, the circumstances were no different from finding Ms. Terwilliger's sister. I needed to locate someone I'd never met. I had a picture, which was what the spell required. What was different was that I'd be initiating the spell myself. It was a difficult piece of magic, and I knew Ms. Terwilliger's coaching had helped me. There was also the moral dilemma of working that type of spell on my own. My conscience had an easier time handling magic when I felt coerced.

"I couldn't try until next month," I said, thinking back to the spell book. "I mean, I have the picture with me, but the spell's got to be done during a full moon. This is the last night for the current one, and I'd never be able to get the components in time."

"What do you need?"

I told him, and he nodded along, promising he could get them.

I scoffed. "Where are you going to get anise and hyssop at this time of night? In this town?"

"This town's full of quirky boutique shops. There's some herbal place that sells soaps and perfume made of anything you can imagine. I guarantee they've got what you need."

"And I guarantee they're closed." He swept me into another flourish-filled spin, and I kept up with him perfectly.

The song was wrapping up. The time had flown by faster than I'd thought. I'd forgotten about the onlookers. I'd even forgotten I was with a vampire. I was simply dancing with Adrian, which felt easy and natural, so long as I didn't think about our audience.

His roguish look returned. "Don't worry about that. I can find the owner and talk her into making an exception."

I groaned. "No. Not compulsion." Compulsion was an ability vampires had to force their wills on others. All vampires had it to a small extent, and spirit users had it in excess. Most Moroi considered it immoral. Alchemists considered it a sin.

The song ended, but Adrian didn't release me right away. He leaned a little closer. "Do you want to wait another month to find Marcus?"

"No," I admitted.

Adrian's lips were a breath away. "Then we'll meet in two hours by the hotel's service door." I gave a weak nod, and he stepped back, releasing my hands. "Here's one last sign of good relations." With a bow that could've come straight out of a Jane Austen novel, he gestured to the bar and spoke loudly. "Thank you for the dance. May I escort you to get a drink?"

I followed without a word, my head spinning with what I'd need to do in two hours. At the bar, Adrian astonished me by ordering ginger ale. "Nice restraint," I said, realizing he'd need to stay sober to work spirit. I hoped he hadn't indulged too much already. For him, the only thing better than an open bar would be a case of cigarettes showing up at his door.

"I'm a master of self-control," he declared.

I wasn't so sure of that but didn't contradict him. I sipped my Diet Coke, and we stood there in comfortable silence. Two Moroi men sidled up the bar near us, talking with the volume and exuberance of those who hadn't held back on sampling free liquor.

"Well, no matter how liberal that girl is, she's certainly easy on the eyes," one guy said. "I could look at her all day, especially in that dress."

His friend nodded. "Definitely an improvement over Tatiana. Too bad about what happened to her, but maybe a change of scenery was for the best. Did that woman ever smile?" They both laughed at the joke.

Beside me, Adrian's own smile vanished, and he went perfectly still. Tatiana, the former Moroi queen, had been Christian's great-aunt. She'd been viciously murdered this summer, and though Adrian rarely spoke about her, I'd heard from a number of people that they'd been close. Adrian's lips twisted into a snarl, and he started to turn around. Without hesitation, I reached out and grabbed his free hand, holding it tightly.

"Adrian, don't," I said softly.

"Sydney, they can't say that." There was a dangerous look in his eyes, one I'd never seen.

I squeezed his hand harder. "They're drunk, and they're stupid. They're not worth your time. Please don't start a scene here—for Sonya's sake." I hesitated. "And for me."

His face was still filled with rage, and for a moment, I thought he would ignore me and throw a glass at one of those guys. Or worse. I'd seen angry spirit users, and they were terrifying. At last, that fury faded, and I felt his hand relax in mine. He closed his eyes briefly, and when he opened them again, they were dazed and unfocused.

"No one really knew her, Sydney." The sorrow in his voice broke my heart. "They all thought she was some draconian bitch. They never knew how funny she was, how sweet she could be. You can't . . . you can't imagine how much I miss her. She didn't deserve to die like that. She was the only one who understood me—even more than my own parents. She accepted me. She saw the good in my soul. She was the only one who believed in me."

He was standing in front of me, but he wasn't with me. I recognized the rambling, consuming nature of spirit. It messed with its users' minds. Sometimes it made them scattered and distant, like he was now. Sometimes it challenged people's grip on reality. And sometimes, it could create a despair with devastating consequences.

"She wasn't the only one," I told him. "I believe in you. She's at peace, and nothing they say can change who she was. Please come back to me."

He still stared off into someplace I couldn't follow. After a few frightening moments, he blinked and focused on me. His expression was still sad, but at least he was in control again. "I'm here, Sage." He removed his hand and glanced around to make sure no one had seen me holding it. Thankfully, the bride and groom had taken to the dance floor, and everyone was too mesmerized watching them. "Two hours."

He knocked back the rest of his drink and walked away. I watched him until he disappeared into the crowd, and then I returned to my own table, glancing at the clock along the way. Two hours.

Ian jumped out of his seat at my approach. "Are you okay?"

No Moroi well-wishers were around, so only Stanton was nearby to hear him. She seemed to share his concern. "I'm sorry you had to endure that, Miss Sage. As always, your dedication to our work is admirable."

"I do what I can to help, ma'am," I said. I was still worried about Adrian and hoped he wouldn't slip back into spirit's grip again.

"Did he hurt you?" asked Ian, pointing. "Your hands?"

I looked down and realized I'd been rubbing my hands together. They were warm from where Adrian had touched me. "Huh? Oh, no. Just, um, trying to rub the taint off. In fact . . . I should probably go wash up. Be right back."

They seemed to find this a perfectly reasonable idea and didn't stop me as I hurried to the restroom. Free of their concern, I breathed a sigh of relief. I'd dodged two bullets here, by not letting the Alchemists know that I was friendly with a vampire and also that I was plotting magic with him.

"Sydney?"

I was so distracted when walking out of the restroom that I hadn't noticed Rose standing nearby with Dimitri Belikov. They stood arm in arm, smiling at my surprise. I hadn't seen Dimitri tonight, and his black and white guardian attire told me why. He was on duty here and had undoubtedly been one of the shadows darting among the trees of the greenhouse, keeping a watch on everyone. He must be on a break now because there was no way he'd be standing so casually here, even with Rose, otherwise. And really, "casual" for Dimitri meant he could still leap into battle at any moment.

They were a striking couple. His dark-haired, dark-eyed looks matched hers, and they were both dazzlingly attractive. It was no wonder Adrian had fallen for her, and I felt surprised at how uncomfortable that memory made me. Like Sonya and Mikhail, there was a bond of love between Rose and Dimitri that was almost palpable.

"Are you okay?" asked Rose, eyes kind. "I can't believe Adrian did that to you." She reconsidered. "Then again, I kind of can believe it."

"I'm fine," I said. "I think the other Alchemists were more appalled than I was." I remembered belatedly that even if Rose and Dimitri knew I knew Adrian from Palm Springs, I still couldn't act too at ease here. I put on my earlier look of outrage. "It was still out of line, though."

"Propriety's never been Adrian's strong suit," Dimitri observed.

Rose laughed at the understatement. "If it makes you feel any better, you guys looked really good together out there. Made it hard to believe you're mortal enemies . . . or whatever it is Alchemists think." She gestured to my dress. "You even coordinated."

I'd totally forgotten what I was wearing. It was a short-sleeved silk dress, almost entirely black save for some splashes of royal blue on the skirt. That was a bolder color than I would normally wear, but the black tempered it. Thinking back to Adrian's shades of blue, I realized our palettes had indeed complemented each other.

You guys looked really good together

I don't know what expression I wore, but laugh again.

"Don't look so panicked," Rose said, eyes shining. "It was nice seeing a human and a Moroi look like they belong together."

Belong together.

Why did she keep saying things like that? Her words were messing with the cool, logical demeanor I tried to maintain. I knew she was speaking in that friendly, diplomatic way that everyone was pushing so hard for. But as progressive as Rose and Dimitri were, I knew even they would be shocked if they knew the truth about Adrian's feelings and that monumental kiss.

I spent the rest of the reception with a knot of anxiety building within me. Fortunately, I didn't have to hide it. Moroi and Alchemist alike expected me to feel that way. In fact, Stanton soon got her own share of "diplomacy" when a middle-aged Moroi guy asked her to dance, obviously taking a cue from Adrian's display of goodwill. Apparently, as outrageous as Adrian's behavior had been, some Moroi thought it had been a smart move and decided to follow suit. Stanton could hardly refuse after encouraging me, so she took the dance floor with gritted teeth. No one asked Ian to dance, which was probably just as well. He didn't look at all disappointed.

Adrian stayed away, presumably to gather my spell components. Time ticked down, and as the two-hour mark approached, I realized that although I'd brought Marcus's picture with me on this trip (I rarely let it out of my sight), it was still in my room. I excused myself from Ian, telling him I needed to go back to the inn to change shoes and would take one of the cars that had been ferrying wedding guests around town.

Ian's face immediately grew protective. "Do you want me to go with you? It's not safe out there."

I shook my head. "No, you need to stay here. Stanton's in more danger." She was standing near the bar, speaking to two Moroi men. I wondered if she had another dance in her future. "Besides, it's early, so there's still more of them here than out there. At least the inn is run by humans."

Ian couldn't fault my Alchemist logic and reluctantly let me go. Catching a town car was easy, and I was able to make the round trip in almost the perfect amount of time. I even changed shoes so that I'd have proof for my story. Although I'd worn heels to the wedding, I'd packed flats in my suitcase, just in case. That was just smart planning for any occasion.

When I reached the service door, however, I realized my clever planning had failed. Filled with haste and anxiety, I'd left my warm, heavy shawl in the car, which was probably long gone. Now, waiting for Adrian in the bitter Pennsylvania cold, I wrapped my arms around myself and hoped I wouldn't freeze before he showed up.

He was good to his word, though, and arrived at exactly the appointed time with a tote bag over one shoulder. Even better, he was completely back to his normal self. "Ready to go," he told me.

"Seriously?" I asked, my teeth chattering. "You found everything?"

He patted the bag. "You ask, I deliver. Now where do we need to do this?"

"Somewhere remote." I scanned around. Beyond the hotel's parking lot was a vacant field that I hoped would suffice. "There."

Walking across the well-salted parking lot wasn't a problem, but once we "off-roaded" into the snowy field, even my practical flats were of no use. I was also so cold that I suspected my skin was as blue as my dress.

"Stop," said Adrian at one point.

"We need to go a little farther," I protested.

Adrian, who'd had the sense to put on a wool coat, was taking it off. "Here."

"You'll be cold," I protested, though I didn't stop him when he stepped forward and helped me put the coat on. He was taller than me, so the three-quarter length was mercifully full length on me. Its scent was a mix of smoke and cologne.

"There." He pulled the coat more tightly around me. "I've got long sleeves and the jacket. Now come on—let's hurry."

He didn't have to tell me twice. Aside from the temperature, we had to do this before we were caught by others. Even I wasn't going to be able to explain this away to the Alchemists.

The moon was still crisp and bright when we finally found an acceptable spot. I sifted through Adrian's bag, amazed that he'd come through with everything, from the mirror to the dried leaves and flowers. He stayed quiet as I set it all up, only speaking when I was just about ready to go.

"Is there anything I can do?" he asked gently.

"Just keep watch," I said. "And catch me if I pass out."

"Gladly."

I'd memorized the spell when Ms. Terwilliger and I had performed it. Still, I was nervous about going solo, especially since the environment was so distracting. It was kind of hard to find the mental focus I needed while kneeling in snow. Then I thought back to Stanton and the lies the Alchemists were telling me. A spark of anger flared in me, creating warmth of a different sort. I used that to direct my thoughts as I stared at Marcus's picture. He was Adrian's age, with shoulder-length blond hair and a pensive look in his blue eyes. The tattoo on his check was a tangle of indigo crescents. Slowly, I managed to sink into the spell.

I felt that same euphoria as the mirror shifted into a city image. No fog blocked me this time since presumably Marcus wasn't wielding the kind of protective magic that Ms. Terwilliger's sister had been using. The scene before me showed what looked like a very modest studio apartment. A mattress lay on the floor, and an ancient TV sat in one corner. I looked around for any identifying features but found nothing. The room's one window finally gave me a clue. Outside in the distance, I could see a Spanish-style building that looked like a church or monastery. It was made of white stucco, with red-roofed domed towers. I tried to get a closer look, to fly up like I had in the other spell, but suddenly, I became aware of the Pennsylvania cold seeping into me. The image shattered, and I was back to kneeling in the field.

"Ugh," I said, putting my hand to my forehead. "So close."

"Did you see anything?" Adrian asked.

"Nothing that'll help."

I stood and felt a little dizzy but managed to stay upright. I could see Adrian ready and waiting to catch me in case I did indeed keel over. "You okay?"

"I think so. Just a little light-headed from the blood sugar drop." I slowly gathered up the mirror and bag. "I should've had you get orange juice too."

"Maybe this'll help." Adrian produced a silver flask from his suit jacket's inner pocket and handed it toward me.

So typical, Adrian helpfully offering alcohol. "You know I don't drink," I said.

"A few sips won't get you drunk, Sage. And it's your lucky night—it's Kahlua. Packed with sugar *and* coffee-flavored. Trade me and try."

Grudgingly, I handed him the bag and then took the flask as we began walking back to the hotel. I took a tentative sip and grimaced. "That is *not* coffee-flavored." No matter how much people tried to dress up alcohol, it always tasted awful to me. I didn't understand how he could consume so much. But, I could taste the sugar, and after a few more sips, I felt steadier. That was all I drank since I didn't want to get dizzy for different reasons.

"What'd you see?" asked Adrian, once we reached the parking lot.

I described the spell's scene and sighed in frustration. "That could be any building in California. Or the Southwest. Or Mexico."

Adrian came to a halt and slung the bag over one shoulder. "Maybe. . . ." He took out his phone from his jacket and typed in a few things. I shivered and tried to be patient as he searched for what he needed. "Did it look like this?"

I peered at the screen and felt my jaw drop. I was looking at a picture of the building from my vision.

"Yes! What is it?"

"The Old Mission Santa Barbara." And then, just in case I needed help, he added, "It's in Santa Barbara."

"How did you know that?" I exclaimed. "What that building is, I mean."

He shrugged. "Because I've been to Santa Barbara. Does this help you?"

My earlier dismay transformed into excitement. "Yes! Based on the window's position, I can get a pretty good idea of where the apartment is. You may have found Marcus Finch." Caught up in my elation, I squeezed his arm.

Adrian rested a gloved hand on my cheek and smiled down at me. "And to think, Angeline said I was too pretty to be useful. Looks like I might have something to offer to the world after all."

"You're still pretty," I said, the words slipping out before I could stop them. Another of those intense moments hung between us, the moonlight illuminating his striking features. Then it was shattered by a voice in the darkness.

"Who's there?"

Both of us flinched and jerked back as a black-and-white-clad figure seemed to materialize out of the shadows. A guardian. It was no one I knew, but I realized I'd been foolish if I thought we could slip in and out of the hotel unseen. The grounds were probably crawling with guardians, keeping watch for Strigoi. They wouldn't have cared much about two people leaving, but our return would naturally be challenged.

"Hey, Pete," said Adrian, putting on that easygoing smile he excelled at. "Nice to see you. Hope you're not too cold out here."

The guardian seemed to relax a little upon recognizing Adrian, but he was still suspicious. "What are you two doing outside?"

"Just walking Miss Sage back," said Adrian. "She had to get something from her room."

I gave him a puzzled look. The inn wasn't in this direction. Pete looked dazed for a moment. Then he nodded in understanding. "I see. Well, you'd better get back inside before you freeze."

"Thanks," said Adrian, steering me away. "Make sure you get a break and try the canapés. They're amazing."

"You compelled him," I whispered, once we were safely out of earshot.

"Only a little," said Adrian. He sounded very proud of himself. "And being outside to walk you is a valid reason, one he won't think too much about later. Compelling someone into believing a story works best if there's a little truth—"

"Adrian? Sydney?"

We'd almost reached the back of the building now and were suddenly face-to-face with an ivory-clad figure. Sonya stood before us, a fur stole wrapped around her. Once again, I was struck by her beauty and the happy glow she seemed to radiate. She gave us a puzzled smile.

"What are you two doing out here?" she asked.

Both of us were speechless. Adrian had no brash words or tricks. Sonya was a spirit user too, and compulsion wouldn't work on her. Frantically, I groped for some excuse that wasn't: *We were out using illicit magic in a continuing effort to uncover secrets the Alchemists don't want me to know about.*

"You can't tell," I blurted out to her. I held up the flask. "Adrian was letting me sneak some of his Kahlua. Stanton'll kill me if she finds out."

Sonya looked understandably startled. "I didn't think you drank."

"Tonight's been kind of stressful," I said. It was hardly a lie.

"And it's coffee-flavored," Adrian pointed out, as though that might aid our cause.

I wasn't sure if Sonya was buying it, so I attempted a change in subject. "Congratulations, by the way. I didn't have a chance to talk to you earlier. You look beautiful."

Sonya let go of her inquisitiveness and offered me a smile. "Thank you. It's kind of unreal. Mikhail and I have been through so much . . . there were times I never thought we'd reach this moment. And now . . ." She glanced down at the diamond sparkling on her hand. "Well, here we are."

"What are you doing out here, Mrs. Tanner?" Adrian had recovered himself and was back to his outgoing self. "Shouldn't you be inside gazing adoringly at your husband?"

She chuckled. "Oh, we've got a lifetime of that ahead. Honestly, I just needed to get out of the crowd." Sonya took a deep breath of the crisp, cold air. "I should probably get back soon. We're about to throw the bouquet. You aren't going to miss your chance, are you?" That was to me.

I scoffed. "I think I'll sit this one out. I've already caused too much speculation tonight."

"Ah, yes. Your infamous dance." Sonya glanced between us, and a bit of her earlier puzzlement returned. "You two look very good together." Awkward silence fell for a few seconds, and then she cleared her throat. "Well, I'm getting in where it's warm. Hope you'll change your mind, Sydney."

She disappeared through the service door, and I resisted the urge to beat my head against the wall. "She knows we're lying. She can tell." Spirit users were good at reading subtle cues from people, with Sonya being one of the best.

"Probably," agreed Adrian. "But I doubt she's going to guess we were out working magic in a field."

A terrible thought came to me. "Oh God. She probably

thinks we were off doing—you know—romantic type, um, things—"

That amused Adrian far more than it should have. "See, there you go again. That's the first thought that comes to your mind." He shook his head melodramatically. "I can't believe you keep accusing me of being the obsessed one."

"I'm not obsessed!" I exclaimed. "I'm just pointing out the obvious conclusion."

"Maybe to you. But she's right about one thing: we need to get inside." He anxiously touched his hair. "I think my hair gel's frozen."

I handed him back the flask and opened the door. Just before stepping through, I hesitated and glanced back at him. "Adrian? Thanks for helping me."

"What are friends for?" He caught the door from me and motioned for me to go inside.

"Yeah, but you went above and beyond tonight for something that has nothing to do with you. I appreciate that. You didn't have to help. You don't have the same reasons I have for cracking open the Alchemists."

Not knowing what else to say, I gave him a small nod of thanks and went inside. As the warmth and noise of the crowd swallowed us, I thought I heard him say, "I have different reasons."

CHAPTER 5

I LEFT SHORTLY THEREAFTER with the Alchemists and didn't expect to see Adrian for a little while. He was staying on with the other Moroi a couple more days in Pennsylvania, so there was no chance of a repeat flight together. My trip back to California was quiet and uneventful, though my mind raced with all the developments of the last couple of days. Between Ms. Terwilliger's cryptic warning and my new lead on Marcus, I had plenty to occupy me.

A text message from Eddie greeted me when I hailed a cab at the Palm Springs airport: *We're eating at Marquee's. Wanna join us?* A follow-up message soon came: *You can drive us back.* I directed the driver to take me to a suburb on the far edge of the city rather than Amberwood's home in Vista Azul. I was hungry, seeing as there'd been no dinner served on the plane in coach, and besides, I wanted my car back in my own hands.

When I arrived at the restaurant, I found Eddie and

Angeline sitting on one side of a booth with Jill on the other. Immediately, I knew why they'd chosen to eat so far from our school. Being away meant Eddie and Angeline could go out as a couple. Back at Amberwood, everyone thought we were related. Eddie, Jill, and I passed ourselves off as siblings, while Angeline was our cousin. Eddie and Angeline had recently started dating, so they'd had to hide their relationship from our classmates to avoid raising suspicions. We already seemed to attract enough attention as it was.

Angeline was cuddled up in Eddie's arm. Even he looked like he was having a good time, which was nice to see. He took his responsibilities so seriously and was often so tense that it seemed as though it wouldn't take much to make him snap in two. Angeline—though uncouth, unpredictable, and often inappropriate—had proven remarkably good for him. That didn't make him any less diligent in his guardian duties, of course.

Things were a little different on the opposite side of the table. Jill looked miserable, slumped into the seat with her arms crossed. Her light brown hair hung forward, covering part of her face. After ill-fated romances with a guy who wanted to become a Strigoi and with Eddie's human roommate, Jill had come to realize that Eddie might very well be the guy for her. It was fitting, too, because for a long time, he'd harbored a secret crush on her, fiercely dedicated to her in the way a knight served his liege lady. He'd never believed he was worthy of Jill, and without any signs of her affection, he'd turned to Angeline—just when Jill had come around and wanted him. At times, it seemed like some sort of Shakespearean comedy . . . until I looked at Jill's face. Then I'd feel conflicted because I knew if Eddie returned her affection, Angeline would be the one with that sad, sad expression. It was kind of a mess and made me glad to be free of any romantic entanglements.

"Sydney!" Jill beamed when she saw me, brushing her hair away. Maybe it was because she needed the distraction, or maybe it was because Adrian's new attitude toward me had lifted some of her moodiness. Regardless, I welcomed a return to the old friendliness in her rather than the brooding and accusing looks she'd harbored since I rejected him.

"Hey, guys." I slid into the booth beside her. Immediately, I opened up my cell phone's picture album and handed it to her since I knew she'd want to know about the wedding right away. Despite all the intrigue that had gone down there, I had managed to take some pictures without the other Alchemists noticing. Even if she'd seen some of it through Adrian's eyes, Jill would still want to examine everything in detail.

She sighed with happiness as she scanned the pictures. "Look at Sonya. She's so pretty." Angeline and Eddie leaned across the table to get a look. "Oh. And there's Rose and Lissa. They look great too." There was an odd note in Jill's voice as she spoke. She was friends with Rose, but her half sister was still a bit of an enigma. Jill and Lissa hadn't even known they were sisters until recently, and the volatile political environment had forced Lissa to behave more as a queen than a sister toward Jill. It was a difficult relationship for both of them.

"Did you have a fun time?" Eddie asked me.

I considered my answer for several moments. "I had an interesting time. There's still a lot of tension between the Alchemists and your people, so some of it was a little weird."

"At least Adrian was there. Must have been nice to have

someone you know," said Angeline, in well-meaning ignorance. She pointed to a picture I'd taken of the reception hall. My intent had been to get a full shot of the venue for Jill, but Adrian had happened to walk into the shot, posed and perfect like some handsome spokesmodel hosting the event. "Always so pretty." Angeline shook her head in disapproval. "Everyone there is. I guess that means there weren't any celebratory wrestling matches?"

It was a sign of Angeline's progress that she'd deduced that so quickly. Her people, the Keepers, lived in the wilds of West Virginia, and their openness to romance between vampires, dhampirs, and humans was only one of their more bizarre customs. Friendly fights broke out often, and Angeline had had to learn that such behaviors weren't acceptable out here in mainstream America.

"Not while I was there," I said. "But hey, maybe something went down after I left." That brought grins to Jill's and Eddie's faces and a hopeful look to Angeline's.

A waitress came by, and I ordered Diet Coke and a salad. Maybe I'd loosened up in my tight calorie counting, but I swore I could still taste the sugar from all the wedding cake I'd eaten after the spell.

Angeline tightened her hold on Eddie's arm and smiled up at him. "If you ever get to see my home, you can fight my brother Josh to show that you're worthy of me."

I had to swallow a laugh. I'd seen the Keepers' community and knew she was absolutely serious. I worked to keep a straight face. "Aren't you breaking a lot of rules by being together without that having happened yet?"

Angeline nodded, looking a little glum. "My mom would be

so scandalized if she knew. But I guess this is a unique situation."

Eddie smiled indulgently at her. I think sometimes he thought we were exaggerating about the Keepers. He was going to be in for a shock if he ever did visit them. "Maybe I can fight a bunch of your relatives to make up for it," he said.

"You might have to," she said, not realizing he was joking.

It was hardly romantic banter, but Jill looked decidedly uncomfortable discussing their relationship. She turned to me, very obviously trying not to look at them. "Sydney, what are we going to do about Christmas?"

I shrugged, unsure what she was asking. "The usual, I guess. Give presents. Sing songs. Have Yuletide duels." Angeline lit up at that.

Jill rolled her eyes. "No, I mean, we're going to be on winter break in a few weeks. Is there any way . . . is there any way we can go home?"

There was a plaintive note in her voice, and even Eddie and Angeline broke their mutual admiration to stare at me. I shifted under their scrutiny. Angeline wasn't as concerned about visiting the Keepers, but I knew Eddie and Jill missed their friends and family. I wished I could give them the answer they wanted to hear.

"I'm sorry," I said. "You'll be staying at Clarence's for break. We can't risk . . . well, you know." I didn't need to emphasize the need for Jill's safety. We were all familiar with that refrain. Ian's comment about how fragile the throne was drove home the importance of what we did.

Jill's face fell. Even Eddie looked disappointed. "I figured," she said. "I just hoped . . . that is, I miss my mom so much."

"We can probably get a message to her," I said gently.

I knew that was no substitute for the real thing. I was able to make occasional phone calls to my own mom, and hearing her voice was a million times better than any email could be. I even got to talk to my older sister, Carly, sometimes, which always cheered me up since she was so bright and funny. My younger sister, Zoe . . . well, she was a different story. She wouldn't take my calls. She'd nearly been initiated into the Alchemists—to take on this mission, in fact—when I'd stolen it from her. I'd done it to protect her from committing to the Alchemists so young, but she'd seen it as an insult.

Looking at Jill's sad face, I felt my heart clench. She had been through so much. Her new royal status. Targeted by assassins. Fitting in to a human school. Her disastrous and deadly romances. And now enduring Eddie and Angeline. She handled it all with remarkable strength, always resolutely going through with what she *had* to do even if she didn't want to do it. Lissa was praised for being such an exemplary queen, but there was a regality and strength to Jill as well that many underestimated. Glancing up, I caught a spark in Eddie's eyes as he too seemed to recognize and admire that about her.

After dinner, I took them back to Amberwood and was pleased to see that my car was in perfect shape. I drove a brown Subaru named Latte, and Eddie was the only other person I trusted behind the wheel. I dropped him off at the boys' dorm and then took Angeline and Jill back to ours. As we were walking in the door, I caught sight of Mrs. Santos, a teacher I knew by reputation.

"You guys go ahead," I told Jill and Angeline. "I'll see you tomorrow."

They left, and I walked across the lobby, waiting patiently

for Mrs. Santos to finish a discussion with our dorm matron, Mrs. Weathers. When Mrs. Santos started to turn around and leave, I caught her attention.

"Mrs. Santos? I'm Sydney Melrose. I wondered if I could—"

"Oh, yes," she said. "I know who you are, dear. Ms. Terwilliger raves about you all the time at our department meetings." Mrs. Santos was a kindly-looking woman with silver and black hair. Rumor had it she'd be retiring soon.

I flushed a little at the praise. "Thank you, ma'am." She and Ms. Terwilliger were both history teachers, though Mrs. Santos's focus was on American history, not world. "Do you have a minute? I wanted to ask you something."

"Of course."

We stepped off to the side of the lobby, out of the incoming and outgoing dorm traffic. "You know a lot about local history, right? Southern California?"

Mrs. Santos nodded. "I was born and raised here."

"I'm interested in nontraditional architecture in the Los Angeles area," I told her, the lie rolling easily off my lips. I'd thought about this in advance. "That is, non-Southwest styles. Do you know any neighborhoods like that? I'd heard there were some Victorian ones."

She brightened. "Oh, yes. Absolutely. Fascinating subject. Victorian, Cape Cod, Colonial . . . there are all sorts. I don't have all the information on me, but I could email you when I get home tonight. There are several I know off the top of my head, and I know a historian who could help you with others."

"That'd be great, ma'am. Thank you so much."

"Always happy to help a star pupil." She winked as she

started to walk away. "Maybe next semester you'll do an independent study with me. Provided you can tear yourself away from Ms. Terwilliger."

"I'll keep it in mind," I said.

As soon as she was gone, I texted Ms. Terwilliger. *Mrs. Santos is going to tell me about historical neighborhoods.* The response came quickly: *Excellent. Come over right now.* I scowled as I typed back: *I just got here. Haven't even been in my room.* To which she replied: *Then you can get here that much faster.*

Maybe that was true, but I still took the time to put my suitcase back in my room and change out of my travel clothes. Ms. Terwilliger lived pretty close to the school and looked as though she'd been pacing in circles when I arrived at her house.

"Finally," she said.

I glanced at the time. "It's only been fifteen minutes."

She shook her head and again wore the same grim expression she'd had out in the desert. "Even that might be too much. Follow me."

Ms. Terwilliger's home was a little bungalow that could have doubled as a New Age store or possibly a cat shelter. The level of clutter set my teeth on edge. Spell books, incense, statues, crystals, and all sorts of other magical items sat in piles in all rooms of the house. Only her workshop, the room she led me to, was neat and orderly—even to levels I approved of. Everything was clean and organized, to the point of being labeled and alphabetized. A large worktable sat in the center of the room, completely cleared off, save for a stunning necklace I'd never seen before. The chain was made of intricate gold loops, and the pendant was a deep red cabochon stone in a lacy gold setting.

"Garnet?" I asked.

"Very good," she said, lifting the necklace. The candlelight in the room seemed to make every part of it glitter.

"It's lovely," I said.

She held it out to me. "It's for you."

I stepped back uneasily. "For . . . me? I . . . I mean, thank you, but I can't accept a gift like that."

"It's not a gift," she said. "It's a necessity. One that might save your life. Take it and put it on."

I refused to touch it. "It's magical, isn't it?"

"Yes," she said. "And don't give me that look. It's no different from any of the charms you've made for yourself."

"Except that anything you'd make . . ." I swallowed as I stared into the depths of that bloodred jewel. "It's going to be a lot more powerful than anything I can create."

"That's exactly the point. Now here." She thrust it so close to me that it nearly swung out and hit me in the face.

Steeling myself, I reached out and took it from her. Nothing happened. No smoke or sparks. No searing pain. Seeing her expectant look, I fastened it around my neck, letting the garnet lie next to my cross.

She sighed, her relief nearly palpable. "Just as I'd hoped."

"What?" I asked. Even if I sensed nothing special about it, the garnet felt heavy around my neck.

"It's masking your magical ability," she said. "No one who meets you should be able to tell that you're a magic user."

"I'm *not* a magic user," I reminded her sharply. "I'm an Alchemist."

A small flicker of a smile played over her lips. "Of course you are—one who uses magic. And to a particularly powerful person, that would be obvious. Magic leaves a mark on your blood that permeates your whole body."

"*What?*" I couldn't have been more shocked if she'd said I'd just contracted a deadly disease. "You never told me that before!"

"It wasn't important," she said with a small shrug. "Until now. I need you hidden. Do not take that off. Ever."

I put my hands on my hips. "Ma'am, I don't understand."

"All will be revealed in time—"

"*No,*" I said. At that moment, I could have been talking to Stanton or any of the countless others who'd used me and fed me pieces of information throughout my life. "It will be revealed *now.* If you've gotten me into something dangerous, then you either need to get me out of it or tell me how to."

Ms. Terwilliger stared at me for several quiet moments. A gray tabby cat rubbed up against my legs, ruining the seriousness of the moment. "You're right," she said at last. "I do owe you an explanation. Have a seat."

I sat down on one of the stools by the table, and she sat opposite me. She clasped her hands together in front of her and seemed to be having a hard time gathering her thoughts. I had to force myself to stay calm and patient. Otherwise, the panic that had been gnawing at me since the desert would completely consume me.

"You remember that woman you saw in the picture?" she asked at last.

"Your sister."

Ms. Terwilliger nodded. "Veronica. She's ten years older than me and looks half my age, as you could undoubtedly tell. Now, it isn't difficult to create an illusion. If I wanted to appear young and beautiful, I could—emphasis on *appear*. But Veronica? She's actually managed to make her body young and vibrant. It's an advanced, insidious kind of magic. You can't defy age like that without making some sacrifices." She frowned, and my heart pounded. Creating youth made all my Alchemist sensibilities reel. It was nearly as bad as Strigoi immortality, maybe worse if she was talking about a *human* doing it. That kind of twisted magic had no place in this world. Her next words drove home the wrongness of it all. "Or, in her case, sacrificing others."

Sacrifice. The very word seemed to poison the air. She stood up and walked over to a shelf, producing a newspaper clipping. Wordlessly, she handed it to me. It was a recent article, from three days ago, talking about a nineteen-year-old UCLA student who'd been found comatose in her dorm room. No one knew what had caused it, and the girl was hospitalized with no indication of when or if she'd wake up.

"What is this?" I asked, not sure I wanted to know the answer.

I inspected the article more closely, especially the picture it contained. At first, I wondered why the paper would show a sleeping old woman. Then, reading the fine print, I learned that the coma victim also displayed some unexplained physical symptoms: gray-streaked hair and dry, cracked skin. Doctors were currently investigating rare diseases. I cringed, unable to believe what I saw. She was hideous, and I couldn't look at her for very long.

And just like that, I suddenly understood. Veronica wasn't sacrificing victims with knives and stone altars. She was conducting some kind of perverse magic on these girls that bent the rules of nature, putting them in this hideous state. My stomach twisted, and I gripped the table for support.

"This girl was one of Veronica's victims," confirmed Ms. Terwilliger. "That's how she maintains her youth and beauty—by taking it from others. When I read this, I thought—almost hoped—some other magic user was doing it. Not that I'd wish this on anyone. Your scrying spell confirmed she was in the area, however, which means it's my responsibility to deal with her."

I dared a look down at the article again and felt that nausea well up again. The girl was nineteen. What would it be like to have the life sucked out of you at so young an age? Maybe the coma was a blessing. And how corrupt and twisted would you have to be to do that to someone?

I didn't know how exactly Ms. Terwilliger would "deal with" her sister and wasn't sure I wanted to find out. And yet, if Veronica really was doing things like this to innocents, then yes, someone like Ms. Terwilliger needed to stop her. A magical attack of this magnitude was one of the most terrible things I could imagine. It brought back all my ingrained fears about the wrongness of magic. How could I justify using it when it was capable of such horror? Old Alchemist lessons came back to me: *Part of what makes the Moroi particularly dangerous is their ability to work magic. No one should be able to twist the world in that way. It's wrong and can easily run out of control.*

I tuned back into the present. "How do I fit into this, ma'am? I already figured out where she is. Why am I in danger?"

"Sydney," Mrs. Terwilliger said, looking at me strangely. "There are few young women out there with your abilities. Along with youth and beauty, she intends to suck someone's magic away and use it to make herself that much more power-ful. You, my dear, would be the ultimate coup for her."

"She's like Strigoi," I murmured, unable to repress a shiver. Although those undead vampires could feast on anyone, they preferred Moroi because they had magic in their blood. Drinking Moroi blood made Strigoi more powerful, and a chill-ing thought suddenly hit me. "Practically a human vampire."

"Something like that," Ms. Terwilliger agreed. "This amulet should hide your power, even from someone as strong as her. She shouldn't be able to find you."

A calico cat jumped up on the table, and I ran a hand over her sleek fur, taking comfort in the small contact. "The fact that you keep saying 'should' makes me a little nervous. Why would she even come looking in Palm Springs? Does she know about me yet?"

"No. But she knows *I'm* here, and she may check on me once in a while—so I need to hide you in case she does. I'm in a bind, however, because I need to find her but can't actively do the hunting. If she finds out I'm investigating, she'll know that I know she's here. I can't alert her. If I have the element of sur-prise on my side, I'm more likely to stop her." She frowned. "I'm honestly surprised she would come so close to me in California at all. Regardless, I need to keep a low profile until it's time to strike."

Ms. Terwilliger looked at me meaningfully, and I felt a sink-ing feeling in my stomach as I began to put together what she was saying. "You want me to hunt her."

"It's not hunting so much as gathering some data. You're the only one I can trust to do this. She and I can sense each other if we're close, no matter how much we try to hide our magic. I know this is going to sound shocking, but I actually think it'd be best if you hunted her—even if you're the one she's after. You're one of the few I can trust completely, and you're resourceful enough to pull something like this off."

"But I'd be putting myself out there. You just said I'd be a big catch for her." The twists and turns here were mindboggling.

"Yes. Which is why I gave you the amulet. She won't sense your magic, and if you're cautious in your investigation, she should have no reason to notice you."

I still wasn't following the logic here. "But why *me*? You have a coven. If you can't do it yourself, then there must be someone else—a stronger witch—who can do it."

"Two reasons," she said. "One is that you have excellent investigative skills—more so than others older than you. You're intelligent and resourceful. The other reason . . . well, if another witch goes after her, she might very well kill Veronica."

"Would that be such a bad thing?" I didn't like violence and killing by any means, but this might be a case where it was justified, if it could save other lives. "You said you were going to 'take care of her.'"

"If I have no choice . . . if I must kill her, then I will." She looked dejected, and I had a moment of empathy. I loved my two sisters. What would I do if I was ever in a deadly conflict with one of them? Of course, it was hard to imagine Zoe or Carly committing this kind of atrocity. "However, there are other ways of neutralizing and subduing a magic user. If there's any way—any way at all—I can do that, I will. My coven sisters won't feel that way, which is why I need your help."

"I can't." I pushed the stool back and stood up, nearly stepping on a cat in the process. "There must be some other way you can do this. You know I'm already bogged down in supernatural affairs." I actually couldn't bring myself to admit the real reason I wanted to dodge this. It was about more than just risking my life. So far, all my magical interactions had been with Ms. Terwilliger. If I signed on for this, I would be plunging into the world of witches, something I'd sworn I would never do.

Ms. Terwilliger tapped the article, and her voice was quiet when she spoke. "Could you let this happen to other girls, knowing there's a way you could stop it? I've never heard of any of her victims waking up. The way this spell works, Veronica needs to renew it every few years, and it requires five victims within one month. She did this once before, and it caught me off guard. This time, we have warning. Four more people could suffer this fate. Do you want that?"

There it was. She'd called me on the other part that had been nagging me because she knew me too well. I couldn't let innocents suffer, not even if it meant risking myself or facing the fears that haunted me. If I could stop this, I had to. No one deserved the fate of that girl in the paper. "Of course not."

"And let's not forget that you could soon be one of her victims."

I touched the garnet. "You said I'm hidden."

"You are, for now. And I hope against all hope you'll stay that way." I'd never seen her so grim before, and it was hard to watch. I was used to her prattling, bumbling, no-nonsense nature. "But here's something I've never told you about how magic users sense each other."

Something I'd learned over the years: it was never a good thing when people said, "Here's something I never told you. . . ." I braced myself.

86

"Untrained magic users have a particular feel that's unique from the more experienced," she explained. "There's a oh, wildness about the magic that surrounds you. It's easy for advanced witches to sense. My coven keeps track of novice magic users, but those are tightly guarded secrets. Veronica won't have access to those names, but there are spells she can use that can pick up on some of that untamed magic if it's near her. It's how she probably found this poor girl." Ms. Terwilliger nodded toward the article.

The idea of me having some "wild" magical aura was as shocking as her saying I had magic in my blood.

"When she absorbs a victim," Ms. Terwilliger continued, "she gets a burst of that wildness. It fades quickly, but when she possesses it, it can briefly enhance her ability to scry for another untrained victim. The more victims she takes, the stronger that ability will grow. There's a chance," Ms. Terwilliger said gravely, "that it could be enough to break apart the garnet. I don't know." She spread out her hands.

"So you're saying . . . with each victim she attacks, the chance that she'll find me increases."

"Yes."

"All right. I'll help you hunt for her." I shoved all my fears and doubts aside. The stakes were too high. My life, the other girls . . . Veronica had to be stopped for all our sakes. Someone like her couldn't be allowed to go on like this.

"There's more," added Ms. Terwilliger.

Really?

"More than hunting an evil witch who wants to drain me of my life and power?"

"If we can stop Veronica from finding less powerful victims, we can save their lives and limit her ability to find you." She produced a small velvet bag and emptied it out onto the table. Several small agate circles fell out. "These are charms that have some ability to mask magic. Not as strong as the garnet—that would take too long. But they're a quick fix that might save some of these other girls' lives."

I knew where this was going. "And you want me to deliver them."

"I'm sorry. I know I'm giving you some very difficult tasks here."

This was getting worse and worse. "Difficult? That's an understatement. And putting aside the fact that you want me to find a woman who could suck my life away, there's also the very small detail that the Alchemists would flip out if they knew I was involved with any of this."

Ms. Terwilliger didn't answer right away. She just watched me. A black cat jumped up beside her and joined in the staring. Its yellow-eyed gaze seemed to say, *Do the right thing*.

"Where do I start?" I asked finally. "Finding that neighborhood is part of it, right?"

"Yes. And I'll tell you where to find her potential victims, if you'll do the legwork of warning them. My coven keeps track of them. They'll be girls very much like you, ones with power who refuse to train and have no mentor to look after them. Once we have a clear fix on Veronica herself . . ." Ms. Terwilliger's eyes hardened. "Well, then. That's when I'll step in."

Once more, I wondered if I really wanted to know what that entailed.

A moment later, she added, "Oh, and I thought it would be a good idea to obscure your appearance as well."

I brightened. I couldn't explain it, but somehow, that made me feel immensely better. "There are a lot of spells for that, right?" I'd seen a number of them in my studies. Even if I had to use magic, it was better to at least look different.

"Yes. . . ." She drummed her fingers against the table. "But the amulet might not be able to hide you wearing an 'active' spell, which would then defeat the whole purpose. What I was actually hoping was that your 'brother' Adrian might be able to help."

My legs felt weak, and I sat back down. "Why on earth should Adrian be involved in this?"

"Well, he seems like he'd do anything for you." I eyed her, wondering if there was a double meaning in that. Her gaze was far away, her thoughts turned inward. She'd meant her words honestly. "Veronica wouldn't be able to detect vampire magic. His power . . . that spirit element he was telling me about . . . it can confuse the mind, right? Affect what others can see?"

"Yes. . . ."

She focused on me again, nodding in satisfaction. "If he could accompany you, help muddle whoever meets you . . . well, that would offer an extra level of protection."

I still didn't know what all I'd be doing to hunt Ms. Terwilliger's sister, but it sounded like, at the very least, there'd be a drive to Los Angeles in my future. Me, trapped in another small space with Adrian while he continued with that infuriating "loving from afar." I was so caught up in the emotional turmoil that idea caused that it took me a moment to realize the larger issue I was letting myself get sucked into.

"Do you realize what you're asking?" I said quietly. I touched the garnet again. "To be a part of this, you're asking me to expose myself to both human magic *and* vampire magic. Everything I try to avoid."

Ms. Terwilliger snorted, and for the first time tonight, I saw a return of her usual amused attitude. "Unless I'm mistaken, you've been exposing yourself to both kinds of magic for some time now. So, it can't go against your beliefs that much." She paused meaningfully. "If anything, it seems like it goes against the Alchemists' beliefs."

"The Alchemists' beliefs are my beliefs," I said quickly.

She arched an eyebrow. "Are they? I would hope your beliefs would be *your* beliefs."

I'd never thought about it that way before, but I suddenly hoped desperately that her words were true.

CHAPTER 6

I FOLLOWED MS. TERWILLIGER'S instructions diligently. I never took the garnet off, not even when I slept or showered. When school started the next morning, I wore it under my shirt to avoid any questions. It didn't exactly scream "magical amulet," but it was certainly conspicuous. To my surprise, Ms. Terwilliger wasn't in her first-period history class, making me wonder if she was doing some investigating of her own.

"Ms. T on some secret mission?"

I flinched and realized I'd been lost in my own thoughts. I turned and found Trey Juarez kneeling by my desk. Class hadn't started yet, and a confused-looking substitute teacher was trying to make sense of the chaos of Ms. Terwilliger's desk. Trey grinned at my surprise.

"Wh-what?" I asked. Had he somehow found out about Veronica? I tried to keep cool. "What makes you say that?"

"I was just joking," he said. "This is the second year I've had her, and she's never missed a day." He gave me a puzzled look.

"Unless you really do know something I don't?"

"No," I said quickly. "I'm just as surprised as you are."

Trey scrutinized me a few moments. We were good friends here at Amberwood, with only one teeny-tiny problem hanging between us.

His family was tied to the Warriors of Light.

Last month, the Warriors had tried to kill Sonya in a barbaric execution ritual. Trey had been one of the contenders for the "honor" of killing her, though he'd thrown the match at the last minute. I'd tried to appeal to the Warriors to release Sonya, but they hadn't listened. She and I were both saved when a raiding party of dhampirs showed up and defeated the Warriors. Stanton had helped orchestrate that raid—but hadn't bothered to fill me in that I was being used as a distraction. It was part of what had fueled my distrust of her and the Alchemists.

Trey had been blamed for getting me involved with the ritual, and the Warriors had ostracized his father and him. Just as I had been pressured by the Alchemists, Trey had had Warrior doctrine drilled into him his whole life. His father was so ashamed of the fallout that he would barely speak to Trey now. I knew how much Trey wanted his father's approval, so this silence was more painful to him than the Warriors' treatment.

Our allegiances made things difficult. When I'd once tentatively hinted to Trey that we still had unresolved issues between us, he'd responded with a bitter laugh. "You have nothing to worry about anymore," he'd told me. "I'm not hiding any secret plans from you—because I don't know any. They won't tell us anything. I'm not one of them, as far as they're concerned. I've been cut off forever, and it'd take a miracle for them to ever take us back." There'd been something in his dark eyes that told me if he ever could find that miracle, he'd jump on it. I'd tried asking about that, but he wouldn't discuss it any further. "I want to be your friend, Melbourne," he had said. "I like you. We're never going to resolve our differences. Might as well ignore them since we have to be together every day."

Amazingly, our friendship had managed to survive all that drama. The tension was always there, lurking between us, but we tried to ignore it. Although he knew about my involvement in the vampiric world, he had no idea I was taking behind-the-scenes magic lessons with our history teacher, of course.

If he thought I was lying about Ms. Terwilliger's absence today, he didn't push the matter. He nodded toward the sub. "This is going to be a blow-off day."

I dragged my mind away from magical intrigue. After being homeschooled for most of my life, some parts of the "normal" school world were a mystery. "What's that mean, exactly?"

"Usually teachers leave subs a lesson plan, telling them what to do. I saw the one Ms. Terwilliger left. It said, 'Distract them.'" Trey shook his head in mock sympathy. "I hope you can handle the wasted academic time. I mean, she'll probably say something like, 'Work on homework.' But no one will."

He was right. I wasn't sure if I could handle this. "Why wouldn't they?"

This seemed to amuse him immensely. "Melbourne, sometimes you're the only reason I come to class. I saw her sub plan for your independent study, by the way. It said you didn't even have to stick around. You're free to run wild."

Eddie, sitting nearby, overheard and scoffed. "To the library?"

This made both of them laugh, but my mind was already

spinning with possibilities. If I really didn't have to stay for my last class, I'd be free to leave campus early. I could go into Los Angeles to look for Veronica and—no. Adrian wasn't back. For a moment, I toyed with the idea of investigation without his spirit magic, but Ms. Terwilliger's warnings echoed through my mind. The hunt would have to wait.

But I could still look for Marcus Finch.

Santa Barbara was two hours away. That meant I had enough time to drive up there, do some investigating of Marcus, and still comfortably make it back by the school's curfew. I hadn't intended to go look for him until this weekend but realized now that I shouldn't waste this opportunity. Ms. Terwilliger's task weighed heavily on me as well, but I couldn't do anything about it until Adrian returned tonight.

Marcus Finch had been a mystery to me since the moment I'd discovered he was an ex-Alchemist. Realizing that I might actually get some answers *today* made my heart pound in overtime. It was one thing to suspect the Alchemists had been holding out on me. It was an entirely different matter to accept that I might be on the verge of having those suspicions confirmed. It was actually kind of terrifying.

As the day progressed, I became more and more resolved to make the drive. I had to face this sooner or later, and I might as well get it over with. For all I knew, Marcus had simply been sightseeing in Santa Barbara and could be gone already. I didn't want to repeat the scrying spell if I could help it.

Sure enough, when I showed up for what would normally be my independent study at the end of the day, the sub (looking extremely worn out after a day of following in Ms. Terwilliger's footsteps) told me I was free to go. I thanked her and hurried off to my dorm room, conscious of the clock that was now ticking. I didn't know exactly what I'd be facing in Santa Barbara, but I planned to be prepared for anything.

I changed out of my Amberwood uniform, opting for jeans and a plain black blouse. Kneeling by my bed, I pulled out a large metal box from underneath it. At first glance, the box looked like a makeup kit. However, it had an intricate lock that required both a key and combination. Inside was my Alchemist chemistry set, a collection of chemicals that would probably get me kicked out of school if found since it looked like it was capable of manufacturing illegal drugs. And really, some of the compounds probably were pretty questionable.

I selected some basics. One was a formula that was usually used to dissolve Strigoi bodies. I didn't expect to encounter any Strigoi in Santa Barbara, but the compound could also be used to disintegrate metal pretty handily. I chose a couple other mixtures—like one that could create a spy-worthy smoke screen—and carefully wrapped them all up before slipping them into my messenger bag. Then I locked the box again and slid it back under the bed.

After a little consideration, I took a deep breath and produced another hidden box. This was a new one in my collection. It contained various charms and potions I'd made under Ms. Terwilliger's instruction. Staring at its contents, I felt my stomach twist. Never in my wildest dreams had I imagined I'd have such a kit. When we'd first met, I'd only created charms under duress. Now I had several that I'd willingly made, and if what she'd said about her sister was true, I'd need to start making more. With great reluctance, I picked a variety of these as well and packed them up with the Alchemist chemicals. After a moment's consideration, I put a couple in my pocket for quick access.

The drive to Santa Barbara was easy this time of day. December had cooled off some of southern California's weather, but the sun was still out, making it seem warmer than it really was. And, as I drove up the coast, the desert gave way to more temperate conditions. Rain increased in the middle and northern parts of the state this time of year, making the landscape lush and green. I really did love Palm Springs and Amberwood, but there were times I wouldn't have minded if Jill's assignment had taken us up here.

Finding the Old Mission Santa Barbara wasn't difficult. It was a well-known tourist attraction and pretty easy to spot once you were nearby. The sprawling church looked exactly as it had in my vision save that it was lit by mid-afternoon sunshine rather than twilight. I pulled off to the side of the road in a residential neighborhood and gazed up at the beautiful stucco and terra-cotta masterpiece. I wished I had the time to go on a tour, but, as they so often did, my personal desires had to take a backseat to a larger goal.

Now came the more difficult part—having to figure out where the studio I'd seen might be. The neighborhood I parked in provided a view that was similar to the one I'd observed in the spell. The angles weren't exact, however, and this street only contained houses. I was almost certain the studio I'd seen had been in an apartment building. Keeping the mission in view, I drove a few more streets over and found what I'd hoped for: several blocks containing apartment complexes.

One looked too nice to have what I'd seen. The studio had seemed pretty bare bones and run down. The other two buildings on the street looked like more likely candidates. I drove to each one and walked around their grounds, trying to imagine what the angle might be when viewed from a higher window. I wished I'd had a chance to actually look down to the parking lot in the vision. It would have given me a better idea of the floor. After much thought, I finally deduced the studio had been on the third or fourth floor. Since one of the buildings only had two floors, that gave me a pretty positive hit on the correct place.

Stepping inside the building made me glad I'd packed hand sanitizer in my bag. The halls looked like they hadn't been swept in over a year. The walls were dirty, their paint chipped. Bits of trash sat on the floor. Cobwebs hung in some of the corners, and I prayed spiders were the only creepy-crawly inhabitants. If I saw a roach, I was probably going to bolt. The building had no front desk I could make inquiries at, so I flagged down a middle-aged woman as she was leaving. She paused, regarding me warily.

"Hi," I said, hoping I looked non-threatening. "I'm trying to find a friend of mine, but I don't know which apartment he lives in. Maybe you know him? His name is Marcus. He has a blue tattoo on his face." Seeing her blank look, I repeated the question in Spanish. Comprehension showed in her expression, but once she'd heard my entire question, her only response was a brief headshake. I didn't even have time to show her Marcus's picture.

I spent the next half hour doing the same thing whenever I saw residents going in or out. I stayed outside this time, preferring a brightly lit public area to the dingy interior. Some of the people I talked to were a little sketchy, and a couple of guys looked me over in a way I definitely didn't like. I was about to give up when a younger boy approached me. He appeared to be about ten and had been playing in the parking lot.

"I know the guy you're looking for," he told me in English. "But his name's not Marcus. It's Dave."

Considering how difficult Marcus had been to find, I wasn't entirely surprised he'd been using another name. "You're sure?" I asked the boy. I showed him the picture. "This is the guy?"

He nodded eagerly. "That's the one. He's real quiet. My mom says he's probably doing bad things."

Great. Just what I needed. "Do you know where he lives?"

The boy pointed upward. "At the top. 407."

I thanked him and went back inside, heading up to the fourth floor on stairs that creaked the entire way. The apartment was near the end of the hall, next to one that was blasting obnoxious music. I knocked on 407 and didn't get a response. Not sure if the occupant had heard me, I knocked more loudly and received the same result.

I eyed the doorknob, considering melting it with my Alchemist chemicals. Immediately, I dismissed the thought. Even in a disreputable building like this, a neighbor might be concerned to see me breaking into an apartment. I didn't want to attract any attention. This situation was getting increasingly frustrating, and I couldn't spend all day here.

I ran through my choices. Everyone said I was so smart. Surely there was some solution here that would work? Waiting around in the hall wasn't an option. There was no telling how long it could take for Marcus or "Dave" to show up. And honestly, the less time spent in the dirty hall, the better. If only there was some way to get inside that didn't involve actually destroying—

That's when the solution came to me. I groaned. It wasn't one I liked, but it would get the job done.

I went back outside and waved hello to the boy as he practiced jumping off the steps. "Was Dave home?" he asked.

"No."

The boy nodded. "He usually isn't."

That, at least, would be helpful for this next crazy plan. I left the boy and walked around the side of the building, which was mercifully deserted. There, clinging to the outer wall, was the most rickety fire escape I'd ever seen. Considering how rigid California safety standards were, I was astonished that this hadn't been reported. Of course, if it had, it didn't seem likely this building's owner would've been quick to act, judging from the rest of the conditions I'd seen.

Double checking that no one was around, I stood in the fire escape's shadow, hoping it more or less concealed me. From the messenger bag, I produced one of my charms: a necklace made of agate and crow feathers. I slipped it over my head and recited a Greek incantation. I felt the warmth of magic run through me but saw no ostensible changes. Theoretically, I should be invisible for those who didn't know to look for me. Whether that had actually happened, I couldn't say. I supposed I'd find out if someone came by and demanded to know why I was climbing into an apartment via the fire escape.

Once I stepped onto it, I nearly terminated the plan. The entire fire escape squeaked and swayed. The scaffolding was so rusty, I wouldn't have been surprised if it disintegrated beneath my feet. I stood frozen where I was, trying to work up the courage to go on. I reminded myself that this could be my one chance to find Marcus. The boy in the parking lot had confirmed he lived here. I couldn't waste this opportunity.

I gulped and kept going, gingerly moving from floor to floor. When I reached the fourth, I stared down in amazement, unable to believe the fire escape was still intact. Now I had a new problem. I'd figured out where Marcus's studio was, and it was one window over from the fire escape's landing. The distance wasn't that great, but on the narrow ledge between them would feel like miles. Equally daunting was the fact that I'd have to get through the window. It was shut, which made sense if he was in hiding. I had a couple magical amulets capable of melting glass, but I didn't trust myself to be able to use them on the narrow ledge—which meant I had to see just how good my aim had become in PE.

Still conscious of the precarious fire escape, I took out a small pouch of powder from my messenger bag. Sizing up the distance, I threw the pouch hard toward the window, reciting a spell—and missed. The pouch hit the side of the building, throwing up a dusty cloud, and began eating away at the stucco. I winced as the wall dissolved. The spell eventually burned itself out but left a noticeable hole behind. It hadn't gone all the way through, and I supposed given the state of the building, no one would probably even notice.

I had one pouch left and had to make it count. The pane was fairly big, and there was no way I could miss this time. I threw hard—and made contact. The powder smashed against the window. Immediately, a reaction spread out and began melting the glass. It dripped down like ice out in the sun. Now, watching anxiously, I wanted the reaction to go on for as long as possible. I needed a big enough hole to get through. Fortunately, when it stopped, I felt confident I could make it inside—if I could get over there.

I wasn't afraid of heights, but as I crept along the ledge, I felt like I was on top of a skyscraper. My heart was in my throat, and I pondered the logistics of surviving a four-floor drop. My palms began to sweat, and I ordered them to stop. I wasn't going to come all this way just to have my hands slip at the last minute.

As it turned out, it was my foot that slipped. The world spun, and I frantically flung my arms out, just barely grabbing the inside of the window. I pulled myself toward it, and with a surge of adrenaline-fueled effort managed to hook my other leg inside. I took a deep breath and tried to quiet my pounding heart. I was secure. I was going to make it. A moment later, I was able to pull myself up and swing my other leg around the ledge, tumbling into the room.

I landed on the floor, my legs weak and shaky as I worked to steady my frantic breathing. That was close. If my reflexes had been a little slower, I would've found out exactly what four floors could do to the human body. While I loved science, I wasn't sure that was an experiment I needed to try. Maybe being around dhampirs so much had helped improve my physical skills.

Once I'd recovered, I was able to assess my surroundings. Here I was, in the exact same studio I'd seen in my vision. Glancing behind me, I sized up the mission, verifying I had the same vantage. Yup. Exactly the same. Inside, I recognized the mattress on the floor and the same meager belongings. Across the room, the door leading out had a number of very new, very state-of-the-art locks. Dissolving the outer doorknob wouldn't have done any good.

"Now what?" I muttered. I'd made it inside. I didn't have Marcus, but I theoretically had his apartment. I was unsure what I was looking for but might as well start somewhere.

First, I examined the mattress, not that I expected much. It couldn't hide belongings like mine could. It could, however, hide rats and God only knew what else underneath it. I gingerly lifted a corner, knowing I must be grimacing, but there was nothing underneath—alive or otherwise. My next target was a small, disorderly pile of clothes. Going through someone's dirty laundry (because I assumed it was dirty, if it was sitting on the floor) wasn't much better than looking at the mattress. A whiff of fabric softener told me that these clothes were, in fact, recently washed. They were ordinary guy clothes, probably a young guy's clothes, which fit with Marcus's profile. Jeans. T-shirts. Boxers. As I sifted through the pile, I nearly started folding them and had to remind myself that I didn't want to leave any sign of my passing. Of course, the melted window was kind of a dead giveaway.

A couple of personal items sat nearby, a toothbrush and deodorant with a scent inexplicably called as "Ocean Fiesta." Aside from a rickety wooden chair and the ancient TV, there was only one other form of comfort and entertainment in the barren room: a battered copy of *The Catcher in the Rye*. "Great," I muttered, wondering what it said about a person who owned no other personal possessions. "Marcus Finch is pretentious and self-entitled."

The studio's bathroom was claustrophobic and barely had enough space for a single shower stall, toilet, and dripping sink. Judging from the mildew on the floor, a good deal of water sprayed out when the shower was used. A large black spider scurried down the drain, and I hastily backed out.

Defeated, I went to investigate a narrow closet door. After all my work, I'd found Marcus Finch but hadn't actually *found* him. My search had revealed nothing. I had limited time to wait for him, and honestly, if I were him and returned home to a melted window, I would promptly walk out the door and never return. If he ran, I'd have no choice but to keep scrying and—

"Ahh!"

Something jumped out at me as I opened the closet door— and it wasn't a rat or a roach.

It was a man.

The closet was tiny, so it was a miracle he had even fit inside. I had no time to process the spatial logistics, however, because his fist shot out and clipped me on the side of the face.

In my life, I'd been slammed up against brick walls and bitten by a Strigoi. I'd never been punched, however, and it wasn't an experience I wanted to repeat. I stumbled backward, so surprised that I couldn't even react right away. The guy lunged after me, grabbing my upper arms and shaking me as he leaned close.

"How did you guys find me?" he exclaimed. "How many more are coming?"

Pain radiated through the side of my face, but somehow, I managed to gather my senses. Last month, I'd taken a self-defense class with a slightly unstable Chihuahua breeder who looked like a pirate. Despite Malachi Wolfe's unorthodox behavior, he'd actually taught us some legitimate skills, and they came back to me now. I kneed my attacker in the stomach. His blue eyes went wide with shock as he released me and fell to the ground. It didn't keep him down for long, though. He scrambled back to his feet and came after me, but by then, I'd grabbed the chair and was using it to keep him at bay the way a lion tamer would.

"Back off," I said. "I just want to—"

Ignoring my threats, the guy pushed forward and grabbed one of the chair's legs, pulling it away from me. He had me backed into a corner, and despite some tricks Eddie had taught me, I wasn't confident in my own ability to throw a punch. Nonetheless, I put up a good fight when my attacker tried to grab me again. We struggled and fell to the floor. I kicked and clawed like crazy, making things as difficult as possible. It was only when he managed to pin me with his entire body that my flailing got stifled. I had enough freedom to reach a hand into my pocket, however.

"Who sent you?" he demanded. "Where are the others?"

I didn't answer. Instead, I pulled out a small vial and flipped the cap off with one hand. Immediately, noxious yellow vapor with the consistency of dry ice spilled out of it. I thrust it toward the guy's face. He recoiled in disgust, and tears sprang into his eyes. The substance itself was relatively harmless, but its fumes acted as a kind of pepper spray. He let go of me, and with strength I didn't even know I had, I managed to roll him over and hold him down. I drove my elbow into his wrist, and he made a small grunt of pain. With my other arm, I waved the vial with as much menace as I would a machete. This wouldn't fool him for long, but hopefully it'd buy me some time to reassess my situation. Now that he was still, I was finally able to get a good look at him and was relieved to see I'd at least achieved my goal. He had a young, handsome face with an indigo tattoo on his cheek. It was an abstract design that looked like a latticework of crescent moons. A faint silver gleam edged some of the blue lines.

"Nice to meet you, Marcus."

Then, the most astonishing thing happened. Through his watering eyes, he'd been trying to get a good look at me too. Recognition appeared on his face as he blinked me into focus.

"Sydney Sage," he gasped. "I've been looking for you."

I didn't have any time to be surprised because I suddenly heard the click of a gun, and a barrel touched the back of my head.

"Get off him," a voice demanded. "And drop the smoke bomb."

CHAPTER 7

I MIGHT HAVE BEEN DETERMINED to find Marcus, but I certainly wasn't going to argue against a gun.

I raised my hands in the air and slowly stood up, keeping my back to the newcomer. Just as carefully, I stepped away from Marcus and set the vial on the floor. Fumes still wafted out of it, but the reaction would burn itself out soon. Then I dared a peek behind me. When I saw the girl who stood there, I could barely believe my eyes.

"Are you okay?" she asked Marcus. He was unsteadily getting to his feet. "I left as soon as you called."

"You!" I couldn't quite manage anything more articulate.

The girl standing before me was close to my age, with long, tangled blond hair. She still had the gun on me, but a small smile appeared on her face.

"Nice to see you again."

The feeling wasn't mutual. I'd last seen this girl when I faced down the Warriors in their arena. She'd been toting a gun there as well and had had a perpetual snarl on her face. She'd pushed me around and threatened me, making no secret of how heretical she thought my defense of Sonya was. Although she seemed much calmer now than she had with those fanatics, I still couldn't dismiss what she was—or what the implications were. I turned to Marcus in disbelief. He was cradling the wrist I'd nailed with my elbow.

"You . . . you're one of them! One of the Warriors of Light!"

I don't think I'd ever been so let down in my life. I'd had so many hopes pinned on Marcus. He'd become larger than life in my mind, some rebel savior who was going to tell me all the secrets of the world and free me from being another cog in the machine of the Alchemists. But it was all a lie. Clarence had mentioned Marcus had convinced the Warriors to leave him alone. I'd assumed it was because Marcus had some incredible leverage he could use against the Warriors, but apparently, the key to his influence was that he was one of them.

He looked up from his wrist. "What? Those nuts? Hell, no."

I almost pointed at the girl but decided it would be best not to make any sudden moves. I settled for a nod in her direction and noticed all the locks on the door had been undone. I'd been so caught up in the struggle with Marcus that I hadn't heard them. "Really? Then how come one of them just saved you?"

"I'm not really one of them." She spoke almost casually, but the gun contradicted her tone. "I mean, I guess I kind of am. . . ."

"Sabrina's a spy," explained Marcus. He looked much more at ease too, now that I wasn't assaulting him. "A lovely one. She's been undercover with them for over a year. She's also the one who told me about you."

Once again, it was hard knowing how to respond to that. I

also wasn't sure if I bought this spy story. "What exactly did you tell him?"

He shot me a movie star smile. His teeth were so white that I wondered if he had veneers. It seemed out of character for a rogue who lived on the run, but nothing about this day was really turning out like I'd expected. "She told me about this Alchemist girl who defended a Moroi and then helped lead a dhampir raiding party."

Lead? Hardly. No one—notably Stanton—had felt the need to enlighten me about that raid until I was in the middle of it. I didn't want to tip my hand too early, though. "The Alchemists sanctioned that raid," I said.

"I saw the way you spoke," said Sabrina. Her eyes flicked between Marcus and me, fierce for me and admiring for him. "It was inspiring. And we watched you for a while, you know. You spent an awful lot of time with the Moroi and dhampirs in Palm Springs."

"It's my job," I said. She hadn't really seemed inspired at the time. Mostly she'd looked disappointed at not having a chance to use the gun on me.

Marcus's smile turned knowing. "From what I heard, you and those Moroi almost looked like friends. And then, here you are, looking for me. You're definitely the dissident we'd hoped for."

No, this was not turning out at all like I'd planned. In fact, it was pretty much the opposite of what I'd planned. I'd been so proud of my ability to track down Marcus, little knowing that he'd been watching me already. I didn't like that. It made me feel vulnerable, even if they were saying some of things I'd hoped to hear. Needing to feel like I was in control, I tried to play it cool and tough.

"Maybe there are other Alchemists about to show up," I said.

"They would've been here already," he said, calling my bluff. "They wouldn't have sent you alone . . . though I did panic when I first saw you. I didn't realize who you were and thought there were others right behind you." He paused, and that cocky attitude turned sheepish. "Sorry about, um, punching you. If it makes you feel better, you did something pretty serious to my wrist."

Sabrina's face filled with concern. "Oh, Marcus. Do you need to see a doctor?"

He tested the movement of his wrist and then shook his head. "You know we can't. Never know who might be watching at a hospital. Those places are too easy to monitor."

"You really are hiding from the Alchemists," I said in amazement.

His nodded, almost looking proud. "You doubted? I figured you'd know that."

"I suspected, but I didn't hear it from them. They deny you exist."

He seemed to find that funny. In fact, he seemed to find everything funny, which I found slightly irritating. "Yup. That's what I've heard from the others."

"What others?"

"Others like you." Those blue eyes held me for a moment, like they could see all my secrets. "Other Alchemists wanting to break free of the fold."

I knew my own eyes were wide. "There . . . there are others?"

Marcus settled on the floor, leaning against the wall and still cradling his wrist. "Let's get comfortable. Sabrina, put the gun away. I don't think Sydney's going to give us any trouble."

Sabrina didn't look so sure of that, but after several moments, she complied. She joined him on the floor, positioning herself protectively next to him. "I'd rather stand," I told them. No way would I willingly sit on that filth. After rolling around with Marcus, I wanted to go bathe myself in hand sanitizer.

He shrugged. "Suit yourself. You want some answers? You give me some first. Why'd you come looking for me off the Alchemist clock?"

I didn't like being interrogated, but what was the point of being here if I wasn't going to engage in a dialogue?

"Clarence told me about you," I said at last. "He showed me your picture, and I saw how you'd tattooed over the lily. I didn't even know that was possible." The tattoo never faded.

"Clarence Donahue?" Marcus looked genuinely pleased. "He's a good guy. I suppose you'd be friends with him if you're in Palm Springs, huh?"

I started to say we weren't friends but then reconsidered. What else were we?

"Getting this isn't easy," added Marcus, tapping the blue tattoo. "You'll have to do a lot of work if you want to do it."

I stepped backward. "Whoa, I never said that's what I wanted. And why in the world would I do it anyway?"

"Because it'll free you," he said simply. "It prevents you from discussing vampire affairs, right? You don't think that's all it does, do you? Think. What stops it from exerting other control?"

I pretty much had to just give up on any expectations for this conversation because every topic was crazier than the last. "I've never heard of anything like that. I've never felt anything like that. Aside from it protecting vampire information, I'm in control."

He nodded. "Probably. The initial tattoo usually only has the talking compulsion in it. They only start adding other components with re-inks if they've got a reason to worry about you. People can sometimes fight through those and if they do . . . well, then it's off to re-education."

His words sent a chill through me, and I rested a hand on my cheek as I flashbacked to the meeting I'd had when I was given the Palm Springs assignment. "I was re-inked recently . . . but it was routine." Routine. Normal. Nothing like what he was suggesting.

"Maybe." He tilted his head and gave me another piercing look. "You do anything bad before that, love?"

Like helping a dhampir fugitive? "Depends on your definition of bad."

Both of them laughed. Marcus's laugh was loud and rollicking and actually pretty infectious—but the situation was far too dire for me to join in.

"They may have reinforced your group loyalty then," he said, still chuckling. "But it either wasn't very strong or else you fought through it—otherwise you wouldn't be here." He glanced over at Sabrina. "What do you think?"

Sabrina studied me with a critical eye. I still had a hard time believing her role in all of this. "I think she'd be a good addition. And since she's still in, she could help us with that . . . other matter."

"I think so too," he said.

I crossed my arms over my chest. I didn't like being discussed as though I weren't there. "A good addition to what?"

111

"Our group." To Sabrina, he said, "We really need a name for it, you know." She snorted, and he returned his attention to me. "We're a mix. Some are former Warriors or double agents like Sabrina. Some are ex-Alchemists."

"And what do you do?" I gestured around us. "This doesn't exactly look like a high-tech base of operation for some covert team."

"Look at you. Pretty and funny," he said, looking delighted. "We do what you do—or what you want to do. We like the Moroi. We want to help them—on our own terms. The Alchemists theoretically want to help them too, but we all know that's based on a core of fear and dislike—not to mention a strict control of its members. So, we work in secret, seeing as the Alchemists aren't fans of those who break from the fold. They *really* aren't fans of me, which is why I end up in places like this."

"We keep an eye on the Warriors too," said Sabrina. She scowled. "I hate being around those nuts, having to play along with them. They claim they only want to destroy the Strigoi— but, well, the things I've heard them say against the Moroi too . . ."

I thought back to one of my more disturbing memories of the Warrior arena. I'd heard one of them make a mysterious comment about how someday, they'd deal with the Moroi too.

"But what do you guys actually *do*?" Talking about rebellions and covert operations was one thing, but actually effecting change was another. I'd visited my sister Carly at her college and seen a number of student groups who wanted to change the world. Most of them sat around drinking coffee, talking a lot and doing little.

Marcus and Sabrina exchanged glances. "I can't quite get

into our operations," he said. "Not until I know you're on board with breaking your tattoo."

Breaking your tattoo. There was something sinister—not to mention permanent—about those words, and I suddenly wondered what I was doing here. Who were these people, really? Why was I even humoring them? Then another, almost terrifying thought hit me: *Am I doubting them because of the tattoo's control? Is it making me skeptical around anyone who questions the Alchemists? Is Marcus telling the truth?*

"I don't really understand that either," I told them. "What it means to 'break' the tattoo. Do you just mean putting ink over it?"

Marcus stood up. "All in good time. Right now, we've got to get out of here. Even if you were discreet, I assume you used Alchemist resources to find me?"

I hesitated. Even if these guys were legitimate and had good intentions toward the Moroi, I certainly wasn't going to reveal my involvement with magic. "Something like that."

"I'm sure you're good, but we can't take the chance. This place has been compromised." He cast a wistful glance around the studio. Honestly, I thought he should be grateful I'd given him a reason to leave.

Sabrina rose as well, her face hardening. "I'll make sure the secondary location is ready."

"You're an angel, as always," he told her.

"Hey, how did you know I was coming?" I asked. "You had time to hide and call her." What I really wanted to know was how he'd seen me through the invisibility spell. I'd felt the magic fill me. I was certain I'd cast the spell correctly, but he'd discovered me. The spell wouldn't work if someone knew to look for you, so maybe he'd happened to glance out the window when I was scaling the fire escape? Worst timing ever.

"Tony warned me." Marcus flashed me another of those dazzling grins. I think he was trying to make me smile back. "Good kid."

Tony? Then I knew. The boy in the parking lot. He'd pretended to help me and then sold me out. He must have spoken to Marcus while I climbed the fire escape. Maybe Marcus only answered to some secret knock. At least I had the comfort of knowing I'd cast the spell correctly. It simply hadn't worked because Marcus had advance warning that some girl was coming after him.

He began packing up his meager belongings into a backpack. "*The Catcher in the Rye* is a great book, by the way." He winked. "Maybe someday we'll have a literary discussion."

I wasn't interested in that. Watching him, I saw that he kept favoring his uninjured wrist. I couldn't believe I'd caused damage like that and felt a little guilty, despite everything that had happened. "You should get that taken care of," I said. Sabrina nodded in agreement.

He sighed. "I can't. At least, not through conventional means. The Alchemists have eyes everywhere."

Conventional means.

"I, uh, might be able to help you get it healed through unconventional means," I said.

"You know some off-the-grid doctor?" asked Sabrina hopefully.

"No. But I know a Moroi spirit user."

Marcus froze, and I kind of liked that I'd thrown him off guard. "Seriously? We've heard of them but never met one.

That woman they had—Sonya? She was one, right? She was gone before we could find out more."

Talking about Adrian made me nervous, but Sabrina probably already knew he existed if they'd been watching me. "Yeah, she was one, and there's another in Palm Springs. I could take you to him and let him heal you."

Excitement lit Marcus's features. Sabrina looked at him in horror. "You can't just go off with her." Was that concern or jealousy in her voice?

"Why not?" he asked. "She's taking a leap of faith with us. We can't do any less. Besides, I'm dying to meet a spirit user. The safe house isn't that far from Palm Springs. You make sure everything's in order and then come pick me up later."

Sabrina didn't like that, not at all. Maybe I didn't understand the dynamics of their group yet, but it was obvious she regarded him as a leader and was insanely protective. In fact, I suspected her feelings for him were more than professional. They went back and forth on whether he'd be safe or not, and I listened without a word. All the while, I wondered if *I'd* be safe heading off with some unknown guy. *Clarence trusted him,* I reminded myself. *And he's pretty paranoid.* Besides, with Marcus's wrist out of commission, I could probably take him.

He finally convinced Sabrina to let him go but not before she snarled, "If anything happens to him, I'm coming after you." Apparently her hard-core character in the arena hadn't been entirely faked.

We parted ways from her, and before long, Marcus and I were on the road to Palm Springs. I tried to get more information out of him, but he wouldn't bite. Instead, he kept complimenting me and saying things that were only one step away from pickup lines. Judging from the way he'd bantered with Sabrina too, I didn't think there was anything particularly special about me. I thought he was just used to women fawning all over him. He *was* cute, I'd give him that, but it took a lot more than that to win me over.

It was sunset when we pulled up to Adrian's apartment, and I belatedly wondered if I should've given him some advance warning. Too late now.

We walked up to the door, and I knocked three times. "It's open," a voice called from within. I stepped inside, and Marcus followed.

Adrian was working on an abstract painting of what looked like a crystalline building from some fantasy world. "Unexpected treat," he said. His eyes fell on Marcus and widened. "I'll be damned. You found him."

"Thanks to you," I said.

Adrian glanced over at me. A smile started to form—and then instantly dried up. "What happened to your face?"

"Oh." I lightly touched the swollen spot. It still smarted but wasn't as painful as it had been earlier. I spoke my next words without thinking. "Marcus hit me."

I'd never seen Adrian move so fast. Marcus had no chance to react, probably because he was exhausted from our earlier encounter. Adrian shoved Marcus up against a wall and—to my complete and utter astonishment—punched Marcus. Adrian had once joked that he never dirtied his hands, so this was something I never could have prepared myself for. In fact, if Adrian was going to attack someone, I would've expected something magical and spirit-driven. Yet . . . as I watched him, I could see that anything as thoughtful as magic was far from

Adrian's mind. He had kicked into primal mode. See a threat. Go after it. It was yet another surprising—yet fascinating—side of the enigma that was Adrian Ivashkov.

Marcus quickly got his bearings and responded in kind. He pushed Adrian back, wincing a little. Even with his injury, he was still strong. "What the hell? Who are you?"

"The guy that's going to kick your ass for hurting her," said Adrian.

He tried another punch, but Marcus dodged and managed to land a hit that knocked Adrian back into one of his easels. When Marcus swung again, Adrian eluded him with a maneuver that was straight out of Wolfe's class. I would've applauded him if I wasn't so appalled by the situation. I knew some girls thought it was sexy to have men fight over them. Not me.

"You guys, stop!" I cried.

"No one's going to throw you around and get away with it," said Adrian.

"What happened with us has nothing to do with you," retorted Marcus.

"*Everything* about her has to do with me."

The two circled around each other, waiting for the other to pounce. "Adrian," I exclaimed. "It was an accident."

"Doesn't look like an accident," he replied, never taking his eyes off Marcus.

"You should listen to her," growled Marcus. The easygoing guy I'd met earlier was gone, but I guess being attacked would do that to you. "It might save you from getting your pretty face wrecked. How much styling did you have to do to get your hair like that?"

"At least I brush my hair," said Adrian.

Marcus lunged forward—but not directly at Adrian. He grabbed a painting off an easel and used it as a weapon. Adrian again managed a dodge, but the painting didn't fare so well. The canvas tore, and Marcus tossed it aside, ready for the next advance.

Adrian spared the canvas a brief glance. "Now you've really pissed me off."

"Enough!" Something told me they weren't going to listen to reason. This required direct intervention. I stalked across the room and pushed myself between them.

"Sydney, get out of the way," ordered Adrian.

"Yeah," agreed Marcus. "For once he's got something worthwhile to say."

"No!" I held out my hands to separate them. "Both of you back off—*now*!" My voice rang through the apartment, and I refused to budge. "Back. Off," I repeated.

"Sydney. . . ." Adrian's voice was a little more uncertain than when he'd told me to get out of the way.

I looked back and forth between them, giving each guy a healthy glare. "Adrian, it really was an accident. Marcus, this is the guy who's going to help you, so show some respect."

This, more than anything, seemed to derail them.

"Wait," said Adrian. "Did you say 'help'?"

Marcus was equally flabbergasted. "*This* asshole is the spirit user?"

"You're both acting like idiots," I scolded. The next time I had nothing to do, I'd have to get a book on testosterone-driven behavior. This was out of my league. "Adrian, can we talk somewhere in private? Like the bedroom?"

Adrian agreed, but not before giving Marcus one last

menacing look. I told Marcus to stay where he was and hoped he wouldn't take off or call in someone else with a gun. Adrian followed me to his bedroom and shut the door behind us.

"You know," he said, "under normal circumstances, you inviting me to the bedroom would be the highlight of my day."

I crossed my arms and sat on the bed. I did so out of simple fatigue, but a moment later, I was struck by what I was doing. *This is where Adrian sleeps. I'm touching the covers he's wrapped in every night. What does he wear? Does he wear anything?*

I jumped up.

"It really was an accident," I told him. "Marcus thought I was there to abduct him."

Adrian, having no such hang-ups with the bed, sat down. He winced, probably from the blow to the stomach. "If someone like you showed up to abduct me, I'd let you."

Even when he was in pain, it never stopped with him. "I'm serious. It was just instinct, and he apologized over and over in the car once he realized who I was."

That got his attention. "He knew you?"

I gave him a recap of my day in Santa Barbara. He listened avidly, nodding along, his expression shifting back and forth between intrigue and surprise.

"I didn't realize when I brought him back here that you'd inflict more damage," I said, once I'd finished the story.

"I was defending your honor." Adrian gave me that devil-may-care smile that always managed to both infuriate and captivate me. "Pretty manly, huh?"

"Very," I said dryly. I didn't like violence, but him doing something so out of character for me actually *was* kind of incredible. Not that I'd ever tell him that. "You did Wolfe proud. Do you think you can manage not to have any more 'manly' displays while he's here? Please?"

Adrian shook his head, still smiling. "I've said over and over, I'd do anything for you. I just keep hoping it'll be something like, 'Adrian, let's go hot tubbing' or 'Adrian, take me out for fondue.'"

"Well, sometimes we have to—did you say fondue?" Sometimes it was impossible to follow Adrian's train of thought. "Why in the world would I ever say that?"

He shrugged. "I like fondue."

I didn't even know what to say about that. This whole day was getting more and more exhausting. "I'm sorry I'm not asking for something as glamorous as melted cheese. But for now, I need to find out about Marcus and his group—and the tattoo."

Adrian recognized the situation's severity. He stood up and gently touched the lily on my cheek. "I don't trust him. He could be using you. But then . . . I don't like the idea of this controlling you either."

"That makes two of us," I admitted, losing some of my earlier toughness.

He traced the line of my cheek for a few breathless moments and then dropped his hand. "It might be worth helping him to get some answers."

"Will you promise not to get in any more fights? Please?"

"I promise," he said. "So long as he doesn't start one."

"I'll have him promise too." I just hoped their "manly" natures wouldn't get the better of them. As I ruminated on this, something I'd nearly forgotten about tumbled to the forefront of my mind. "Oh . . . Adrian, I've got one more favor to ask you. A big one."

"Fondue?" he asked hopefully.

"No. It's about Ms. Terwilliger's sister. . . ."

I told him what I'd learned. The amusement in his face faded and turned to disbelief. "You just mention this now?" he exclaimed when I finished. "That some soul-sucking witch might be after you?"

"She doesn't know I exist." I felt surprisingly defensive. "And I'm the only one who can help, at least according to Ms. Terwilliger. She thinks I'm some super-investigator."

"Well, you do have that Sherlock Holmes thing going for you," he said. His joking didn't last; he was too upset. "But you still should've told me! You could've called."

"I was kind of busy with Marcus."

"Then your priorities are off. This is a *lot* more important than his band of Merry Men. If we need to take out some evil sorceress before she gets to you, then of course I'll help." He hesitated. "With one condition."

I eyed him warily. "What's that?"

"Let me heal you too."

I jerked backward, almost more shocked than if he'd suggested hitting me again. "No! Absolutely not! I don't need it. I'm in better shape than him."

"You want to go back to Amberwood with that on your face? You're not going to be able to hide that, Sage. And if Castile sees it, he really will come after Marcus." Adrian crossed his arms defiantly. "That's my price."

He was bluffing, and I knew it. Maybe it was egotistical, but I knew he wasn't going to let me go into a dangerous situation without him. He did, however, have a point. I still hadn't seen the mark Marcus had left, but I didn't want to explain it back at school. And yes, there was a good chance Eddie would want to hunt down my assailant. Being beat up by an avenging dhampir might make working with Marcus difficult.

Yet . . . how could I agree? At least the magic I used was on my terms. And although my tattoo had trace amounts of vampire magic, I took comfort in knowing it was tied to the "normal" four elements, the ones we understood. Spirit was still an unknown entity, with abilities that continually surprised us. How could I subject myself to rogue vampire magic?

Guessing my inner turmoil, Adrian's face softened. "I do this all the time. It's an easy spell. No surprises."

"Maybe," I said reluctantly. "But each time you use spirit, you're more likely to go crazy."

"Already crazy about you, Sage."

At least this was familiar territory. "You said you wouldn't bring that up."

He simply regarded me without comment. Finally, I threw my arms up. "Fine," I said, with more boldness than I felt. "Just get it over with."

Adrian didn't waste any time. Stepping forward, he reached out and rested his hand on my cheek once more. My breath caught and my heart rate went up. It would be so, so easy for him to pull me to him and kiss me again. A tingling warmth spread over my skin, and for a moment, I thought it was just my normal reaction to him. No, I realized. It was the magic. His eyes locked onto mine, and for the space of a heartbeat, we were suspended in time. Then he removed his hand and stepped away.

"Done," he said. "Was that so bad?"

No, it hadn't been bad at all. The throbbing pain was gone. All that was left was the constant inner voice nagging me that what had just happened was wrong. That same voice tried to tell me that Adrian had left a taint behind . . . but that was hard to believe from him. I released the breath I'd been holding.

"Thank you," I said. "You didn't have to do that."

He gave me one of those small smiles. "Oh, believe me, I did."

A moment of awkward silence hung between us. I cleared my throat. "Well. We should get back out to Marcus. Maybe we'll have time for dinner before Sabrina shows up, and you guys can patch things over."

"I doubt even a moonlight stroll would fix things between us."

His words reminded me of something else I'd meant to bring up when he got back to town, something that had taken a very low priority. "Your coat—you never took it back after the wedding. It's in my car."

He waved dismissively. "Keep it. I've got others."

"What am I going to do with a wool coat?" I asked. "Especially here in Palm Springs?"

"Sleep with it," he suggested. "Think of me."

I put my hands on my hips and tried to stare him down, which wasn't easy since he was so tall. That, and because his words suddenly returned me to the disorienting feeling I'd had sitting on his bed. "You said you weren't going to bring up any romantic stuff around me."

"Was that romantic?" he asked. "I was just making the suggestion, since the coat's so heavy and warm. I figured you'd think of me since it was such a nice gesture. And yet, once again, you're the one who finds romantic subtext in everything I say."

"I do not. You know that's not what I meant."

He shook his head in mock sympathy. "I tell you, Sage. Sometimes I think I'm the one who needs to take out the restraining order on *you*."

"Adrian!"

But he was already out the door, knowing laughter echoing behind him.

CHAPTER 8

I THINK ADRIAN WOULD'VE gone hunting Ms. Terwilliger's sister with me then and there. Amberwood's curfew wouldn't allow it, and besides, it was something I wanted to do in daylight. To his credit, he did heal Marcus without them getting into a fistfight, so that was progress. Marcus lost a little of his animosity and tried to engage Adrian in conversation about what spirit could do. Adrian gave wary responses and looked relieved when Sabrina showed up to take Marcus away. He gave me a mysterious farewell, simply saying he'd text me soon about the "next stage." I was too tired to ask for more details and headed back to my dorm to sleep off what had been a pretty crazy day.

I was awakened at the crack of dawn by heavy pounding at my door. I squinted at the clock, grimacing when I saw that it was an hour earlier than I usually got up. I stayed in bed, hoping whoever it was would go away. If there was something really urgent happening, someone would've called me on my cell phone. The display showed no missed calls, however.

Unfortunately, the knocking didn't stop. With a feeling of dread, I finally dragged myself up, half-afraid of what I'd find outside my door.

It was Angeline.

"Finally," she said, inviting herself into my room. "I thought you'd never answer."

"Sorry," I said, shutting the door behind her. "I was busy sleeping."

She walked right up to my bed and sat down like she owned it. I really didn't know her schedule, but she always struck me as a late riser. Apparently not today. She was dressed in a school uniform, with her brilliant red hair pulled back in what was, for her, a rather tidy ponytail.

"I have a problem," she said.

My feeling of dread grew. I turned on my coffeemaker, which I always had ready with fresh grounds and water. Something told me I was going to need a cup to get through this. "What's going on?" I asked, settling into my desk chair. I made no attempt at even guessing. When it came to Angeline, her problems could range from throwing a desk in rage or accidentally spilling hydrochloric acid on another student. Both had happened recently.

"I'm failing math," she said.

This was unwelcome but not unexpected news. Angeline's mountain community, while still educating its children, didn't quite match the standards of Amberwood's elite curriculum. She struggled in a number of her classes but had managed to scrape by so far.

"I'm already in trouble in my Spanish class," she added. "But that piñata I made got me some extra credit, so I'm hanging in there okay for now."

I'd heard about the piñata. It had been for her class's cultural day, and she'd been so thorough with her papier-mâché that none of her classmates had been able to open it through normal means. Angeline had ended up beating it against a wall and had to be stopped by her teacher when she'd produced a lighter.

"But if I slip there *and* in math, I could get expelled."

That dragged me away from the flammable piñata and back to the present. "Ugh," I said, having no better way to articulate my thoughts. The problem with a school that had high standards was . . . well, it had high standards. Trouble in one class might be tolerated, but not two. And if Angeline got kicked out, we'd be down one level of security for Jill—not to mention the fact that I'd probably get blamed for it all.

"Ms. Hayward told me I need to get a tutor. She says I either need to get better or at least show I'm trying."

That was promising, I supposed. Even if a tutor couldn't help, hopefully the school would be lenient with her good faith effort.

"Okay," I said. "We'll get you a tutor."

She frowned. "Why can't you do it? You're smart. You're good at math."

Why couldn't I? Well, first I had to stop an evil sorceress from sucking the youth and power from innocent girls. Then I had to crack the secrets and lies that the organization I'd been born into was telling me.

Instead I said, "I'm busy."

"You have to do it. It'd be easy for you," she protested.

"Really busy," I said. "I'm surprised Eddie can't do it."

His name brought a smile to her face. "He offered, but his grades are just average. I need someone really good."

"Then I'll get you someone really good. I just can't do it myself right now."

Angeline didn't like that answer, but at least she didn't flip over my desk. "Okay. Fine. Just hurry up."

"Yes, your majesty," I muttered, watching her strut out of my room in a huff.

At least Angeline's academic problems were something a little easier to deal with than the other supernatural intrigues occupying my time. Since I was already awake and had coffee, I decided there was no point in going back to sleep. I showered and dressed, then caught up on some extra homework while I waited for breakfast. When the serving time started in our cafeteria, I headed downstairs and lingered near the entrance. It only took about five minutes before my friend Kristin Sawyer came by. She always went running before class started and was usually one of the first in line for breakfast afterward. She was also in AP calculus with me.

"Hey," I said, falling in step with her. "Good run?"

"Great run," she said. There was still a little sweat on her dark skin. "A lot nicer now that the weather's cooler." She eyed me curiously. "I don't usually see you here this early. I don't usually see you eat breakfast."

"It's the most important meal of the day, right?" I selected oatmeal and an apple. "Besides, I have a favor to ask you."

Kristin nearly dropped the plate of scrambled eggs one of the servers handed to her. Her brown eyes widened. "You have a favor to ask *me*?"

While I wasn't responsible for my human friends in the same way I was the Moroi and dhampirs, I still had a tendency to look after them. I'd helped Kristin a number of times.

"Yeah . . . my cousin Angeline needs a math tutor."

There was an expectant look on Kristin's face, like she was waiting for me to finish my story. Then understanding hit. "Who, me? No. No way."

"Oh, come on. It'd be easy." I followed her to a table, having to hurry to catch up. I think she thought that if she walked quickly enough, she might be able to escape my request. "She's in remedial math. You could tutor her in your sleep."

Kristin sat down and gave me a long, level look. "Sydney, I saw your cousin punch a grown man and throw a speaker at someone. Do you really think I'm going to sign on for a job that makes her do work she doesn't want to do? What if she gets frustrated at what I'm telling her? How do I know she won't stab me with a compass?"

"You don't," I admitted. "But I think it's unlikely. Probably. She really wants to improve her grade. Otherwise, she could get kicked out."

"Sorry." Kristin actually did look legitimately apologetic. "You know I'd do almost anything for you—but not this. You're going to have to find someone who's not afraid of her."

I thought about her words over and over as I headed off to history class. She was right. But the only people completely at ease around her were Eddie and Jill, and they were off the list as tutors. I wondered if maybe I should offer up money to someone when I went to calculus later.

"Miss Melbourne."

Ms. Terwilliger was back in her classroom, no doubt to the relief of yesterday's sub. She waved me up to her messy desk and handed me a single sheet of paper. "Here's the list we discussed."

I scanned it. It contained the names of six girls as well as their addresses. These must be the ones she'd mentioned, girls with known magical aptitude but no coven or teacher to look out for them. All the addresses were in the Los Angeles metropolitan area.

"I trust Mrs. Santos got you the other information you needed for your project?"

"Yes." Mrs. Santos had emailed me the historical neighborhoods she knew about, and I'd narrowed them down to a couple likely candidates. "I'll start working on the, uh, project this weekend."

Ms. Terwilliger arched an eyebrow. "Why are you putting it off? I've never known you to procrastinate on an assignment."

I was a little startled. "Well . . . normally I don't, ma'am. But this is going to take some extra time—travel time—and I don't have enough of it on school days."

"Ah," she said, realization hitting her. "Well, then, you may use your independent study for it. That'll give you extra time. And I'll tell Mrs. Weathers you may be coming in after curfew. I'll make sure that she's accommodating. This project is of the utmost importance."

There was no protest I could make. "I'll start today, then."

As I was walking back to my desk, a voice said, "Jeez, Melbourne. Just when I thought that independent study you had with her couldn't get any easier . . . now you don't even have to show up for class?"

I paused to give Trey a smile. He was Ms. Terwilliger's assistant during this class period, meaning he did a lot of filing and photocopying.

"It's a very important assignment," I said.

"I guess. What is it?"

"It'd bore you." I did a double take as I looked him over. I didn't even have to grope for a change in conversation. "What happened to you?"

His eyes were bloodshot, and the unkempt state of his black hair suggested he hadn't had a shower this morning. There was a sallow, almost sickly hue to his normally tan skin. He gave me a weak smile and lowered his voice. "Craig Lo's brother scored us some beer last night. It was from some microbrewery. I guess that's good."

I groaned. "Trey, I thought you were better than that."

Trey managed as much of an indignant look as he could in his hungover state. "Hey, some of us like to have a little fun now and then. You should give it a shot sometime. I already tried to help you with Brayden, but you messed that up."

"I didn't mess anything up!" Brayden was a barista who worked with Trey, one who rivaled me when it came to a love of academia and random knowledge. Our brief relationship had been full of facts and low on passion. "He broke up with *me*."

"You wouldn't guess it. Did you know he writes all this lovesick poetry about you on his breaks?"

I was taken aback. "He . . . he does?" The reason Brayden had broken up with me was because my various duties to my vampire family had constantly interfered with the two of us, forcing me to neglect him and cancel a lot. "I feel kind of bad he took it that hard. I'm surprised he'd have such a, I don't know, outburst of passion."

Trey snorted. "I don't know that it's that passionate. He's more concerned about form and sits around with books detailing iambic pentameter and sonnet analysis."

"Okay, that sounds more like him." The bell was about to ring, so I had started to return to my seat when I noticed something on Trey's desk. "You're not done with that?"

It was a big homework assignment we had for our chemistry class, involving a number of complicated acid and base problems. It was due in our next period, and it seemed unlikely Trey would finish in time since all he had on the paper so far was his name.

"Yeah . . . I was going to finish it last night, but . . ."

"Right. The beer. Having fun." I didn't even bother to hide my disapproval. "That's a huge part of our grade."

"I know, I know." He looked down at the papers with a sigh. "I'll finish as much as I can before then. Partial credit's better than no credit."

I studied him for a moment and then made a decision that went against many of my basic principles. I reached into my messenger bag and handed him my completed homework.

"Here," I said.

He took the pages with a frown. "Here what?"

"It's the assignment. Use my answers."

"I. . . ." His jaw dropped. "Do you know what you're doing?"

"Yes."

"I don't think you do. You're giving me your homework."

"Yes."

"And telling me to pass it off as my homework."

"Yes."

"But I didn't actually do the work."

"Do you want them or not?" I asked in frustration. I started to take the papers back, but he pulled them close.

"Oh, I want them," he said. "I just want to know what *you* want in return. Because this doesn't really make up for getting me ostracized from my family and friends." He kept his tone light, but I heard the edge of bitterness. There it was. No matter how friendly he and I were, our respective allegiances to the Warriors and the Alchemists would always be between us. Maybe it was a joke now . . . but someday it wouldn't be.

"I need a favor," I explained. "A small one, really. Has nothing to do with any of that . . . stuff."

Trey looked understandably wary. "Which is?"

The bell rang, so I spoke quickly. "Angeline needs a math tutor or else she'll fail. And if she fails, she'll get kicked out of school. It wouldn't be hard for you at all. And it'd look good on your college applications."

"Your cousin's a little unstable," he said. But he didn't say no, so I thought that was a good sign.

"You used to think she was hot," I reminded him.

"Yeah, that was before. . . ." He didn't finish, but I knew. Before he found out she was a dhampir. The Warriors had the same taboos the Alchemists did about relationships between the races.

"Okay," I said. "I understand. I'll just take my homework and go." I held out my hand, but he didn't give the papers back.

"Wait, I'll do it. But if she injures me, I hope you'll feel really bad. Basketball season just started, and the team will fall apart if I'm sidelined because of her."

I grinned. "I'll be devastated."

Angeline was not so thrilled when I told her at lunch. She flushed with rage and looked like she was about ready to throw her tray across the cafeteria.

"You expect me to work with that . . . that . . . vampire hunter?" she demanded. I wondered if she'd had another name in mind but had held back in some remarkable show of restraint. "Especially after what they tried to do to Sonya?"

"Trey's not like the rest of them," I said defensively. "He refused to kill her and even went through the trouble of getting me in to help her—which ended up severely messing up his life, I might add."

Eddie looked amused, despite the grim subject. "You should also add that he wants very, very badly to get back to that old life."

I pointed at Eddie with my fork. "Don't tell me you think Trey's a bad choice too."

"For tutoring?" He shook his head. "Nah, he's fine. I'm just saying you shouldn't be so quick to assume everything's happy and bright with him. It seems pretty likely his group's working against us."

"He's my friend," I said, hoping my firm tone would put an end to the discussion. After a few more assurances, Eddie convinced Angeline to work with Trey, reminding her she needed to keep her grades up. Still, Eddie's words haunted me. I believed absolutely that Trey was my friend but again wondered when that rift between us would rear its ugly head.

When Eddie and Angeline left to go to their afternoon classes, I asked Jill to hang back at the table for a minute. "What's Adrian doing right now?"

"He's in his painting class," she said promptly.

"The bond must be running strong today, huh?" I asked. Sometimes her view of his mind and experiences was clearer than others.

She shrugged. "No, but it's eleven on Tuesday."

"Right," I said, feeling foolish. I knew everyone's schedules;

it was necessary for my job. "I should've realized that. Do you think he'd be able to meet up with me after school?"

"To go on that witch hunt? Yeah, he'd probably leave right now."

Jill knew what Adrian knew, so she'd also been briefed about my search for Veronica. While I'd learned to accept Jill's knowledge as part of confiding in Adrian, it was still a little shocking for me to hear these forbidden topics discussed openly. Seeing my stunned reaction, Jill smiled a little.

"Don't worry," she said. "I keep Adrian's secrets. And yours." The bitterness in her voice also caught me off guard.

"Are you mad at me?" I asked, puzzled. "You're not . . . you're not still upset about what happened between Adrian and me, are you? I thought you'd eased up on that." Although Adrian's proclamation of loving me against the odds had been unsettling, his more relaxed attitude had come through in her until now.

"Adrian has," she said. "He doesn't see the danger of you running around with another guy."

I was lost. "Another guy? You don't mean . . . Marcus? That's crazy."

"Is it?" asked Jill. The bond was so strange at times. Jill was jealous on Adrian's behalf. "He's human, you're human. You've both got this rebel Alchemist thing going on. And I saw him. He's pretty cute. There's no telling what could happen."

"Well, I know what could happen: nothing," I said. Even through a psychic bond, Marcus could win over girls. "I just met him. I don't even know if I can entirely trust him, and I certainly don't have any feelings for him. Look, I get that you want to help Adrian, but you can't be mad at me about what happened. You know why I turned him down—especially after Micah." Micah was Eddie's human roommate, and even though she knew human-vampire relationships couldn't get serious, she'd still been surprised at just how complex and difficult the situation had been.

"Yeah. . . ." She frowned, no doubt conflicted over Adrian's feelings and what she knew was true. "But maybe with Adrian, I don't know. Maybe things could be different. Or maybe there's at least a way to make them less painful for him."

I looked away, unable to meet her eyes. I didn't like to think of Adrian in pain, but what else could I do? What did either of them expect me to do? We all knew the rules.

"I'm sorry," I said, picking up my tray and standing. "I never asked for any of this. Adrian will get over me."

"Do you really want him to get over you?" she asked.

"What? Why would you even ask something like that?"

She didn't answer and instead made a great show of stirring around her mashed potatoes. When I realized she wasn't going to elaborate, I shook my head and walked off toward the exit. All the while, I could feel her watching me as that question echoed in my mind: *Do you really want him to get over you?*

CHAPTER 9

AS JILL HAD SAID, Adrian was more than happy to begin our hunt that afternoon. In fact, when I finally got ahold of him, he offered to pick me up when classes ended, in order to maximize our time. I didn't mind this since it meant I'd get to ride in the Mustang. Admittedly, I would've preferred to drive it myself, but I'd take what I could get.

"When are you going to name the car?" I asked him once we were on the road to Los Angeles.

"It's an inanimate object," he said. "Names are for people and pets."

I patted the Mustang's dashboard. "Don't listen to him." To Adrian, I said, "They name boats all the time."

"I don't really understand that either, but maybe I would if my old man ever fronted me the money for a private yacht." He shot me a quick, amused look before returning his attention to the road. "How can someone as cold and logical as you be so obsessed with something as frivolous as this?"

I wasn't sure which part bothered me the most—being called cold or obsessed. "I'm just giving the proper respect to a beautiful machine."

"You named your car after coffee. That's a sign of respect?"

"The *highest* respect," I said.

He made a noise that sounded like a cross between a scoff and a laugh. "Okay, then. You name it. Whatever you want, I'll go along with."

"Really?" I asked, a bit startled. True, I'd been badgering him about naming the car, but I wasn't sure I wanted to be the one to wield that sort of power. "It's a big decision."

"Life or death," he said, deadpan. "Better choose carefully."

"Yeah, but you're the so-called creative one!"

"Then this'll be good practice for you."

I fell silent for a good part of the drive, struck by the gravity of the dilemma that lay before me. What should the name reflect? The car's sunny yellow color? Sleek lines? Powerful engine? The task was overwhelming.

Adrian pulled me out of my thoughts when we began nearing the outer Los Angeles suburbs. "We're not actually going into the city, are we?"

"Huh?" I'd been waging a mental debate between Summer Wind and Gold Dust. "Oh, no. We're heading north. Take the next exit."

Mrs. Santos had provided me with two neighborhoods known for their Victorian-style houses. I'd researched them extensively online, even going so far as to look at satellite pictures. I'd finally chosen one that most resembled my vision and crossed my fingers I'd have the same luck as I'd had in finding Marcus's apartment. Surely the universe owed me a few favors.

Unfortunately, things didn't look too promising when we finally reached the street I'd been given. It was a peaceful residential area, filled with those same distinctive houses, but nothing that quite matched the one I'd seen in my vision. We drove up and down the street as I scanned each side, hoping maybe I'd missed something.

"Ugh," I said, slouching back into my seat. No luck. The universe had apparently cut me off. "We'll have to check the other location, but seriously, it didn't look like a match."

"Well, it can't hurt to—" Adrian suddenly made an abrupt turn onto a side street we'd nearly driven past. I jerked upright as he clipped the curb.

"What are you doing? Think about your tires!"

"Look." He made another turn, putting us on a parallel street. Most of it was contemporary California housing . . . but one block had more Victorian houses. I gasped.

"There it is!"

Adrian came to a stop on the side of the street opposite from the house of my vision. Everything was there, from the wrapping porch to the hydrangea bush. And now, in the full light of day, I could make out the sign in the front yard: OLD WORLD BED-AND-BREAKFAST. Smaller print identified it as a historic site.

"Well, there we go." Adrian was clearly very pleased with his find, despite the risk to the car's tires. "Maybe Jackie's sister is staying here."

"Odd choice to run nefarious magical activities out of," I remarked.

"I don't know. Seeing as there aren't any ancient castles in the neighborhood, then why not a bed-and-breakfast?"

I took a deep breath. "Okay, then. Let's go make some

inquiries. You sure you can muddle the minds of those who see me?"

"Easy," he said. "Easier still if you were wearing your wig."

"Oh, shoot. I forgot." I ducked down and retrieved a shoulder-length brown wig that Ms. Terwilliger had supplied me with. Even with Adrian's magic, we wanted to take extra precautions. While it would be good if people were visited by an unmemorable blonde, it'd be better still if they were visited by an unmemorable brunette. I tugged the wig on, hoping no one had seen my transformation. I lifted my head. "Does it look okay?"

Adrian's face showed approval. "It's cute. You look even brainier, which I didn't think was possible."

We left the car, and I wondered if I wanted to look brainier. A lot of people already thought I was boring. Blond hair might be the only exciting thing I had going for me. Then I thought for a minute about my recent experience scaling a fire escape, breaking and entering, and getting into a fistfight with a fugitive. Not to mention that I was now hunting a powerful evil witch alongside a vampire who could control people's minds.

Okay, maybe I wasn't so boring after all.

We stepped inside to find a cute little lobby with an ornate desk and a sitting area with wicker furniture. Stuffed rabbits dressed in ball gowns adorned the shelves, and the walls actually had oil paintings of Queen Victoria. The owners apparently took their theme very literally, though I wasn't sure how the rabbits fit in.

A girl my age sat at the desk and glanced up in surprise from a magazine. She had short platinum hair and hipster glasses. Tons of necklaces hung around her neck in a gaudy display that went against my minimalist sensibilities. Hot pink plastic beads, a sparkly green star, a gold and diamond locket, a dog tag . . . it was mind-boggling. Even worse, she was chewing gum loudly.

"Hi," she said. "Can I help you?"

We'd had a whole routine planned, but Adrian immediately went off script. He slung his arm around me. "Yeah, we're looking for a weekend getaway, and a friend of ours swears this is top-of-the-line romance." He pulled me closer. "Our anniversary's coming up. We've been dating for one year, but man, it hardly seems like it."

"That's for sure," I said, trying to keep my jaw from dropping. I forced what I hoped was a happy smile.

The girl glanced back and forth between us, her expression softening. "That's so sweet. Congratulations."

"Can we check the place out?" Adrian asked. "I mean, if there are any vacant rooms?"

"Sure," she said, standing up. She spit her gum into a trash can and walked over to us. "I'm Alicia. My aunt and uncle are the owners."

"Taylor," I said, shaking her hand.

"Jet," said Adrian. I nearly groaned. For inexplicable reasons, "Jet Steele" was a pseudonym Adrian really liked using. In our rehearsal today, he was supposed to be called Brian.

Alicia glanced back and forth between us, a small frown on her face that soon smoothed out. I had to guess it was Adrian's compulsion, confusing her perceptions of us a bit. "Follow me. We have a few vacant rooms you can see." With one last puzzled look at us, she turned and headed toward a stairway.

"Isn't this great, sweetie?" Adrian asked loudly as we walked up the creaking stairs. "I know how much you like rabbits.

Didn't you have one when you were little? What was his name, Hopper?"

"Yeah," I said, resisting the urge to punch him on the arm. Hopper? Really? "Best rabbit ever."

"Oh, neat," said Alicia. "Then I'll take you to the Bunny Suite first."

The Bunny Suite had more of those well-dressed stuffed rabbits as part of the decor. The quilt covering the king-size bed also had a border of alternating hearts and rabbits stitched in. Several books sat on the mantel above the wood-burning fireplace, including *The Tale of Peter Rabbit* and *Rabbit, Run*. Until that moment, I hadn't realized just how absurdly far a theme could be taken.

"Wow," said Adrian. He sat down on the bed and tested its bounciness, giving it a nod of approval. "This is amazing. What do you think, buttercup?"

"I have no words," I said honestly.

He patted the spot beside him. "Want to try it out?"

I answered with a look and felt relieved when he stood up. Adrian and beds stirred up too many conflicting feelings in me.

After that, Alicia showed us the Morning Glory Suite, the Velvet Suite, and the London Suite, all of which competed to outdo the others in tackiness. Nonetheless, despite the absurdity of Adrian's ruse, the tour had given me the opportunity to take note of the other labeled doors in the hallway. We followed Alicia back downstairs.

"We don't get to see the Sapphire Suite or the Prince Albert Suite?" I asked.

Alicia shook her head. "Sorry. Those are occupied. I can

give you a brochure with some pictures, if you want."

Adrian had his arm around me again. "Angel cake, wasn't the Prince Albert Suite where Veronica stayed? She's not still here, is she?"

"I'm not sure," I said. This, at least, was similar to what we'd rehearsed. I glanced over at Alicia. "You probably can't tell us that, huh? If our friend Veronica's here? She's really pretty, has long dark hair."

"Oh, yeah," said Alicia, brightening. "Of course I remember her. She was in the Velvet Suite, actually, and just checked out yesterday."

I resisted the urge to kick the desk. So close. We'd missed her by a day. Yes, the universe was definitely done giving me breaks. I wouldn't be able to cast the scrying spell until the next full moon, which was a month away.

"Oh, well," said Adrian, still with that easy smile. "We'll see her for Christmas anyway. Thanks for your help."

"Do you want to book a room?" Alicia asked hopefully.

"We'll get back to you on that," I said. I actually wouldn't have put it past Adrian to book one and then claim it was part of our cover. "We're checking out a few places. A one-year anniversary isn't something you want to make a hasty decision on."

"But," said Adrian, giving her a wink, "I've got a good feeling about the Bunny Suite."

Alicia walked us out, her eyes widening when she saw the Mustang. "Wow, nice car."

"It's an amazing car," I said.

"That's our baby—well, until we have real ones. Don't you think it needs a name?" asked Adrian. "I keep trying to convince

Taylor." Once again, I had to fight the urge to punch him.

"Oh, definitely," said Alicia. "That kind of car . . . it's like royalty."

"See?" Adrian shot me a triumphant look. "And Alicia's an expert on royalty. Didn't you see all those paintings?"

"Thanks for your help," I told her, steering him forward. "We'll be in touch."

We got in the car, and after waving goodbye to Alicia, Adrian drove away. I stared blankly ahead. "Much like with the Bunny Suite, I have no words to describe what just happened. I mean, really? Our anniversary? Jet?"

"I look more like a Jet than a Brian," he argued. "Besides, that was a much better story than the one about how we wanted to pay a surprise birthday visit to our 'friend' Veronica."

"I don't know about that. But it *did* give us the information we needed. Which isn't good."

Adrian grew serious. "Are you sure? Maybe Veronica left the area altogether. Maybe you and the other girls are out of danger."

"That would be good, I guess . . . except, it just means some other poor girl somewhere else would suffer instead, and we wouldn't have any way to stop it." From my purse, I pulled out Ms. Terwilliger's list of magic-using girls. "One of these addresses is in Pasadena. We can at least swing through on our way back and warn her."

The girl we sought was named Wendy Stone. She was a student at Cal Tech, which seemed like an odd vocation for a wannabe witch. Of course, Ms. Terwilliger had said these were girls who weren't actively studying the magical path. They simply possessed magical ability, and I supposed the fact that they had no mentors suggested that they might actually be resistant to their inborn abilities—kind of like me.

Wendy lived in an apartment near campus that was easy to find. It was a no-nonsense, primarily student residence, but it seemed like a luxury palace after Marcus's building. As we passed busy students carrying backpacks and talking about classes, I felt a pang of longing that I hadn't experienced in a while. Inheriting the Alchemist mantle meant I couldn't go to college. College was a dream I'd held on to for a long time, though enrolling at Amberwood had helped ease some of my longing. Now, in this buzz of academia, a surge of jealousy sprang up in me. What would it be like to have this kind of life? To have your days solely devoted to the pursuit of knowledge, with no intrigue or life-threatening situations? Even Adrian, with his part-time art classes, was able to have some sort of collegiate experience.

"Don't be so down," he said when we reached Wendy's floor. "You might get to college someday."

I looked over at him in wonder. "How did you know that's what I was thinking?"

"Because I know you," he said simply, no mockery in his eyes. "Your aura got sad, and I figured being on a college campus had something to do with it."

I couldn't meet his gaze and turned away. "I don't like that."

"What, that someone actually knows what's important in your life?"

Yes, that was exactly it. But why *did* it bother me? Because it was Adrian, I realized. Why was it that a vampire understood me so well? Why not one of my friends? Why not one of my *human* friends?

"You can be Jet if you want," I said brusquely, trying to get us back on track and cover up my troubled feelings. After all, this wasn't Sydney's Therapy Hour. "But we are *not* posing as a couple again."

"Are you sure?" he said. His tone was lighter now, turning him back into the Adrian I knew. "Because I've got a lot more terms of endearment to use. Honey pie. Sugarplum. Bread pudding."

"Why are they all high-calorie foods?" I asked. I didn't want to encourage him, but the question slipped out before I could stop it. "And bread pudding isn't really that romantic."

We had reached Wendy's door. "Do you want me to call you celery stick instead?" he asked. "It just doesn't inspire the same warm and fuzzy feelings."

"I want you to call me Sydney." I knocked on the door. "Er, Taylor."

A girl with freckles and frizzy red hair answered. Her eyes narrowed warily. "Yes?"

"We're looking for Wendy Stone," I said.

She scowled. "Are you from the registrar's office? Because I told them the check's on its way."

"No." I lowered my voice and made sure there were no witnesses. "My name's Taylor. We're here to talk to you about, um, magic."

The transformation was sudden and startling. She went from suspicious and cautious to shocked and outraged. "No. *No.* I've told you guys a hundred times I don't want to be involved! I can't believe you'd actually show up at my door to try to convert me to your little coven freak show."

She tried to shut the door, but Adrian managed to stick his

foot in and block it. Very manly. "Wait," he said. "That's not what this is about. Your life might be in danger."

Wendy turned incredulous. "So you guys are threatening me now?"

"No, nothing like that. Please," I pleaded. "Just let us talk to you for five minutes inside. Then we'll leave and never bother you again."

Wendy hesitated and then finally gave a nod of resignation. "Fine. But I'm getting my pepper spray."

Her apartment was neat and tidy, save for a pile of papers and engineering books scattered on the floor. We'd apparently interrupted her homework, which brought back my wistfulness. She made good on her promise to get the pepper spray and then stood before us with crossed arms.

"Talk," she ordered.

I showed her the picture of Veronica. "Have you ever seen this woman?"

"Nope."

"Good." Or was it? Did that mean Veronica might have Wendy tagged as a future hit and was waiting to pounce? "She's dangerous. I'm not exactly sure how to put it. . . ."

"She finds girls with magic and sucks away their souls," supplied Adrian helpfully.

Wendy did a double take. "I'm sorry, what did you say?"

"That's not exactly the case," I said. "But it's close enough. She seeks out girls with power and takes it for herself."

"But I don't use magic," Wendy countered. "Like I told you, I don't want anything to do with it. There's a witch who lives in Anaheim who's always telling me how much potential I have and how I should be her apprentice. I keep telling her no, and

I've never even tried any spells. This soul-sucking lady has no reason to come after me."

Ms. Terwilliger had warned me some of the girls might say this. In fact, she'd said most would have this argument.

"It doesn't matter," I said. "That won't stop her."

Wendy looked terrified now, and I didn't blame her. My reaction had been similar. It was frustrating to know the very thing you were trying to get away from might come after you.

"Then what should I do?" she asked.

"Well, avoid her if you can. If she comes to see you . . . I mean, don't let her in. Don't be alone with her." That was slightly lame advice, and we all knew it. "If you do see her, I'd tell that witch in Anaheim. In fact . . . I know you don't want to, but if I were you, I'd get in touch with that witch now and try to get her help. Maybe even learn a few defensive spells. I understand you don't want to—believe me, I really do—but it could save your life. Also . . . " I held out the agate charm. "You should take this and wear it at all times."

Wendy eyed the charm as though it were a poisonous snake. "Is this some trick to get me to learn magic after all? You come here with this whole act about how if I don't learn, I could get my soul sucked away?"

Again, I had to give her points. I would think exactly the same thing. "We're telling the truth," I insisted. "There's no proof I can offer—well, wait. Give me your email address, and I'll send you this article about another girl it happened to."

Wendy looked like she was on the verge of using the pepper spray. "I think I would've heard if some girl had her soul magically sucked away."

"It wasn't really obvious to those who don't know about the

magical world. Let me send it to you, and then you can make your own decisions. It's the best I can offer."

She reluctantly agreed and wrote down her email address. Adrian stepped forward to take it from her, but he must have moved too quickly because she suddenly thrust the can of pepper spray in his direction.

"Stay back!" she exclaimed. At the exact same moment, I sprang in front of him, terrified he was about to get a face full of pepper spray. I cast the first spell I could think of, a simple one that created a flashy—but harmless—show of colored light. A shielding spell would've been much more useful, but I hadn't practiced any yet. That would have to be rectified, in case our future errands involved more pepper spray.

"*You* back off," I warned.

As I'd hoped, the brilliant display was terrifying to someone anti-magic like Wendy. She retreated to the far side of her apartment and thankfully didn't use the spray.

"G-get out," she stammered, eyes full of fear.

"Please take precautions," I said. I set the charm on the floor. "And please wear this. I'll email you the article."

"Get out," she repeated, making no move toward the charm.

As Adrian and I walked out of her building and into the sun, I sighed loudly. I was dismayed enough that I didn't even have the chance to feel down about being at a college.

"That didn't go so well," I said.

He thought about it, then grinned. "I don't know, Sage. You threw yourself in the line of pepper spray for me. You must like me just a *little* bit."

"I—I figured it'd be a shame to ruin your pretty face," I stammered. In truth, I hadn't been thinking of anything that specific. All I'd known was that Adrian was in danger. Protecting him had been instinctual.

"Still, that spell was kind of badass."

I managed a small smile. "It was harmless, and that's the thing. Wendy didn't know any better. The reason Veronica goes after these girls is that they don't have any magical protection—and that's exactly why they probably can't stop her. I don't think pepper spray will help, but maybe the article will convince her. Oh, shoot. I'll have to make a fake email address for Taylor."

"No worries," said Adrian. "I already have a Jet Steele one you can use."

This actually made me laugh. "Of course you do. For all the online dating you do, right?"

Adrian didn't comment one way or the other, which bothered me more than it should have. I'd meant it as a joke . . . but was there truth to it? If rumors—and some of my own observations—were true, Adrian had experience with a lot of women. A *lot*. Thinking of him with others upset me, far more than it should have. How many other girls had he kissed with that same intensity? How many had been in his bed? How many had felt his hands upon their bodies? He couldn't have loved them all. Some—probably most—had been conquests, girls whose faces he forgot the next morning. For all I knew, I was just the ultimate conquest for him, a test for his skills. You probably couldn't find a greater challenge than a human with hang-ups about vampires.

And yet, thinking back on all the things said and unsaid between us, I was pretty sure that wasn't true. No matter how crazy this romantic entanglement was, he loved me—or thought he did. I was no superficial conquest. It'd probably be better if

I was, though. Without an emotional connection, he'd eventually give up and easily find comfort in someone else's arms. This would probably be a good time for me to suggest he do that anyway.

But I stayed silent.

CHAPTER 10

THE NEXT MORNING, I sought out Ms. Terwilliger before class to give her a recap of yesterday's adventures. She leaned against her desk, sipping a cappuccino as I spoke. Her expression grew darker as the story progressed, and she sighed when I finished.

"Well, that's unfortunate," she said. "I'm glad you were able to find the Stone girl, but that kills our lead on Veronica until the next full moon. It could be too late by then."

"You're sure there's no other scrying spell?" I asked.

She shook her head. "Most that I could attempt would alert her that I was looking for her. There is one that might mask me while I'm using it . . . but it also might not be able to penetrate any shielding she's using to hide herself."

"It's still worth a try, isn't it?" I asked. The warning bell rang, and students began trickling into the classroom. She shot me a smile as she straightened up.

"Why, Miss Melbourne, I never thought I'd hear you

suggesting such things. But you're right. We'll talk about it this afternoon. It's something I'd like you to see."

That anti-magic gut instinct started to rear its ugly head . . . and then stopped. Somewhere, against my wishes, I'd gotten caught up in all of this. I was too concerned now about Veronica's other victims to pay attention to my usual worries. In Alchemist eyes, using magic was bad. In my eyes, leaving innocents in danger was worse.

With no other critical situations to contend with, I found that the day flew by. When I rejoined Ms. Terwilliger for our independent study, I found her packed up and waiting for me to arrive. "Field trip," she told me. "We need to work on this at my place." A wistful look crossed her features. "Too bad we can't stop at Spencer's."

Caffeine and magic didn't mix, which was another good reason for staying away from the arcane. I started to point out that since I wasn't working any magic, I didn't have the same restrictions. A moment later, I decided that would be mean. Ms. Terwilliger had enough going on with a bloodthirsty sister on the loose. She didn't need to be taunted too.

The cats were waiting at the door when we arrived at her house, which was slightly terrifying. I'd never seen all of them at once and counted thirteen. I had to assume that number was by design.

"I have to feed them first," she told me as they swarmed at her feet. "Then we'll get to work."

I nodded wordlessly, thinking her plan was a good one. If those cats weren't fed soon, it seemed likely they would turn on us. I didn't like our odds.

Once they had food to distract them, Ms. Terwilliger and I

went to her workshop. There was little I could do except observe. Magic often required that the person doing the spell be the one to put in all the labor. I assisted with a little measuring, but that was about it. I'd seen her do a couple of quick, flashy spells in the past but never anything of this magnitude. It was clear to me that this was a very, very powerful feat. She had nothing to link her to Veronica, no hair or picture. The spell required the caster to use the image in her mind of the person being sought. Other components, herbs and oils, helped enhance the magic, but for the most part, the work was all on Ms. Terwilliger. Watching her prepare triggered a mix of emotions in me. Anxiety was one, of course, but it was paired with a secret fascination at seeing someone with her strength cast a spell.

When everything was in place, she spoke the incantation, and I nearly gasped as I felt power surge up in the room. I'd never sensed it from another person before, and the intensity nearly knocked me over. Ms. Terwilliger was staring at a spot a few feet in front of her. After several long moments, a glowing dot appeared in the air. It grew bigger and bigger, turning into a flat, shimmering disc, which hung there like a mirror. I stepped backward, half-afraid the disc would keep expanding and consume the room. Eventually, it stabilized. Tense silence surrounded us as she stared at that glowing surface. A minute passed, and then the oval began to shrink and shrink until it was gone. Ms. Terwilliger sank with exhaustion and caught the side of her table for support. She was sweating heavily, and I handed her some orange juice we'd had ready.

"Did you see anything?" I asked. There'd been nothing visible to me, but maybe only the caster could see what the spell revealed.

She shook her head. "No. The spell was unable to touch her mind. Her shielding must be too strong."

"Then we can't do anything until next month." I felt my stomach drop. I hadn't realized until that moment how much I'd been hoping this spell would work. So much of my life involved problem solving, and I felt lost when I ran out of options.

"You and Adrian can keep warning the other girls," said Ms. Terwilliger. Color was starting to return to her face. "At the very least, it might slow Veronica down."

I looked at the time on my cell phone. This spell had taken longer than I thought. "I don't think we can do a round trip to Los Angeles today. I'll get him tomorrow, and we'll see if we can finish off the list."

Once I was convinced she wouldn't pass out from magical exertion, I made motions to leave. She stopped me as I was about to walk out the door.

"Sydney?"

I glanced back, suddenly uneasy. The problem with having so many people call me by nicknames was that when someone called me by my actual name, it usually meant something serious was happening.

"Yes?"

"We keep talking about warning others, but don't forget to look after yourself as well. Keep studying the book. Learn to protect yourself. And keep the charm on."

I touched the garnet, hidden under my shirt. "Yes, ma'am. I will."

Marcus's promised text came as I was driving back to school, telling me to meet him at a nearby arcade. I knew the place and had actually been to its adjacent mini-golf course once before, so I had no difficulty heading over there. Marcus was waiting for me just inside the door, and thankfully, Sabrina wasn't around wielding a gun.

I hadn't spent a lot of time in arcades and didn't really understand them. They hardly meshed with my father's style of education. For me, it was a mass of sensory overload that I wasn't quite ready for. The smell of slightly burnt pizza filled the air. Excited children and teenagers darted back and forth between games. And everywhere, everything seemed to be flashing and beeping. I winced, thinking maybe my dad had been on to something in avoiding these places.

"This is where we're going to discuss covert activities?" I asked in disbelief.

He gave me one of his movie star smiles. "It's not an easy place for people to spy on you. Besides, I haven't played Skee-Ball in years. That game is awesome."

"I wouldn't know."

"What?" It was kind of nice to catch him by surprise again, even if it was for something so trivial. "You've been missing out. Spot me some money for tokens, and I'll show you." Apparently, being an on-the-run renegade leader didn't pay well.

He found the Skee-Ball machines instantly. I bought him a cupful of tokens and handed them over. "Have at it."

He promptly put a token in and threw his first ball. It landed completely outside of the rings, making him scowl. "You don't waste any time," I remarked.

His eyes were on the game as he made his second throw, which again missed. "It's a survival tactic. When you spend enough time on the run . . . hiding out all the time . . . well, you take advantage of these moments of freedom. And when pretty girls spirit you away."

"How do you know we're free? How can you be so sure the Alchemists haven't been watching me?" I asked. I was pretty sure I wasn't being watched and mostly wanted to test him.

"Because they would've showed up on that first day."

He had a point. I put my hands on my hips and tried to be patient. "How long are you going to play? When can we talk?"

"We can talk now." His next ball hit the ten-point ring, and he whooped with joy. "I can talk and throw. Ask away. I'll give you as many shocking secrets as I can."

"I'm not easily shocked." But I wasn't going to waste this opportunity. I glanced around, but he was right. No one was going to eavesdrop in this noisy place. We could barely hear each other as it was. "What'd you do to get kicked out of the Alchemists?"

"I didn't get kicked out. I left." This round ended, and he put in his next token. "Because of a Moroi girl."

I froze, unable to believe what I'd heard. Marcus Finch had started his great rebellion . . . because he'd been involved with a Moroi? It rang too close to my own situation. When I didn't say anything, he glanced over and took in my expression.

"Oh. *Oh.* No, nothing like that," he said, realizing my thoughts. "That's not a line even I would cross."

"Of course not," I said, hoping I was doing a good job at hiding my nervousness. "Who would?"

He returned to the game. "We were friends. I was assigned to Athens, and she lived there with her sister."

That derailed me. "Athens . . . you were in Athens? That was one of the places I wanted to be assigned. I went to St.

Petersburg instead, but I always kept hoping that, maybe, *maybe*, I'd get reassigned to Greece. Or even Italy." I was nearly babbling, but he didn't seem to notice.

"What's wrong with St. Petersburg? Aside from the high Strigoi count."

"What's wrong is that it wasn't Athens or Rome. My dad specifically requested that I *not* be assigned to either place. He thought it'd be too distracting."

Marcus paused again to give me a long, level look. There was sympathy in his expression, as though my entire history and family drama were playing before his eyes. I didn't want him to feel sorry for me and wished I hadn't said anything. I cleared my throat.

"So tell me about this girl in Athens."

He took the hint. "Like I said, she was a friend. So funny. Oh, man. She cracked me up. We used to hang out all the time—but you know how that's kind of frowned upon."

I almost laughed at his subtle joke. Kind of? That was an understatement. Field Alchemists weren't supposed to interact with Moroi unless it was absolutely necessary for some business matter or related to stopping and covering up Strigoi. My situation was a little unique, since my mission actually required me to talk to her on a daily basis.

"Anyway," he continued. "Someone noticed, and I got a lot of unwelcome attention for it. Around the same time, I started hearing all these rumors . . . like about Alchemists holding Moroi against their will. And even some Alchemists interacting with the Warriors."

"*What?* That's impossible. We would never work with those freaks." The idea of Moroi prisoners was outlandish, but it was that second part that truly stumped me. I couldn't even process it. He might as well have said the Alchemists were working with aliens.

"That's what I thought." He threw another ball, looking supremely pleased when it scored thirty points. "But I kept hearing whispers, so I started asking questions. A lot of questions. And, well, that's when things really went bad. Questions don't always go over so well—especially if you're a nuisance about them."

I thought about my own experience. "That's certainly true."

"So that's when I walked. Or, well, ran. I could see the signs. I'd crossed a line and knew it was only a matter of time before I had a one-way ticket to re-education." Another new round started, and he gestured me forward. "Want to give it a try?"

I was still stunned enough by his earlier words that I stepped forward and took a ball. The Alchemists were logical, organized, and reasonable. I knew there were Alchemists who wished we could do more to fight the Strigoi, but there was no way our group would work with trigger-happy zealots. "Stanton told me we only tolerate the Warriors. That we're just keeping an eye on them."

"That's what I was told too." He watched me line up a shot. "There's kind of a learning curve to this, by the way. It may take you a few—"

I threw and hit the fifty-point ring. Marcus could only stare for a few seconds, his earlier smirk vanishing.

"You said you'd never played!" he exclaimed.

"I haven't." I threw another fifty pointer.

"Then how are you doing that?"

"I don't know." Fifty points again. "You just base your force on the ball's weight and distance to the ring. It's not that hard. This is kind of a boring game, really."

Marcus was still dumbstruck. "Are you some kind of super-athlete?"

I nearly scoffed. "You don't need to be an athlete to play this."

"But . . . no . . ." He looked at the rings, then at me, and then back to the rings. "That's impossible. I've been playing this since I was a kid! My dad and I used to go to our town's carnival over and over in the summer, and I'd spend at least an hour playing this each time."

"Maybe you should have made it two hours." I tossed another ball. "Now tell me more about the Warriors and the Alchemists. Did you ever get any proof?"

It took him several moments to tune back into the conversation. "No. I tried. I even got cozy with the Warriors for a while—that's how I met Clarence. My group has found a few dark secrets about the Alchemists and saved other Moroi from the Warriors, but we were never able to make a connection between the two groups." He paused dramatically. "Until now."

I picked up the next ball. This mundane activity was helping me analyze his startling words. "What happened?"

"It was a fluke, really. We've got a guy working with us now who just left the Alchemists and broke his tattoo," he explained. He said it like it was no big deal, but I still couldn't shake how uneasy "breaking the tattoo" made me feel. "He'd overheard something that matched up to something Sabrina uncovered. Now we've just got to get the evidence linking it all."

"How are you going to pull that off?"

"Actually, *you're* going to pull it off."

He spoke just as I was releasing another ball. My shot went

wide, missed the rings and even the machine entirely. The ball bounced off the wall and landed at the feet of some startled girls. Marcus retrieved the ball and gave them an apologetic smile, which made them gush about how it was no problem at all. As soon as they were gone, I leaned toward Marcus.

"What did you say?"

"You heard me. You want to join our group? You want to break your tattoo?" He looked annoyingly smug. "Then this is all part of the process."

"I never said I wanted to do any of those things!" I hissed. "I just wanted to find out more about them."

"And I bet you'd really love to know if there are factions in the Alchemists working with the Warriors."

He was right. I did want to know that.

He caught hold of my hand. "Sydney, I know this is a lot to take in. I don't blame you for doubting, and that's exactly why we need you. You're smart. You're observant. You question. And just like me, those questions are going to get you in trouble—if they haven't already. Get out now while you can—on your own terms."

"I just met you! I'm not breaking away from the group that raised me." I pulled my hand back. "I was willing to hear you guys out, but now you've gone too far."

I turned and headed toward the door, unwilling to listen anymore. Yet as I walked away, his words crawled over me. Even though I'd been forgiven for my involvement with Rose, my record still probably had a black mark. And even though I hadn't pushed hard about Marcus Finch, had even bringing him up raised Stanton's suspicions? How long until little things added up?

I pushed open the doors and stepped out into bright

sunlight. It chased away the darkness of what I'd just heard. Marcus was right behind me and touched my shoulder.

"Sydney, I'm sorry. I'm not trying to scare you." That cocky attitude was gone. He was deadly earnest. "I just sense something about you . . . something that resonates with me. I think we're on the same side, that we want the same things. We've both gotten close to the Moroi. We want to help them—without being lied to or used."

I eyed him warily. "Go on."

"Please, hear us out."

"I thought I just did."

"You heard *me* out," he corrected. "I want you to meet the others and hear their stories. They'll tell you more about what they went through. They'll tell you about this." He tapped his tattoo. "And when you hear more about that task . . . well, I think you'll want to do it."

"Right. The big, mind-blowing thing that's going to unveil an Alchemist-Warrior conspiracy." He remained serious, which bothered me more than if he'd suddenly revealed this to be one big joke. "So, what? You're going to get the others, and we'll all have an arcade day?"

He shook his head. "Too dangerous. I'll gather them in some other place and then tell you where to meet us, but it's got to be last minute again. Can't risk detection."

"I can't go on some epic road trip," I warned. "No one cares much about LA trips, but traipsing all over the state is going to get that unwanted attention you were talking about."

"I know, I know. It'll be close. I just have to make sure it's secure." He was back to his excited, cheery self. "Will you do it? Come join us?"

In spite of myself, I *was* curious. Even though I refused to believe in any connection between the Warriors and the Alchemists, I wanted to find out what leads this group thought they had. I also just wanted to see this mysterious group of his, period. What had Adrian called them? Marcus's Merry Men? And, of course, there was the tattoo. Marcus kept alluding to its secrets but still hadn't given me the details.

"I'll do it," I said at last. "On one condition."

"Name it."

"I want to bring someone with me," I said. "You can trust him, I swear. But after Sabrina pulled a gun on me, you have to understand why I'd be a little nervous about walking into your clique."

Marcus looked like he might almost consider it but then suddenly recoiled. "Not Adrian?"

"No, no. This guy's a dhampir. No one who'd be interested in turning you over to the Alchemists, especially if you really are working to protect Moroi. You say you've got a good feeling about me? Then trust me that you have nothing to worry about with him. He'd just be there to make me feel a little safer."

"You have nothing to worry about with *us*," Marcus said. "We won't hurt you."

"I want to believe you. But I don't quite have that same good feeling you have yet."

He didn't say anything right away and then burst into laughter. "Fair enough. Bring your friend." He shook my hand, as though we were sealing some great bargain. "I'll be in touch later with the details. You won't regret it, Sydney. I swear it."

CHAPTER 11

MARCUS DISAPPEARED TO WHEREVER it was he was hiding out, and I drove home. What he'd said to me still seemed outlandish. I kept telling myself none of it could be true. It made things a lot easier to handle.

Back at Amberwood, I found the usual buzz of evening student activity. It felt comforting after my shocking outing, far removed from fanatics and cryptic spells. My phone buzzed with a text message the minute I stepped into my dorm room. It was from Jill: *Come see us when you're back.* I sighed. No rest for the wicked, it would seem. I left my purse in my room and then trudged down to the second floor, unsure of what I'd find.

Jill opened her door, looking immensely relieved to see me. "Thank God. We have a situation."

"We *always* have a situation," I said. I stepped inside and saw Angeline sitting on the floor, back against the wall and a miserable expression on her face. "What happened?"

She looked up quickly. "It wasn't my fault."

The sinking feeling in my stomach increased. "It never is, is it? I repeat: what happened?"

When Angeline refused to say, Jill spoke up. "She gave Trey a concussion with an algebra book."

Before I could even start to parse that, Angeline leapt to her feet. "The doctor said it wasn't a concussion!"

"Wait." I glanced between them, half hoping they'd burst into laughter at the joke they must be playing on me. "You did something to Trey that actually required medical attention?"

"I barely touched him," she insisted.

I sat down on Jill's bed and resisted the urge to crawl under its covers. "No. You can't do this. Not again. What did the principal say? Oh, God. Where are we going to send you?" After Angeline's brawl with a motivational group, it had been made very clear that further fighting would get her expelled.

"Eddie took the blame," said Jill. A small smile crossed her face as she spoke. "There weren't really many witnesses, so Eddie said they were playing around in the library and tossing the book back and forth. He claimed he got careless and threw the book too hard . . . and that it accidentally hit Trey on the head."

Angeline nodded. "That's kind of what really happened with us."

"No, it wasn't," protested Jill. "*I* saw it. You got mad when Trey told you it shouldn't be that hard to understand that x always has a different value."

"He implied that I was stupid!"

Variables didn't seem like too hard a concept to me, but I could tell under Angeline's bravado that she really was flustered. I always had the impression that back among the Keepers, Angeline had been a queen among her peers. Here she was constantly trying to keep up academically and socially, adrift in a world very different from the one she'd grown up in. That would make anyone insecure. And while I questioned if Trey had ever said she was stupid, I could understand how some of his snarky commentary could be perceived that way.

"Did Eddie get in any serious trouble?" I asked. I doubted he'd get expelled for something like this, but it would be just my luck that he'd get the punishment he'd saved Angeline from.

"Detention," said Jill.

"He accepted it very bravely," added Angeline.

"I'm sure he did," I said, wondering if either girl knew they were wearing mirror expressions of adoration. "Look, Angeline, I know the tutoring process must be frustrating, but you *have* to watch your temper, okay? Trey's just trying to help."

She looked skeptical. "He's got kind of an attitude sometimes."

"I know, but people aren't exactly lining up to fill his position. We need you here. Jill needs you here. Eddie needs you here." I saw some of her indignation fade at the mention of her friends and duty. "Please try to work with Trey."

She gave a weak nod, and I stood up to leave. Jill hurried after me into the hallway. "Hey, Sydney? How was your outing with Marcus?"

"It was fine," I said, certainly not about to dredge up Marcus's alarming revelations. "Informative. And I learned how to play Skee-Ball."

Jill almost looked offended. "You played Skee-Ball? I thought you were supposed to be learning about the Alchemists' secret history."

"We multitasked," I said, not liking her tone.

I left before she could comment further and texted Eddie when I reached my room. *I heard what happened. Sorry. And thanks.* His response was quick: *At least it wasn't a concussion.*

I braced myself for snark when I went to meet Adrian the next day. Jill had probably told him about my arcade trip, which would probably elicit a comment like, "Nice to know you're so dedicated to crack the Alchemists. Way to keep your eye on the ball."

When I pulled up in front of Adrian's apartment building, he was already waiting out front for me. As soon as I saw his grim face, my heart stopped. I jumped out of the car, just barely pausing to grab the keys as I went.

"What's wrong?" I exclaimed, jogging up to him.

He rested a hand on my shoulder, but I was too worried to care about the touch. "Sydney, I don't want you to freak out. There's no lasting damage."

I looked him over. "Are you okay? Were you hurt?"

For a moment, his somber expression turned puzzled. Then, he understood. "Oh, you think it's me? No, I'm fine. Come on."

He led me around the back of his building, to the private parking lot used by residents. I came to a halt, my jaw dropping as I took in the terrible, ghastly scene. A couple other residents were milling around, and a police officer stood nearby taking notes. Around us, seven parked cars had their tires slashed.

Including the Mustang.

"No!"

I ran over to its side, kneeling and examining the damage. I felt like I was in the middle of a war, kneeling by a fallen comrade on the battlefield. I was practically on the verge of shouting, "Don't you die on me!"

Adrian crouched beside me. "The tires can be replaced. I think my insurance will even cover it."

I was still horrified. "Who did this?"

He shrugged. "Some kids, I guess. They hit a few cars one block over yesterday."

"And you didn't think that was worth mentioning to me?"

"Well, I didn't know they were going to come here too. Besides, I knew you'd flip out and want to set up twenty-four-hour surveillance on this place."

"That's not a bad idea." I glanced up at his building. "You should talk to the landlord about it."

Adrian didn't seem nearly as concerned as he should have been. "I don't know that he'd go for it. I mean, this isn't really a dangerous neighborhood."

I pointed at the Mustang. "Then how come this happened?"

Even though we could take Latte to Los Angeles, we still had to wait around to finish up with the police and then get a tow truck. I made sure the tow truck driver knew that he better not get a scratch on the car, and then I watched mournfully as it was hauled away. Once that sunny splash of yellow disappeared around a corner, I turned to Adrian.

"Ready to go?"

"Do we have enough time?"

I looked at my cell phone and groaned. We'd burned up a lot of time handling the vandalism aftermath. And yet, I hated to wait until tomorrow, seeing as I'd already lost time yesterday while dealing with Marcus. I called Ms. Terwilliger and asked if she'd cover for me if I came in after curfew.

"Yes, yes, of course," she said, in a tone that suggested she couldn't understand why I'd even bothered calling her. "Just talk to more of those girls."

Ms. Terwilliger had given me six names. We'd already taken care of Wendy Stone. Three of the girls lived relatively close together, and they were our goal tonight. The last two were closer to the coast, and we hoped to reach them tomorrow. Adrian tried making conversation with me throughout the drive, but my mind was still on the Mustang.

"God, I'm an idiot," I said, once we'd almost reached our destination.

"That's never a term I'd use to describe you," he said promptly. "Articulate. Well dressed. Smart. Organized. Beautiful. I'd use those terms, but never 'idiot.'"

I nearly asked why "beautiful" had come after "organized" and then remembered the actual concern. "I'm obsessing about that car when girls' lives are on the line. It's stupid. My priorities are messed up."

My eyes were on the road, but I could tell he was smiling. "If your priorities were really messed up, you would've followed that tow truck. Yet here you are, off to help perfect strangers. That's a noble thing, Sage."

"Don't rule yourself out," I said. "You're pretty noble too, going on all these outings with me."

"Well, it's not the same as Skee-Ball, but it'll have to do. How was that anyway? Did you really learn anything?"

"I learned a lot—some pretty unbelievable stuff, actually. I'm still waiting to get some proof, though."

Luck was with us initially. The first two girls were home, though their reactions were similar to Wendy Stone's. This time, I'd had the foresight to bring the newspaper article, in the hopes it would make a stronger impression. That ghastly picture at least gave them pause, but I left not knowing if they'd really take me seriously or use the agate charms.

Our good fortune ran out when we reached the last name. She too was a college student, meaning we had another campus visit. Her name was Lynne Titus, and she lived in a sorority house. I admit, as I knocked on the door, I was fully prepared to find a group of girls dressed in pink, having a pillow fight in their living room. But when we were shown in, we discovered an orderly home not all that different from Wendy's building. Some girls were coming and going, while others sat around with textbooks and papers.

"Lynne?" asked the girl who'd let us inside. "You just missed her."

I knew this shouldn't be a surprise. These girls had lives. They wouldn't all be waiting around for me to come by and talk to them. I glanced uneasily at a window, taking note of the purpling sky. "Any idea when she'll be back?"

The girl shook her head. "No, sorry. I don't know where she went."

Adrian and I exchanged looks. "You're free from your curfew," he reminded me.

"I know. But that doesn't mean I want to spend all night waiting for Lynne." I did some mental calculations. "I suppose we could wait a couple of hours. Three at most."

Adrian seemed supremely delighted by this, and I couldn't help but wonder if he was more excited at hanging out on a college campus . . . or at spending time with me. "What's fun to do around here?" he asked our hostess. He glanced around at the quiet academic environment. "No raging parties here, huh?"

The girl put on a disapproving expression. "We're a very serious sorority. If you're looking for parties, I guarantee there's one going on just down the street. Those girls have one every night." Adrian shot me a hopeful look.

"Oh, come on," I said. "Can't we find some nice museum?"

"We want to stay close, in case Lynne comes back," Adrian said. Something told me if the party had been all the way across campus, he still would've pushed for it. "Besides, if you want to go to college so badly, you should see the full scope of what it has to offer. And aren't you a fan of Greek stuff?"

That was hardly what I had in mind, and he knew it. I reluctantly agreed but warned him he couldn't drink. I was sporting the brown wig and presumed he was using spirit to mask us further. Alcohol would diminish his ability to pull it all off. Plus, I just didn't want to see him drunk.

It was easy to find the party house because we could hear the music blasting from it. A guy and a girl openly drinking beer from plastic cups challenged us at the door. "This is Greek only," the girl said. She looked as though she might fall off her stool. "Who are you with?"

I pointed vaguely toward Lynne's sorority. "Um, them."

"Alpha Yam Ergo," said Adrian, without hesitation. I expected the door squad to point out that most of those weren't even Greek letters. Maybe it was because Adrian spoke so confidently—or because they'd had too much beer—but the guy waved us inside.

It was almost like being back at the arcade, an overwhelming flood of stimuli. The house was crowded and loud, with smoke hanging in the air and alcohol flowing freely. Several people offered us drinks, and some girl invited us—three times—to play beer pong, forgetting that she'd already spoken to us. I regarded it all in amazement, trying to keep the disgust off my face.

"What a waste of tuition. This is ruining all my collegiate dreams," I shouted to Adrian. "Isn't there anything to do that's not drinking or being stupid?"

He scanned around, able to see more of the room from his greater height. He brightened. "That looks promising." He caught hold of my hand. "Come on."

In a surprisingly nice and spacious kitchen, we found several girls sitting on the floor painting blank T-shirts. Judging from the sloppy job and paint spills, they too had been indulging in alcohol. One girl had a cup of beer next to an identical cup of paint, and I hoped she wouldn't mix them up.

"What are you doing?" I asked.

One of the girls glanced up and grinned. "Making shirts for the winter carnival. You want to help?"

Before I could say no, Adrian was already on the ground with them. "Do I ever." He helped himself to a white T-shirt and a brush with blue paint on it. "What are we putting on these?" The girls' shoddy work made that a valid question.

"Our names," said one girl.

"Winter stuff," said another.

That was good enough for Adrian. He set to work painting snowflakes on the shirt. Unable to help myself, I knelt down to get a better look. Whatever his faults, Adrian *was* a decent artist. He mixed in a few other colors, making the snowflakes intricate and stylized. At one point, he paused to light a clove cigarette, sharing one of the girls' ashtrays. It was a habit I didn't really like, but at least the rest of the smoke in this place masked his.

As he was finishing up the shirt and writing out the sorority's name, I noticed that all the other girls had stopped to stare.

"That's amazing," said one, her eyes wide. "Can I have it?"

"I want it," insisted another.

"I'll make each of you one," he assured them. The way they looked at him was an unwelcome reminder of the breadth of his experience with other women. I shifted a little closer to him, just so they wouldn't get any ideas.

He handed the white shirt to the first girl and then set to work on a blue shirt. Once he fulfilled his promise to each girl, he sifted through the T-shirt stack until he found a men's-size black one. "Gotta pay tribute to my fraternity."

"Right," I scoffed. "Alpha Yam Ergo."

Adrian nodded solemnly. "A very old and prestigious society."

"I've never heard of them," said the girl who'd claimed the first shirt.

"They don't let many people in," he said. In white paint, he wrote his fake fraternity's initials: AYE.

"Isn't that what pirates say?" asked one of the other girls.

"Well, the Alpha Yams have nautical origins," he explained. To my horror he began painting a pirate skeleton riding a motorcycle.

"Oh, no," I groaned. "Not the tattoo."

"It's our logo," he said. Adrian and I had once had to investigate a tattoo parlor, and to distract the owner, he'd gone in and pretended to be interested in a tattoo that sounded very much like what he was drawing now. At least, I assumed he'd been pretending. "Isn't it badass?"

"Badass" wasn't quite the word I would've used, but despite it being such a ridiculous image, he actually did a good job. I

made myself comfortable, drawing my knees up to me and leaning against the wall. He soon stopped with his banter and grew
completely absorbed in his work, meticulously painting the skeleton's bones as well as that of a skeleton parrot sitting on the
pirate's shoulder. I studied his features as he worked, fascinated
by the joy in his eyes. Art was one of the few things that seemed
to anchor him and drive that darkness in him away. He seemed
to glow with an inner light, one that enhanced his already handsome features. It was another rare and beautiful glimpse of
the intense, passionate nature lying beneath the jokes. It came
through in his art. It had come through when he kissed me.

Adrian suddenly glanced up at me. Our gazes locked, and I
felt like he could read my mind. How often did he think about
that kiss? And if he really was crazy about me, did he imagine
more than just kissing? Did he fantasize about me? What kinds
of things did he think about? His lips on my neck? His hand on
my leg? And was that leg bare . . . ?

I was afraid of what my eyes might betray and quickly looked
away. Desperately, I groped for some witty and nonsentimental
comment. "Don't forget the ninja throwing stars."

"Right." I could feel Adrian's gaze on me a few moments
longer. There was something tangible to it, a warmth that envel-
oped me. I didn't look back until I was certain his attention was
again on the shirt. He added the stars and then sat back trium-
phantly. "Pretty cool, huh?"

"It's not bad," I said. In truth, it was kind of amazing.

"You want one too?" The smile he gave me stirred up those
warm feelings again. I couldn't help but smile back.

"We don't have the time," I managed to say. "We've got to
check on Lynne."

"I'll make you a fast one."

"Not the pirate," I warned. He found a small purple shirt and began painting on it in silver. "Purple?"

"It's your color," he insisted. A thrill ran through me at his words. Adrian could see auras, the light that surrounded all people and was tied into their personalities. He'd told me that mine was yellow, a color most intellectuals had. But he'd also said I had flares of purple, which indicated a passionate and spiritual nature. Those weren't qualities I usually thought I possessed . . . but sometimes, I wished I did.

I watched, enthralled, as he painted a large silver heart with flames edging one side. The whole design was Celtic in style. It was beautiful.

"Where did you get that from?" I asked in awe. I'd seen a lot of his work but never anything like this.

His eyes were on his heart, completely caught up in his work. "Just something kicking around in my head. Reminds me of you. Fiery and sweet, all at the same time. A flame in the dark, lighting my way." His voice . . . his words . . . I recognized one of his spirit-driven moments. It should've unnerved me, but there was something sensual about the way he spoke, something that made my breath catch. *A flame in the dark.*

He swapped out the silver paintbrush for a black one. Before I could stop him, he wrote over the heart: AYE. Underneath it, in smaller letters, he added: HONORARY MEMBER.

"What are you doing?" I cried. The spell had shattered. "You ruined it!"

Adrian regarded me with a mischievous look. "I figured you'd be flattered at being accepted as an honorary member."

"How can I get in?" asked one of the girls.

In spite of my outrage, I took the shirt when he offered it to me. I held it up gingerly, careful not to mess up the paint job. Even through the ridiculous words, the fiery heart was still stunning. It shone through, and I couldn't stop admiring it. How could someone so irreverent create something so beautiful? When I finally looked up again, I found Adrian watching me. That earlier thrall seized me, and I found myself unable to move.

"You haven't painted anything," he said softly.

"That's because I have zero creativity," I told him.

"Everyone's got *some* creativity," he insisted. He handed me the silver brush and slid over to join me against the wall. Our legs and arms touched. He laid out his own AYE shirt across his lap. "Go ahead. Add something, anything."

I shook my head in protest and tried to hand him the brush. "I can't draw or paint. I'll ruin it."

"Sydney." He pushed the brush back into my hand. "It's a pirate skeleton, not the *Mona Lisa*. You're not going to decrease its value."

Maybe not, but I had a hard time imagining what I could possibly add to this. I could do a lot of things, but this was out of my league—especially compared to his skill. Something in his expression drove me, however, and after a lot of thought, I gave my best shot at drawing a tie around the skeleton's neck. Adrian frowned.

"Is that a noose?"

"It's a tie!" I cried, trying not to feel offended.

He laughed, clearly delighted at this. "My mistake."

"He can go to a boardroom meeting," I added, feeling a need to defend my work. "He's very proper now."

Adrian seemed to like that even more. "Of course he is.

Proper and dangerous." A little of his mirth faded, and he grew pensive as he studied me, holding me in his gaze. "Just like you."

I'd been so worried about the artistic challenge that I wasn't aware of just how close he'd moved to me until now. So many details came into focus. The shape of his lips, the line of his neck. "I'm not dangerous," I breathed.

He brought his face toward mine. "You are to me."

And somehow, against all reason, we were kissing. I closed my eyes, and the world around me faded. The noise, the smoke . . . it was gone. All that mattered was the taste of his mouth, a mix of cloves and mints. There was a fierceness in his kiss, a desperation . . . and I answered, just as hungry for him. I didn't stop him when he pulled me closer, so that I almost sat on his lap. I'd never been wrapped around someone's body like that, and I was shocked at how eagerly mine responded. His arm went around my waist, pulling me onto him further, and his other hand slid up the back of my neck, getting entangled in my hair. Amazingly, the wig stayed on. He took his lips away from my mouth, gently trailing kisses down to my neck. I tipped my head back, gasping when the intensity returned to his mouth. There was an animalistic quality that sent shock waves through the rest of my body. Some Alchemist voice warned me that this was exactly how a vampire would feed, but I had no fear. Adrian wouldn't hurt me, and I needed to know just how hard he could kiss me and—

"Oh my God!"

Adrian and I jerked apart as though someone had thrown cold water on us, though our legs stayed entangled. I glanced around in a panic, half expecting to see an outraged Stanton standing over us. Instead, I looked up into the terrified face of a girl I didn't know. She wasn't even looking at us.

"You guys won't believe what happened!" she exclaimed, directing her words to our fellow artists. She pointed vaguely behind her. "Over across the street at Kappa, they found one of their girls unconscious, and they can't wake her up. I don't know what happened, but it sounds like she was attacked. There's police out front and everything."

Adrian and I stared at each other for one shocked moment. Then, wordlessly, we both stood up. He held my hand to steady me until my trembling legs strengthened. *I'm weak because of this news,* I told myself. *Not because I was just making out with a vampire.*

But those dangerous and intoxicating kisses faded almost instantly when we returned to Lynne's sorority. It was busy with frightened people, and campus security moved in and out, allowing us to step right inside the open door.

"What happened?" I asked a brunette standing nearby.

"It's Lynne," she said, biting her lips. "They just found her in an empty auditorium."

Something in the way she spoke made me uneasy. "Is she . . . alive?"

The girl nodded. "I don't know . . . I think so, but they said there's something really wrong. She's unconscious and looks . . . well . . . *old.*"

I met Adrian's eyes and vaguely noticed he had silver paint in his hair. I'd still been holding the brush when I'd wrapped my arms around him. "Damn," he murmured. "Too late."

I wanted to scream in frustration. We'd been so close to warning her. She'd allegedly left just before we'd arrived. What if we'd come sooner? What if we'd visited her before the other two girls? I'd chosen the order randomly. Worse, what if we'd been able to find her instead of having art time with the drunken sorority girls?

What if I hadn't been all over Adrian? Or maybe he'd been all over me. Whatever you wanted to call it, I hadn't exactly resisted.

The more we learned, however, the more unlikely it seemed we would've been able to do anything if we'd stuck around Lynne's house and investigated. Nobody knew where she'd gone. Only one person had seen her leave, a girl with curly blond hair who frustrated the campus police with her vague answers.

"I'm sorry," she kept saying. "I just . . . I can't remember the girl she left with."

"Nothing?" asked one of the officers. "Height? Age? Hair color?"

The girl frowned, looking as though she was using every ounce of mental effort. At last, she sagged in defeat and shook her head. "I'm sorry."

"Did she have black hair?" I suggested.

The girl brightened a little. "Maybe. Er, wait. It might have been brown. No. Red, maybe?"

Adrian and I stepped away, knowing we could do no more. "That girl seems awfully confused," I said as we walked back to my car.

"She certainly does," he agreed. "Sound familiar?"

"Very," I muttered, recognizing the signs of magic.

No one could deny it. Veronica had been here. And we'd been too late to stop her.

CHAPTER 12

I FELT LIKE A FAILURE when I delivered Ms. Terwilliger the news before classes the next day.

She told me, her face pale and grim, that there was nothing I could've done. But I didn't know if I believed that. I still berated myself with the same questions as last night. What if I hadn't spent the previous day with Marcus? What if I hadn't spent so much time making sure the Mustang was taken care of? What if I hadn't been engaged in a massive public display of affection on the floor with Adrian? I'd let personal matters interfere, and now a girl had paid with her life. I wanted to skip school and warn the others immediately, but Ms. Terwilliger assured me that Veronica wouldn't be able to feed so quickly. She told me waiting until later in the day would be fine.

I gave a reluctant nod and returned to my desk, figuring I'd try to read until class started. I didn't expect to have much success. "Miss Melbourne?" she called. I glanced back and saw that her sad expression had lightened up a little. She almost looked amused, which seemed weird, given the situation.

"Yes, ma'am?"

"You might want to do something about your neck."

I was totally lost. "My neck?"

She reached into her purse and handed me a compact mirror. I opened it and surveyed my neck, still trying to figure out what she could be talking about. Then I saw it. A small, brownish purple bruise on the side of my neck.

"What on earth is that?" I exclaimed.

Ms. Terwilliger snorted. "Although it's been a while for me, I believe the technical term is a hickey." She paused and arched an eyebrow. "You do know what that is, don't you?"

"Of course I know!" I lowered the mirror. "But there's no way—I mean, we barely—that is—"

She held up a hand to silence me. "You don't have to justify your private life to me. But you might want to consider how you can actually keep it private in the next fifteen minutes."

I was practically out of my seat before she finished speaking. When I emerged from the building, I had the amazing fortune to find the campus shuttle just pulling up. I hurried onto it, and although the ride to my dorm only took a few minutes, it felt like forever. All the while, my mind reeled with what had happened.

I have a hickey. I let Adrian Ivashkov give me a hickey.

How in the world had that happened? The devastating news about Lynne had allowed me to ignore the full impact of my indiscretion, but there was no avoiding that now. Against every principle I possessed, I'd allowed myself to get drawn into kissing Adrian. And not just kissing. Thinking about the way our bodies had been pressed together made me feel as flushed as I had last night.

No, no, no! I couldn't think about that. I had to forget it had happened. I needed to make sure it didn't happen again. What had come over me? I didn't feel the way he felt about me. He was Moroi. And even if he hadn't been, he was undoubtedly the most unsuitable guy for me in the world. I needed someone serious, someone with the potential to get a job that had medical benefits. Someone like Brayden.

Yeah, how'd that work out for you, Sydney?

What happened with Adrian had been wrong. It had obviously been some twisted act of lust, probably brought on because he was so forbidden. That was it. Women fell for that kind of thing. When I'd researched relationship books, I'd seen one called *Bad Boys and the Women Who Love Them*. I'd ignored it because Brayden was pretty much the opposite of a bad boy. Maybe it would be worth getting that book now.

A flame in the dark. I needed to forget that Adrian had ever called me that. I had to.

We had another minute before we would reach my dorm, so I sent a quick text to Adrian: *I have a hickey! You can't ever kiss me again*. I honestly hadn't expected him to be awake this early, so I was surprised to get a response: *Okay. I won't kiss you on your neck again*.

So typical of him. *No! You can't ever kiss me ANYWHERE. You said you were going to keep your distance.*

I'm trying, he wrote back. *But you won't keep your distance from me.*

I didn't dignify that with a response.

When we reached my dorm, I asked the driver how long she'd wait before returning to main campus. "I'm leaving right now," she said.

"Please," I begged. "Wait sixty seconds. I'll pay you."

She looked offended. "I don't take bribes."

But when I sprinted back out of the dorm—in a scarf—she was still there. I made it back to Ms. Terwilliger's class just as the bell rang. She flashed me a knowing look but said nothing about my wardrobe change.

While I was in class, I received a text from Marcus. *Can you meet today? San Bernardino, 4 p.m.*

Well, he'd warned me about short notice. San Bernardino was an hour away. I'd given Eddie a heads-up about the meeting happening this week, and he'd agreed to go. I just hoped he didn't have anything planned this afternoon. I texted back that we'd be there, and Marcus sent me an address.

When class ended, a girl from my English class caught my attention and asked if she could borrow some notes since she'd been out sick yesterday. Eddie was gone by the time I finished with her, so I didn't get a chance to ask him about San Bernardino until lunch.

"Sure," he said, snapping into that fierce guardian mode.

Jill already knew about our errand because I'd told Adrian about it. I felt a little bad about taking Eddie from Jill. Okay, *really* bad. Removing Eddie was a serious risk, though I reminded myself that he wasn't always with her every single second. Sometimes it was impossible, which was why we'd acquired Angeline. Still, if anyone in the Alchemists found out I was using her main bodyguard for personal errands, I'd be in big trouble. Well, actually, I'd probably be in big trouble regardless, seeing as I was meeting with a group of rebels. I turned to Angeline, who was trying to decipher some notes about the quadratic equation.

"Angeline, you need to stay with Jill until we're back," I said. "And you should both actually just stay in your dorm, to be extra safe. Don't wander campus."

Jill accepted this, but Angeline looked up in dismay. "I'm supposed to meet Trey for math. How do you expect me to pass?"

I was helpless against an academic argument. "Study in the dorm lobby. That should be safe enough. Jill can just do home-work with you."

Angeline didn't seem entirely pleased about that alterna-tive, but she didn't protest it. She started to return to her notes and then did a double take. "Why are you wearing that scarf?" she asked. "It's so hot today." It was true. The unseasonable temperatures had returned.

Eddie, to my surprise, said, "I wondered the same thing."

"Oh, um . . . " *Please don't blush, please don't blush,* I ordered myself. "I've just been cold today."

"That's weird," said Jill, perfectly deadpan. "For someone who always seems to be so cold, you sure can warm up pretty fast."

It was straight out of Adrian's playbook. Jill knew perfectly well why I had on the scarf, and I gave her a warning look. Eddie and Angeline appeared completely mystified. I stood up, even though I'd barely touched my food. Probably none of them would find that weird.

"Well, I've got to go. I'll find you later, Eddie." I hurried off before any of them could question me further.

I'd been a little hesitant to let Eddie in on Marcus. Eddie certainly wasn't going to turn Marcus or me in to the Alchemists for sideline plotting. That being said, I also didn't want Eddie to think the Alchemists were involved in nefarious schemes against the Moroi. That might very well be something Eddie would relay back to his own people, which could in turn cause all sorts of diplomatic problems. Even this hint of the Alchemists potentially being in contact with the Warriors was dangerous. I decided that having Eddie as protection was worth the risk of him hearing something he shouldn't. He was my friend, and I trusted him. Still, I had to give him a little background information as we made the drive to San Bernardino.

"Who are these people exactly?" he asked.

"Ex-Alchemists," I said. "They don't like all the procedures and red tape and just want to interact with Moroi and dhampirs on their own terms."

"That doesn't sound so bad." I could hear caution in his voice. Eddie was no fool. "Why do you want me along?"

"I just don't know much about them. I think their intentions are good, but we'll see." I thought very carefully on how to phrase my next words. I had to give him a heads-up. "They've got a lot of conspiracy theories. Some even, um, think there might be Alchemists working with Warriors."

"*What?*" It was a wonder Eddie's jaw wasn't on the floor.

"They don't have any hard proof," I added quickly. "They've got a Warrior girl who spies for them. She thinks she overheard something . . . but it all sounds sketchy to me. They want me to help, but I don't think there's anything to uncover. I mean, the Alchemists helped raid the Warriors, right? Disrupting their crazy execution ritual wouldn't exactly foster good relations."

"I suppose not," he admitted, but it was clear he wasn't entirely at ease.

I decided to move on to safer territory. No need to worry

about Marcus and his Merry Men (I couldn't get Adrian's name out of my head) until we heard them out.

"How is everything?" I asked. "With Angeline? Jill? I've been so busy with, uh, stuff that I feel like we haven't talked much."

Eddie didn't answer right away. "Quiet with Jill, which is good. We want things to be as boring as possible for her. Things are better with her and Micah too. At first, a lot of his friends wouldn't talk to her after the breakup. But he's gotten over her enough that they can just be friends . . . so, the others have decided they can too."

"That's a relief."

When we'd first come to Amberwood, Jill had had trouble fitting in. Dating Micah had opened up a lot of social circles for her, and I'd worried about what would happen after they split up. Things had worsened when I'd forbidden her from modeling for a local and very assertive fashion designer, Lia DiStefano, who risked exposing Jill. Jill had felt like she'd lost everything, so I was glad to see things were coming together for her again.

"Jill's easy to like," I added. "I bet most of them were happy to stay friends with her."

"Yeah." It was all he said, but there was a lot of emotion in that one word. I glanced over and saw a dreamy look on his face. So. Micah might be over Jill, but Eddie wasn't. I wondered if he even knew it. "How's Angeline?"

The dreaminess became a frown. "Confusing."

I laughed. "That's pretty accurate."

"She goes from one extreme to another. When we first started going out, she, uh, couldn't stay away from me." I didn't entirely know what that entailed, and I really didn't want to think about it. "Now I can hardly get five minutes alone with her. She's started going to basketball games for some reason. I think she's just kind of dumbstruck at a game that's got so many rules, compared to whatever insanity the Keepers do for fun. And she's really into fixing that math grade too. I guess that's a good thing." He didn't sound too sure. I, however, was thrilled.

"I think the idea of getting kicked out really scared her. Despite all the tough adjustments she's had here, she doesn't want to go back home." When Rose had been on the run, I'd hidden Dimitri and her with the Keepers. That was where we'd first met Angeline, and even back then, she'd begged Rose to take her away from that rural world. "Give her time. This'll settle down, and her, uh, enthusiasm will come back."

We reached the address in San Bernardino, a hardware shop that seemed like a strange location for a secret meeting. I pulled into the parking lot and texted Marcus that we were here. No response came.

"That's weird," I said. "I hope he didn't change his mind."

Eddie was over his girl troubles and had that sharp guardian look in his eyes again. "I bet we're being watched. If they're as paranoid as you say, this probably isn't the place we're meeting. They've sent you here and are looking for signs to see if you were followed."

I turned to him in amazement. "I never would've thought of that."

"That's why you've got me along," he said with a smile.

Sure enough. Ten minutes later, Marcus texted with another address. We must have passed the test. This new location was in another loud, busy place: a family-friendly restaurant with actors walking around in giant animal costumes. It was, if possible, more absurd than the arcade.

"He picks the weirdest places," I said.

Eddie's eyes were everywhere. "It's brilliant actually. Too loud to be overheard. One exit in the back, one in the front. And if the Alchemists did show up, I'm guessing they wouldn't create a scene around this many children?"

"I guess."

Marcus met us in the lobby and waved us forward. "Hey, gorgeous. Come on, we've got a table." He paused to shake Eddie's hand. "Nice to meet you. We can always use more for the cause."

I'm not sure what I'd expected of the Merry Men. Maybe a bunch of rough-and-tumble outcasts with battle scars and eye patches, like Wolfe. Instead, what we found were a guy and girl sharing a plate of chicken fingers. They had golden lilies on their cheeks.

Marcus directed us to two chairs. "Sydney, Eddie. This is Amelia and Wade."

We shook hands. "Sabrina's not with you?" I asked.

"Oh, she's here," said Marcus, an enigmatic note in his voice.

I picked up on the subtext and glanced around. I wasn't the only one who'd brought protection. Sabrina was hidden somewhere in the crowd, watching and waiting. Maybe in an animal costume. I wondered if she'd brought her gun in here.

Amelia slid the plate toward us. "Want some? We've got mozzarella sticks on the way."

I declined. Even with my resolution to eat more, I drew the line at deep fryers. "Let's talk," I said. "You're supposed to tell me about the tattoos and this mysterious task you have for me."

Wade chuckled. "She gets down to business."

"That's my girl," said Marcus. I could almost hear an

unspoken *That's why we need her for the cause*. He waited for our waitress, who was dressed like a cat, to bring the mozzarella sticks and take our drink orders. At least, I think it was a waitress. Gender was a little hard to determine under the mask.

"The tattoo process is simple," Marcus said, once our privacy was back. "I told you that the Alchemists are able to put Moroi compulsion in it, right? To limit communication . . . and other things, if needed."

I still didn't know if I bought the idea of mind control in the tattoos, but I let him go on.

"When Moroi help make the blood ink, the earth users put in the compulsion that prevents you from discussing vampires. That earth magic is in harmony with the other three physical elements: air, water, and fire. That harmony gives the tattoo its power. Now, if you can get a hold of charmed ink and have a Moroi undo the earth magic in it, that'll shatter the bond with the other elements and kill any compulsion locked in. Inject that 'broken' ink into your tattoo, and it breaks the harmony of your elements as well—which in turn breaks any suggestions the Alchemists put in."

Eddie and I stared.

"That's 'all' I have to do?" I asked in disbelief.

"It's easier than you might think," said Amelia. "The hard part is . . . well, Marcus added another part to the process. Not technically necessary . . . but helpful."

We'd been here ten minutes, and I was already getting a headache. "You decided to do some improvisation?"

The laughter that elicited from Marcus was just as infectious as before . . . except, once again, the scene didn't really warrant laughing. He paused, like he was waiting for us to join in, and continued when we didn't. "That's one way of looking at it. But she's right—it's helpful. Before I'll let anyone do it, they have to perform a task. Some task that involves directly going against the Alchemists."

Eddie couldn't hold back anymore. "What, like an initiation ritual?"

"More than that," said Marcus. "I have a theory that doing something like that, something that challenges all the training you've had, will weaken the compulsion a little. Usually it's something that involves infiltration and helps our cause. That weakening makes it easier for the other ink to take effect. It's also a good test. Deactivating the tattoo doesn't mean you're ready to walk away. It doesn't undo years of mental conditioning. I try to find people who think they're ready to rebel, but sometimes, when they're faced with actually taking action, they crack. Better to know sooner rather than later, before we interfere with the tattoo."

I turned toward Amelia and Wade. "And you've both done this? You did some dare, and then your tattoos were deactivated?" They nodded in unison.

"We just have to seal it with indigo now." Seeing my confusion, Wade explained, "Even after breaking the elements in the tattoo, it can still be repaired. Someone could forcibly re-ink and compel you. Tattooing over it with indigo ink makes sure you can never be controlled again."

"And here I thought yours was just a style choice," I said to Marcus.

He absentmindedly traced the crescent pattern. "Oh, the design was. But the ink was mandatory. It's a special concoction that's hard to get a hold of, and I have to go down to a guy in

Mexico to get it. I'm taking Amelia and Wade there in a couple weeks to seal theirs. You could come too."

I didn't even acknowledge that crazy idea. "Seems like that blue ink would kind of be a tip-off to the other Alchemists that something's up."

"Oh, we ran away from the Alchemists," said Amelia. "We're not part of them anymore."

Once again, Eddie jumped in. "But you were just talking about infiltration. Why not keep doing other covert tasks once you've broken the elements? Especially if it frees you? Your tattoos look the same as Sydney's right now. If you really think there's something suspicious going on, then work from the inside and hold off on sealing with the indigo ink."

"Too risky," said Marcus. "You could slip up and say something that the tattoo wouldn't have let you before. Or, if you're not cautious, they might catch you going off to meet with others. Then you've got a date with re-education—where they could repair the tattoo."

"Seems like it'd be worth the risk for more information," I said. "If you're careful enough."

Marcus shook his head, no longer flippant. "I've known others who tried that. They thought no one was on to them. They were wrong. We don't make that mistake anymore." He touched his tattoo again. "This is the way we do it now. Complete your mission, break the tattoo, leave the Alchemists, and get sealed. Then we work from the outside. Also saves us from getting caught up in all the Alchemist routine and menial tasks."

"So there are others?" I asked, picking up on what he'd said.

"Of course." That amusement returned. "You didn't think it was just the three of us, did you?"

I honestly hadn't known. "So this is what you're offering me. A fairy tale about my tattoo, if I just complete some traitorous mission for you."

"I'm offering you freedom," Marcus corrected. "And the ability to help Moroi and dhampirs in a way that's not part of some larger conspiracy. You can do it on your own terms."

Eddie and I exchanged glances. "And speaking of conspiracy," I said. "I'm guessing this is the part where you tell me about the alleged Alchemist and Warrior connection—the one you need me to prove."

My sarcasm was lost on the threesome because they all grew excited. "Exactly," said Marcus. "Tell her, Wade."

Wade finished off a chicken finger covered in ranch dressing and then leaned toward us. "Just before I joined Marcus, I was assigned to the St. Louis facility. I worked in operations, handling a lot of visitor access, giving tours . . . not the most interesting work."

I nodded. This, at least, was familiar territory. Being in the Alchemists meant taking on all sorts of roles. Sometimes you destroyed Strigoi bodies. Sometimes you made coffee for visiting officials. It was all part of the greater cause.

"I saw a lot of things. I mean, you can probably guess." He looked troubled. "The harsh attitudes. The rigid rules. Moroi visited, you know. I liked them. I was glad we were helping them, even though everyone around me acted as though helping such 'evil' creatures was a terrible fate that we'd been forced into. I accepted this because, you know, I figured what we're told is true. Anyway, there was one week . . . I swear, it was just nonstop Strigoi attacks all over the country. Just one of those things. The guardians took out most of them, and field Alchemists were pretty busy covering up. Even though most of it was taken care of, I just kept wondering about why we were always dealing with the aftermath when we have so many resources. I mean, I didn't think we should start going after Strigoi, but it just seemed like there should be a way to help the Moroi and guardians be more proactive. So . . . I mentioned it to my supervisor."

Marcus and Amelia wore deadly earnest expressions, and even I was hooked. "What happened?" I asked softly.

Wade's gaze looked off into the past. "I was chastised pretty bad. Over and over, all my superiors kept telling me how wrong it was for me to even think things like that about the Moroi, let alone talk about them. They didn't send me to re-education, but they suspended me for two weeks, and each day, I had to listen to lectures about what a terrible person I was and how I was on the verge of corruption. By the end, I believed them . . . until I met Marcus. He made me realize I didn't have to be in that life anymore."

"So you left," I said, suddenly feeling a little more kindly toward Marcus.

"Yes. But not before completing the mission Marcus gave me. I got a hold of the classified visitor list."

That surprised me. The Alchemists were always hip deep in secrets. While most of our goings-on were recorded diligently, there were some things that our elite leaders didn't want the rest of the society to know about. Again, all for the greater good. The classified list would detail people allowed access—that the higher-ups wanted kept secret. It wasn't something the average Alchemist could see.

"You're young," I said. "You wouldn't be allowed access to something like that."

Wade snorted. "Of course not. That's what made the task so difficult. Marcus doesn't have us do easy assignments. I had to do a lot of dangerous things—things that made me glad to escape afterward. The list showed us the link to the Warriors."

"Did it say 'Top Secret Vampire Hunter Meeting'?" asked Eddie. Things like that, aside from his deadly protective skills, were why I liked having him along.

Wade flushed at the jibe. "No. It was all coded, kind of. It didn't list full names, just initials. Even I couldn't get the actual names. But one of the entries? Z. J."

Marcus and his Merry Men all looked at me expectantly, as though that were supposed to mean something to me. I glanced at Eddie again, but he was just as baffled.

"What's that stand for?" I asked.

"Zebulon Jameson," said Marcus. Once again, there was an expectation. When I didn't answer, Marcus turned disbelieving. "You were there with the Warriors. Don't you remember him? Master Jameson?"

I did, actually. He was one of the Warriors' high officials, an intimidating man with a salt-and-pepper beard who'd worn old-fashioned golden ceremonial robes.

"I never caught his first name," I said. "But isn't it kind of a leap to assume that's who Z. J. was? Maybe it was, I don't know, Zachary Johnson."

"Or Zeke Jones," supplied Eddie.

The cat came by with a refill for Marcus's lemonade, and I soon had proof that it was a woman. "Thanks, love," Marcus said, giving her a smile that nearly made her swoon and drop the tray. When he turned back to us, he was all business. "That's where Sabrina comes in. Not long before Wade got the list, she overheard Master Jameson talking to one of his cronies about an upcoming trip to St. Louis and how he was going to find out about leads on some missing girl. The timing lines up."

"It's an awfully big coincidence," I said. Yet even as I spoke, I was reminded of something Sonya Karp always said about the world of Moroi and Alchemists: *There are no coincidences.*

"What missing girl were they talking about?" asked Eddie carefully.

I met his eyes and immediately understood what he wasn't saying. A missing girl that the Warriors were interested in. There was one missing girl that the Moroi were very, very interested in as well. And whom the Alchemists were determined to keep safe. She was the reason I was stationed in Palm Springs in the first place. In fact, I was pretending to be her sister.

Jill.

I said nothing and focused on Marcus again.

He shrugged. "I don't know, just that finding her would create a lot of problems for the Moroi. The details aren't important yet. First we have to prove the connection."

Those details were immensely important to Eddie and me, but I wasn't sure how much Marcus and friends knew about Jill. I wasn't about to show too much interest.

"And that's what you want me to do?" I asked, recalling the arcade discussion. "How would you like me to do that? Go visit Master Jameson and ask him?"

"Every visitor is recorded on video if they're going through the secure access point," said Wade. "Even the top secret ones. All you have to do is steal a copy of that footage. They store it all in their computers."

These people had a very different idea than me of what "all you have to do" meant.

"I'm a field Alchemist in Palm Springs," I reminded them. "I'm not a computer hacker. I'm not even in St. Louis! How would I walk in and steal something?"

Marcus tilted his head to study me, allowing some of that golden hair to slip forward. "It's more of that resourceful vibe I get off you. Couldn't you find some way to get to St. Louis? Some reason to visit?"

"No! I'd have no . . ." I trailed off, flashing back to the wedding. Ian, with his lovesick eyes, had invited me to visit him in St. Louis. He'd had the audacity to use church services as a way to further his chances with me.

Marcus's eyes sparkled. "You've already thought of something, haven't you? Brilliant, just like I thought." Amelia looked mildly put out at hearing me complimented.

"It'd be a long shot," I said.

"That's kind of how we roll," said Marcus.

I still wasn't on board. "Look, I know someone there, but I'd have to get permission to even go, which wouldn't be easy." I stared at each of them in turn. "You know how it is. You were all in the Alchemists. You know we can't just take vacations whenever we want."

Wade and Amelia actually had the grace to look embarrassed, but Marcus was undaunted. "Can you let this chance pass? Even if you don't want to join us or alter your tattoo, just think about it. You saw the Warriors. You saw what they're capable of. Can you even imagine what could happen if they had access to Alchemist resources?"

"It's all circumstantial," argued the scientist in me.

"Sydney," said Eddie.

I turned to him and saw something in his eyes I'd never expected to see: pleading. He didn't care about Alchemist conspiracies or Marcus's Merry Men. What he cared about was Jill, and he'd heard something that made him think she was in danger. That was unacceptable in his world. He would do anything in his power to keep her safe, but even he knew stealing information from the Alchemists was out of his league. It was pretty much out of mine too, but he didn't know that. He believed in me, and he was silently begging me to help.

Marcus pushed his advantage. "You have nothing to lose—I mean, if you aren't caught. If you get the footage and we find nothing . . . well, so be it. False alarm. But if we get hard proof that Jameson was there, then I don't have to tell you how big that is. Either way, you should break your tattoo and join us. Besides, after a stunt like this, would you really want to stick around?" He eyed me. "But that part's up to you. Just help us for now."

Against my better judgment, my mind was starting to figure out how I could pull this off. "I'd need a lot more information about operations," I murmured.

"I can get you that," said Wade promptly.

I didn't answer. This was crazy—a crazy idea from a crazy group. But I looked at Marcus's tattoo and the way the others followed him—the way even Sabrina followed him. There was a dedication, an ardent belief that had nothing to do with Marcus's silly flirting. They might really be on to something.

"Sydney," said Eddie again. And this time: "Please."

I could feel my resolve weakening. A missing girl, who could cause lots of trouble if found. If they were really talking about Jill, how could I risk anything happening to her?

But what if I was caught?

Don't get caught, an inner voice said.

With a sigh, I looked back up at Wade. "All right," I said. "Give me the scoop."

CHAPTER 13

WADE TOLD ME EVERYTHING he knew. It was all useful, but I didn't know if it would be enough. First, I had to get to St. Louis . . . and that was going to be tricky. I braced myself for the phone calls I'd have to make, hoping I had enough Alchemist wiles to pull them off.

Before I took on that task, I just wanted the normality and comfort of my own room. Eddie and I drove back to Amberwood, analyzing every detail of our meeting. He was chomping at the bit to make progress, and I promised I'd keep him in the loop.

I had just reached my door when my phone rang. It was Ms. Terwilliger. I swear, sometimes I thought she had a sensor outside my room so that she'd know the instant I returned.

"Miss Melbourne," she said. "We need to meet."

My heart stopped. "There hasn't been another victim, has there? You said we have time."

"We do," she replied. "Which is why we need to meet sooner rather than later. Reading up on spells is one thing, but you

199

require some hands-on practice. I refuse to let Veronica get to you."

Her words triggered a mix of emotions. Naturally, I had my knee-jerk reaction against practicing magic. It was quickly squashed by the realization that Ms. Terwilliger cared about me and was so concerned about keeping me safe. My own personal desire to not be in a coma was also a strong motivator.

"When do you want to meet, ma'am?" I asked.

"Tomorrow morning."

I realized tomorrow was Saturday. Already? Where had the week gone? I was driving Adrian to pick up his car in the morning, which hopefully wouldn't take a long time. "Could we meet at noon? I've got an errand to run."

"I suppose so," said Ms. Terwilliger, with some reluctance. "Meet me at my place, and then we'll go out to Lone Rock Park."

I was about to lie back on my bed and froze. "Why do we have to go out to the middle of the desert?" Lone Rock Park was remote and rarely saw many tourists. I hadn't forgotten how terrifying it was the last time she'd brought me out into the wilderness. At least this time we'd be in daylight.

"Well, we can hardly practice on school grounds," she pointed out

"True. . . ."

"Bring your book, and the components you've been working on."

We disconnected, and I jotted out a quick text to Adrian: *Need to be fast tomorrow. Meeting Ms. T at 12.* His response wasn't entirely unexpected: *Why?* Adrian naturally needed to know everything that was going on in my life. I texted back that Ms. Terwilliger wanted to work on magical protection. This time, he did surprise me: *Can I watch? Wanna know how she's protecting you.*

Wow, Adrian actually asked? He had a history of simply inviting himself along on outings. I hesitated, still confused after our heated moment at the sorority. He'd never mentioned it again, though, and his concern now touched me. I texted back that he could come along and was rewarded with a smiley face.

I didn't entirely know what to wear to "magical training," so I opted for comfortable layers the next morning. Adrian gave me a once-over when he got into Latte. "Casual mode, huh? Haven't seen that since the Wolfe days."

"I don't know what she has in mind," I explained, doing a U-turn on his street. "Figured this was best."

"You could have worn your AYE shirt."

"Wouldn't want to get it dirty," I said, grinning.

That was partially true. I still thought the fiery heart he'd painted was exquisite. But each time I looked at the shirt, too many memories seized me. What had I been thinking? That was a question I'd asked myself a hundred times, and every answer I came up with sounded fake. My preferred theory was that I'd simply been caught up in how serious Adrian had been about his art, how the emotion and passion had seized hold of him. Girls liked artists just as much as bad boys, right? Even now, something stirred in my chest when I thought about the enraptured look on his face. I loved that he possessed something so powerful in him.

But, as I told myself constantly, that was no excuse for climbing all over him and letting him kiss me—*on my neck.* I'd bought and downloaded the "bad boy" book online, but it had been completely useless in advising me. I finally decided the best way—if not the healthiest one—was to act like the moment had never happened. That didn't mean I forgot it. In fact, as I sat beside him in the car, I had a difficult time not thinking about how it had felt to be pressed up against him. Or how his fingers had felt entangled in my hair. Or how his lips had—

Sydney! Stop. Think of something else. Conjugate Latin verbs. Recite the periodic table.

None of those did any good. To Adrian's credit, he continued to withhold any commentary about that night. Finally, I found distraction in telling him about my trip to San Bernardino. Rehashing the conspiracy, rebel groups, and break-ins pretty much killed any passionate feelings I still had. Adrian didn't like the idea of Alchemists working with Warriors or of the tattoo controlling me. But he also didn't like me walking into danger. I tried to downplay the near impossibility of breaking into the St. Louis facility, but he clearly didn't believe me.

Ms. Terwilliger texted me twice not to be late to our meeting. I kept an eye on my watch, but the care of a Mustang was not something I took lightly, and I had to take my time at the mechanic's shop to make sure the Mustang was in pristine condition. Adrian had wanted to go with basic tires, but I'd urged him to upgrade, convincing him the extra cost would be worth it. And once I inspected them, I congratulated myself on the choice. Only after I was satisfied the car hadn't been unnecessarily scratched did I finally allow him to pay. We drove both cars back to Vista Azul, and I was pleased to see my timing was perfect. We weren't late, but Ms. Terwilliger was waiting on her porch for us.

We designated Adrian as our carpool driver. "Jeez," I said when she hurriedly got in the car. "Do you have somewhere to be after this?"

The smile she gave me was strained, and I couldn't help but notice how pale she looked. "No, but we do have a schedule to follow. I cast a large spell this morning that won't last forever. The countdown is on."

She wouldn't say any more until we reached the park, and that silence unnerved me. It gave me the opportunity to imagine all sorts of frightening outcomes. And although I trusted her, I suddenly felt relieved that Adrian was along as a chaperone.

Although it wasn't the busiest place, Lone Rock Park still had the occasional hiker. Ms. Terwilliger—who was actually in hiking boots—set off across the rocky terrain, searching for a suitably remote space to do whatever it was she had in mind. A few stratified rock formations dotted the landscape, but I couldn't really appreciate their beauty. Mostly I was aware that we were out here when the sun was at its fiercest. Even if it was almost winter, we'd still be feeling the heat.

I glanced over at Adrian as we walked and found him already looking at me. From his jacket pocket, he produced a bottle of sunscreen. "I knew you'd ask. I'm nearly as prepared as you are."

"Nearly," I said. He'd done it again, anticipating my thoughts. For half a heartbeat, I pretended it was just the two of us out on a pleasant afternoon hike. It seemed like most of the time we spent together was on some urgent mission. How nice would it be to just hang out without the weight of the world on us? Ms. Terwilliger soon brought us back to our grim reality.

"This should do," she said, surveying the land around her. She had managed to find one of the most desolate areas in the park. I wouldn't have been surprised to see vultures circling overhead. "Did you bring what I asked for?"

"Yes, ma'am." I knelt on the ground and rifled through my bag. In it was the spell book, along with some herbal and liquid compounds I'd mixed up at her request.

"Take out the fireball kindling," she instructed.

Adrian's eyes went wide. "Did you just say 'fireball'? That's badass."

"You see fire all the time," I reminded him. "From Moroi who can wield it."

"Yeah, but I've never seen a human do anything like that. I've never seen *you* do anything like that."

I wished he didn't look so awestruck because it kind of drove home the severity of what we were about to attempt. I would've felt better if he'd treated it like it was no big deal. But this spell? Yeah, it was kind of a big deal.

I'd once performed another spell that involved throwing a painstakingly made amulet and reciting words that made it burst into flames. That one had a huge physical component, however. This spell was another of those mental ones and essentially involved summoning fire out of thin air.

The kindling Ms. Terwilliger had referred to was a small drawstring bag filled with ashes made from burnt yew bark. She took the bag from me and examined its contents, murmuring in approval. "Yes, yes. Very nice. Excellent consistency. You burned it for exactly the right amount of time." She handed the bag back. "Now, eventually you won't need this. That's what makes this spell so powerful. It can be performed very quickly, with very little preparation. But you have to practice first before you can reach that point."

I nodded along and tried to stay in student mode. So far, what she was saying was similar to what the book had described. If I thought of all this as a classroom exercise, it was much less daunting. Not really scary at all.

Ms. Terwilliger tilted her head and looked past me. "Adrian? You might want to keep your distance. A considerable distance."

Okay. Maybe a little scary.

He obeyed and backed up. Ms. Terwilliger apparently had no such fear for herself because she stayed only a few feet away from me. "Now then," she said. "Apply the ashes, and hold out your hand."

I reached into the bag, touching the ashes with my thumb and forefinger. Then I lightly rubbed all my fingers together until my whole palm had a fine gray coating on it. I set the bag down and then held out my hand in front of me, palm up. I knew what came next but waited for her instruction.

"Summon your magic to call the flame back from the ashes. No incantation, just your will."

Magic surged within me. Calling an element from the world reminded me a little of what the Moroi did, which felt strange. My attempt started off as a red glimmer, hovering in the air above my palm. Slowly, it grew and grew until it was about the size of a tennis ball. The high of magic filled me. I held my breath, scarcely able to believe what I had just done. The red flames writhed and swirled, and although I could feel their heat, they didn't burn me.

Ms. Terwilliger gave a grunt that seemed to be equal parts amusement and surprise. "Remarkable. I forget sometimes what a natural you really are. It's only red, but something tells me, it won't take long before you can produce blue ones without the ashes. Calling elements out of the air is easier than trying to transform one substance into another."

I stared at the fireball, entranced, but soon found myself getting tired. The flames flickered, shrank, and then faded away altogether.

"The sooner you get rid of it, the better," she told me. "You'll just use up your own energy trying to sustain it. Best to throw it at your adversary and quickly summon another. Try again, and this time, throw it."

I called the fire once more and felt a small bit of satisfaction at seeing it take on more of an orange hue. I'd learned in my very first childhood chemistry lessons that the lighter a flame was, the hotter it burned. Getting to blue anytime soon still seemed like a long shot.

And speaking of long shots . . . I threw the fireball.

Or, well, I tried. My control of it faltered when I attempted to send it off toward a bare patch of ground. The fireball splintered apart, the flames disappearing into smoke that was carried off by the wind.

"It's hard," I said, knowing how lame that sounded. "Trying to hold it and throw it is just like an ordinary physical thing. I have to do that while still controlling the magic."

"Exactly." Ms. Terwilliger seemed very pleased. "And that's where the practice comes in."

Fortunately, it didn't take too many attempts before I figured out how to make it all work together. Adrian cheered me on when I successfully managed to throw my first fireball, resulting in a beautiful shot that perfectly hit the rock I'd been aiming for. I flashed Ms. Terwilliger a triumphant look and waited for the next spell we'd be moving on to. To my surprise, she didn't seem nearly as impressed as I expected her to be.

"Do it again," she said.

"But I've got it down," I protested. "We should try something else. I was reading the other part of the book—"

"You have no business doing that yet," she scolded. "You think this is exhausting? You'd pass out attempting one of the more advanced spells. Now." She pointed at the hard desert floor. "Again."

I wanted to tell her that it was impossible for me not to read ahead in a book. It was just how I operated with all my classes. Something told me now was not the best time to bring that up.

She made me practice the throw over and over. Once she was convinced I had it down, she had me work on increasing the fire's heat. I finally managed to get up to yellow but could go no farther. Then I had to work on casting the spell without the ashes. Once I reached that milestone, it was back to practicing the throws. She picked various targets for me, and I hit them all effortlessly.

"Just like Skee Ball," I muttered. "Easy and boring."

"Yes," Ms. Terwilliger agreed. "It's easy hitting inanimate objects. But moving targets? Living targets? Not quite so easy. So, let's move on to that, shall we?"

The fireball I'd been holding above my hand vanished as shock shattered my control. "What do you mean?" If she expected me to start aiming at birds or rodents, she was in for a rude awakening. There was no way I was going to incinerate something *alive*. "What am I supposed to hit?"

Ms. Terwilliger pushed her glasses up her nose and backed up several feet. "Me."

I waited for the punch line or at least some further

explanation, but none came. I glanced behind me at Adrian, hoping perhaps he might shed some light on this, but he looked as astounded as I felt. I turned back to the singed ground where my earlier fireballs had struck.

"Ms. Terwilliger, you can't ask me to hit you."

Her lips twitched into a small half smile. "I assure you, I can. Go ahead, you can't hurt me."

I had to think a few moments for how to phrase my next response. "I'm a pretty good shot, ma'am. I can hit you."

This earned an outright laugh. "Hit, yes. Hurt, no. Go ahead and throw. Our time is running out."

I didn't know how much time had passed exactly, but the sun was definitely lower in the sky. I looked back at Adrian, silently asking for help in dealing with this insanity. His only response was a shrug.

"You're a witness to this," I told him. "You heard her tell me to do it."

He nodded. "You're totally blameless."

I took a deep breath and summoned my next fireball. I was so frazzled that it started off red, and I had to work to heat it up. Then I looked up at Ms. Terwilliger and braced myself for the shot. It was more difficult than I expected—and not just because I was worried about hurting her. Throwing something at the ground required almost no thought. The focus there was on aim and little else. But facing a person, seeing her eyes and the way her chest rose and fell while breathing . . . well, she was right. It was entirely different from hitting an inanimate object. I began to tremble, unsure if I could do it.

"You're wasting time," she warned. "You're sapping energy again. *Throw*."

The command in her voice jolted me to action. I threw.

The fireball flew from my hand, straight at her—but it never made contact. I couldn't believe my eyes. About a foot in front of her, it hit some kind of invisible barrier, smashing apart into small flames, which quickly dissipated into smoke. My jaw dropped.

"What is that?" I exclaimed.

"A very, very powerful shielding spell," she said, clearly enjoying my reaction. She lifted up a pendant that had been hanging under her shirt. It didn't look like anything special, just a piece of unpolished carnelian wrapped in silver wire. "It took incredible effort to make this . . . and requires more effort still in order to maintain it. The result is an invisible shield—as you can see—that's impervious to most physical and magical attacks."

Adrian was by my side in a flash. "Hang on. There's a spell that makes you invulnerable to everything, and you only now just thought to mention it? You've been going on this whole time about how Sydney's in danger! Why don't you just teach her this one? Then your sister can't touch her." Although it didn't seem like Adrian was about to attack her as he had Marcus, he was almost just as upset. His face was flushed, his eyes hard. He had clenched his fists at his side, but I didn't even think he noticed. It was more of that primal instinct.

Ms. Terwilliger remained strong in the face of his outrage. "If it were that simple, then believe me, I would. Unfortunately, there are a number of problems. One is that Sydney, prodigy that she is, is nowhere near strong enough to cast this. *I'm* hardly strong enough. The other problem is that it has an extremely short time frame, which is why I've been so adamant about a schedule. It only lasts six hours and requires so much effort that you can't just cast it and permanently keep it on you at all times. I'm already worn out and will be even more so once it fades. I won't be able to cast it—or hardly any other magic—for at least another day. That's why I need Sydney to be prepared at all times."

Neither Adrian nor I said anything right away. I'd taken note of her weary state when she got in the car but hadn't thought much more about it. As we'd continued to practice out here, I'd observed her sweating and looking more fatigued, but I'd written it off to the heat. Only now could I fully appreciate the extent of what she had done.

"Why would you go to so much effort?" I asked.

"To keep you alive," she snapped. "Now, don't make this a waste. We've only got one more hour before it wears off, and you need to be able to aim at someone without thinking twice. You hesitate too much."

She was right. Even knowing that she was invulnerable, I still had a difficult time attacking her. Violence just wasn't something I embraced. I had to push down all my inner worries and treat it exactly like Skee-Ball. *Aim, throw. Aim, throw. Don't think.*

Soon, I was able to fight past my anxieties and throw without hesitation. She even tried moving around a little, just to give me a better feel for what it'd be like with a real foe, but I didn't find it to be much of a challenge. She was simply too tired and unable to run around or dodge me. I actually started to feel bad for her. She looked like she was about ready to pass out, and I felt guilty sizing up my next shot and—

"Ahh!"

Fire arced from Ms. Terwilliger's fingertips just as I released my fireball. My shot went wide, the ball disintegrating before it got anywhere near her. The fire she'd released passed me, about a foot away. With a weary grin, she sank to her knees and exhaled.

"Class dismissed," she said.

"What was that?" I asked. "I don't have a magic shield on me!"

She didn't display my same concern. "It was nowhere near you. I made sure of that. It was simply to prove that no matter how 'boring and easy' this seems, all bets are off when someone is actually attacking *you*. Now then. Adrian, would you be kind enough to bring me my bag? I have some dried dates in there that I think both Sydney and I would appreciate right about now."

She was right. I'd been so caught up in the lesson that I hadn't noticed how exhausted I had become. She was in worse shape, but the magic had definitely taken its toll on me. I'd never worked with amounts this big for so long, and my body felt weak and drained as the usual blood-sugar drop occurred. I began to understand why she kept warning me away from the really difficult stuff. I practically inhaled the dried dates she'd brought for us, and although the sugar helped, I was desperate for more. Adrian gallantly helped us both walk back to the parking lot at the park's entrance, keeping one of us on each arm.

"Too bad we're out in the middle of nowhere," I grumbled, once we were all in Adrian's car. "I think you'd be amazed at how much I could eat right now. I'll probably faint before we're back to some civilization and restaurants."

"Actually," said Adrian. "You might be in luck. I think I saw a place not far from here when we were driving in."

I hadn't noticed anything, but I'd been too preoccupied worrying about Ms. Terwilliger's upcoming lesson. Five minutes after we were back on the highway, I saw that Adrian was right about a restaurant. He exited onto a drab little road, pulling into the gravel parking lot of a small but freshly painted white building.

I stared at the sign out front in disbelief.

"Pies and Stuff?"

"You wanted sugar," Adrian reminded me. The Mustang kicked up dust and gravel, and I winced on behalf of the car. "And at least it's not Pies and Bait or anything like that."

"Yeah, but the 'Stuff' part isn't exactly reassuring."

"I thought it was more the 'Pie' part that had you upset."

Despite my misgivings, Pies and Stuff was actually a cute and clean little establishment. Polka-dot curtains hung in the windows, and the display case was filled with every pie imaginable as well as "stuff" like carrot cake and brownies. We were the only people under sixty in the whole place.

We ordered our pie and sat down with it in a corner booth. I ordered peach, Adrian had French silk, and Ms. Terwilliger went with pecan. And of course, she and I had the waitress bring us coffee as soon as humanly possible since we'd had to abstain, painfully, for the magic. I took a sip and immediately felt better.

Adrian ate his slice at a reasonable rate, like a normal person, but Ms. Terwilliger and I dug in as though we hadn't eaten in a month. Conversation was irrelevant. Only pie mattered. Adrian regarded us both with delight and didn't try to interrupt until we'd practically licked the plates clean.

He nodded toward mine. "Another piece?"

"I'll take more coffee." I eyed the sparkling plate and couldn't help but notice that inner voice that used to nag me about calories was quiet these days. In fact, it didn't seem to be around anymore at all. I'd been so angry about Adrian's food "intervention," but his words had ended up having a bigger impact than I'd expected. Not that it had anything to do with him *personally*, of course. Lightening up my dieting restrictions was just a reasonable idea. That was it. "I feel pretty good now."

"I'll get you another cup," he told me. When he returned, he even had a mug for Ms. Terwilliger. "Figured you'd want one too."

She smiled in appreciation. "Thank you. You're very astute." As she drank, I couldn't help but notice she still looked tired, despite the fact that we'd just replenished with sugar. She no longer seemed in danger of passing out, but it was obvious she hadn't recovered as quickly as I had.

"Are you sure you're okay?" I asked her.

"Don't worry, I'll be fine." She sipped more coffee, her face lost in thought. "It's been years since I performed the shield spell. I forgot how much it takes out of me."

I was again struck by all the trouble she'd gone through for me. Ever since she'd identified me as a potential magic user, I'd done nothing but resist her and even be antagonistic.

"Thanks," I told her. "For everything . . . I wish there was a way I could make it up to you."

She set her cup down and stirred in more sugar. "I'm happy to do it. There's no need to reciprocate. Although . . . once this is all over, I'd like very much if you'd meet my coven. I'm not asking you to join," she added quickly. "Just to talk. I think you'd find the Stelle very interesting."

"Stelle," I repeated. She'd never called them by name before. "The stars."

Ms. Terwilliger nodded. "Yes. Our origins are Italian, though as you've seen already, the magic we use comes from a number of cultures."

I was at a loss for words. She'd gone to so much trouble for me . . . surely it wasn't a big deal just to *talk* to the other witches, right? But if it was such a small thing, then why was I terrified? The answer came to me a few moments later. Talking to others, seeing the larger organization, would kick my involvement with magic up to the next level. It had taken me a long time to come around to the magic I already used. I'd overcome many of my fears, but some part of me treated it as just some sideline activity. Like a hobby. Meeting other witches would change everything. I would have to accept that I was part of something so much bigger than just the occasional dabbling. Meeting a coven seemed official. And I didn't know if I was ready to be considered a witch.

"I'll think about it," I said at last. I wished I could give her more, but my protective instincts had seized me.

"I'll take what I can get," she said with a small smile. Her phone chimed, and she glanced down. "Speaking of the Stelle, I need to talk to one of my sisters. I'll meet you at the car." She finished her coffee and headed outside.

Adrian and I followed a few minutes later. I was still troubled about the coven and caught hold of his sleeve to keep him back. I spoke softly.

"Adrian, when did I reach this point? Trying to crack open the Alchemists and practicing magic in the desert?" Last summer, when I'd been with Rose in Russia, I couldn't even tolerate the idea of sleeping in the same room with her. I'd had too many Alchemist mantras running through my mind, warning me of vampire evils. And now, here I was, in league with vampires and questioning the Alchemists. That girl in Russia had nothing in common with the one in Palm Springs.

No, I'm still the same person at heart. I had to be . . . because if I wasn't, then who was I?

Adrian smiled at me sympathetically. "I think it's been a culmination of things. Your curious nature. Your need to do the right thing. It's all led you to this point. I know the Alchemists have taught you to think a certain way, but what you're doing now—it's not wrong."

I raked my hand through my hair. "And yet, despite all of that, I can't bring myself to have one tiny conversation with Ms. Terwilliger's coven."

"You have boundaries." He gently smoothed one of my way-ward locks. "Nothing wrong with that."

"Marcus would say it's the tattoo holding me back."

Adrian dropped his hand. "Marcus says a lot of things."

"I don't think Marcus is trying to deceive me. He believes in his cause, and I'm still worried about mind control . . . but hon-estly, it's hard to believe I'm being held back when I'm out here doing stuff like this." I gestured outside, to where Ms. Terwilliger was. "Alchemist dogma says this magic is unnatural and wrong."

Adrian's smile returned. "If it makes you feel better, you actually looked natural out there—back in the park."

"Doing . . . what? Throwing fireballs?" I shook my head. "There's nothing natural about that."

"You wouldn't think so, but . . . well. You were . . . amazing, throwing that fire like some kind of ancient warrior goddess."

Annoyed, I turned away. "Stop making fun of me."

He caught my arm and pulled me back toward him. "I am absolutely serious."

I swallowed, speechless for a moment. All I was aware of was how close we were, that he was holding me to him with only a few inches between us. *Almost as close as at the sorority.* "I'm not a warrior or a goddess," I managed at last.

Adrian leaned closer. "As far as I'm concerned, you're both."

I knew that look in his eyes. I knew because I'd seen it before. I expected him to kiss me, but instead, he ran his finger along the side of my neck. "There it is, huh? Badge of honor."

It took me a moment to realize he was talking about the hickey. It had faded but wasn't entirely gone. I pulled away. "It is not! It was a mistake. You were out of line doing that to me."

His eyebrows rose. "Sage, I distinctly remember every part of that night. You didn't seem that unwilling. You were practically on top of me."

"I don't really remember the details," I lied.

He moved his hand from my neck and rested a fingertip on my lips. "But I'll stick to just kissing these if it makes you feel better. No mark." He started to lean toward me, and I jerked away.

"You will not! It's wrong."

"What, kissing you, or kissing you in Pies and Stuff?"

I glanced around, suddenly aware that we were creating a dinner show for the senior citizens, even if they couldn't hear us. I backed up.

"Both," I said, feeling my cheeks burn. "If you're going to attempt something inappropriate—something you said you wouldn't do anymore—then you could at least pick a better place."

He laughed softly, and the look in his eyes confused me further. "Okay," he said. "The next time I kiss you, I promise it'll be in a more romantic place."

"I—what? No! You shouldn't try at all!" I began moving toward the door, and he fell in step with me. "What happened to loving me from a distance? What happened to not, um, bringing up any of this stuff?" For someone who was allegedly just going to watch from afar, he wasn't doing a very good job. And I was doing an even worse job of being indifferent.

He moved in front of the door and blocked my way. "I said I wouldn't—if you don't want me to. But you're kind of giving me mixed signals, Sage."

"I am not," I said, amazed that I could even say that with a straight face. Even I didn't believe it. "You're presumptuous and arrogant and a whole lot of other things if you think I've changed my mind."

"You see, that's just it." There he was again, moving into my space. "I think you like the 'other things.'"

I shook off my daze and pulled away. "I like *humans*."

Another Alchemist lesson came to mind. *They look like us, but don't be deceived. The Moroi don't display the malice of the Strigoi, but creatures who drink blood and manipulate nature have no place in our world. Work with them only as you must. We are not the same. Keep your distance as much as possible. It's for the good of your soul.*

Adrian didn't look like he believed this either, but he stepped away and headed outside. I followed a few moments later, thinking I'd played with fire more than once today.

CHAPTER 14

SUNDAY ROLLED AROUND, and the day started off quietly. We were nearing the point when Veronica might strike again, and my stomach was in knots over what her next step would be . . . and how stuck we were on how to stop her. Then I received help from an unexpected source when my phone rang with an unknown number on the display.

Normally, I wouldn't answer something like that, but my life was hardly normal these days. Besides, it was a Los Angeles area code.

"Hello?"

"Hi! Is this Taylor?"

It took me a moment to remember my secret identity. I did not, however, recall giving my actual number to any of the girls we'd warned about Veronica.

"Yes," I said warily.

"This is Alicia, from Old World Bed-and-Breakfast."

"Hi," I said, still puzzled as to why and how she'd be calling me.

Her voice was as cheery and bright as when we'd met her. "I wanted to know if you'd thought any more about getting a room for your anniversary."

"Oh, well . . . that. We're still deciding. But, uh, probably we're going to go with something closer to the coast. You know, romantic beach walks and all that."

"I can totally understand," she said, though she sounded disappointed at the loss of a sale. "If you change your mind, just let me know. We're running a special this month, so you could get the Bunny Suite at a really good price. I remember you saying it reminded you of your pet rabbit. What was his name?"

"Hopper," I said flatly.

"Hopper! That's right. Such a sweet name."

"Yeah, awesome." I tried to think of a polite way to phrase my next question but simply chose directness. "Look, Alicia, how did you get this number?"

"Oh, Jet gave it to me."

"He did?"

"Yup." She'd apparently gotten over her disappointment and now sounded bright and chirpy again. "He filled out an info card while you guys were here and put down your number."

I nearly groaned. Typical.

"Good to know," I said. I wondered how often Adrian gave my number out. "Thanks for following up."

"Happy to. Oh!" She giggled. "I nearly forgot. Your friend is back."

I froze. "What?"

"Veronica. She checked back in yesterday."

My first reaction was excitement. My second one was panic. "Did you tell her we were asking about her?"

"Oh, no. I remembered you saying you wanted to surprise her."

I nearly sank in relief. "Thank you. We, uh, wouldn't to ruin that. We'll have to stop by and visit—but don't tell her."

"You can count on me!"

We disconnected, and I stared at the phone. Veronica was back. Just when we thought we'd lost all leads on her. I immediately called Ms. Terwilliger but was sent to voice mail. I left a message and then followed up with a text, saying I had urgent news. My phone rang again, just as I was about to call Adrian. I almost hoped Alicia had more to tell me, but then I saw that it was Stanton's number. After first taking a deep breath, I tried to answer in as calm a way as possible.

"Miss Sage," she said. "I received your message yesterday."

"Yes, ma'am. Thank you for calling me back."

I'd called her yesterday, just before meeting up with Adrian. Ms. Terwilliger's magical training had taken priority at the time, but I hadn't forgotten my deal with Marcus.

"I have a, um, favor to ask," I continued.

Stanton, who was rarely surprised, was clearly surprised now. "You're certainly entitled to ask . . . but you're just not usually the type who does."

"I know, and I feel bad. So, if you have to say no, I understand." In truth, if she said no, I would have a number of problems on my hands, but it was best not to sound too eager. "Well, I've been thinking about how I have to spend Christmas here— with the Moroi. And I definitely understand that, ma'am. It's part of the mission, but . . . well, I'd be lying if I said that didn't bother me. So, I was wondering if there's any way at all I'd be allowed to go to one of the big holiday services. It would make me feel . . . oh, I don't know. More connected. Purified, even. I'm just always surrounded by them here, by that taint, you know? I feel like I can't even breathe half the time. That probably sounds ridiculous."

I cut my rambling off. When Marcus had first suggested taking advantage of knowing someone in St. Louis, I'd immediately thought of Ian. Then I realized that wasn't enough. Alchemists on assignment couldn't just ask for casual time off to visit friends. Time off for something more spiritual and group-oriented—say, the Alchemists' annual holiday services—was a different matter. Lots of Alchemists were given clearance to travel and attend those services. They were tied to our faith and group unity. In fact, Ian had even brought it up at the wedding in the hopes of luring me to visit him. Little had he known his trick would pay off. Kind of.

"It doesn't sound that ridiculous," Stanton said. That was promising, and I tried to unclench my fist and relax.

"I was thinking maybe I could go before we're out for winter break," I added. "Jill can stay within the confines of the school, so there shouldn't be too much risk. And Eddie and Angeline are always with her. I could just hop over to St. Louis for a quick weekend trip."

"St. Louis?" I could almost see her frown through the phone. "There are services in Phoenix as well. That would be much closer."

"I know, ma'am. It's just. . . ." I hoped being genuinely nervous would help me sound convincing. "I, uh, was hoping I could also see Ian again."

"Ah. I see." There was a long pause. "I find that more surprising than you wanting to attend services. From what I saw at the wedding, you didn't seem to be that charmed by Mr. Jansen."

So. I'd been right that Stanton had noticed his crush on me. However, she'd also noticed I didn't return his affection. She was observant, even to little details, which brought Marcus's warnings back to me, about how the Alchemists paid attention to everything we did. I started to understand his fears and why he pulled his recruits out of the Alchemists so quickly. Was I already attracting attention? Were all the little things I did—even asking for this—slowly building a case against me?

Again, I hoped my anxiety simply made me sound like a flustered, love-struck girl, one Stanton would feel sorry for and shake her head over. St. Louis wasn't that much farther away by plane, and the end result was the same. "Well, that was business, ma'am. I didn't want to get distracted from our goal."

"Of course." Her next pause was only a few seconds long, but it felt like an hour. "Well, I see no reason why you can't go. You've done an admirable job in your work, and—from a personal point of view—I can understand why you'd want to be with familiar faces again. You've spent more time with the Moroi than many Alchemists ever will in their lives, and you didn't hesitate when that Ivashkov pushed himself onto you at the wedding."

I didn't really hesitate when he pushed himself onto me at the sorority, either. Or did I push myself on him?

"Thank you, ma'am."

She authorized me to go next weekend and said I could use Alchemist funds to book my travel arrangements. When we got off the phone, I contemplated calling Ian but then decided on a more impersonal approach. I jotted out a quick email telling him that I'd be in town and that I hoped we could meet up. After a few moments of thought, I then texted Marcus: *Arrangements made.*

Lunchtime came around, and Eddie texted to ask if I could meet Jill and him in my dorm's cafeteria. I headed downstairs at the appropriate time and found a glum Eddie sitting by himself at a table. I wondered where Angeline was and noted he hadn't mentioned her in his text. Rather than bring that up, I focused on who he had mentioned.

"Where's Jill?"

He nodded toward the opposite side of the cafeteria. I followed his gaze and saw Jill standing near a table, laughing and talking. She held a tray and looked as though she'd been stopped on her way back from the food line. Micah and some other guys were at the table, and I was happy to see he did indeed seem comfortable with being her friend again.

"That's nice," I said, turning back to my own food. "I'm glad she's getting along with everyone."

Eddie stared at me in amazement. "Don't you see what's going on?"

I'd been about to bite into an apple and stopped. I hated these kinds of loaded questions. They meant I'd missed out on some social subtlety—something that wasn't my strong suit. Glancing back at Jill, I tried to make my best guess.

"Is Micah trying to get back together with her?"

"Of course not," said Eddie, like I should've known. "He's going out with Claire Cipriano now."

"Sorry. I can't keep track of everyone's dating lives. I'll add it to my to-do list after, you know, busting Alchemist conspiracies and finding out whether the Warriors are after Jill."

Eddie's gaze was locked on Jill, and he nodded, making me think he hadn't actually heard a word I'd said. "Travis and Juan want to ask her out."

"So? She learned her lesson about human and vampire dating." I wished I had. "She'll tell them no."

"They still shouldn't be bothering her," he growled.

Jill didn't seem to be particularly bothered by their attention. In fact, I liked seeing her bright and smiling for a change. Confidence suited her and emphasized her royal status, and she clearly was enjoying whatever banter was going on. One thing I'd learned in my social education was that flirting wasn't the same thing as going out with someone. My friend Julia was an expert at the difference. If it made Jill happy, I certainly had no problems with it.

Honestly, it looked like the person who was most bothered by Jill's suitors was Eddie. He theoretically had the excuse of wanting to protect her, but this seemed pretty personal. I decided to bring him back to his own romantic life, the one he should actually be concerned about.

"Where's Angeline?"

Jill began walking toward us. Looking relieved, Eddie turned back to me. "Well, that's what we wanted to talk to you about."

Whenever anyone wanted to talk to me, it meant something weird was about to happen. Actual emergency issues were never given an introduction. They were just delivered immediately. This premeditated stuff was a wild card.

"What's going on?" I asked once Jill sat down. "With Angeline?"

She exchanged a knowing glance with Eddie. "We think Angeline's up to something," she said. A moment later, she clarified, "Something bad."

Not this again. I turned to Eddie. "Is she still being distant?"

"Yeah. She had lunch with us yesterday." He frowned. "But she was acting weird. She wouldn't explain why she's been so busy."

Jill concurred. "She actually got really upset the more we kept questioning her. It was strange. I think she's in some kind of trouble."

I leaned back in my chair. "The kind of trouble Angeline gets into is usually spontaneous and unexpected. You're talking like she's masterminding something in secret. That's not her style. At worst, she's harboring an illicit wardrobe."

Eddie looked like he wanted to smile but couldn't quite manage it. "True."

Jill apparently wasn't convinced. "You have to talk to her. Find out what's going on."

"Can't *you* talk to her?" I asked, looking between their faces. "You live with her."

"We tried," protested Jill. "I told you. She just got mad the more we talked."

"Well, I can understand that," I snapped. "Look, I'm sorry something weird is going on with her. And I don't want her in trouble, believe me. But there's only so much hand-holding I can do with her. I fixed her math problem. My job is to make sure she stays in school and doesn't blow your cover. Everything else is extraneous, and I just don't have time for that. And if she wouldn't talk to you, why on earth do you think she'd talk to me?"

I'd spoken a bit more harshly than I intended. I really did care about them all. I also didn't want trouble in the group. Nonetheless, it was always a little frustrating when they came to me with dramas like this, as though I were their mother. They were some of the smartest, most competent people I knew. They didn't need me, and Angeline was no criminal genius. Figuring out her motives couldn't be that difficult.

Neither one of them had an immediate response for me. "You just always seem to get through to people," Jill said at last. "You're good at communication."

That certainly wasn't a compliment I heard very often. "I don't do anything special. I'm just persistent. Keep trying, and maybe you'll get through." Seeing Jill start to protest, I added, "Please. Don't ask me to do this right now. You both know I've got a lot going on."

I gave each of them a meaningful look. Both knew about Marcus, and Jill also knew about Ms. Terwilliger's sister. After a few moments, that knowledge set in, and they both looked a little embarrassed.

Eddie gave Jill a gentle nudge. "She's right. We should keep working on Angeline ourselves."

"Okay," said Jill. My relief was short-lived. "We'll try a little more. Then, if it still doesn't work, Sydney can step in."

I groaned.

When I parted ways from them later, I couldn't help but think again about Marcus's comments in San Bernardino about how Alchemists got caught up in menial tasks. I tried to reassure myself that Jill and Eddie would take care of this on their own, meaning I wouldn't actually have to intervene. Presuming, of course, Angeline really wasn't planning something catastrophic.

Unfortunately, those doubts were soon shaken when I got on the shuttle that would take me to main campus. On weekends, there was only one bus that looped between all buildings, and this one had just picked up at the boys' dorm. I found Trey sitting in it, staring out the window with a happy expression. When he saw me, his smile vanished.

"Hey," I said, taking a seat beside him. He actually looked nervous. "Off to study?"

"Meeting with Angeline, actually."

There was no escaping her today, but at least if she was working on math, it seemed unlikely she'd be staging a coup or committing arson. His troubled expression concerned me, though.

"She . . . she didn't hit you again?" I didn't see any noticeable marks, but with her, you could never tell.

"Huh? No, no. Not recently." He hesitated before speaking again. "Melbourne, how long are you going to need me to do this?"

"I don't know." Mostly I'd been focusing on getting her through the present, not the future. One thing at a time. "She'll have her final coming up before break. If she passes, then I guess you're home free. Unless you want to keep up with it after break—I mean, provided she doesn't wear you out."

This startled him a lot more than I would have expected. "Okay. Good to know."

He looked so forlorn when he left to go to the library that I wondered if those chemistry answers had really been worth it. I liked Trey. I'd never thought inflicting Angeline on him would so radically alter his life. I guessed that was just the kind of effect she had on the world.

I watched him walk away for a few more seconds and then turned toward the science building. One of the teachers, Ms. Whittaker, was an amateur botanist who was always happy to supply Ms. Terwilliger with various plants and herbs. She thought Ms. Terwilliger used them for home craft projects, like potpourri and candles, and I frequently had to pick up the latest supplies. When I walked into her classroom today, Ms. Whittaker was grading exams at her desk.

"Hi, Sydney," she said, barely looking up. "I set it all over there, on the far counter."

"Thanks, ma'am."

I walked over and was surprised to practically find a spice cabinet. Ms. Terwilliger had requested all sorts of leaves, stems, and clippings. It was the most I'd ever had to pick up for her.

"She sure had a big order this time," Ms. Whittaker remarked, as though sensing my thoughts. "Is she really using garlic in potpourri?"

"Oh, that's for some, um, cooking she's doing. You know, holidays and all."

She nodded and returned to her work. One thing that often helped in Alchemist affairs (and witch ones) was that people rarely expected supernatural reasons for weird behaviors and phenomena.

I almost considered visiting Trey and Angeline at the library, just to assess her behavior myself, but decided it'd be better to not get involved. Eddie and Jill would handle it. With nothing else to do, I dared to hope I might actually just be able to stay inside and read today. But, when I returned to my dorm, I was greeted with the astonishing sight of Marcus sitting outside on a bench, playing an acoustic guitar. A group of four girls stood around, listening in awe. I walked up to the circle, my arms crossed over my chest.

"Really?" I asked.

Marcus glanced up and shot me a grin. One of the girls actually cooed.

"Hey, Sydney."

Four sets of eyes turned to me, displaying a mix of both disbelief and jealousy. "Hey," I said. "You're the last person I expected to see here."

"I never do what's predictable." He tossed his hair back and started to put his guitar back in its case. "Sorry, girls. Sydney and I have to talk."

I got more of those stares, which kind of annoyed me. Was it really that unbelievable that a good-looking guy would want to talk to me? His followers dispersed reluctantly, and Marcus and I strolled around the grounds.

"Aren't you supposed to be in hiding?" I asked. "Not panhandling with your guitar?"

"I never asked them for money. Besides, I'm incognito today." He tapped his cheek, and I noticed the tattoo was barely noticeable.

"Are you wearing makeup?" I asked.

"Don't judge," he said. "It lets me move around more freely. Sabrina helped color match me."

We came to a halt in a relatively private copse of trees. "So why are you here? Why didn't you call or text?"

"Because I have a delivery." He reached into his shirt pocket and handed me a folded piece of paper that looked like it had traveled around the world before reaching me. When I opened it and managed to smooth it out, I saw several painstakingly drawn diagrams. I jerked my gaze back to him.

"Wade's floor plans."

"As promised." A little of that self-satisfaction faded, and he actually looked impressed. "You've really got a way to get to St. Louis?"

"Sanctioned and everything," I said. "I mean, aside from the part where I break into their servers. But I've got a few ideas on how to pull that off."

He laughed. "Of course you do. I won't bother asking. Every girl's got her secrets. Maybe someday you'll share yours." From the tone of his voice, he might have been talking about non-professional secrets. "Once this is all over."

"Is it ever over?" I asked. I meant it as a joke, but it came out sounding a bit more melancholy than I would've liked.

He gave me a long, level look. "No, not really. But getting the tattoo sealed in Mexico is kind of fun. I hope you'll go with us. At the very least, we can take in some beaches and margaritas while undoing insidious magic. Do you own a bikini?"

"No. And I don't drink."

"Well, maybe one of these days we could go out for coffee. I know you drink that."

"I'm pretty busy," I said, thinking of everything weighing on me. "And you know, I also haven't decided if I'm going to do the first phase of tattoo breaking."

"You should, Sydney." He was all business again and tapped my cheek. "If nothing else, do that. Don't let them have any more control over you than they have to. I know you think we're a little out there, but this is one thing we're absolutely serious about."

"Hi, Sydney."

I glanced over and saw my friend Julia Cavendish carrying a huge stack of books. A couple seconds later, Marcus looked up at her too. Her eyes went wide, and she stumbled and dropped everything she was carrying. She flushed.

"Oh, God. I'm such an idiot."

I started to help her, but Marcus was by her side in a flash, his movie star grin firmly in place. "Happens to the best of us. I'm Dave."

"J-Julia," she said. In all the time I'd known her, I'd never seen her flustered around a guy. She usually ate them for breakfast.

"There we are." He handed her the books, all neatly stacked.

"Thank you. Thank you so much. You didn't have to do that. I mean, it was my own fault. I'm not usually that clumsy. And I'm sure you're busy. You must have lots to do. Obviously." I'd also never heard Julia ramble.

Marcus patted her on the back, and I thought she might pass out. "Always happy to help a beautiful damsel in distress." He nodded in my direction. "I've got to go. Sydney, I'll be in touch."

I nodded back. As soon as he walked away, Julia dropped the books again and hurried over to me. "Sydney, you have to tell me who that is."

"He already did. Dave."

"Yes, but *who is he*?" She gripped my arm and seemed on the verge of shaking answers out of me.

"Just a guy I know." I thought about it more. "A friend, I guess."

Her breath caught. "You guys aren't—I mean—"

"What? No! Why would you think that?"

"Well, he's gorgeous," she said, as though that were enough

to make us soul mates. "Don't you want to just rip his clothes off?"

"Whoa, no way."

"Really?" She scrutinized me, like I might be joking. "Not even a little?"

"Nope."

She stepped back and started picking up her books. "Jeez, Syd. I don't know what to think of you sometimes. I mean, I'm glad he's available—he is available, right?—but I'd be all over that if I were you."

Jill's words came back to me, about how he was human and had "that rebel Alchemist" thing going for him. Maybe I should start considering him or another ex-Alchemist as a romantic option. Having someone who wasn't a forbidden vampire in my life would make things a lot easier. I tried to dredge up the same reaction other girls had around Marcus, but nothing happened. No matter how hard I tried, I just didn't have that same attraction. His hair was too blond, I decided. And his eyes needed a little more green.

"Sorry," I told Julia. "Just not feeling it."

"If you say so. I still think you're crazy. That's the kind of guy you'd follow to hell and back."

All romantic musings disappeared, and I felt a sinking feeling in my stomach as we slowly headed back toward the dorm. Hell was a good analogy for what I would be walking into. "You actually might be closer to the truth on that than you realize."

She brightened. "See? I knew you couldn't resist."

CHAPTER 15

MS. TERWILLIGER WAS WAITING in the lobby when Julia and I returned to the dorm. "Seriously. Do you have a tracking device on me?" I asked. Julia took one look at our teacher's serious expression and quickly made an exit.

"Just excellent timing," Ms. Terwilliger replied. "I understand you have news."

"Surprisingly, yes."

Ms. Terwilliger's face was hard as she led me back outside to more privacy and yet another top secret outdoor meeting. These days, she hardly resembled the scattered, hippie teacher I'd met when I first started at Amberwood. "Tell me the news," she ordered.

I told her about Alicia's call, and her dismayed expression didn't really inspire me. I'd kind of hoped she'd reveal some amazing, foolproof plan she'd secretly been concocting.

"Well, then," she said once I'd finished. "I suppose I'll have to go out there."

"*I'll* go out there," I corrected.

She favored me with a small smile. "You've done more than enough. It's time I step up and deal with Veronica."

"But you sent me to that place before."

"When we weren't even sure where it was or what she was doing there. This time, we have an eyewitness confirming she's there right now. I can't waste this opportunity." She glanced at a clock near the door and sighed. "I'd go tonight if I could but haven't made the necessary preparations. I'll start working on them now and go in tomorrow evening. Hopefully I won't miss her again."

"No." The defiance in my voice surprised even me. I didn't contradict teachers—or any kind of authority—very often. Okay, never. "She eluded us before. Let us scout it out. You don't want to tip your hand yet, just in case something goes wrong. You'll be ready tomorrow night? Then let us go in the day . . . I mean, provided someone could get me out of school. . . ."

A little of that tension faded, and she laughed. "I suppose I could do that. I hate that I keep putting you in danger, though."

"We passed that point a long time ago."

She couldn't argue against that logic. I made arrangements for Adrian to pick me up the next day—after first scolding "Jet" for giving out "Taylor's" number. When morning came, Ms. Terwilliger was true to her word. I'd been excused from classes for a "research trip." The thing about being a star pupil was that none of my teachers had any problems with me skipping classes. They knew I'd get the work done. I probably could've taken the rest of the semester off.

During the drive, I told Adrian that I'd managed to score a trip to St. Louis in order to pursue Marcus's daunting task.

Adrian's expression grew darker and darker, but he stayed silent on the matter. I knew what a conflict it was for him. He didn't like Marcus. He didn't like me taking on this potentially dangerous mission. However, he also trusted me to make my own decisions. Contradicting me or telling me what to do wasn't in his nature—even though he secretly may have wanted to. His only comment was one of support.

"Be careful, Sage. For God's sake, be careful. I've seen you pull off some crazy shit, but this is extreme, even for you. You're probably the only one who can manage this, but still . . . don't let your guard down, even for a moment."

When I told him about how I was hoping to use Ian to get more in-depth access, Adrian's troubled look turned to one of incredulity.

"Hold on here. Let me make sure I'm following this. You're going to seduce some guy to help you with your espionage."

Seduce Ian? Ugh. "Don't jump to conclusions," I warned. "I'm just going to try to use his feelings for me to get what I want."

"Wow. Cold, Sage. Very cold."

"Hey, now." I felt a little indignant at the accusation. "I'm not going to promise to marry him or something and then dump him later. He wrote me about going to dinner when I'm there. We'll have a nice time, and I'll try to talk him into letting me tour the facility. That's it."

"And 'talking him into it' doesn't involve putting out?"

I glared at him and hoped he could see me in his periphery. "Adrian. Do I really seem like the kind of person who'd do that?"

"Well—" He stopped, and I suspected he'd held back from

some snarky comment. "No, I suppose not. Certainly not with a guy like him. Did you get a dress?"

Here we were again, Adrian randomly jumping topics. "For dinner and the service? I've got plenty."

"I guess that answers my question." He seemed to wage a great mental battle. At last, he said, "I'm going to give you some advice."

"Oh no."

He looked over at me again. "Who knows more about male weakness: you or me?"

"Go on." I refused to directly answer the question.

"Get a new dress. One that shows a lot of skin. Short. Strapless. Maybe a push-up bra too." He actually had the audacity to do a quick assessment of my chest. "Eh, maybe not. But definitely some high heels."

"Adrian," I exclaimed. "You've seen how Alchemists dress. Do you think I can really wear something like that into a church service?"

He was unconcerned. "You'll make it work. You'll change clothes or something. But I'm telling you, if you want to get a guy to do something that might be difficult, then the best way is to distract him so that he can't devote his full brainpower to the consequences."

"You don't have a lot of faith in your own gender."

"Hey, I'm telling you the truth. I've been distracted by sexy dresses a lot."

I didn't really know if that was a valid argument, seeing as Adrian was distracted by a lot of things. Fondue. T-shirts. Kittens. "And so, what then? I show some skin, and the world is mine?"

"That'll help." Amazingly, I could tell he was dead serious.

"And you've gotta act confident the whole time, like it's already a done deal. Then make sure when you're actually asking for what you want that you tell him you'd be 'so, so grateful.' But don't elaborate. His imagination will do half the work for you. "

I shook my head, glad we'd almost reached our destination. I didn't know how much more I could listen to. "This is the most ridiculous advice I've ever heard. It's also kind of sexist too, but I can't decide who it offends more, men or women."

"Look, Sage. I don't know much about chemistry or computer hacking or photosynthery, but this is something I've got a lot of experience with." I think he meant *photosynthesis*, but I didn't correct him. "Use my knowledge. Don't let it go to waste."

He seemed so earnest that I finally told him I'd consider it, though I had a hard time imagining myself wearing anything like he'd described. My answer satisfied him, and he said no more.

When we reached the bed-and-breakfast, I put on the brown wig so that we could be Taylor and Jet again. I braced myself as we approached the door

"Who knows what we're walking into?" I murmured. I'd been very brave while speaking to Ms. Terwilliger, but the reality that I might be going right up to an evil sorceress was sinking in. I had yet to develop the ability to sense magic in others, so I could very well be taken by surprise if she had a way to hide her appearance too. All I could do was have faith that Adrian's spirit and Ms. Terwilliger's charm would mask me. If Veronica was there, we'd just seem like an ordinary couple. I hoped.

Alicia was reading another magazine when we walked in. She still sported the same hipster glasses and clutter of gaudy necklaces. Her face lit up when she saw us. "You're back."

Adrian's arm immediately went around me. "Well, when we heard Veronica was in town again, we wanted to come see her right away. Right, honeydew?"

"Right," I said. At least he was going with healthier nicknames today.

"Oh." Alicia's sunny smile dimmed a little. "She just left."

"You have got to be kidding," I said. How could our luck be this bad? "So, she checked out?"

"No, she's still renting out the Velvet Suite. I think she was just running errands. But. . . ." She turned sheepish. "I may have, uh, ruined the surprise."

"Oh?" I asked very carefully. I felt Adrian's hold on me tense, but there was nothing romantic about it.

"I couldn't resist. I told her she might have some unexpected visitors soon. Good visitors," she added. "I wanted to make sure she didn't stay out too long."

"That's very nice of you," said Adrian. His smile looked as strained as mine felt. In trying to "help" us, Alicia might very well have ruined everything.

What did we do now? I was saved from an immediate decision when a middle-aged woman walked through the door.

"Hello," she told Alicia. "I wanted to get some information about hosting a wedding here. For my niece."

"Of course," said Alicia, glancing back and forth between all of us. She looked a little flustered over who to help, and I was quick to jump in.

"Hey," I said. "Since we're here, can we look at the Bunny Suite again? We can't stop talking about it."

Alicia frowned. "I thought you were going to the coast for your anniversary?"

"We were," said Adrian, following my lead. "But then Taylor was thinking about Cottontail the other night, and we thought we should reconsider." I had to give him credit for jumping in and going along with the story I was making up on the spot. Of course, you'd think he'd remember the name of the fake rabbit *he* had created.

"Hopper," I corrected.

"Is the Bunny Suite still vacant?" he asked. "We can just take a quick peek in while you help her."

Alicia hesitated only a moment before handing over a key. "Sure. Let me know if you have any questions."

I took the key and headed toward the stairs with Adrian. Behind us, I could hear the woman asking if it'd be okay to set up a tent in the backyard and how many hot plates the inn could hold before it became a fire hazard. Once we were on the second floor and out of earshot, Adrian spoke. "Let me guess. You want to go prowl through the Velvet Suite."

I rewarded him with a grin, pleased that he'd guessed my plan. "Yup. Pretty good idea, huh? Hopefully Alicia will be distracted for a while."

"I could have just compelled her," he reminded me.

"You're using too much spirit already."

I found the Velvet Suite and put the key in the lock, hoping Alicia had given us the master key and not one specifically for the Bunny Suite. When she had shown us around last time, she'd only used one key. A click told me we'd lucked out and wouldn't have to use any metal-burning chemicals today.

We'd seen the Velvet Suite during our last visit, and for the most part, it looked the same. Velvet bedding, velvet-covered furniture, and even velvet-textured wallpaper. Only, this time, the room wasn't in the pristine and unoccupied state as before. Signs around the room showed recent use. The bed was unmade, and the scent of shampoo from the bathroom indicated a shower not too long ago.

"Alicia might have been wrong about Veronica checking out," said Adrian. He opened drawer after drawer and found nothing. In the closet, he discovered high-heeled shoes tucked into a corner and a belt on a hanger—things that might be easily missed with frantic packing. "Someone left here in a hurry."

My hopes plummeted. In accidentally revealing our "surprise," Alicia had apparently scared Veronica into skipping out on the room. We found no sign that Veronica would actually return, and as Adrian had said, she seemed to have taken off quickly, based on the kinds of easy-to-forget things that were left behind: a razor in the shower, a bottle of perfume on the bathroom counter, and a stack of takeout menus on the nightstand.

I sat on the bed and sifted through the menus, not really convinced they'd tell me much. Chinese, Indian, Mexican. Veronica had diverse tastes, at least. I reached the bottom of the stack and threw them on the ground.

"She left," I said. I couldn't hide from the truth any longer. "That idiot Alicia tipped her off, and now we've lost her again."

Adrian sat down beside me, his face mirroring my dismay. "We'll find her. We've slowed her down by hiding the others. Maybe it'll buy us time until the next full moon so you can scry again."

"I hope so," I said, though I wasn't optimistic.

He brushed aside the wig's hair and turned my face toward him. "Everything's going to be okay. She doesn't know about you."

I knew he was right, but it was hollow comfort. I leaned my head against his shoulder, wishing I could fix everything. That was my job, right? "All that means is that someone else could suffer in my place. I don't want that. I need to stop her once and for all."

"So brave." He gave me a small smile. His fingertips slid down from my face, lightly stroking the line of my neck, down toward my shoulder. Everywhere he touched, a trail of goose bumps appeared. How did he keep doing this to me? Marcus— who made every girl in the world swoon—had zero effect on me. But one whisper of a touch from Adrian completely undid me. "You could give Castile a run for his money," he added.

"Stop that," I warned.

"Comparing you to Castile?"

"That's not what I'm talking about, and you know it." His hands were too dangerous, as was being with him on a bed. Terrified I might be kissed again, I jerked away, and the sudden movement caught him by surprise. His fingers got tangled in my hair, as well as in my two necklaces, which resulted in him snapping both chains and nearly pulling off the brown wig. I quickly caught the garnet before it could fall off, but the cross slipped away. Thank God I'd kept the important one on. "No more kissing," I warned. I refastened the charm and straightened the wig.

"You mean no more kissing unless it's a romantic place," he reminded me. "Are you saying this place doesn't scream romance?" He nodded around to our tacky velvet surroundings. He then picked up the small cross and held it in the air, growing thoughtful as he studied the way the light played off the gold surface. "You gave this to me once."

"And you gave it back."

"I was angry."

"And now?"

He shrugged. "Now I'm just determined."

"Adrian." I sighed. "Why do you keep doing this? The touch-ing . . . the kissing . . . you know I don't want it."

"You don't act that way."

"Stop saying that. It's obnoxious. Next you'll be saying I'm 'asking for it.'" Why did he have to be so infuriating? Okay . . . I hadn't really sent a clear message back at the sorority. Or Pies and Stuff. But this time I'd done better. "I just pulled away. How much more direct do I have to be?"

"It's not your actions, exactly," he said. He still clutched the cross in his hand. "It's your aura."

I groaned. "No, no, not that. I don't want to hear about auras."

"But I'm serious." He shifted over and stretched out on the bed, lying on his side. He patted the bed near him. "Lie down."

"Adrian—"

"I won't kiss you," he said. "I promise."

"How stupid do you think I am?" I said. "I'm not falling for this."

He gave me a long, level look. "Do you really think I'd assault you or something?"

"No," I said quickly. "Of course not."

"Then humor me."

Warily, I lay down on my side as well, facing him with only a few powerful inches between us. An enraptured, slightly dis-tracted look appeared in his eyes. He'd given himself over to spirit. "Do you know what I see in you now? The usual aura. A steady golden yellow, healthy and strong, with spikes of purple here and there. But when I do this. . . ."

He rested a hand on my hip, and my whole body tensed up. That hand moved around my hip, slipping under my shirt to rest on the small of my back. My skin burned where he touched me, and the places that were untouched longed for that heat.

"See?" he said. He was in the throes of spirit now, though with me at the same time. "Well, I guess you can't. But when I touch you, your aura . . . it *smolders*. The colors deepen, it burns more intensely, the purple increases. Why? Why, Sydney?" He used that hand on me to pull me closer. "Why do you react that way if I don't mean anything to you?" There was a desperation in his voice, and it was legitimate.

It was hard for me to talk. "It's instinct. Or something. You're a Moroi. I'm an Alchemist. Of course I'd have a response. You think I'd be indifferent?"

"Most Alchemist responses would involve disgust, revulsion, and holy water."

That was an excellent point. "Well . . . I'm a little more relaxed around Moroi than most Alchemists. Probably this is just some purely physical response driven by hormones and years of evolution. My body doesn't know any better. I'm as susceptible to lust as anyone else." There was probably a book about that or at least an article in *Cosmopolitan*.

The hint of a smile played over his lips. He was fully in tune with me again. "No, you aren't. I mean, you are, but not without reason. I know you well enough to realize that now. You're not the kind of person who's 'susceptible to lust' without some emotion to back it." He moved his hand back to my hip, sliding it down my leg. I shuddered, and his face moved closer to mine. There was so much in his eyes, so much desire and longing. "See? There it is again. My flame in the dark."

"Don't kiss me," I whispered. It was the only defense I could muster. If he kissed me, I'd be lost. I closed my eyes. "You said you wouldn't."

"I won't." His lips were only a breath away. "Unless you want me to."

I opened my eyes, ready to tell him no, that it didn't matter what my aura allegedly said . . . this couldn't keep happening. There was no emotion backing this desire, and I tried to cling to my earlier argument. I was so comfortable around Moroi now that clearly some primal part of me kept forgetting what he was. This was a base instinct. I was simply having a physical reaction to him, to his hands, to his lips, to his body. . . .

He caught hold of my arm and rolled me over. I closed my eyes again and wrapped my arms around his neck. I felt his lips touch mine, not quite a kiss, just the barest brush of—

The door opened, and I flinched. Alicia stepped inside, gasped, and put a hand up over her mouth to cover a shocked squeal. "O-oh," she stammered. "I'm so sorry . . . I . . . I didn't realize . . ."

Adrian and I jerked away and sat up. My heart was ready to beat out of my chest, and I knew I was blushing. I quickly patted my wig and was relieved to feel it was still in place. He recovered his voice more quickly.

"Sorry . . . we kind of got carried away. We started checking out the other rooms and decided to, uh, try them out." Despite his sheepish words, there was a smug look on his face, the kind you'd expect from a guy who'd just made a conquest. Was it part of the act, or did he really think he'd gotten away with something?

Alicia looked as uncomfortable as I felt. "I see. Well, this room's occupied. It's—" She frowned and did a double take. "It's Veronica's. It looks like she left."

I finally managed to speak. "That's why we thought it was empty," I said hastily. "There was nothing in here."

Alicia thankfully seemed to have forgotten about our compromising position. "That's weird. She didn't formally check out. I mean, she paid in advance in cash, but still. It's so strange."

We made a hurried escape of our own after that, once again feeding Alicia lines about how we'd be in touch. Neither of us spoke much when we got in the car. I was lost in my own thoughts, which were equal parts frustration over Veronica and confusion over Adrian. I refused to acknowledge the latter, though, and opted for my usual tactic. The sooner that moment was forgotten, the better. I was pretty sure I could keep telling myself that. Some part of me — nearly as snarky as Adrian — suggested I pick up a book on denial the next time I was in the self-help section.

"Another dead end," I said once we were on the road. I texted Ms. Terwilliger: *V's gone. No need for action.* Her response came a few minutes later: *We'll keep trying.* I could practically feel her disappointment through the display on my phone. She wasn't the only one. Adrian seemed particularly melancholy on the drive back. He responded whenever I spoke, but it was clear he was distracted.

When he dropped me off at Amberwood later that night, I found everything mercifully quiet. No crises, no dangerous missions. It felt like it had been ages since I had a moment to myself, and I curled up on my bed, taking solace in the ordinary tasks of homework and reading. I fell asleep with my face on my calculus book.

I experienced one of those nonsensical dreams that everyone has. In it, my family's cat could talk, and he was driving Adrian's Mustang. He asked me if I wanted to take a road trip to Birmingham. I told him I had a lot of homework to do but that if he wanted to go to Fargo, I'd consider it.

We were in the middle of negotiating who'd pay for gas when the dream suddenly dissolved to blackness. A cold feeling swept over me, followed by a feeling of dread that rivaled the time Adrian and I had faced down Strigoi in his apartment. A woman's laughter rolled around me, foul and sickening, like some sort of toxic smoke. A voice came out of the darkness, echoing in my mind.

She's kept you well hidden, but it can't stay that way forever. You can't conceal power like yours forever. I've caught your trail. I'll find you.

Hands suddenly reached out of the darkness for me, wrapping around my throat and cutting off my air. I screamed and woke up in my own bed, surrounded in books. I'd left the light on, and it chased some of the dream's terror away. But only some. Sweat poured off me, making my shirt stick to me. I touched my neck, but there was nothing wrong with it. The garnet hung in place but not my cross.

No need to fear a dream, I thought. It didn't mean anything, and really, with everything going on lately, it was a wonder I didn't have nightmares more often. But thinking back on it, I wasn't so sure. There had been something so terrible and real about it, a horror that seemed to reach into my very soul.

I didn't want to sleep after that, so I made a cup of coffee and tried to read again. It worked for a while, but somewhere around four, my body couldn't take it anymore. I fell asleep on my books again, but this time, my sleep stayed dream free.

CHAPTER 16

I GAVE MS. TERWILLIGER a full report on our trip to the inn the next morning. We met at Spencer's, and in a rare show of early rising, Adrian joined us. "I've got a study group meeting soon," he explained. His mood was a lot better, with no mention of yesterday's . . . indiscretion.

Even though there wasn't much to tell, lines of worry creased her face as she heard our story. The true panic came when I mentioned my dream. Ms. Terwilliger's eyes went wide, and she gripped her coffee cup so tightly, I thought it would break.

"She found out," she murmured. "Whether it was that Alicia girl or some other way, Veronica found out about you. I should never have sent you. I thought you'd slip underneath her radar if the other girls were charmed, but I was wrong. I was selfish and naive. It would've been better if she knew I was on to her from the very beginning. You're sure you were masking Sydney's appearance?" That was to Adrian.

"Positive," he said. "Everyone we talked to, all the girls and even Alicia . . . none of them would have a clear idea of what Sydney looks like."

"Maybe she's been spying on you," I suggested. "And saw us together. I haven't been in disguise around here."

"Maybe," Ms. Terwilliger conceded. "But we also know she was active in Los Angeles. She would have to spend considerable time stalking her victims, which wouldn't give her the chance to come here and watch me extensively. Even with her powers, she can't teleport." Her expression hardened with resolve. "Well, there's nothing to be done now but damage control. She doesn't seem to know exactly where you are yet or that you're even connected to me. I'll make you another charm to try to boost this one, but it may not work if she's found a way to reach out to you. And in the meantime, don't worry about offense anymore. You need to focus on defense—particularly invisibility spells. Your best protection against Veronica at this point is for her simply not to find you if she comes looking around Palm Springs."

I'd continued reading the advanced offense spells, despite her warnings. With this new development, though, I knew she was right about defense being more important. Still, I couldn't shake the worry that Veronica had discovered me by watching Ms. Terwilliger, which in turn made me fear for my teacher's safety. "You keep saying she's not after you . . . but are you really sure?"

"She'll avoid me if she can," said Ms. Terwilliger, sounding confident. "I have the power but not the youth and beauty she's after. And even she would draw the line at taking on her sister.

It's the only remnant of human decency she has left."

"Will she still have that attitude when you confront her?" asked Adrian.

Ms. Terwilliger shook her head. "No. Then anything goes. I'd like to meet with you tonight to practice a couple other defensive tactics."

I eyed her carefully. "Are you up for that? No offense, ma'am, but you already look exhausted."

"I'll be fine. Meet me at the park again around ten. I'll get Weathers to let you go. We must keep you safe." She stared off into space for several moments and then focused on me again. "In light of this development . . . it wouldn't be a bad idea for you to find some, ah, more basic means of defense as well."

"Basic?" I asked, puzzled.

"She means like a gun or a knife," supplied Adrian, catching on to what I hadn't.

Ms. Terwilliger nodded. "If you ever confront Veronica, it'll most likely come down to magic fighting magic . . . but, well, one can never say. Having something else for backup might prove invaluable."

I wasn't a fan of this idea. "I have no clue how to knife fight. And I don't like guns."

"Do you like being put into a coma and aging before your time?" asked Adrian.

I shot him a glare, surprised he'd be on board with this. "Of course not. But where would we even get one on such short notice?"

From the look on his face, he knew I had a point. Suddenly, he became enthusiastic again. "I think I know."

"I'm sure you two will figure it out," said Ms. Terwilliger, her mind already moving to something else. She glanced at her watch. "Almost time for classes."

We all stood up, preparing to go our own ways, but I held Adrian back. I couldn't imagine how in the world he would know where to get a gun on no notice. He wouldn't elaborate and simply said he'd meet me after school. Before he left, I remembered something I'd wanted to ask.

"Adrian, did you keep my cross?"

"Your—oh." Looking into his eyes, I could practically see yesterday's events playing through his mind—including us rolling around on the bed. "I dropped it when—ah, well, before we left. You didn't pick it up?"

I shook my head, and his face fell.

"Shit, I'm sorry, Sage."

"It's okay," I said automatically.

"It's *not* okay, and it's my fault. I know how much it means to you."

It did mean a lot to me, but I almost blamed myself as much as him. I should've thought of it before we left, but I'd been a little preoccupied. "It's just a necklace," I told him.

This didn't comfort him. He looked so dejected when we parted ways that I hoped he wouldn't forget about us meeting up later to visit his mysterious gun source. There was nothing to worry about, though. When classes ended, he was outside my dorm in the Mustang and looked much more upbeat, with no more mention of the necklace.

When he told me his gun plan, I was shocked, but after a few moments of thought, I realized he might be on to something. And so, a little less than an hour later, we found ourselves far outside the city, driving up to a forlorn-looking home on a large, barren piece of land. We had reached the Wolfe School of Defense.

"I never thought we'd be here again," I remarked.

Wolfe's house had no windows, and there were no cars in sight as we walked up to the door. "He may not even be home," I murmured to Adrian. "We probably should have called first."

"Wolfe never struck me as a guy who leaves the house very much," said Adrian. He knocked on the door, and almost instantly, we heard a flurry of barking and scampering feet. I grimaced. Wolfe, for reasons I would never be able to understand, kept a herd of Chihuahuas in his house. He'd once told us that they could kill a man upon a single command.

We waited a few minutes, but the barking was the only sign that there was any sort of life inside. Adrian knocked one more time (driving the dogs into an even greater frenzy) and then shrugged. "I guess you were—"

The door suddenly opened—just a slit—and one gray eye peered out at us from underneath a chain. "Oh," came a grizzled voice. "It's you two."

The door closed, and I heard the chain being unlocked. A moment later, Wolfe slipped outside, careful not to let any of the dogs out. He had a patch over his left eye, which was probably just as well since his other eye alone seemed to peer straight through me. "You should've called," he said. "I nearly turned the dogs on you."

Wolfe was dressed in his favorite pair of Bermuda shorts as well as a T-shirt showing a bald eagle riding on a monster truck. The eagle held an American flag in one set of talons and a samurai sword in the other. That seemed a weird weapon choice for such a patriotic shirt, but we'd long since learned not to question his wardrobe. That had come after he'd kicked a woman out of our class who'd dared to ask if he only had one pair of shorts or several identical ones.

"What do you kids need?" he asked. "Next classes don't start until after New Year's."

Adrian and I exchanged glances. "We, um, need a gun," I said. "I mean, just to borrow."

Wolfe scratched his beard. "I don't lend them out to students who haven't taken my gun class. Safety first." I found it promising, however, that he lent out guns at all. It was a sign of his character that he didn't even bother asking why we wanted one.

"I've already had training," I said. That was true. It was mandatory for all Alchemists. I'd done well in it, but as I'd mentioned to Adrian, I really didn't like guns at all. At least a knife had other uses. But a gun? It was only there to injure or kill.

Wolfe arched an eyebrow, the one over his good eye. Clearly, he didn't believe me. "Can you back that up?"

"Do you have a shooting range?" I returned coolly.

He almost looked offended. "Of course I do."

He led us to a building beyond the garage we'd trained in. I'd never been inside this building before, but like his house, it had no windows. The door was covered in enough locks to meet with Alchemist security standards. He let us inside, and I gaped when I saw not only a practice range but also a wall covered in various types of guns. Wolfe gave the small holding space a once-over.

"Earmuffs must be in the house. Be right back."

I continued staring at the wall, knowing my eyes were wide.

"There's no way those are all legal."

Adrian's response was unexpected. "Did you notice his eye patch?"

I dragged my gaze from the arsenal. "Um, yes. From the day we first met him."

"No, no. I mean, I swear it was on his other eye last time."

"It was not," I said immediately.

"Are you sure?" asked Adrian.

I wasn't, I realized. Words and numbers were easy for me to memorize. But other details, like clothing or hair—or eye patches—were sometimes easy for me to miss. "That doesn't make any sense," I finally said. "Why would he do that?"

"He's Malachi Wolfe," said Adrian. "Why wouldn't he do that?"

I couldn't argue against that.

Wolfe returned with ear protection. After examining his wall, he selected a small handgun and then unlocked a cabinet containing ammunition. At least he didn't leave a bunch of loaded guns around.

"I'll do that," I told him. I took the gun from him and effortlessly loaded it. He made a small grunt of approval. He gestured toward the far end of the range, to a large paper cutout showing a human silhouette with various targets marked on it.

"Now then," he said. "Don't worry about hitting the—"

I fired, perfectly emptying the clip into the most difficult targets. I handed the gun to him. He handed it back. Behind him, I could see Adrian staring at me with enormous eyes.

"Keep it," said Wolfe. "You passed. You've gotta buy your own ammunition, but as long as you fill out the rental agreement, you're good to go."

As it turned out, the "rental agreement" was a piece of paper where he wrote the gun type on one side and I put my initials on the other. "Really?" I asked. "That's all I need to do? I mean, I'm glad, but . . ." I didn't really know what else to say.

Wolfe waved off my protests. "You're a good kid. If you say you need a gun, I believe you. Someone giving you trouble?"

I slipped the gun into my messenger bag. "Something like that."

Wolfe glanced over at Adrian. "What about you? You need a gun too?"

"I'm good," said Adrian. "Besides, I haven't had the training. Safety first."

Wolfe opened up the ammunition cabinet again and produced a long wooden tube and a sandwich bag of what looked like small darts. "You want to borrow my blowgun? Not much of a learning curve on this. I mean, you'll never be able to match the skill and cunning of the Amazonian warriors that I stole this from, but it can get you out of a pinch."

"Thanks, but I'll take my chances," Adrian said after several long moments. He almost sounded as though he'd considered it.

I was still hung up on Wolfe's other words, not sure I believed what I'd heard. "You were in the Amazon?"

This time, Wolfe arched the eyebrow above his eye patch. "You don't believe me?"

"No, no, of course I do," I said quickly. "It's just, you've never mentioned it before."

Wolfe gazed off beyond us. "I've been trying for years to forget my time there. But some things, you just can't escape."

A very long and very uncomfortable silence followed. At

last, I cleared my throat. "Well, thank you, sir. We should get going. Hopefully I won't need the gun for very long."

"Keep it as long as you need," he said. "If I want it back, I'll find you."

And on that disturbing note, Adrian and I left. Although I understood Ms. Terwilliger's reasons for "old-fashioned" defense, I was in no way comfortable having a gun around. I'd have to keep it in my car in case school authorities ever did a search of my room and discovered it. My Alchemist and magical kits were already a liability. I was pretty sure there'd be no talking my way out of a gun.

Adrian returned me to Amberwood. I started to open the door and then paused to glance over at him. "Thanks," I said. "For everything. Going to the inn. Suggesting we see Wolfe."

"Hey, that was worth it just to know Wolfe owns a blowgun."

I laughed. "Actually, I'd be more surprised if he didn't. See you later."

Adrian nodded. "Sooner than you think."

"What's that mean?" I asked, suspicion rearing up in me.

He dodged the question and reached underneath his seat. "I called Alicia," he told me, producing a small box. "She couldn't find your cross. Her housekeeping service had already gone through and cleaned the room, but she says she'll check to see if it got caught up in the bedding. Oh, and I also asked about Veronica. She hasn't been back."

That was disheartening news, but I was touched he'd called. "Thanks for trying."

He opened the box and pulled out a necklace with a tiny wooden cross on it. "I got you a replacement. I mean, I know there's no real substitute, but I wanted to get you something.

And don't start about not being able to accept some fancy gift," he said, guessing the protest I was about to make. "It cost me five dollars from a street vendor, and I'm pretty sure the chain is brass."

I bit off my words and took the necklace from him. The cross barely weighed anything. Studying it more closely, I could see a tiny pattern of silver flowers painted on its surface. "The vendor didn't do that. That's your handiwork."

"Well . . . I know you're into simple stuff, but I've always got to have some embellishment."

I ran my finger over the cross's surface. "Why'd you choose morning glories?"

"Because I'm not the biggest fan of lilies."

I smiled at that.

When I returned to my dorm room, I laid the necklace out on my dresser. I gave it one last fond look and then tried to decide how best to spend the rest of my day. Our trip to Wolfe actually hadn't taken that long, so I had plenty of time to catch dinner and make sure I was up to date on my homework. I actually ate with Kristin and Julia for a change, which was kind of a nice break from the drama of my other friends. Of course, most of the meal consisted of Julia gushing about "Dave." By the end, both she and Kristin were demanding to know when I'd bring him by again.

As the evening pushed on, I began to prepare for my meeting with Ms. Terwilliger. I wasn't sure what kind of magic we'd be practicing outdoors but figured I should be ready for anything. I packed a wide variety of items from my kit and even had the foresight to bring a granola bar for post-magic fuel. Once everything was in order, I headed back downstairs. I was nearly out the dorm door when Mrs. Weathers called out to me.

"Sydney?"

I paused to glance back. "Yes, ma'am?"

"Where are you going? It's nearly curfew."

Frowning, I walked over to her desk. "I'm doing an assignment for Ms. Terwilliger."

Mrs. Weathers looked troubled. "Yes, I know you do that a lot for her . . . but I haven't received authorization from her to let you out after hours today." Her expression turned apologetic. "I'm sure this is all on the up-and-up, but, well, rules are rules."

"Of course," I said. "But she said she'd let you know. Are you sure you didn't get anything? A note? A phone call?"

She shook her head. "Nothing. I'm sorry."

"I understand," I murmured, though I wasn't sure I did. Despite her perpetually scattered nature, Ms. Terwilliger was usually good about this sort of thing. Mrs. Weathers assured me she'd let me go if Ms. Terwilliger gave the okay by phone, so I returned to my room and attempted to call her. I went straight to voice mail, and my text went unanswered. Had something happened to her? Had that magical confrontation I'd been dreading finally gone down?

I kicked around my dorm room for the next hour or so, letting all my worries eat at me. Veronica. Marcus. St. Louis. Ms. Terwilliger. The dream. Over and over, I kept imagining the worst outcome for all of them. Just when I thought I'd go crazy, Ms. Terwilliger finally returned my call.

"Why didn't you show up?" she asked as soon as I answered. I felt relieved. She'd gone to the park. That explained the lack of contact since there was no signal out there.

"I tried! Mrs. Weathers wouldn't let me out. You forgot to give me permission."

"I most certainly didn't. . . ." Her words trailed off uncertainly. "That is, I thought I did. . . ."

"It's okay," I said. "You've had a lot on your mind."

"It's not okay." She sounded angry, but it was at herself, not me. "I need to be on top of this."

"Well, you can call Mrs. Weathers now," I said.

"Too late. I'm already back home. We'll have to attempt this again another time."

"I'm sorry," I said. "I tried."

Ms. Terwilliger sighed. "I know you did. It's not your fault. It's mine. I'm letting all of this wear me down, and now I'm getting sloppy. I've already taken too many risks at your expense, and it's put Veronica on your trail. I can't let her get any farther."

A chill ran through me as I thought of those comatose girls—and the possibility of me joining them. I'd been able to stay cool and collected while investigating, but last night's dream had driven home the dangers I faced. That image of the girl in the newspaper hovered in my mind as I held the phone and paced my room. I stopped in front of a mirror and tried to picture myself like that, aged before my time. I squeezed my eyes shut and turned away. I couldn't let that happen to me. I just couldn't, and I needed Ms. Terwilliger if I was going to stay safe. Maybe I was a prodigy, but I was nowhere near being able to take on someone like her sister.

"Get some rest, ma'am," I said at last. "You sound like you need it."

"I'll try. And you be careful, Miss Melbourne."

"I will."

Being careful was the only thing I could do on my own for now. I just hoped it would be enough.

When we got off the phone, I didn't want to sleep again. I was afraid to, and it wasn't just because of the sheer terror I'd felt in last night's dream. Ms. Terwilliger had explained there was a type of searching spell that sought people in their sleep, and I worried that if Veronica reached out to me again, she might get a fix on my location. The problem was that after last night's sketchy sleep, I was now even more exhausted. My usual coffee and distraction tricks failed, and before I knew it, I was asleep.

I don't know how much time passed before I dreamed. One moment I was lost in the oblivion of sleep. The next, I found myself standing in the room that had hosted Sonya and Mikhail's reception. It looked exactly the same: flowers everywhere, tables covered in white linen and crystal glasses . . . The only difference was that the room was empty and silent. It was eerie, seeing all that richness and glamour with no one to enjoy it. I could've been in a ghost town. I looked down and saw that I wore the same dress from that evening as well.

"I could've made it red, you know. That's a better color for you—not that blue looks bad on you."

Adrian strode toward me, dressed in the same dark blue suit. Understanding hit me. I was in a spirit dream. It was another of that element's incredible feats, the ability for a spirit user to intrude on someone's dreams. No—not intrude. The user was actually able to create the dream itself, controlling every detail.

"It's been a long time since you pulled me into one of these," I said.

"And look at the progress you've made. Last time you were kicking and screaming." He held out a hand. "Want to dance?"

"No music," I said, not that I had any intention of dancing. He had a point about my reaction, though. I hadn't exactly been kicking and screaming, but I had kind of freaked out. I'd been in full possession of all my fears about vampires and magic, and being surrounded in a world completely constructed of that magic had left me frightened and unhinged. And now? Now I had apparently become so comfortable that my biggest concern was that he'd put me in this dress. I gestured to it.

"Can you change me out of this?"

"You can change yourself out of it," he said. "I'm letting go of the control. Just picture yourself the way you are in reality."

I did exactly that, and a moment later, I wore jeans and a pale blue knit top. This obviously disappointed him. "That's what you sleep in?"

"No." I laughed. "I was trying not to sleep at all. It didn't work. Why'd you bring me here?"

He strolled around and picked up one of the crystal goblets, nodding in approval as though he were some sort of glassmaking expert. "Exactly that reason. I saw how much that dream bothered you. I figured if I pulled you into one of these, it'd keep you from one of Veronica's."

I'd never thought of that. Vampire magic was certainly preferable to hers. Looking around, I gained a new appreciation for the room. It became a sanctuary, a place where she couldn't reach me. At least, I hoped not. We really didn't know how her magic would work against Adrian's. For all I knew, she might come walking through the door, carrying Sonya's bouquet.

"Thank you," I said. I sat down at one of the tables. "That was nice of you." It was another one of those incredible moments when Adrian had had the insight to guess my thoughts—or in this case, my fears.

"Well, it was also selfish. I wanted to see you in the dress." He reconsidered. "Actually, I wanted to see you in that red Halloween dress again, but I figured that would be pushing my luck."

I looked away as an image of that dress returned to me. Lia DiStefano had created the costume for me. She'd loosely based it on an ancient Greek dress and ended up with a gauzy confection of red and gold. That was when Adrian had said I was the most beautiful creature walking the earth. It had happened before he expressed his feelings for me, but even then, his words had undone me. I thought about what he was doing for me now and decided to give him a small compensation. I focused again on my clothes, and the blue dress returned.

"Better?" I asked.

His face lit up in a way that made me smile in return. "Yes."

Hoping I wasn't setting myself up for some suggestive answer, I asked, "So what are we going to do?"

"You sure you don't want to dance? I can make some music." My silence spoke for me. "Fine, fine. I don't know. We could play a game. Monopoly? Life? Battleship? Twister? Whatever we do, I am *not* playing Scrabble with you."

We warmed up with Battleship—I won—and then moved on to Monopoly. That took a little work to set up because Adrian could only create things that he could imagine. He couldn't remember all the streets and cards, so we made our best attempt to re-create them. Neither of us could remember one of the yellow streets, so he named it Jet Way.

We proved surprisingly well matched, and I became engrossed in the game. The power shifted back and forth between us. Just when one of us seemed to have all the control, the other would seize it back. I had no doubts about my ability to win—until I lost. I sat there, dumbstruck, staring at the board.

"Have you ever lost a game before?" he asked.

"I . . . yes, of course . . . I just didn't think . . ."

"That *I* could beat you?"

"No, I just . . . it doesn't happen very often." I looked up at him and shook my head. "Congratulations."

He leaned back in his chair and laughed. "I think beating you just improved your opinion of me more than anything else I've ever done."

"I've always had a high opinion of you." I stretched out, surprised to feel kinks in my body. It was strange how these dreams could have such a realistic physical component. "How long have we have been here?"

"I don't know. It's not morning yet." He appeared unconcerned. "What do you want to play next?"

"We shouldn't play anything," I said. I stood up. "It's been hours. I'm asleep, but you aren't. You can't stay up all night."

"I'm a vampire, Sage. A creature of the night, remember?"

"One who's on a human schedule," I chastised.

He still didn't seem worried. "Only one class tomorrow. I'll make it up."

"What about the spirit?" I began to pace restlessly as more of the implications hit me. "You have to be using a lot of it. That's not good for you."

"I'll take my chances." There was an unspoken *for you* at the end of his sentence.

I returned to the table and stood in front of his chair. "You have to be careful. Between this and the Veronica hunt. . . ." I suddenly felt bad. I hadn't thought twice about asking him to help with that. I'd forgotten the risks. "Once we've stopped her, you need to lay off the spirit."

"Don't worry." He grinned. "Once we've gotten rid of that bitch, I'll be celebrating so much that I won't be sober for days."

"Ugh. Not the healthiest way to do it. Have you ever thought about antidepressants?" I knew they helped some spirit users by blocking the magic.

His smile vanished. "I won't touch those things. Lissa took them and hated them. Being cut off from spirit nearly drove her crazy."

I crossed my arms and leaned against the table. "Yeah, but using it will drive you crazy too."

"No lectures tonight, Sage. It mars my stunning Monopoly victory."

He was far too casual for such a serious matter, but I knew him well enough to recognize when he wouldn't yield. "Fine. Then let's end on a high note. Send me back, and get some sleep."

"You sure you'll be okay?" His concern was so intense. I didn't think anyone had ever worried about me that much. Well, maybe Ms. Terwilliger.

"Probably she gave up for the night." I really didn't know, but I couldn't let him keep exerting himself. The thought of Veronica reaching out again terrified me . . . but the thought of Adrian endangering himself almost scared me more. He'd risked so much for me. Could I do any less? "You can check on me tomorrow night, though."

Adrian's face lit up as though I'd just accepted a date. "It's a deal, then."

And like that, the reception hall dissolved around me. I returned to peaceful sleep and just barely heard him say, "Sweet dreams, Sage."

CHAPTER 17

ALTHOUGH OUR MAGICAL PLANS had been derailed, Ms. Terwilliger had asked me to come by her room before classes started in the morning so that we could talk strategy and future assignments. I had just enough time to swing by the cafeteria for breakfast and found Jill, Eddie, and Angeline sitting together. It felt like it had been a long time since we'd all been together in some kind of normal setting, and I welcomed this small moment of bonding. It was a refuge in the storm that had been my life recently.

Jill was grinning about something that Eddie didn't seem to find so funny. "He didn't say anything about it to me," he said.

"Of course not." Jill laughed. "He's too embarrassed."

I sat down with my tray. "Who's too embarrassed?" I assumed any "he" they were talking about must be Adrian, though it was hard to imagine Adrian embarrassed about anything.

"Micah," said Jill. "I talked him into modeling for our sewing club again. And then he got Juan and Travis to do it too. "

"How'd you manage that?" I asked. Jill had originally gotten involved with Lia through the school's sewing club. Back when Jill and Micah had dated, she'd convinced him to model some very badly made clothes. He'd done it out of adoration, though I wasn't sure he'd really enjoyed it.

Jill leaned forward, an excited sparkle in her eyes. "Claire guilted him into it! It was hilarious. But I don't know how he talked Juan and Travis into it. Maybe they owed him a favor."

"Maybe they have ulterior motives," said Eddie. His tone surprised me until I remembered his lesson about the latest social developments around here. What was it? Claire was Micah's new girlfriend. Juan and Travis were his friends, who liked Jill. Eddie didn't like that they liked her. Got it. Apparently, Eddie hadn't kept his opinions to himself because Jill rolled her eyes.

"Will you stop worrying about that?" she asked. She was still smiling but sounded just a *little* annoyed. "They're good guys. And I'm not going to do anything stupid. You don't have to lecture me about humans and Moroi. I get it."

Her jade eyes flicked over to me, and her smile faltered a little. She studied me for several long, troubled moments, and I wondered what she was thinking about. Was she still hoping for some romantic resolution between Adrian and me? Was she wondering why Adrian and I kept getting into intimate situations? I kind of wanted to know that too. She finally dragged her gaze away, letting her happy mood return.

"I'm just looking out for you," Eddie said obstinately.

"You look out for assassins. I can handle these guys. I'm not a child, and besides, these are the most male models we've ever had. It's great. If we could score a couple more, our club could do a whole project on men's clothing."

Eddie still looked way too serious for this discussion. "Maybe Eddie would volunteer," I suggested. "I bet guardian posture would be great on the catwalk."

He blushed, which even I had to admit was adorable. If Jill had been irritated by his earlier overprotectiveness, it was no longer obvious. From her dreamy expression, you'd think Eddie blushing was the most amazing thing she'd ever witnessed. I think he was too overwhelmed at the thought of strutting down a runway to notice.

Angeline had been completely silent so far. I glanced over at her, expecting her to have something funny to say about her boyfriend being encouraged to model. But to my surprise, she wasn't paying attention to the conversation at all. She had a geometry book open and was furiously trying to draw some circles freehand. It killed me to watch, but after Kristin's comment about Angeline stabbing someone with a compass, freehand might be best.

"What do you think, Angeline?" I asked, just to see how engrossed she was. "Do you think Eddie would make a good model?"

"Hmm?" She didn't look up. "Oh, yeah. You should let Jill try some clothes on you."

Now Jill blushed. Eddie's deepened.

Just when I thought this meal couldn't get any more surreal, Trey stopped by. He nudged Angeline's chair with his toe. "Hey, McCormick." He nodded toward her graph paper. "Time to check out your curves."

Rather than answering with some biting response, she looked up instantly, a big smile on her face. "I've been working on them all morning," she said. "I think they're pretty good."

"They look good from where I'm standing," said Trey.

They were actually the worst circles I'd ever seen, but I guessed Trey wanted to encourage her. I was amazed at how seriously she was treating this math grade. It seemed to me that she was putting it above everything else, even her personal life. She gathered up all her things so that she and Trey could go to the library. Eddie looked disappointed but couldn't protest, lest it give away the truth about Angeline and him. Trey knew we weren't all actually related, but Eddie and Angeline's relationship was still kept secret.

I realized then that it was almost time to meet Ms. Terwilliger. I hurriedly finished a banana and told Eddie and Jill I'd see them later. Whether they would talk about male modeling or Jill's dating life, I couldn't guess.

I showed up right on the dot for my meeting but found Ms. Terwilliger's room locked and dark. Even in crisis mode, I supposed she was entitled to run a little late now and then, so I settled down on the hallway floor and read ahead for my English class.

I grew so absorbed that I didn't realize how much time had passed until I heard the warning bell ring and realized students were starting to fill the halls. I glanced up just as the same harried substitute teacher from before came scurrying up to the door with a set of keys. I scrambled to my feet.

"Ms. Terwilliger's out today?" I asked. "Is she okay?"

"They don't tell me the reasons," the sub said brusquely. "They just ask me to be here. I hope she left an assignment this time."

Knowing Ms. Terwilliger, I had a feeling it was going to be another "homework" day. I shuffled into the classroom after the sub, feeling a knot of anxiety in my stomach.

The next hour was agonizing. I barely heard as the sub told us to work on homework. Instead, I kept sneaking glances at my cell phone, hoping a text would come from Ms. Terwilliger. No such luck.

I went from class to class but was too distracted to give anything my full attention. I even shocked myself in English when I nearly mixed up *Henry IV* with *Henry VI* while answering an essay question. Thankfully, I caught myself before committing that embarrassing mistake to paper.

When I returned to Ms. Terwilliger's classroom for my independent study at the day's end, I was expecting the sub to tell me I could leave early again. Instead, I found Ms. Terwilliger herself, rifling through papers on her desk.

"You're back!" I exclaimed. "I thought something had happened to you."

"Not me," she said. Her face was pale and drawn. "But someone else wasn't so lucky."

"No. Not again." I sank into a chair, and all the fears I'd been carrying around today came crashing down on me. "I'd hoped we'd protected those girls."

Ms. Terwilliger sat down opposite me. "It wasn't one of them. Last night, Veronica targeted one of my coven members. Alana."

It took me several moments to truly process that. "Your coven . . . you mean, like a full-fledged witch?"

"Yes."

"Someone like *you*?"

Her face gave me the answer before she spoke. "Yes."

I was reeling. "But you said she only went after young girls."

"Normally she does. That way she can capture youth and

beauty along with power." Ms. Terwilliger didn't look like she had to worry about someone stealing her youth anytime soon. Fatigue and stress were taking their toll on her, making her look older than she was. "Now, some magic users who perform this spell are only concerned about power, not getting younger. That's never been Veronica's style, though. She's vain. She always wanted the superficial benefits—not to mention easier victims. Someone like my coven sister would be more difficult to take, so this is surprising behavior."

"It means *you* could be a target," I said. "You've been saying all this time that you're safe, but now everything's different."

Ms. Terwilliger shook her head, and a bit of steely resolve flashed in her eyes. "No. Maybe she did this to throw me off, to make me think it's someone else behind the spells. Or maybe to make me think she's not interested in you. Whatever the reason, she won't target me."

I admired Ms. Terwilliger for thinking so well of her sister, but I couldn't share her confidence that sisterly affection would overcome an evil quest for youth and power. "No offense, ma'am, but isn't there a slight chance you could be wrong about her coming for you? You said she'd only go after young novices, but obviously, that's not the case. She's already doing things you didn't expect."

Ms. Terwilliger refused to back down. "Veronica may do any number of terrible things, but she won't face me unless she's absolutely forced to." She handed over a new spell book and a small drawstring bag. "Just because she went after an older witch, it doesn't mean you're out of danger. I've marked some pages I want you to go over. There's a spell there I think will prove particularly useful. I've gathered some components for you, and you should be able to cast the rest yourself—just make sure you do it somewhere remote. Meanwhile, I still need to make you that secondary charm. There's just so much to do lately."

A mix of emotions swirled within me. Once again, I was amazed that Ms. Terwilliger would go to such lengths for me. Yet I couldn't shake my fear for her. "Maybe you should make one for yourself, just in case."

She gave me a wan smile. "Still pushing that, hmm? Well, once I've secured yours, I'll see about another. It may take a while, however. What I have in mind for you is particularly complex."

That made me feel even worse. She always looked so worn out lately, and all these things she was doing for me were only intensifying the situation. But no matter how many arguments I made, she refused to listen. I left her classroom feeling upset and confused. I needed to vent to someone. Obviously, my choices were limited in this matter. I texted Adrian: *V attacked a real witch last night. Ms. T won't protect herself. She's only worried about me.* As usual, I received a quick response: *Wanna talk about it?*

Did I? I wasn't the type to sit and analyze my feelings, but I did actually want company. I knew I shouldn't spend more time around Adrian than I had to when my feelings for him were already so mixed. But he was the only person I wanted to talk to. *I have to cast some spells for her now. Want to pick me up and come along?*

My answer was a smiley face.

She'd told me to go somewhere remote, so I picked Lone Rock Park again. When Adrian and I arrived, it was smoldering in the late-afternoon heat, and I found it hard to believe

Christmas was only a couple weeks away. I'd dressed in layers, just like before, and took off my Amberwood hoodie as Adrian and I trekked across the rocky terrain. He took off a coat as well, and I had to do a double take when I saw what he was wearing underneath.

"Really?" I asked. "Your AYE shirt?"

He shot me a grin. "Hey, it's a perfectly good shirt. I think I'm going to see if I can start a chapter on Carlton's campus." Carlton was the college he took art classes at. It was pretty small and didn't even have fraternities or sororities.

"A chapter?" I scoffed. "Don't you mean the *only* chapter?"

"Gotta start somewhere, Sage."

We reached the same spot where I'd practiced with Ms. Terwilliger, and I tried to ignore the scorch marks on the ground. Adrian had decided to turn this into a desert picnic and had brought along a basket containing a blanket and a thermos of lemonade. "I figured we could stop at Pies and Stuff on the way back since I know how much you like that place," he explained, deadpan, as he poured me a cup. "Hopefully this'll tide you over after the spell."

"I wish this was over," I said, running my hand over the weathered leather of Ms. Terwilliger's latest book. It was an old handwritten one called *Summonings and Conjurations*. "I hate living with the uncertainty, worrying that Veronica's lurking behind every corner. My life's already complicated enough without witches coming after me."

Adrian, face serious, stretched out on the blanket and propped his head up with his elbow. "If she's even coming after you."

I sat down cross-legged, careful to keep a lot more distance than in the Velvet Suite. "Ms. Terwilliger won't listen to me. She just keeps stressing over me."

"Let her," he suggested. "I mean, I totally get why you're worried about her. I am too. But we have to accept that she knows what she's talking about. She's been involved with this stuff a lot longer than we have."

I couldn't help but smile at that. "Since when are you involved with magic?"

"Since I started looking after you and being all manly and brave."

"Funny, I don't remember it that way." I worked to keep a straight face. "If you think about all the rides I gave you, me getting you into college . . . well, it kind of seems like I'm looking after you."

He leaned toward me. "I guess we look after each other."

We locked eyes and smiled, but there was nothing sensuous about it. There was no trick here, no sly move on Adrian's part to advance on me. And there was no fear on my part. We were just two people who cared about each other. It reminded me of what had initially drawn us together—before all the romantic complications. We connected. Against all reason, we understood each other, and—as he said—we looked out for each other. I'd never had a relationship quite like that with anyone and was surprised at how much I valued it.

"Well, then, I guess I'd better get to work." I glanced back down at the book. "I haven't had a chance to look at what she wants me to do. It doesn't sound like a defensive book."

"Maybe you're graduating from fireballs to lightning bolts," Adrian suggested. "I bet it'd be a lot like throwing ninja stars. Except, well, you could incinerate people."

When I found the page Ms. Terwilliger had marked, I read the title aloud: "Callistana Summoning."

"What's *callistana* mean?" asked Adrian.

I scrutinized the word, making sure I was deciphering the elaborate script correctly. "I don't know. It's kind of like the Greek word for 'beautiful,' but not quite. The spell's subtitle is 'For protection and advanced warning.'"

"Maybe it's some kind of shield, like the one Jackie had," suggested Adrian. "An easier one."

"Maybe," I agreed. I wouldn't mind a little bit of invulnerability.

I opened up the bag Ms. Terwilliger had given me. Inside, I found dragon's blood resin, a small bottle of gardenia oil, branches of juniper berries, and a glittering smoky quartz crystal, rutilated with lines of gold. Although she'd provided the ingredients, the spell's directions required that I use and measure them in a very specific way, which made sense. As usual, it was the caster's work that powered the magic. Adrian sat up and read over my shoulder.

"It doesn't really say what happens when you cast it," he pointed out.

"Yeah . . . I'm not really excited about that part." Presumably, the caster was supposed to just know what she was doing. If this was some kind of protective shield, then maybe the shield would materialize around me, just as it had for Ms. Terwilliger. "Well, no point in wasting time. We'll find out soon enough."

Adrian chuckled as he watched me walk over to a clear piece of land. "Am I the only one amazed that you now perform magic blindly?"

"No," I assured him. "You're not the only one."

I had to pluck the juniper berries off one by one and make a small ring with them, saying, "Fire and smoke," each time I placed one on the ground. When I finished, I anointed each berry with a drop of the oil and recited, "Breath and life." Inside the circle, I lit a small pile of the resin and rested the smoky quartz on top of it. Then I stepped back and reread the spell, committing the words and gestures to memory. Once I was satisfied I knew it, I handed it to Adrian and shot him a hopeful look.

"Wish me luck," I said.

"You make your own luck," he replied.

I tried not to roll my eyes and turned toward the circle. I recited the spell's complex Greek incantation, pointing in the four cardinal directions as I spoke, per the book's instructions. It was startling how quickly the magic welled up within me, filling me with that blissful power. I spoke the last words, pointing at the juniper circle as I did. I felt the magic pour from me and into the quartz. Then I waited for something to happen.

Nothing did.

I looked back at Adrian, hoping he noticed something I hadn't. He shrugged. "Maybe you did it wrong."

"It worked," I insisted. "I felt the magic."

"Maybe you just can't see it. At the expense of getting myself in trouble here, you should know how amazing you look when you do that stuff. All graceful and—" His eyes went wide. "Um, Sydney? That rock is smoking."

I glanced back at the circle. "That's just the resin that's—"

I stopped. He was right. Smoke was coming out of the quartz. I watched, fascinated, and then slowly, the quartz began to melt. Rather than dissipate into a puddle, though, the liquid began to re-form into a different shape, one that soon hardened into something new and unexpected: a crystalline dragon.

It was small, able to fit in a palm, and glittered just like the dark brown quartz had. The dragon looked more like the serpentine kind usually associated with Chinese culture rather than the winged types of European myth. Every detail was meticulously carved, from the tendrils of its mane to the scales on its hide. It was stunning.

Also, it was moving.

I screamed and backed up, running into Adrian. He put an arm around me and held me as protectively as he could, though it was clear he was just as freaked out. The dragon opened its crystal eyelids and peered at the two of us with tiny golden eyes. It elicited a small croak and then began walking toward us, its small claws scraping against the rocks.

"What the hell is that?" Adrian demanded.

"Do you really think I know?"

"You made it! Do something."

I started to ask what had happened to him looking out for me, but he had a point. I was the one who'd summoned this thing. No matter where we moved or backed up to, the dragon continued to follow and make a small, high-pitched screeching noise that sounded like nails on a chalkboard. I groped for my cell phone and tried to dial Ms. Terwilliger, but there was no reception out here. Darting over to the blanket, I grabbed the spell book and then hurried back to Adrian's side. I flipped to the index, looking up *callistana*. There I found two entries: *Callistana—Summoning* and *Callistana—Banishing*. You would've thought the two would be near each other in the book, but they were pages apart. I flipped to the latter and found the instructions brief and to the point: *Once your callistana has been fed and rested, you may summon and banish it at will for a year and a day.* A short incantation followed.

I looked up at Adrian. "It says we have to feed it."

"Will that make it shut up?" he asked. His arm was around me again.

"I honestly don't know."

"Maybe we can outrun it."

All my instincts about hiding the supernatural world kicked in. "We can't just leave it for some hiker to find! We have to get it some food." Not that I had any clue what to feed it. Hopefully humans and vampires weren't on the menu.

A look of determination crossed Adrian's features. In a great show of bravery, he lunged for the picnic basket and actually managed to scoop the dragon up in it. He slammed down the lid, and the mewling faded but didn't stop.

"Wow," I said. "Manly and brave."

Adrian regarded the basket with dismay. "I just hope that thing doesn't breathe fire. At least it's contained. Now what do we do?"

"Now we feed it." I made a decision. "We take it to Pies and Stuff."

I didn't know if dragons ate pie, but that was the closest food source we had. Besides, I was pretty sure I'd be able to get a cell phone signal there. So, Adrian drove us back to the little diner while I gingerly held the noisy basket. He went inside, and I stayed in the car and tried to call Ms. Terwilliger. I was sent to voice mail and didn't even bother with formalities. Was she never near her phone anymore?

"Call me now," I said through gritted teeth. The dragon's screeching was really starting to get to me.

Adrian returned in about ten minutes carrying two bags. I stared in amazement as he got in the car. "Did you buy out the store?"

"I didn't know what kind it wanted," he protested. Between the two bags, we had half a dozen slices of different kinds of pies. Each one's container was neatly labeled.

"I really don't know either," I said.

Adrian sifted through the bags and pulled out a slice of coconut cream. "If I were a dragon, this is what I'd go for."

I didn't argue, mainly because that statement had no logical argument. He took the lid off the pie and then looked at me expectantly. With a gulp, I opened the basket's lid and prayed the dragon wouldn't climb out and claw my face off. Adrian quickly set the pie down in the basket. Nervously, we both leaned forward to watch.

At first, the dragon looked as though it really would climb out after us. Then it noticed the pie. The little crystal creature sniffed at the slice, circled it a few times, and then began gnawing at the pie in teeny-tiny bites. Best of all, the screeching stopped. We watched in wonder as the dragon made its way through a third of the coconut cream pie. Then, without warning, it rolled over onto its back and began to snore. Adrian and I sat there, frozen, and then finally dared to look at each other.

"I guess you were right about the flavor," I said.

"Do you think you can banish it now?" he asked. "Is it fed and rested enough?"

I retrieved the spell book to double-check the incantation. "Time to find out."

I recited the words. Smoke fluttered from the dragon's body. He began to shimmer, and within moments, we were looking at an inert piece of smoky quartz. In another valiant display, Adrian picked it up but held it as far away as possible as he studied it. The ringing of my phone startled both of us, and he dropped the crystal back into the basket. I looked at the phone's screen and saw Ms. Terwilliger's name.

"You made me summon a dragon!" I exclaimed.

"I most certainly did not," she responded. "Callistanas are a type of demon."

I froze. "A demon."

"Well," she amended. "A very minor and generally benign kind." I didn't reply for a while. "Sydney? Are you still there?"

"You had me summon a demon," I replied, voice stiff. "You know how I feel about evil and the supernatural. You've spent all this time trying to convince me that the magic we do is all for some greater good in the battle against evil, and yet you made me summon a creature of hell."

"Creature of hell?" She snorted. "Hardly. You know nothing about demons. I told you it's benign, didn't I? Callistanas can be very useful. They'll warn you if dark magic is nearby and will even try to defend you if you're attacked—not that they can do much damage."

I wasn't buying it. "If they're so useful, then why don't you have one?"

"Oh, well, I'm at a level where I can sense dark magic on my own. That, and—if you'll forgive my language—callistanas are a real pain in the ass. They make the most irritating noise when they're hungry. Cats are more than adequate for my needs."

"Yeah," I said. "I kind of noticed the noise part. I fed it some pie and turned it back into a rock."

"There, you see?" She sounded happier than I'd heard her in days. "Look at the progress you've made already. No matter what comes of this mess we've found ourselves in, I'm more convinced than ever that I made the right choice in guiding you on the magical path."

I had too much going on to really appreciate the compliment. "So what do I do now?"

"It'll disappear on its own after a year and a day. Until then, you can call it when you need it. You can try to train it. And of course, you'll have to feed it. Whatever you choose to do, it will be loyal to you. It bonds with the first person it sees and will need to spend time with you . . . Sydney? Are you there?"

I'd gone silent again. "The first person it sees?" I finally managed to ask. "Not the caster?"

"Well, usually they're one and the same."

I glanced over at Adrian, who was eating a piece of blackberry pie while listening avidly to my side of the conversation. "What happens if there were two people there when it opened its eyes? Adrian was with me when I summoned it."

Now she paused. "Oh? Hmm, well, I probably should've said something before you cast the spell."

That had to be the understatement of the century. "You should've told me a lot of things before I cast it! What does it mean that the dragon—demon, whatever— saw both of us? Did it bond with both of us?"

"Look at it this way," Ms. Terwilliger said, after several moments of thought. "The callistana thinks of you two as its parents."

CHAPTER 18

I CERTAINLY HADN'T EXPECTED to walk away from today's trip with joint custody of a miniature dragon. (I refused to call it a demon). And, as it turned out, Adrian was already proving not to be the most dedicated of "fathers."

"You can take him for now," he told me when we got back to Amberwood. "I'll handle weekend visitations."

"You don't have anything going on. Besides, we're only a few days from the weekend," I protested. "And you don't know that it's a 'he.'"

"Well, I don't think he'll mind, and besides, I'm not going to investigate to find out the truth." Adrian put the quartz in the basket and closed the lid before handing it over to me. "You don't have to summon him back, you know."

I took the basket and opened the car door. "I know. But I feel kind of bad leaving him as a rock." Ms. Terwilliger had told me it'd be healthier for him if I let him out once in a while.

"See? Motherly instinct already. You're a natural, Sage."

Adrian grinned and handed me a bag of pie slices. He'd kept some for himself. "Look at you. You don't even need to break the tattoo. You think you would've been mothering a baby dragon a month ago?"

"I don't know." But he had a point. It seemed likely I would've run screaming from it back in the desert. Or maybe tried to exorcise it. "I'll take him for now, but you've got to pull your weight at some point. Ms. Terwilliger says the callistana needs to spend time with both of us. Hmm."

"Hmm, what?"

I shook my head. "Just getting ahead of myself. Wondering what I'd do with him if I did go to Mexico."

Adrian gave me a puzzled look. "What about Mexico?"

It had never come up, I realized. All Adrian had known about was Marcus's mission and the initial tattoo breaking, not the sealing. I hadn't been keeping the rest a secret, but suddenly, I felt uncomfortable telling Adrian about it.

"Oh. Well, Marcus says that after I perform this rebellious act, we can break the elements and free me from the tattoo's control. But to truly bind the spell and make sure the tattoo is never repaired, I need to tattoo over it like he did. He calls it sealing. But it takes some special compound that's hard to find. He got his done in Mexico and is going to take some of his Merry Men there so they can do it."

"I see." Adrian's smile had vanished. "So. Are you joining them?"

I shrugged. "I don't know. Marcus wants me to."

"I'm sure he does."

I ignored the tone. "I've thought about it . . . but it's a big step. Not just for the tattoo, either. If I did that, there'd be no going back. I'd be turning my back on the Alchemists."

"And us," he said. "Unless you really are only helping Jill because of your orders."

"You know it's not about that anymore." Again, I didn't like his tone. "You know I care about her and . . . and the rest of you."

His face was hard. "And yet you'd run off with some guy you just met."

"It's not like that! We wouldn't be 'running off' together. I'd be coming back! And we'd be going for a specific reason."

"Beaches and margaritas?"

I was speechless for a few moments. It was so close to what Marcus had joked about. Was that all anyone associated with Mexico?

"I see how it is," I snapped. "You were all in favor of me breaking the tattoo and thinking on my own—but that's only okay if it's convenient for you, huh? Just like your 'loving from afar' only works if you don't have an opportunity to get your hands all over me. And your lips. And . . . stuff."

Adrian rarely got mad, and I wouldn't quite say he was now. But he was definitely exasperated. "Are you seriously in this much self-denial, Sydney? Like do you actually believe yourself when you say you don't feel anything? Especially after what's been happening between us?"

"Nothing's happening between us," I said automatically. "Physical attraction isn't the same as love. You of all people should know that."

"Ouch," he said. His expression hadn't changed, but I saw hurt in his eyes. I'd wounded him. "Is that what bothers you? My past? That maybe I'm an expert in an area you aren't?"

"One I'm sure you'd just love to educate me in. One more girl to add to your list of conquests."

He was speechless for a few moments and then held up one finger. "First, I don't have a list." Another finger. "Second, if I did have a list, I could find someone a hell of lot less frustrating to add to it." For the third finger, he leaned toward me. "And finally, I know that you know you're no conquest, so don't act like you seriously think that. You and I have been through too much together. We're too close, too connected. I wasn't that crazy on spirit when I said you're my flame in the dark. We chase away the shadows around each other. Our backgrounds don't matter. What we have is bigger than that. I love you, and beneath all that logic, calculation, and superstition, I know you love me too. Running away to Mexico and fleeing all your problems isn't going to change that. You're just going to end up scared and confused."

"I already feel that way," I said quietly.

Adrian moved back and leaned into his seat, looking tired. "Well, that's the most accurate thing you've said so far."

I grabbed the basket and jerked open the car door. Without another word, I stormed off toward the dorm, refusing to look back in case he saw the tears that had inexplicably appeared in my eyes. Only, I wasn't sure exactly which part of our conversation I was most upset about.

The tears seemed like they were going to stay put by the time I reached my room, but I still had to calm down. Even once my emotions were settled, it was hard to shake his words. *You're my flame in the dark. We chase away the shadows around each other.* What did that even mean?

At least smuggling a dragon into my room provided a pretty

good distraction. I brought the basket inside, hoping demonic dragons weren't contraband. No one stopped me when I went upstairs, and I was left wondering how I was going to confine him if I did summon him back. The basket didn't seem all that secure, and I certainly wasn't going to let him run loose in my dorm room. When I reached my door, I found Jill standing outside, her pale green eyes wide with excitement.

"I want to see him," she said. The bond was strongest in moments of high emotion, and judging from Adrian's face when the dragon had been chasing us, his emotions had been running pretty strong. I wondered if she'd witnessed our argument too or if that hadn't come through the bond. Maybe the tension between him and me was second nature to her now.

"I can't let him out yet," I said, letting her into my room. "I need something to keep him in. Like a birdcage. Maybe I can get one tomorrow."

Jill frowned in thought, then brightened. "I have an idea." She glanced at my alarm clock. "I hope it's not too late."

And without further explanation, she took off, promising to be back soon. I was still a little shaky from today's magic but hadn't had time to rectify the situation after all the other excitement. So, I sat at my desk with a spell book and ate the rest of the now-soft coconut cream pie, careful to first cut off the part where the dragon had eaten. I didn't know if callistanas had communicable germs, but I wasn't taking any chances.

Jill returned an hour later, bearing a rectangular glass aquarium, like the kind you'd keep fish or gerbils in.

"Where'd you get that?" I asked, moving a lamp off my desk.

"My biology teacher. Our guinea pig died a couple weeks ago, and she's been too sad to replace him."

"Didn't she ask what you needed it for?" I examined the tank and found it spotless, so someone had apparently cleaned it after the guinea pig's unfortunate passing. "We can't have pets."

"I told her I was building a diorama. She didn't question it." Jill eagerly brought the aquarium over to the desk. "We can give it back when you get your own."

I set the quartz crystal inside and slammed on the tank's lid, making sure it was securely attached. After more entreating from Jill, I spoke the summoning words. A bit of smoke appeared, and the quartz transformed back into the dragon. Mercifully, he didn't make any more of that screeching, so I guessed he was still full. Instead, he scampered around the tank, examining his new home. At one point, he tried to climb the side, but his tiny claws couldn't get traction on the glass.

"Well, that's a relief," I said.

Jill's face was filled with wonder. "I think he'll be bored in there. You should get him some toys."

"Toys for a demon? Isn't it enough that I give him pie?"

"He wants *you*," she insisted.

Sure enough, I glanced back at the tank and found the callistana regarding me adoringly. He was even wagging his tail.

"No," I said sternly. "This isn't a Disney movie where I have an adorable sidekick. You aren't coming out."

I cut off a piece of blueberry pie and put it in the tank in case he wanted a midnight snack. No way would I risk a late-night wakeup call. After a moment's thought, I added a stress ball and a scarf.

"There," I told Jill. "Food, a toy, and a bed. Happy?"

The callistana apparently was. He batted the ball around

a few times and then curled up on the nest I'd made with the scarf. He looked more or less content, aside from the fact that he kept watching me.

"Aww," she said. "Look how sweet he is. What are you going to name him?"

Like I needed something else to worry about. "His 'father' can name him. I'm already on the hook for the Mustang."

After a bit more swooning, Jill finally retired for the night. I made my own preparations for bed, always keeping one eye on the dragon. He did nothing threatening, however, and I even managed to fall asleep, though my sleep was restless. I kept imagining he'd find a way out and come get into bed with me. And of course, I had my usual fears about Veronica coming after me.

I did hit one stretch of sound sleep, during which Adrian pulled me into a spirit dream. After our earlier fight, I honestly hadn't expected to see him tonight, a thought that had saddened me. The reception hall materialized around us, but the image wavered and kept fading in and out.

"I didn't think you'd come," I told him.

No wedding clothes tonight. He wore what he'd had on earlier, jeans and the AYE shirt, though both looked a bit more wrinkled. He was dressed as he was in reality, I realized.

"You think I'd abandon you to Veronica?"

"No," I admitted. "What's wrong with the room?"

He looked a little embarrassed. "My control's not all it could be tonight."

I didn't understand . . . at first. "You're drunk."

"I've been drinking," he corrected, leaning against one of the tables. "If I was drunk, I wouldn't be here at all. And really, this is pretty good for four White Russians."

"White what?" I almost sat down but was afraid the chair might dematerialize beneath me.

"It's a drink," he said. "You'd think I wouldn't be into something named that—you know, considering my own personal experience with Russians. But they're surprisingly delicious. The drinks, not real Russians. They've got Kahlua. It might be the drink you've been waiting your whole life for."

"Kahlua does *not* taste like coffee," I said. "So don't start with that." I was insanely curious to know why he'd been drinking. Sometimes he did it to numb spirit, but he seemed to still want to access that magic tonight. And of course, half the time, he didn't even need a reason to drink. Deep inside me, I wondered if our fight had driven him to it. I didn't know whether to feel guilty or annoyed.

"I also had to come tonight to apologize," he said. He sat down, apparently not having the same fears about chairs.

For one inexplicably terrifying moment, I thought he was going to take back the part about me being his flame in the dark. Instead, he told me, "If you need to go to Mexico to finish this process off, then I understand. I was wrong to criticize you for it or even imply that I had some kind of say in it. One of the greatest things about you is that in the end, you always make smart decisions. Can't always say the same for myself. Whatever you need to do, I'll support you."

Those annoying tears almost returned, and I blinked them back. "Thank you. That means a lot . . . and to tell you the truth, right now, I still don't know what I'm going to do. I know Marcus is worried about me eventually getting in trouble and being under their control. Then again, staying part of the Alchemists seems like it'd give me more power, and besides . . . I don't want to leave you. Er, you guys."

He smiled, and it lit up his whole face. *Like a flame in the dark.* "Well, 'we' are certainly happy to hear that. Oh, and I'm also happy to watch our darling little love child dragon while you're in St. Louis."

I grinned back. "As a rock or in his real form?"

"Haven't decided yet. How's he doing right now?"

"He's locked in an aquarium. I'm guessing I'd wake up if he got into bed with me, so he must still be asleep." I hoped.

"Well, I'm sure getting into bed with you would be—"Adrian held back whatever comment he'd been about to utter. He instead gestured to the table, and a Monopoly board appeared. "Shall we play?"

I walked over and peered at the board. It apparently was also suffering from his drinking, seeing as half the streets were blank. The ones that were there had names like "Castile Causeway" and "Jailbait Avenue." "The board's a little incomplete," I said diplomatically.

Adrian didn't seem concerned. "Well, then, I guess that improves your odds."

I couldn't resist that and took a gamble on sitting in one of the chairs. I smiled at him and then began counting money, happy that all was (relatively) right in the world with us again.

CHAPTER 19

SOMEHOW, I STILL LOST.

If Adrian were capable of on-the-fly calculations, I'd swear he was using his powers to affect the way the dice rolled. Most likely, he either had some innate and inexplicable Monopoly skills I just couldn't understand—or he was very, very lucky. But through it all, I had fun, and losing to him was a lot better than having Veronica haunt me in my sleep. He continued the dream visits for the next few days, and although I never felt completely safe from her, I at least didn't have her occupying the forefront of my mind at all times. That honor was saved for my weekend trip to St. Louis, which came around more quickly than I expected.

Once I was on the plane, the reality of what I was about to attempt hit me. This was it, the point of no return. In the safety of Palm Springs, I'd been able to maintain a somewhat cool and collected attitude. St. Louis had seemed far away back then. Now the tasks ahead of me seemed daunting and kind of crazy. And *dangerous*. There was no part of this that wouldn't get me into serious trouble. Lying to Stanton. Breaking into top secret servers. Even charming information out of Ian could have repercussions.

And really, who was I to think I would have any ability to lure secrets from him? I wasn't like Rose or Julia. They had men fawning all over them. But me? I was socially awkward and pretty inept when it came to romance. Maybe Ian liked me, but that didn't mean I'd have some magical power over him. Of course, if that part of the plan with him failed, then I'd be free of my other tasks.

Every single part of this was overwhelming, and as I stared out the plane's window, watching St. Louis grow closer and closer, my feelings of dread grew. My palms were too sweaty to hold a book, and when I refused food, it was because of the queasiness in my stomach, not some obsession with calories.

I'd gone back and forth on whether to get a hotel room or stay at the facility itself, which provided guest housing for visiting Alchemists like me. In the end, I opted for the former. The less time I spent under the watchful eyes of my masters, the better.

It also meant I didn't have to worry about my outfit attracting attention. I hadn't exactly followed all of Adrian's suggestions, but the dress I'd purchased for this trip was a bit racier than my normal business casual wardrobe. Okay, a lot racier. It would have been completely out of place among the modest and neutral-colored attire Alchemists usually wore. But when Ian met me in the hotel's lobby for dinner, I knew I'd made the right choice.

"Wow," he said, eyes widening. "You look amazing."

Apparently, his Alchemists sensibilities weren't offended by my outfit. It was a form-fitting minidress that went about to my mid-thigh, with an open back and a disconcertingly low V-neck that gave me cleavage I hadn't even known was possible. Any demureness the dress's long sleeves might have offered was undone by the fabric combination: a beige underdress covered in black and maroon lace. It gave the illusion that I was wearing lace with nothing underneath. The saleswoman had assured me that every part of the dress was supposed to fit that snugly (for once in my life, I'd actually suggested a larger size) and that I needed at least four-inch black heels to make it all work. With the help of a lot of hairpins, I'd even managed to pull my hair up into a bun, which wasn't easy with my layered haircut.

I felt conspicuous walking through the lobby, but no one gave me any shocked looks. The few I did get were admiring ones. The hotel was pretty posh, and I was just one of a number of women dressed in holiday cocktail dresses. Nothing scandalous or out of the ordinary. *You can do this, Sydney.* And wearing a revealing dress wasn't nearly as difficult as breaking into a server, right?

Right?

I smiled as I approached Ian and gave him a quick hug, which was weird both because it was with Ian and because I felt naked in the dress. This femme fatale thing was harder than I'd thought it'd be.

"I'm glad I got to see you again," I said. "I know what an inconvenience this must be, with no notice."

Ian shook his head so adamantly that I almost expected to hear rattling. "N-no. No trouble at all."

Satisfied he'd gotten a look, I slipped on my coat, a

mid-length black trench, and gestured toward the exit. "Time to brave the elements?"

He hurried ahead of me to open the door. A scattering of snowflakes drifted down, resting on my coat and hair. My breath made a frosty cloud in the air, and I had a momentary flashback to traipsing across that field with Adrian. Little had I known that search for Marcus would lead to me running errands for him in a tight dress.

Ian had parked in the hotel's front circle drive. He drove a Toyota Corolla, which was made even more boring by the fact that he'd chosen it in white. A little air freshener shaped like a tree hung from the rearview mirror, but rather than the usual pine scent, a small label declared it to be "New Car Scent." Mostly it smelled like plastic. I put on a brave face. Marcus really owed me one.

"I made us a reservation at this really great seafood place," he told me. "It's close to the facility, so we can head on over to the service right away."

"Sounds great," I said. I never ate seafood in any landlocked state.

The restaurant was called Fresh Cache, which didn't improve my opinion of it. Still, I had to give it credit for attempts at a romantic atmosphere. Most of the lighting came from candles, and a pianist in the corner played covers of easy-listening songs. More well-dressed people filled the tables, laughing and chatting over wine and shrimp cocktails. The host showed us to a corner table, covered with burgundy linen and decorated with a scattering of green orchids. I'd never seen any up close and was actually quite taken with how exotic and sensual they were. If only I was here with anyone but Ian.

I was hesitant to take my coat off. It made me feel exposed, and I had to remind myself of the consequences of Alchemists and Warriors working together. As soon as the dress was unleashed again, I had the satisfaction of seeing Ian melt once more. I remembered Adrian's advice about confidence and put on a smug smile, hoping I gave the impression that I was doing Ian a great favor by allowing him to be in my presence. And, to my complete and utter amazement, it seemed to work. I even allowed myself to indulge in a dangerous thought: maybe it wasn't the dress wielding such power here.

Maybe it was *me*.

Opening the menu, I began skimming for a beef or poultry option. "What do you recommend?"

"The mahi mahi is great here," he said. "So is the swordfish."

The waiter stopped by, and I ordered a chicken Caesar salad. I figured they couldn't really mess up the anchovies in the dressing.

We were left alone to wait, with nothing to do now but move on to small talk. Ian picked up the ball. "I suppose you still can't tell me much about where you're at, huh?"

"Afraid not. You know how it is." I buttered a sourdough roll with what I was pretty sure was exactly half a tablespoon. I didn't want to go too crazy, but I could allow myself a little indulgence since I ordered a salad. "I can tell you I'm in the field. I just can't say much else."

Ian's attention shifted off my neckline as he stared into the candle's flame. "I miss that, you know. Being in the field."

"You used to be, right? What happened?" I hadn't thought much about it lately, but when Ian had accompanied Stanton and me to the Moroi court, he had been pulled from his post to make the trip. He'd been assigned somewhere in the south, Florida or Georgia, I thought.

"Those Moroi holding us prisoner is what happened." He shifted his gaze back to me, and I was startled at the fierceness I saw. "I didn't handle it very well."

"Well, none of us did."

He shook his head. "No, no. I really didn't handle it well. I kind of freaked out. They sent me to anger management training afterward."

I nearly dropped the roll. I had in no way expected that. If someone had asked me to name the top ten people who needed anger management, Ian wouldn't have even made the bottom of the list. My father, however, would have been near the top.

"How—how long were you there?" I stammered.

"Two weeks, and then I was good to go."

Admittedly, I didn't know the extent of the rage that had landed him in anger management, but I found it interesting that two weeks was good enough to deem him ready to work again. Meanwhile, Keith's scheme to use Moroi to make money had earned him at least two months in re-education—maybe more, since I hadn't heard any updates in a while.

"But they wouldn't let me work in the field," Ian added. "Figure I shouldn't be around Moroi for a while. So that's why I'm stuck here."

"In the archives."

"Yes."

"Doesn't sound so bad," I told him. I wasn't entirely lying. "Lots of books."

"Don't fool yourself, Sydney." He began tearing a pumpernickel roll into pieces. "I'm a glorified librarian."

Maybe so, but that wasn't my concern. What was my concern was Wade telling me that the archives were on a secure level, one floor up from the surveillance room that held security footage. He'd drawn me a map of each floor, making sure I memorized the layout and the best ways to get in and out.

"I'd still love to see them," I said. "I mean, the history they contain is amazing." Again, not entirely a lie. I leaned forward, resting my elbows on the table, and had the satisfaction of seeing his eyes drop to my plunging neckline again. This wasn't that difficult! Really, I didn't know why I hadn't been using my "womanly charms" a long time ago. Actually, I never really knew I had any, until now. "Could you get me in for a tour? Of the archives specifically. You seem like the kind of guy who could get access to . . . a lot of places."

Ian choked on his roll. After a bout of coughing, he glanced up at my face, then my cleavage (again), and then back to my face. "I'd, um, love to, but it's not really open to the public— I mean, even the Alchemist public. Only those with special scholar access are allowed in. We could look at the general access parts of the building, though."

"Oh. I see." I looked down at my plate, pouting slightly, but didn't say anything else. As the waiter arrived with our food, I hoped my silence was making him reconsider what he could be missing out on.

Eventually, Ian couldn't take it anymore. He cleared his throat, maybe because there was still bread stuck in it. "Well, I might be able to . . . you see, the problem is just getting you down to the secure levels. Once you're through that checkpoint, it's not hard to get you into the archives—especially if I'm working."

"But you can't do anything about the main checkpoint?" I coaxed, as if all real men should be able to do that.

"No, I mean . . . maybe. I've got a friend who works there. I don't know if he's got a shift tomorrow, but he still might be able to help. He owes me some money, so I can use this as a trade. I hope."

"Oh, Ian." I flashed him a smile that I hoped rivaled one of Marcus's. "That's amazing." I remembered what Adrian had said. "I'd be so, *so* grateful if you could pull it off."

My reaction clearly delighted Ian, and I wondered if Adrian had been right about how "so, so grateful" was translated. "I'll call him tonight after the service," Ian said. He looked determined now. "Hopefully we can make it happen before your flight tomorrow."

I rewarded him by hanging on his every word for the rest of dinner, as though I'd never heard anything quite so fascinating. All the while, my heart raced with the knowledge that I was now one step closer to fulfilling Marcus's task, one step closer to potentially proving a connection to a bunch of gun-toting zealots and the organization I'd served my whole life.

The salad was tiny, so I agreed to see the dessert menu after dinner. Ian suggested we share, but that was a little too intimate for me, not to mention unhygienic. So, I ate an entire lemon tart by myself, confident in the knowledge that I was still a long ways from the five-pound mark. When Adrian had told me I'd look healthier if I gained a little weight, he'd added that it would improve my bra size. I couldn't even imagine what that would do for this dress.

The Alchemist center in St. Louis was contained inside a giant, industrial building that went undercover as a manufacturing plant. Moroi facilities—the court and their schools—usually posed as universities. How ironic that "creatures of the night" would live among beautifully landscaped gardens while "servants of the light" like us skulked in ugly buildings with no windows.

Inside, however, everything was pristine, bright, and well-organized. A receptionist checked us in when we arrived at the main desk and buzzed us through, along with many others who arrived for the service. There were golden lilies everywhere. For many, this was a fun-filled family event, and lots of children trailed their Alchemist parents. It made me feel strange as I watched them, these kids who had been born into our profession. I wondered how they'd feel ten years from now. Would they be excited to step up to the plate? Or would they start questioning?

The center had three floors aboveground and five underneath. People off the street could hardly just come wandering in, but we still took precautions by keeping the more benign offices on the main floor. As we all walked down the corridor to the auditorium, we passed Payroll, Travel, and Maintenance. All the offices had clear windows looking into them from the hall, maintaining the Alchemist ideal that we had nothing to hide.

The secure offices belowground weren't quite so open, however.

I'd been in this facility once before for a training seminar, and it had actually taken place in the auditorium we entered for the service. Despite the spiritual theme of tonight's event, the room bore little resemblance to a church. Someone had gone to the effort of decorating the walls with red-bowed evergreen garlands and setting pots of poinsettias on the stage. The room had a state-of-the-art audio-visual system, including a giant screen that gave a larger-than-life look at whatever was happening onstage. The auditorium's seating was so efficient that even those in the farthest corners had a pretty clear view, so I think the screen was just for emphasis.

Ian and I found two seats near the middle of the auditorium. "Aren't you going to take off your coat?" he asked hopefully.

No way was I going to unleash the dress in this den of taupe and high collars. Besides, if I kept the coat on, it would just give him something to keep looking forward to. Adrian would be proud of my ability to manipulate the opposite sex . . . and I couldn't help but wonder just how well Adrian would be able to stand up to this dress. Clearly, I was getting overly confident with this new power.

"I'm cold," I said, pulling the coat tighter. It was kind of ridiculous since the lights from the stage and high number of bodies had already made the room stifling, but I figured since it was so cold outside, I could get away with it.

For someone who always seems to be so cold, you sure can warm up pretty fast.

"Sydney? Is that you?"

I froze, not from the shock of hearing my name, but from the voice that had said it. I'd know that voice anywhere. Slowly, I turned away from Ian and looked up into my father's face. He was standing in the aisle, wearing a heavy wool suit, with melted snowflakes in his graying dark blond hair.

"Hi, Dad," I said. Then I saw who was standing beside him. "Zoe?"

It was all I could do not to jump up and hug her. I hadn't seen or spoken to my younger sister since that night I'd been pulled out of bed and sent on my Palm Springs mission. That was the mission she believed I'd stolen from her, no matter my protests. It was the mission that had driven her away from me.

I eyed her now, trying to assess where we stood. She didn't wear the blatant hatred she had at our last meeting, which was a good sign. Unfortunately, she didn't look all that warm and friendly either. She was cautious, studying me carefully— almost warily. She did not, I noticed, have a golden lily on her cheek yet.

"I'm surprised to see you here," said my father.

His parting words to me had been "Don't embarrass me," so I wasn't really astonished by his low expectations. "It's the holidays," I said. Forcing a smile now was far more difficult than it had been with Ian. "It's important to be here with the group. Do you know Ian Jansen?"

Ian, wide-eyed, jumped up and shook my father's hand. Clearly, he hadn't expected a parental meeting so soon. "It's a pleasure to meet you, sir."

My father nodded gravely and looked back and forth between the two of us. Whatever surprise he'd had at seeing me here had just been trumped by me being here with a date. Glancing at Ian, I tried to guess how he'd appear to someone like my dad. Clean cut, respectful, an Alchemist. The fact that Ian tended to bore me was irrelevant. I doubted my father had ever thought much about me dating, but if so, he probably hadn't thought I'd get a catch like this.

"Would you like to join us, sir?" asked Ian. I had to give him credit; he'd overcome his initial shock and was now in proper suitor mode. "It would be an honor."

At first, I thought Ian was just laying it on thick. Then I

realized meeting my father might actually very well be an honor. Jared Sage wasn't a rock star, but he did have a reputation among the Alchemists that, by their standards, was outstanding. My father seemed to like the flattery and agreed. He took a seat beside Ian.

"Sit by your sister," he told Zoe, nodding in my direction.

Zoe obeyed and stared straight ahead. She was nervous too, I realized. Looking her over, I felt an ache from how much I'd missed her. We'd inherited the same brown eyes from our father, but she'd gotten Mom's brown hair, which made me a little jealous. Zoe also looked a lot more put together than the last time I'd seen her. She wore a pretty dark brown cashmere dress and didn't have a single hair out of place. Something about her appearance bothered me, and I couldn't quite put my finger on it at first. It soon hit me. She looked older. She looked like a young lady, like my peer. I supposed it was silly of me to feel sad, since she was fifteen, but I kind of wished she could stay a little kid forever.

"Zoe." I kept my voice low, not that I needed to worry about the men overhearing. My dad was interrogating Ian. "I've been wanting to talk to you for so long."

She nodded. "I know. Mom tells me each time you call." But there was no apology for dodging my calls.

"I'm sorry about the way we left things. I never meant to hurt you or one-up you. I thought I was doing you a favor, saving you from getting involved."

Her mouth tightened, and something hard flashed in her eyes. "I don't mind being involved. I *want* to be involved, you know. And it would've been great! Being in the field at fifteen. I could have a stellar career. Dad would be so proud."

I chose my next words very carefully so that she wouldn't

take offense. "Yeah, but another year with Dad will really be, um, stellar. He's got so much experience—and you want to get as much as you can, believe me. Even if you have to wait for an assignment at sixteen, you'll still be ahead of the rest of us."

Each word out of my mouth made me feel sick, but Zoe seemed to buy it. I wasn't bothered by her wanting to be part of the cause—but it killed me that she was clearly doing it to impress our dad. "I suppose. And I *am* learning a lot. I wish I could at least get some field experience—even if it's not my own post. It's all theory with Dad. I've never even seen a Moroi."

"I'm sure he'll fix that." I didn't like encouraging this, but at least she was speaking to me.

The lights dimmed, ending our conversation. Organ music filled the room, and the scent of frankincense drifted around us. Incense and resin were common components in magic, and my mind was instantly starting to make associations from the spell books I'd painstakingly copied. *Frankincense is used to heal burns. It can also be used when casting divining or purifying spells—*

I immediately stopped that train of thought. Even if I was keeping it to myself, thinking about magic in the middle of an Alchemist church service was pretty sacrilegious. I shifted uncomfortably, wondering what all these people would think if they knew the truth about me: that I practiced magic and had kissed a vampire. . . .

Alchemist priests were called hierophants. They performed blessings and offered moral advice, when needed. In day-to-day affairs, they wore suits, but for this occasion, the lead hierophant wore robes that reminded me uncomfortably of the robes some of the Warriors had donned. It was yet another reminder of our shared history—and maybe our shared future. Marcus had been right. This was a mystery I had to solve, regardless of where I stood on breaking the tattoo.

I'd attended services like this off and on throughout my life and knew the Latin prayers by heart. I chanted along with the rest of the congregation and listened avidly as the hierophant reaffirmed our goals, his voice echoing through the sound system. Even though the Alchemists' religion had loose connections to Christianity, there was very little mention of God or Jesus or even Christmas. Most of his sermon was about how we had to help protect humanity from the temptation of following Strigoi who offered unholy immortality. That warning, at least, wasn't exaggerated.

I'd heard stories and even seen for myself what happened when humans decided to serve Strigoi. Those Strigoi promised to turn their servants as a reward. Those humans helped Strigoi spread their evil and became monsters themselves, no turning needed. Keeping those dark vampires hidden was for the good of weak humans who couldn't protect themselves. I paid especially close attention when the hierophant mentioned the Moroi offhandedly in his sermon, as a means to an end in defeating the Strigoi. He didn't exactly inspire warm and fuzzy feelings about them, but at least he wasn't calling for Moroi and dhampir destruction either.

I agreed with a good part of the message, but it no longer filled me with the fire it once had. And when the hierophant started droning on and on about duty, obedience, and what was "natural," I really began feeling disconnected. I almost wished there was more talk of the divine, like you'd find at a normal church service. With everything going on in my life, I wouldn't have minded a connection to a higher power. Sometimes, when I listened to the hierophant, I wondered if everything he was saying had just been made up by a bunch of people sitting around in the Middle Ages. No holy mandate required.

I felt like a traitor when the service ended. Maybe Adrian's joke had been right: I didn't even need Marcus to break my tattoo and connection to the group. Glancing at my companions—and even the other Alchemists in the room—it was clear I was alone. All of them looked captivated by the sermon, devoted to the cause.

I was again eerily reminded of the Warriors and their fanatical devotion. *No, no, whatever else the Alchemists are guilty of, we have nothing to do with that kind of unhinged behavior.* And yet . . . it was more complicated than that, I realized. The Alchemists didn't shoot first and ask questions later or make our members battle each other. We were civilized and logical, but we did have a tendency to just do what we were told. That was the similarity, one that could be dangerous.

Zoe and my father walked out with Ian and me. "Isn't it amazing?" she asked. "Hearing that . . . well, it just makes me so glad Dad decided to raise another Alchemist in the family. It's good to boost our numbers."

Had that truly been his motivation? Or was it because he didn't trust me after I'd helped Rose?

It was infuriating that the only conversation I could have with Zoe centered around Alchemist rhetoric, but I'd take it over the silence of the last few months. In my heart, I longed to talk the way we used to. I wanted it back. Even though she'd warmed up a little, that old familiarity that had once existed between us was gone.

"I wish we had more time," I told her once our groups were ready to part in the parking lot. "There's so much I want to talk to you about."

She smiled, and there was a genuineness in it that warmed me. Maybe the distance between us wasn't irreparable. "Me too. I'm sorry about . . . well, the way things were. I hope we get some time together soon. I . . . I've missed you."

That nearly broke me down, as did her hug. "We'll be together soon, I promise."

Ian—whom my father now seemed to regard as a future son-in-law—drove me back to my hotel and couldn't stop gushing about how awesome it had been to meet Jared Sage. As for me, I could still feel where Zoe had hugged me.

Ian promised he'd get in touch with me in the morning about a tour of the archives. Then, weirdly, he closed his eyes and leaned forward. It took me a moment to realize that he expected a good-night kiss. Seriously? That was how he went about it? Had he ever even kissed anyone before? Even Brayden had displayed a little more passion. And, of course, neither guy measured up to Adrian.

When I did nothing, Ian finally opened his eyes. I gave him another hug—with the coat on—and told him how happy I was that he'd met my dad. That seemed to satisfy him.

Adrian made his nightly check-in with me once I was asleep later on. Naturally, he wanted to know about my dress. He also kept trying to find out how exactly I'd won Ian over and seemed amused at the few details I decided to give him. But mostly I couldn't stop talking about Zoe. Adrian soon gave up on the other topics and simply listened to me gush.

"She spoke to me, Adrian!" I paced around the reception hall, clasping my hands in excitement. "And she wasn't mad. By the end, she was happy to see me. Do you know what that's like? I mean, I know you don't have any brothers or sisters, but to have someone you haven't seen in a while welcome you back?"

"I don't know what it's like," he said quietly. "But I can imagine."

I was too caught up in my own joy at the time, but later, I wondered if he was talking about his incarcerated mother.

"It's nice to see you so happy," he added. "Not that you've been miserable lately, but you've had a lot to worry about."

I couldn't help but laugh at that and came to a halt. "Are you saying evil witches and espionage are stressful?"

"Nah." He walked over to me. "All in a day's work for us. But I'm going to make my way to bed now. You seem like you can get by without me tonight."

He'd visited me every night since Veronica's dream. Most of the trips were short now, but I still knew it was a lot of effort and spirit for him. "Thank you. I feel like I can't say that to you enough."

"You don't have to say it at all, Sage. Good luck tomorrow."

Right. Stealing top secret info from a highly secure facility.

"Thanks," I said again. A little of my mood dimmed, but not all of it. "No matter what happens, though, patching things up with Zoe makes me feel like this mission is already a success."

"That's because you haven't been caught." He cupped my face in his hands and leaned close. "See that you aren't. I don't want to have to dream visit you in prison . . . or wherever it is bad Alchemists go."

"Hey, at least I'd have you for company, right?"

He gave me a rueful headshake, and the dream vanished around me.

CHAPTER 20

IAN WOKE ME THE NEXT MORNING with a super-early phone call. At first, I thought maybe he hoped to sneak in before the other Alchemists woke up, but it turned out he just wanted to get breakfast beforehand. Seeing as he'd managed to get me access, I couldn't very well refuse. He'd originally wanted to go to the facility in the late morning, but I talked him into going closer to noon. It meant lingering longer over breakfast, but it was worth the sacrifice. However, I was strictly back to khakis and a linen top. Espionage aside, cocktail dresses and breakfast buffets just didn't mix. As a concession, however, I unbuttoned *two* buttons at the top of my shirt. Openly wearing that into the facility was practically R-rated, and Ian seemed thrilled by the "scandalous" act.

Sunday at the facility was much quieter than the previous night. Although Alchemists never really got a break from their duties, most of the center worked normal weekday business hours. I had no difficulties checking in through the main reception again, but as predicted, we had a small delay in getting to the secure area. The guy on duty wasn't the friend who owed Ian a favor. We had to wait for him to come out from the back room, and even then, it took Ian a bit of cajoling to convince his colleague to let me in. I think it was obvious to both of them that Ian was just trying to impress me, and finally, the first guy relented to what seemed like a harmless errand. After all, I was a fellow Alchemist, and I was only going on a tour of a library. What could possibly go wrong?

They searched my purse and made me walk through a metal detector. I had two spells in mind that I could perform without physical components, so at least I didn't have to explain any crystals or herbs. The trickiest part was a thumb drive I'd hidden in my bra. They might not have questioned me carrying one in my purse, but I hadn't wanted to risk it being called out. That being said, if the thumb drive did show up on the scan, I was going to have a much more difficult time explaining why I was hiding it. I tensed as I stepped under the scanner, bracing myself to either run or attempt a Wolfe move. But, as hoped, it was too small to find, and we were waved through. That was one obstacle down, though it didn't make me any less tense.

"Did you end up trading this for the money he owed you?" I asked once Ian and I were descending toward the archives.

"Yeah." He made a face. "I tried to just swap it out for half of what he owed, but it was all or nothing for him."

"So how much is this trip costing you?"

"Fifty dollars. It's worth it, though," he added quickly.

Dinner had cost about the same. This was turning into an expensive weekend for Ian, particularly since I was the only one truly reaping the rewards. I couldn't help but feel a bit guilty and had to remind myself again and again that this was for an important cause. I would've offered to pay him back for it all, but something told me that would counteract everything I'd been working to achieve with my "womanly charms."

The archives were sealed with electronic locks that opened when Ian scanned his card key. As we stepped inside, I nearly forgot that coming in here was just a cover for the larger plan. Books and books and books surrounded me as well as scrolls and documents written on parchment. Old and delicate items were sealed under glass, with notes and signs against a far wall on how to access digital copies of them on computers. A couple of Alchemists, young like us, worked at tables and were transcribing old books into their laptops. One of them looked excited about her job; the other guy looked bored. He seemed to welcome the distraction of us entering.

I must have worn an appropriately awed expression because when I turned to Ian, he was watching me with pride. "Pretty cool, huh?" Apparently being a glorified librarian had just become a much more exciting job for him. "Follow me."

He didn't have to tell me twice. We began by exploring the full extent of the archives room, which stretched back much farther than I initially realized. The Alchemists prized knowledge, and it was obvious from this collection, which dated back centuries. I lingered at the shelves, wanting to read every title. They came in different languages and covered a full range of topics useful to our trade: chemistry, history, mythology, the supernatural . . . it was dizzying.

"How do you organize it?" I asked. "How can you find anything?"

Ian pointed to small placards on the shelves that I hadn't

noticed. They bore alphanumeric codes that were part of no filing system I recognized. "These catalog it all. And here's the directory."

He led me to a touch screen panel embedded in the wall. I pressed it and was presented with a menu of options: AUTHOR, TIME PERIOD, SUBJECT, LANGUAGE. I touched SUBJECT and was led through a series of more and more specific topics until I finally realized I'd been searching for "Magic" in the supernatural section. It gave me a list of titles, each with its own code in the organizational system.

To my surprise, there were actually a number of books on magic, and I burned with curiosity. Did the Alchemists have records of witches? Or was it all speculation? Most likely these were moral books preaching the wrongness of humans even considering such feats.

"Can I browse some of the books?" I asked him. "I mean, I know I can't sit and read all afternoon, but there's so much history . . . I just kind of want to be a part of it. I'd be so, so grateful."

I really didn't think that would work twice, but it did.

"Okay." He pointed toward a small office in the back. "I need to catch up on a few things. Do you want to meet back here in an hour?"

I thanked him profusely and then returned to the touch screen. I yearned to investigate the magic books but had to remind myself why I was here. As long as I was in the archives, I might as well do some research that would help our cause. I flipped through the menus until I located the section on the Alchemists' early history. I'd hoped to find a reference to vampire hunters in general or the Warriors specifically. No luck.

The best I could do was follow the codes to shelves and shelves detailing our group's formation. Most of the books were dense and written in an antiquated style. The really old ones weren't even in English.

I skimmed a few and soon realized a task like this would take longer than an hour. The newer books had no mention of the Warriors, which didn't surprise me, seeing as that information was now covered up. If I was going to locate any references to vampire hunters, it would be in the oldest books. They didn't have much in the way of tables of contents or indices, and there was no way I could do a full read. Remembering my real mission here, I put the books away after about ten minutes and sought out Ian. That earlier tension returned, and I began to sweat.

"Hey, is there a restroom in here?"

I prayed there wasn't. I'd seen one down the hall when we'd come to this level. Part of my plan depended on getting out of the archives.

"Down the hall, by the stairs," he said. Some work issue had required his attention, and if my luck held, it would keep his eyes off the clock. "Knock on the door when you get back. I'll tell the scribes to let you in."

I'd had a knot of anxiety in my stomach all day that I'd been trying to ignore. Now there was no getting around it. It was time for the unthinkable.

Subtlety had no role in Alchemist security. The hallway contained cameras at each end. They faced each other, providing a long, continuous shot of the corridor. The restrooms were located at one end of the hall, almost directly under a camera. I went inside the ladies' room and verified there were no other people—or cameras—within. At least the Alchemists allowed some privacy.

Casting the invisibility spell was easy. Getting out was a little more difficult. The cameras' position made me think the restroom door was too flush with the wall for either camera to really get a good look at it. The door opened inward, so I was able to slip out and feel confident no camera had picked up a ghostly door opening. The door to the stairs was the real beast. It was in the range of one of the cameras. Ms. Terwilliger had told me the invisibility spell would protect me from video and film. So, I had no fear of being spotted. I simply had to take the risk of the camera recording the door opening by itself.

Although I knew security guards watched live feeds of the cameras, there were too many for them to scrutinize every second. If no sudden movement appeared on this one, I doubted any guard would notice. And if things stayed tame on this level, no one would have any reason to review the footage. But the operations level . . . well, if everything went according to plan, this sleepy Sunday was about to get a lot more exciting there.

I slipped in and out of the stairwell, opening the door with absolutely as little space as possible. The operations level was even more secure than the archives, with heavy, industrial-looking doors that required both key cards and codes. I had no illusions about cracking any of it. Entry into the security office, much like the rest of this task, relied on an odd mix of logic and luck. The one thing you could count on with Alchemists was reliability. I knew how schedules tended to work. Lunch breaks were taken on the hour at typical lunch times: eleven, twelve, and one. This was why I'd asked Ian to schedule our visit to this time, when I could be relatively certain workers would be moving in and out of the room. Noon was five minutes away, and I crossed my fingers someone would exit soon.

As it turned out, someone entered. A man came whistling down the hall. When he reached the door, the smell of fast-food hamburgers gave away his lunch choice. I held my breath as he scanned his card and punched in the numbers. The lock clicked, and he pushed the door open. I scurried in behind him and cleared the door without having to catch it or open it farther. Unfortunately, he came to a halt sooner than I expected, and I brushed against him. I immediately shrank away, and he scanned around, startled.

Please don't think there's an invisible person here. How terrible would that be to have made it this far, only to be detected now? Fortunately, magical subterfuge wasn't the first thing Alchemists turned to as a reason for anything. After a few more puzzled moments, he shrugged and called a greeting to one of his coworkers.

Wade had described the room perfectly. Monitors covered one wall, flipping back and forth between different camera views. A couple of guards kept an eye on the footage, while others worked away at computers. Wade had also told me which workstation contained the files I needed. I approached it—careful to avoid any other contact mishaps. A woman was already seated at the station.

"I was thinking of Thai carryout," she told one of her coworkers. "I've just got to finish this report."

No! She was about to take her lunch break. For my plan to work, that couldn't happen. If she left, she would lock her computer. I needed it accessible for this plan to work. She was running late on her lunch, which meant I had to act now.

This room wasn't exempt from surveillance. Even the watchers had watchers. Fortunately, there was only one camera. I selected an empty computer with a screen facing the camera and stood behind it. Wires and cords snaked out of the computer's panel, and the fans whirred steadily inside. I rested my hand on the panel and did one more quick assessment. The computer's back was out of the camera's view, but it would do no good if it was in the middle of someone else's line of vision. Everyone seemed preoccupied, though. It was time to act.

I created a fireball—a small one. I kept it in the palm of my hand and rested it right next to the panel. Despite its size, I summoned as much heat as I could. Not quite blue, but getting there. It took effect quickly, and within seconds, the cords and panel began to melt. The scent of burnt plastic rolled over me, and smoke drifted upward. It was enough. I let the fireball fade, and then I sprinted away from the computer just in time. Everyone had now noticed the burning computer. An alarm went off. There were cries of surprise, and someone yelled for a fire extinguisher. They all rose from their chairs to hurry over and look—including the woman who'd been at the computer I needed.

There was no time to waste. I sat immediately in her chair and plugged in the thumb drive. With gloved hands, I grabbed hold of the mouse and began clicking through directories. Wade hadn't been able to help much at this point. We'd just hoped finding the files would be intuitive. All the while, I was conscious of the time—and that someone might notice a mouse moving by itself. Even after they put out the fire, the Alchemists hovered around the smoking computer, trying to figure out what had happened. Overheating wasn't uncommon, but a fire happening that quickly definitely was. And these were computers that contained highly sensitive information.

I felt like there were a million directories. I checked a few likely candidates, only to hit a dead end. Each time I hit a dead end, I would silently swear at the wasted time. The other Alchemists weren't going to stay away forever! Finally, after more stressful searching, I found a directory of old surveillance footage. It contained folders linked to every camera in the building—including one marked MAIN CHECKPOINT. I clicked it open and found files named by date. Wade had told me that eventually these files were cleared and moved to archives, but the day I needed was still here. The cameras recorded one frame every second. Multiplied by twenty-four hours, that made for a huge file—but not nearly the size continuous filming would create. The file would fit on my thumb drive, and I began copying it over.

The connection was fast, but it was still a big transfer. The screen told me it had ten seconds to go. *Ten seconds.* The computer's owner could be back by then. I allowed myself another peek at the Alchemists. They were all still puzzling out the mystery. The thing about scientists like us was that a technological failure like this was fascinating. Also, it never occurred to any of them to look for a supernatural explanation. They tossed around theories with each other and started to take the melted computer apart. My file finished copying, and I sprang out of the chair, just as the woman began walking back toward it. I'd been fully prepared to risk another "ghost door" while they were distracted, but the fire alarm had summoned others in the hallway. People moved in and out with such frequency that I had no trouble holding the door open just long enough for me to sneak through.

I practically ran back to the archives level and had to calm myself when I reentered the restroom. I uncast the invisibility spell and waited for my breathing to slow. The thumb drive was back in my bra, the gloves back in my purse. Studying myself in the mirror, I decided that I looked innocent enough to return to the archives.

One of the scribes let me in. It was the engrossed girl, and she gave me a look that said opening the door was a waste of her time. Ian still appeared to be engulfed with work in the back, which was a relief. I'd been gone far longer than a bathroom trip would require and had worried he'd wonder where I was at. Things could've gone badly if he'd sent the girl to find me, both because I wasn't in the restroom and because she'd be *really* annoyed at the interruption. Over in the history section, I sat on the floor with a book picked at random, which I only pretended to read. I was too anxious and keyed up to parse the words, no matter how many times I tried to reassure myself. There was no reason for the Alchemists to suspect me of causing the fire. There was no reason for them to think I'd stolen data. There was no reason for them to think I was connected to any of this.

Ian found me when the hour was up, and I feigned disappointment at having to leave. In reality, I couldn't get out of this building fast enough. He drove me to the airport and chattered nonstop about the next time we'd get to see each other. I smiled and nodded appropriately but reminded him our work had to come first and that my post was particularly consuming. He was obviously disappointed but couldn't deny the logic. The Alchemist greater good came first. Even better, he didn't try one of those awful kisses again—though he did suggest we set up some times for video chatting. I told him to email me, secretly vowing I'd never open up any message from him.

I didn't relax until the plane took off, when the potential for an Alchemist raid seemed pretty low. The most paranoid part of me worried there could be a party waiting for me at the Palm Springs airport, but for now I had a few hours of peace.

I'd just assumed I'd deliver the drive to Marcus and leave it at that. But now, with it in my possession, my curiosity got the better of me. I had to get to the bottom of this mystery. Was the Z. J. who'd visited the Alchemists really Master Jameson?

With fresh coffee in hand, I opened the file on my laptop and began to watch.

Even with one frame per second, the footage went on forever. Most of it was nothing but a quiet checkpoint, with the most exciting parts being when the guards changed position or took breaks. Plenty of Alchemists passed in and out, but relative to the overall time span, they were few and far between. Ian actually showed up once, off to start his shift.

I wasn't even halfway through when the plane began its descent. Disheartened, I resigned myself to an evening of more of the same when I got back to the dorm. At least I'd be able to make some decent coffee to get me through. I was almost tempted just to push the file off on Marcus tomorrow and let him deal with reviewing it . . . but that nagging voice urging me to find out for myself won. It wasn't just because of my curiosity either. I didn't really think Marcus would fabricate anything, but if I could see for sure that—

There he was on the screen.

He wasn't in those over-the-top robes, but there was no mistaking Master Jameson's old-fashioned beard. He wore business casual clothing and seemed to be smiling at something a man beside him was saying. The man had a lily on his cheek but was no one I knew.

Master Jameson. With the Alchemists.

Marcus and his Merry Men's conspiracy had panned out. A suspicious part of me wanted to believe this was a setup, that maybe they'd altered and planted this. But, no. I'd taken it myself, off an Alchemist server. It was possible Marcus had more insiders running errands for him, but this hadn't been easy for me, even with magical assistance. Besides, why would Marcus go to so much trouble to make me believe this? If it was some twisted way to get me to join him, there were a million other ways he could have attempted it, with evidence much easier to fake.

Something in my gut told me this was real. I hadn't forgotten the similarities in our rituals or how the Warriors had wanted our groups to merge. Maybe the Alchemists and the Warriors weren't best friends yet, but someone had at least humored Master Jameson with a meeting. The question was, what had happened at that meeting? Had the Alchemist in the footage sent Jameson packing? Were the two of them together right now?

Regardless of the outcome, this was undeniable proof that the Alchemists and Warriors were still in contact. Stanton had told me we merely kept an eye on them and had no interest in hearing them out.

Once again, I had been lied to.

CHAPTER 21

SOME PART OF ME BEGGED FOR there to be a mistake. I watched the footage three more times, tossing crazy theories around in my head. Maybe Master Jameson had a twin who wasn't a fanatic who hated vampires. No. The video didn't lie. Only the Alchemists did.

I couldn't ignore this. I couldn't wait. I needed to resolve this immediately. If not sooner.

I sent Marcus a text as soon as my plane was on the ground: *We meet tonight. No games. No runaround. TONIGHT.*

There was no response from him by the time I got back to my dorm. What was he doing? Reading *Catcher in the Rye* again? If I'd known what dive he was holed up in, I would've marched over there right then. There was nothing I could do but wait, so I called Ms. Terwilliger both as a distraction and to buy some freedom.

"Nothing to report," she told me when she answered. "We're

still just watching and waiting—although, your extra charm is almost complete."

"That's not why I'm calling," I said. "I need you to get me a curfew extension tonight." I felt bad using her for something totally unrelated, but I had to do this.

"Oh? Are you paying me an unexpected visit?"

"Er—no. This is for something else."

She clearly thought that was funny. "Now you use my assistance for personal matters?"

"Don't you think I've earned it?" I countered.

She laughed, something I hadn't heard from her in a while. She agreed to my request and promised to call the dorm's front desk right away. As soon as we hung up, my phone chimed with the expected message from Marcus. All the text contained was an address that was a half hour away. Assuming he was ready for me now, I grabbed my messenger bag and got on the road.

In light of my past meetings with Marcus, I wouldn't have been surprised if he'd led me to a department store or karaoke bar. Instead, I arrived at a vintage music shop, the kind that sold vinyl records. A large CLOSED sign hung on the door, emphasized by dark windows and an empty parking lot. I got out of my car and double-checked the address, wondering if my GPS had led me astray. My earlier zeal gave way to nervousness. How careless was this? One of Wolfe's first lessons was to avoid sketchy situations, yet here I was, exposing myself.

Then, from the shadows, I heard my name whispered. I turned toward the sound and saw Sabrina materialize out of the darkness, carrying a gun as usual. Maybe if I showed her the one in my glove compartment, we could have a bonding moment.

"Go around back," she said. "Knock on the door." Without another word, she returned to the shadows.

The back of the building looked like the kind of place that screamed mugging, and I wondered if Sabrina would come to my aid if needed. I knocked on the door, half expecting some kind of speakeasy situation where I'd be asked for a password like "rusted iguana." Instead, Marcus opened the door, ready with one of those smiles he kept hoping would win me over. Strangely, tonight it put me at ease.

"Hey, gorgeous, come on in."

I stepped past him and found we were in the store's back room, which was filled with tables, shelves, and boxes of records and cassette tapes. Wade and Amelia stood against a wall in mirrored stances, their arms crossed over their chests.

Marcus shut the door behind me and locked it. "Glad to see you back in one piece. Judging from your text—and your face—you found something."

All the rage I'd been holding in since my discovery came bursting out. I retrieved my laptop from my bag and had to resist the urge to slam it against a table. "Yes! I can't believe it. You were right. Your insane, far-fetched theory was right. The Alchemists have been lying! Or, well, some of them. I don't know. Half of them don't know what the other half's doing."

I expected some smug remark from Marcus or at least an "I told you so." But that handsome face was drawn and sad, reminding me of the picture I'd seen of him and Clarence. "Damn," he said softly. "I was kind of hoping you'd come back with a bunch of boring video. Amelia, go swap with Sabrina. I want her to see this."

Amelia looked disappointed to be sent away, but she didn't

hesitate to obey his order. By the time Sabrina came back in, I had the video cued up to the correct time. They gathered around me. "Ready?" I asked. They nodded, and I could see a mix of emotions in all of them. Here it was, the conspiracy theory they'd all been waiting to prove. At the same time, the implications were staggering, and the three of them were well aware of how dangerous what they were about to see could be.

I played the video. It was only a few seconds long, but they were powerful ones as that bearded figure appeared on the screen. I heard an intake of breath from Sabrina.

"It's him. Master Jameson." She looked between all our faces. "That's really the Alchemist place? He's really there?"

"Yes," said Wade. "And that's Dale Hawthorne with him, one of the directors."

That triggered a memory. "I know that name. He's one of Stanton's peers, right?"

"Pretty much."

"Is it possible she wouldn't know about a visit like this?" I asked. "Even at her level?"

It was Marcus who answered. "Maybe. Although, walking him right in there—even to the secure level—is pretty ballsy. Even if she doesn't know about the meeting, it's a safe bet others do. If it were completely shady, Hawthorne would've met him off-site. Of course, the secure list means this wasn't out in the open either."

So, it was possible Stanton hadn't lied to me—well, at least not about the Alchemists being in contact with the Warriors. She'd certainly lied about the Alchemists knowing about Marcus since he'd said he was a notorious figure to most higher-ups. Even if she was ignorant about Master Jameson, it didn't change the fact that other Alchemists—important ones—were keeping some dangerous company. Maybe I didn't always like their procedures, but I'd desperately wanted to believe they were doing good in the world. Maybe they were. Maybe they weren't. I just didn't know anymore.

When I dragged my eyes from the frozen frame of Master Jameson, I found Marcus watching me. "Are you ready?" he asked.

"Ready for what?"

He walked over to another table and returned with a small case. When he opened it, I saw a small vial of silver liquid and a syringe.

"What is—oh." Realization hit me. "That's the blood that'll break the tattoo."

He nodded. "Pulling the elements out creates a reaction that turns it silver. It takes a few years, but eventually, the gold in your skin will fade to silver too."

All of them were looking at me expectantly, and I took a step back. "I don't know if I'm ready for this."

"Why wait?" asked Marcus. He pointed at the laptop. "You've seen this. You know what they're capable of. Can you keep lying to yourself? Don't you want to go forward with your eyes open?"

"Well . . . yes, but I don't know if I'm ready to have some strange substance injected into me."

Marcus filled the syringe with the silver liquid. "I can demonstrate on my tattoo if it'll make you feel better. It won't hurt me, and you can see that there aren't any dire side effects."

"We don't know for sure that they've done anything to me," I protested. He had a logical argument, but I was still terrified of taking this step. I could feel my hands shaking. "This could be a waste. There may be no group loyalty compulsion in me."

"But you also don't know for sure," he countered. "And there's always a *little* loyalty put in the initial tattoo. I mean, not enough to make you some slave robot, but still. Wouldn't you feel better knowing everything's gone?"

I couldn't take my eyes off the needle. "Will I feel any different?"

"No. Although you could walk up to someone on the street and start telling them about vampires." I couldn't tell if he was joking or not. "Then you'd just get thrown into a psych ward."

Was I ready for this? Was I really going to take the next step into becoming part of Marcus's Merry Men? I'd passed his test—which he'd been right about. Clearly, this group wasn't useless. They had eyes on the Alchemists and the Warriors. They also seemingly had the Moroi's best interests at heart.

The Moroi—or, more specifically, Jill. I hadn't forgotten Sabrina's offhand remark about the Warriors being interested in a missing girl. Who else could it be but Jill? And did this Hawthorne guy have access to her location? Had he passed it on to Master Jameson? And would this information put those around her at risk, like Adrian?

They were questions I didn't have the answers to, but I had to uncover them.

"Okay," I said. "Do it."

Marcus didn't waste any time. I think he was afraid I'd change my mind—which, perhaps, was not an unfounded fear. I sat down in one of the chairs and tipped my head to the side so that he'd have access to my cheek. Wade gently held my head with his hands. "Just to make sure you stay still," he told me apologetically.

Before Marcus started, I asked, "Where'd you learn to do this?"

His face had been solemn with the task ahead, but my question made him smile again. "I'm not technically tattooing you, if that's what you're worried about," he said. I was actually worried about *a lot* of things. "These are just some small injections, just like being re-inked."

"What about the process itself? How'd you find out about it?" It was probably a question I should have asked before I sat down in this chair. But I hadn't expected to be doing this so soon—or suddenly.

"A Moroi friend of mine theorized about it. I volunteered to be a guinea pig, and it worked." He switched to business mode again and held up the needle. "Ready?"

I took a deep breath, feeling like I was standing on the edge of a precipice.

Time to jump.

"Go ahead."

It hurt about as much as re-inking did, just a number of small pricks on my skin. Uncomfortable, but not really painful. In truth, it wasn't a long process, but it felt like it took forever. All the while, I kept asking myself, *What are you doing? What are you doing?* At last, Marcus stepped back and regarded me with shining eyes. Sabrina and Wade smiled too.

"There you go," Marcus said. "Welcome to the ranks, Sydney."

I took my compact out of my purse to check the tattoo. My skin was pink from the needle's piercing, but if this process continued to be like re-inking, that irritation would fade soon.

Otherwise, the lily looked unchanged.

I also didn't feel that changed on the inside. I didn't want to storm the Alchemist facility and demand justice or anything like that. Taking him up on his dare to tell an outsider about vampires was probably my best bet to see if my tattoo had been altered, but I didn't really feel like doing that either.

"That's it?" I asked.

"That's it," Marcus said. "Once we get it sealed, you won't have to worry about—"

"I'm not getting it sealed."

All those smiles vanished.

Marcus looked confused, as though he might have misheard. "You have to. We're going to Mexico next weekend. Once that's done, the Alchemists won't ever be able to get to you again."

"I'm not getting it sealed," I repeated. "And I'm not going to Mexico." I gestured toward my laptop. "Look what I was able to pull off! If I stay where I'm at, I can keep finding out more. I can find out what else the Alchemists and Warriors are doing together." *I can find out if Jill is in danger.* "Getting permanently marked and becoming an outcast kills all those opportunities for me. There's no going back after that."

I think Marcus almost always got his way, and this new development totally threw him off. Wade took up the argument. "There's no going back *now*. You're leaving a trail of bread crumbs. Look at what you've done. You already made inquiries about Marcus. Even if you haven't gotten super-friendly with the Moroi, the Alchemists still know you spend a lot of time with them. And one day, someone may realize you were there when the data was stolen."

"No one knows it was stolen," I said promptly.

"You hope they don't," corrected Wade. "These little things are enough to raise red flags. Keep doing more, and you'll make it worse. They'll finally notice you, and that's when it'll be over."

Marcus had recovered from his initial shock. "Exactly. Look, if you want to stay where you're at until we go to Mexico, that's fine. Make your peace with it or whatever. After that, you need to escape. We'll keep working from the outside."

"You can do whatever you want." I began packing up my laptop. "I'm going to work from the inside."

Marcus caught hold of my arm. "You're setting yourself up for a fall, Sydney!" he said sternly. "You're going to get caught."

I pulled away from him. "I'll be careful."

"Everyone makes mistakes," said Sabrina, speaking up for the first time in a while.

"I'll take that risk." I slung my bag over my shoulder. "Unless you guys are going to forcibly stop me?" None of them answered. "Then I'm going. I'm not afraid of the Alchemists. Thank you for everything you've done. I really do appreciate it."

"Thank you," said Marcus at last. He shook his head at Wade, who looked like he wanted to protest. "For getting the data. I honestly didn't think you'd be able to pull it off. I figured you'd return empty-handed, though I still would've broken the tattoo for you. A for effort, you know. Instead, you just proved what I'd thought before: you're remarkable. We could really use you."

"Well, you know how to get in touch with me."

"And you know how to get in touch with us," he said. "We'll be here all week if you change your mind."

I opened the door. "I won't. I'm not running away."

Amelia called goodbye to me when I got into my car, oblivious to the fact that I'd just defied her beloved leader. As I drove back to Amberwood, I was amazed at how free I felt—and it had nothing to do with the tattoo. It was the knowledge that I had defied everyone—the Alchemists, the Warriors, the Merry Men. I didn't answer to anyone, no matter the cause. I was my own person, able to take my own actions. It wasn't something I had a lot of experience with.

And I was about to do something drastic. I hadn't told Marcus and the gang because I'd been afraid they really would stop me. When I got back to Amberwood, I went straight to my room and dialed Stanton. She answered on the first ring, which I took as a divine sign that I was doing the right thing.

"Miss Sage, this is unexpected. Did you enjoy the services?"

"Yes," I said. "They were very enlightening. But that's not why I'm calling. We have a situation. The Warriors of Light are looking for Jill." I wasn't going to waste any time.

"Why on earth would they do that?" She sounded legitimately surprised, but if there was one thing in all of this that I believed wholeheartedly, it was that the Alchemists were exceptional liars.

"Because they know if Jill's whereabouts got out, it could throw the Moroi into chaos. Their focus is still on the Strigoi, but they wouldn't mind seeing thing go bad for the Moroi."

"I see." I always wondered if she paused to gather her thoughts or if it was simply for effect. "And how exactly did you learn this?"

"That guy I know who used to be with the Warriors. We're still friendly, and he's been having doubts about them. He mentioned hearing them talk about finding a missing girl that could cause all sorts of trouble." Maybe it was wrong to drag Trey into this lie, but I seriously doubted Stanton would interrogate him anytime soon.

"And you assume this is Miss Dragomir?"

"Come on," I exclaimed. "Who else would it be? Do you know any other Moroi girls? Of course it's her!"

"Calm down, Miss Sage." Her voice was flat and untroubled. "There's no need for theatrics."

"There's a need for action! If they might be on to her, then we need to get out of Palm Springs immediately."

"That," she said crisply, "is not an option. A lot of planning went into getting her to her current location."

I didn't believe that argument for a second. Half our job was doing damage control and adapting to rapidly changing situations. "Yeah? Well, did you also plan on those psycho vampire hunters finding her?"

Stanton ignored the jab. "Do you have any evidence at all that the Warriors actually have concrete data about her? Did your friend supply you with details?"

"No," I admitted. "But we still need to do something."

"There's no 'we' here." Her voice had gone from flat to icy. "*You* do not decide what we do."

I nearly protested and then caught myself. Horror set in. What had I just done? My initial intent had been to either get Stanton to take legitimate action or else find out if she might accidentally reveal knowledge of a Warrior connection. I'd thought mentioning Trey would give me valid backup since I could hardly tell her the real reason I feared for Jill. Yet, somehow, I'd gone from a request to a demand. I'd practically yelled an order at her. That wasn't typical Sydney behavior. That wasn't typical Alchemist behavior. What had Wade said? *You're leaving a trail of bread crumbs.*

Was this because I'd broken the tattoo?

This was no crumb. This was a full loaf. I was on the verge of insubordination, and my mind could suddenly imagine that list Marcus kept warning about, the one that kept track of every suspicious thing I did. Was Stanton already updating that list right now?

I had to fix this, but how? How on earth did I take this back? My mind was racing frantically, and it took several moments for me to calm down and start thinking logically. The mission. Focus on the mission. Stanton would understand that.

"I'm sorry, ma'am," I said at last. *Be calm. Be deferential.* "I'm just . . . I'm just so worried about this mission. I saw my dad at the services, you know." That would be a fact she could check on. "You had to have seen how it was that night I left. How bad things are between us. I . . . I have to make him proud. If things fall apart here, he'll never forgive me."

She didn't respond, so I prayed that meant she was listening intently . . . and believing me.

"I want to do a good job here. I want to fulfill our goals and keep Jill hidden. But there have already been so many complications no one predicted—first Keith and then the Warriors. I just never feel like she's fully safe now, even with Eddie and Angeline. It eats at me. And—" I was no actress who could muster tears, but I did my best to make my voice crack. "And *I* never feel safe. I told you, when I asked to go to the services, how overwhelming it is with the Moroi. They're everywhere—and the dhampirs too. I eat with them. I'm in class with them. Being with other Alchemists this last weekend was a lifesaver. I mean, I'm not trying to dodge my duties, ma'am. I understand we have to make sacrifices. And I've gotten better around them, but sometimes the stress is just unbearable—and then when I heard this thing about the Warriors, I cracked. All I could think about was that I might fail. I'm sorry, ma'am. I shouldn't have flipped out on you. I was out of control, and it was unacceptable."

I cut off my rant and tensed as I waited for her response. Hopefully I'd given her enough to dismiss any thoughts of me being a dissident. Of course, I might have just come off as a totally weak and unstable Alchemist who needed to be pulled from this mission. If that happened . . . well, maybe I'd have to take Marcus up on Mexico.

Her characteristic pause was especially painful this time. "I see," she said. "Well, I'll take this all into consideration. This mission is of the utmost importance, believe me. My earlier questioning of your information was not some weakening of our resolve. Your concerns have been heard, and I will decide the best course of action."

It wasn't exactly what I wanted, but hopefully she would be true to her word. I really, really wanted to believe she was on the up-and-up. "Thank you, ma'am."

"Is there anything else, Miss Sage?"

"No, ma'am. And . . . and I'm sorry ma'am."

"Your apology is noted."

Click.

I'd paced while I'd talked and now stood staring at the phone. A gut instinct told me I really had driven Stanton to take some sort of action. The mystery was whether that action would prove beneficial or catastrophic for me.

Falling asleep was difficult after that, and it had nothing to do with Veronica for a change. I was too keyed up, too anxious about what had happened with Marcus and Stanton. I tried to seize that feeling of freedom again, using it to strengthen me. It was only a spark this time, flickering with my new uncertainties, but it was better than nothing.

I fell asleep sometime around three. I had a vague sense of a couple hours passing before I was swept into one of Adrian's dreams, back in the reception hall. "Finally," he said. "I almost gave up checking in. I thought you were going to pull an all-nighter." He'd stopped wearing his suit in these dreams, probably because I always showed up in jeans. Tonight he wore jeans also, along with a plain black T-shirt.

"Me too." I wrung my hands and began pacing here as well. The nervous energy from my waking self had carried over into the dream. "A lot of stuff's kind of happened tonight."

The dream felt real, solid. Adrian was sober. "Didn't you just get back? How much could've happened?"

When I told him, he shook his head in amazement. "Man, Sage. It's all or nothing with you. Never a dull moment."

I came to a halt in front of him and leaned against a table. "I know, I know. Do you think I just made a huge mistake? God, maybe Marcus was right, and there was some compulsion forcing me to be loyal in the tattoo. I'm free for one hour and completely go over the edge with my superior."

"It sounds like you covered your tracks," he said, though a small frown appeared on his face. "But I would be disappointed if they sent you somewhere less stressful. That seems like it might be the worst-case scenario from everything you said."

I started laughing, but it was the hysterical kind. "What in the world's happened to me? I was doing crazy stuff way before

Marcus broke the tattoo tonight. Meeting with rebels, chasing evil sorceresses, even buying that dress! Yelling at Stanton is just one more thing on a long list of insanity. It's just like I said at Pies and Stuff: I don't know who I am anymore."

Adrian smiled and clasped my hands, taking a few steps toward me. "Well, first off, *I'm* the expert in insanity, and this is nothing. And as for who you are, you're the same beautiful, brave, and ridiculously smart caffeinated fighter you've been since the day I met you." Finally, he put "beautiful" at the top of his list of adjectives. Not that I should have cared.

"Sweet talker," I scoffed. "You didn't know anything about me the first time we met."

"I knew you were beautiful," he said. "I just hoped for the rest."

He always got this glint in his eyes when he complimented my looks, like he was seeing so much more than just my actual appearance. It was disorienting and heady . . . but I didn't mind. And that wasn't the only thing I suddenly found overwhelming. How had he gotten so close to me without me even realizing it? It was like he had secret stealth abilities. His hands were warm on mine, our fingers locked together. I still had remnants of that earlier joy within me, and being connected to him amplified those feelings. The green of his eyes was as lovely as usual, and I wondered if mine had the same effect on him. There was a little amber mixed with the brown that he had once said looked like gold.

He's the only one who never tells me to do anything, I realized. Oh, sure, he asked me to do lots of things, often with cajoling and fast talking. But he made no demands on me, not like the Alchemists or Marcus. Even Jill and Angeline tended to preface their requests with, "You have to . . ."

"Speaking of that dress," he added, "I still haven't seen it."

I laughed softly. "You couldn't handle it."

He raised an eyebrow at that. "Is that a challenge, Sage? I can handle a lot."

"Not if our history is any indication. Each time I wear some moderately attractive dress, you lose it."

"That's not exactly true," he said. "I lose it no matter what you're wearing. And that red dress was not 'moderately attractive.' It was like a piece of heaven here on earth. A red, silky piece of heaven."

I should've rolled my eyes. I should've told him I wasn't here for his personal entertainment. But there was something in the way he was looking at me and something in the way I felt tonight that made me want to see his reaction. Breaking the tattoo hadn't affected anything between us, but it—and the deeds I'd done this weekend—had left me feeling bold. For the first time, I wanted to take a risk with him, despite my usual set of logical arguments. Besides, there was nothing dangerous in letting him look.

I manipulated the dream the way he'd taught me. A few moments later, the lacy minidress replaced my jeans and blouse. I even summoned the heels, which bumped my height up. I was still nowhere near as tall as him, but the small boost brought our faces closer together.

His eyes widened. Still holding my hands, he took a step back so that he could take in the whole look. There was almost something tangible to the way his gaze swept my body. I could practically feel every place it touched. By the time his eyes reached mine again, my breathing was heavy, and I was acutely aware that there really wasn't that much clothing between the two of us. Maybe there was something dangerous in letting him look after all.

"A piece of heaven?" I managed to ask.

He slowly shook his head. "No. The other place. The one I'm going to burn in for thinking what I'm thinking."

He'd moved toward me again. His hands released mine and moved to my waist, and I noticed I wasn't the only one breathing heavily. He pulled me to him, bringing our bodies together. The world was all heat and electricity, thick with tension that was only one spark away from exploding around us. I was balancing on another precipice, which wasn't easy to do in heels.

I wrapped my arms around his neck, and this time I was the one who drew him closer. "Damn," he murmured.

"What?" I asked, never taking my eyes off his.

He ran his hands over my hips. "I'm not supposed to kiss you."

"It's okay."

"What is?"

"It's okay if I kiss you."

Adrian Ivashkov wasn't easy to surprise, but I surprised him then when I brought his mouth toward mine. I kissed him, and for a moment, he was too stunned to respond. That lasted for, oh, about a second. Then the intensity I'd come to know so well in him returned. He pushed me backward, lifting me so that I sat on the table. The tablecloth bunched up, knocking over some of the glasses. I heard what sounded like a china plate crash against the floor.

Whatever logic and reason I normally possessed had melted away. There was nothing but flesh and fire left, and I wasn't going to lie to myself—at least not tonight. I wanted him. I arched my back, fully aware of how vulnerable that made me and that I was giving him an invitation. He accepted it and laid me back against the table, bringing his body down on top of mine. That crushing kiss of his moved from my mouth to the nape of my neck. He pushed down the edge of my dress and the bra strap underneath, exposing my shoulder and giving his lips more skin to conquer. A glass rolled off and smashed, soon followed by another. Adrian broke off his kissing, and I opened my eyes. He had an exasperated look on his face.

"A table," he said. "A goddamned table."

A few moments later, the table was gone. I was in his apartment, on his bed, and was glad that I no longer had silverware underneath me. With the venue change complete, his lips found mine again. The urgency in the way I responded surprised even me. I never would've thought myself capable of a feeling so primal, so removed from the reason that usually governed my actions. My nails dug into his back, and he trailed his lips down the edge of my chin, down the center of my neck. He kept going until he reached the bottom of the dress's V-neck. I let out a small gasp, and he kissed all around the neckline, just enough to tease.

"Don't worry," he murmured. "The dress stays on."

"Oh? Is that your decision to make?"

"Yes," he said. "You're not losing your virginity in a dream. If that's even possible. I don't want to deal with the philosophical side of it. And besides, there's no need to rush anyway. Sometimes it's worth lingering on the journey for a while before getting to the destination."

Metaphors. This was the cost of making out with an artist.

I nearly said as much. Then his hand slid up my bare leg, and I was lost again. Maybe the dress was staying on, but he didn't mind taking liberties with it. That hand slipped under my dress, running along the side of my leg and up to my hip. I burned where he touched me, and everything within me became focused on that hand. It was moving far too slowly, and I grabbed it, ready to urge it on.

Adrian chuckled and caught hold of my wrist, pulling my hand away and pinning it down against the covers. "Never thought I'd be the one slowing you down."

I opened my eyes and met his. "I'm a quick study."

All that burning and animal need within me must have shone through because he caught his breath and lost the smile. He released my wrist and cupped my face in his hands, bringing his face down only a whisper away from mine. "Good God, Sydney. You are—" The passion in his eyes turned to surprise, and he suddenly looked up.

"What's wrong?" I asked, wondering if this was some weird part of "the journey."

He grimaced and began to fade away before my eyes. "You're being woken up."

CHAPTER 22

I OPENED MY EYES, groggy from the sudden shock of being pulled out of the dream. My body felt sluggish, and I squinted against the light. The lamp I'd left on last night was joined by sunlight streaming in through the window, but my phone's display still showed a freakishly early hour. Someone knocked at my door, and I realized that was what had woken me up. I ran a hand through my disheveled hair and rose unsteadily from the bed.

"If she needs a geography tutor now, I really am going to Mexico," I muttered. But when I opened the door, it wasn't Angeline standing outside my door. It was Jill.

"Something big just happened," she said, hurrying in.

"Not to me it didn't."

If she noticed my annoyance, she didn't show it. In fact, as I studied her more closely, I realized she probably had no idea (yet) about what had happened between Adrian and me. From what I'd learned, spirit dreams weren't shared through the bond unless the shadow-kissed person was directly brought into it.

I sighed and sat down on my bed again, wishing I could go back to sleep. The heat and excitement of the dream was fading, and mostly I felt tired now. "What's wrong?"

"Angeline and Trey."

I groaned. "Oh, lord. What's she done to him now?"

Jill settled into my desk chair and put on a steely look of resolve. Whatever was coming was bad. "She tried to get him to sneak into our dorm last night."

"What?" I really did need more sleep because my brain was having trouble understanding the reasoning behind that. "She's not *that* dedicated to her math grade . . . is she?"

Jill gave me a wry look. "Sydney, they weren't working on math."

"Then why were they—oh. Oh no." I fell backward onto the bed and stared up at the ceiling. "No. This can't be happening."

"I already tried saying that to myself," she told me. "It doesn't help."

I rolled over to my side so that I could look at her again. "Okay, assuming this is true, how long has it been going on?"

"I don't know." Jill sounded as tired as me—and a lot more exasperated. "You know how she is. I tried to get answers out of her, but she kept going on about how it wasn't her fault and how it just happened."

"What'd Trey say?" I asked.

"I never got a chance to talk to him. He got hauled away as soon as they were caught." She smiled, but there wasn't much humor in it. "On the bright side, he got in a lot more trouble than she did, so we don't have to worry about her getting expelled."

Oh no. "Do we have to worry about *him* getting expelled?"

"I don't think so. I heard about other people trying this, and they just get detention for life. Or something."

Small blessing. Angeline was in detention so much that they'd at least have bonding time. "Well, then I guess there isn't much to be done. I mean, the emotional fallout's going to be a mess, of course."

"Well . . ." Jill shifted nervously. "That's just it. You see, first Eddie needs to be told—"

I shot up out of my bed. "I am *not* doing that."

"Oh, of course not. No one would ever expect you to do that." I wasn't so sure but let her continue. "Angeline's going to. It's the right thing to do."

"Yes. . . ." I still wasn't letting down my guard.

"But someone still needs to talk to Eddie afterward," she explained. "It's going to be hard on him, you know? He shouldn't be left alone. He needs a friend."

"Aren't you his friend?" I asked.

She flushed. "Well, yeah, of course. But I don't know that it'd be right since . . . well, you know how I feel about him. Better to have someone more reasonable and objective. Besides, I don't know if I'd do a good job or not."

"Probably better than me."

"You're better at that stuff than you think. You're able to make things clear and—"

Jill suddenly froze. Her eyes widened a little, and for a moment, it was like she was watching something I couldn't see. No, I realized a moment later. There was no "like" about it. That was exactly what she was doing. She was having one of those moments where she was in sync with Adrian's mind. I saw her blink and slowly tune back into my room. Her eyes focused on me, and she paled. Just like that, I knew that she *knew*.

Rose had said that sometimes in the bond, you could sift through someone's recent memories even if you hadn't actually been tuned into the bond at that moment. As Jill looked at me, I could tell she'd seen it all, everything that had happened with Adrian last night. It was hard to say which of us was more horrified. I replayed everything I'd done and said, every compromising position I'd literally and figuratively put myself in. Jill had just "seen" me do things no one else ever had—well, except for Adrian, of course. And what had she actually felt? What it was like to kiss me? To run her—his?—hands over my body?

It was a situation I had in no way prepared for. My occasional indiscretions with Adrian had come through to Jill as well, but we'd all brushed those off—me in particular. Last night, however, had taken things to a whole new level, one that left both Jill and me stunned and speechless. I was mortified that she'd seen me so weak and exposed, and the protective part of me was worried that she'd seen anything like that at all, period.

She and I stared at each other, lost in our own thoughts, but Jill recovered first. She turned even redder than when she'd mentioned Eddie and practically leapt out of the chair. Turning her eyes away from mine, she hurried to the door. "Um, I should go, Sydney. Sorry to bother you so early. It probably could've waited. Angeline's going to talk to Eddie this morning, so whenever you get a chance to find him, you know, that'd be great." She took a deep breath and opened the door, still refusing to make eye contact. "I've gotta go. See you later. Sorry again."

"Jill—"

She shut the door, and I sank back into the bed, unable to stand. It was official. Whatever residual heat and lust I'd felt from being with Adrian last night had completely vanished in the wake of Jill's expression. Until that moment, I hadn't really and truly understood what it meant to be involved with someone who was bonded. Everything Adrian said to me, she heard. Every emotion he had for me, she experienced. Every time he kissed me, she felt it. . . .

I thought I might be sick. How had Rose and Lissa handled this? Somewhere in my addled mind, I recalled Rose saying she'd learned to block out a lot of Lissa's experiences—but it had taken a few years to figure it out. Adrian and Jill had only been bonded for a few months.

The shock of understanding what Jill had seen cast a shadow over everything that had been sensual and thrilling last night. I felt like I had been on display. I felt cheap and dirty, especially as I remembered my own role in instigating things. That sickening feeling in my stomach increased, and there was no stopping the avalanche of thoughts that soon followed.

I'd let myself spin out of control last night, carried away by desire. I shouldn't have done any of that—and not just because Adrian was a Moroi (though that was certainly problematic too). My life was about reason and logic, and I'd thrown all of that out the window. They were my strengths, and in casting them aside, I'd become weak. I'd been high on the freedom and risks I'd experienced last night, not to mention intoxicated by Adrian and how he'd said I was beautiful and brave and "ridiculously smart." I'd melted when he'd looked at me in that absurd dress. Knowing he'd wanted me had muddled my thoughts, making me want him too. . . .

There was no part of this that was okay.

With great effort, I dragged myself from the bed and managed to pick out some clothes for the day. I staggered to the shower like a zombie and stayed in for so long that I missed breakfast. It didn't matter. I couldn't have eaten anything anyway, not with all the emotions that were churning inside me. I barely spoke to anyone as I walked through the halls, and it wasn't until I sat down in Ms. Terwilliger's class that I finally remembered there were other people in the world with their own problems.

Specifically, Eddie and Trey.

I was certain there was no way they could be as traumatized as Jill and I were by last night's events. But it was obvious both guys had had a rough morning. Neither one spoke or made eye contact with others. I think it was the first time I'd ever seen Eddie neglect his surroundings. The bell cut me off before I had a chance to say anything, and I spent the rest of class watching them with concern. They didn't look like they were going to engage in any testosterone-driven madness, so that was a good sign. I felt bad for both of them—especially Eddie, who'd been wronged the most—and worrying on their behalf helped distract me from my own woes. A little.

When class ended, I wanted to talk to Eddie first, but Ms. Terwilliger intercepted me. She handed me a large yellow envelope that felt like it had a book inside. There was no end to the spells I had to learn. "Some of the things we discussed," she told me. "Tend to them as soon as you get the chance."

"I will, ma'am." I slipped the envelope into my bag and glanced around for Eddie. He was gone.

Trey was in my next class, and I took my usual seat beside

him. He gave me a sidelong look and then turned away.

"So," I said.

He shook his head. "Don't start."

"I'm not starting anything."

He stayed silent a few moments and then turned back to me, a frantic look in his eyes. "I didn't know, I swear. About her and Eddie. She never mentioned it, and obviously, they don't talk about it around here. I never would've done that to him. You have to believe that."

I did. No matter what Trey's other faults were, he was good-hearted and honest. If anyone was at fault for bad behavior here, it was Angeline.

"I'm actually more surprised that you'd get involved with someone like her, period." I didn't need to elaborate that "someone like her" referred to her being a dhampir.

Trey put his head on his desk. "I know, I know. It all just happened so fast. One day she's throwing a book at me. The next, we're making out behind the library."

"Ugh. That's a little more information than I needed," Glancing up, I saw that our chemistry teacher was still getting organized, giving Trey and me a little more time. "What are you going to do now?"

"What do you think? I have to end it. I shouldn't have let it get this far."

The Sydney from three months ago would have said of course he needed to end it. This one said, "Do you like her?"

"Yes, I—" He paused and then lowered his voice. "I think I love her. Is that nuts? After only a few weeks?"

"No—I don't know. I'm not really good at understanding that stuff." And by not really good, I actually meant terrible.

"But if you feel like that . . . maybe . . . maybe you shouldn't throw it away."

Trey's eyes widened, and surprise completely replaced his blue mood. "Are you serious? How can you say that? Especially you of all people. You know how it is. You've got the same rules as us."

I could hardly believe what I was saying. "Her people don't, and they seem to be fine."

For a moment, I thought I saw a flicker of hope in his eyes, but then he shook his head again. "I can't, Sydney. You know I can't. It would eventually end in disaster. There's a reason our kinds don't mix. And if my family ever found out . . . God. I can't even imagine. There'd be no way I'd ever get back in."

"Do you really want to?"

He didn't answer that. Instead, he just told me, "It can't work. It's over." I'd never seen him look so miserable.

Class started, and that ended the discussion.

Eddie wasn't in our cafeteria at lunch. Jill sat with Angeline at a corner table and looked as though she was delivering a stern lecture. Maybe Jill hadn't felt comfortable consoling Eddie, but she certainly had no problem speaking out on his behalf. I didn't really want to hear Angeline's excuses or meet Jill's eyes, so I grabbed a sandwich and ate outside. I didn't have enough time to check Eddie's cafeteria, so I sent him a text.

Want to go out for coffee later?

Don't feel sorry for me, he responded. I hadn't known if he'd answer at all, so that was something.

I just want to talk. Please.

His next text wasn't nearly so fast, and I could almost imagine his mental battle. *Okay, but after dinner. I have a study group*. A moment later, he added, *Not Spencer's*. Trey worked at Spencer's.

Now that the Angeline drama was on hold, I was able to return to my own messed-up love life. I couldn't shake that image of Jill's expression. I couldn't forgive myself for losing control. And now, I had Trey's words bouncing around my head. *It would eventually end in disaster. There's a reason our kinds don't mix.*

As though summoned by my thoughts, Adrian texted me. *You want to get the dragon today?*

I'd forgotten all about the callistana. He'd stayed with Adrian during my St. Louis trip, and now it was my turn. Since Adrian couldn't transform him back into quartz, the dragon had been in his true form all weekend.

Sure, I wrote back.

My stomach was in knots when I drove to Adrian's place later. I'd had the rest of the day to think about my options, and I'd finally reached an extreme one.

When he opened the door, his face was aglow—until he saw mine. His expression transformed to equal parts exasperation and sadness. "Oh no. Here it comes," he said.

I stepped inside. "Here what comes?"

"The part where you tell me last night was a mistake and that we can't ever do it again."

I looked away. That was exactly what I'd been going to say. "Adrian, you know this can't work."

"Because Moroi and humans can't be together? Because you don't feel the same way about me?"

"No," I said. "Well, not entirely. Adrian . . . Jill saw it all."

For a moment, he didn't seem to understand. "What do you—oh. Shit."

"Exactly."

"I never even think of that anymore." He sat down on the couch and stared off into space. The callistana came scurrying into the room and perched on the arm of the couch. "I mean, I know it happens. We even talked about it with other girls. She understands."

"Understands?" I exclaimed. "She's fifteen! You can't subject her to that."

"Maybe you were an innocent at fifteen, but Jill's not. She knows how the world works."

I couldn't believe what I was hearing. "Well, I'm not one of your other girls! I see her every day. Do you know how hard it was to face her? Do you know what it feels like to know she saw me doing that? And, God, what if there'd been more?"

"So, what's this mean exactly?" he asked. "You finally come around, and now you're going to just end things because of her?"

"Kissing you isn't exactly 'coming around.'"

He gave me a long, level look. "There was a lot more than kissing, Miss 'I'm a Quick Study.'"

I tried not to show how embarrassed I was about that now. "And that's exactly why this is all over. I'm not going to let Jill see that again."

"So you admit it could happen again?"

"Theoretically, yes. But I'm not going to give us the chance."

"You're going to avoid ever being alone with me again?"

"I'm going to avoid you, period." I took a deep breath. "I'm going to go with Marcus to Mexico."

"What?" Adrian jumped up and strode over to me. I immediately backed up. "What happened to you working undercover?"

"That only works if I can stay undercover! You think I can pull that off if I'm sneaking around with you?"

"You're with me half the time already!" I couldn't tell if he was angry or not, but he was clearly upset. "Nobody notices. We'll be careful."

"All it takes is one slipup," I said. "And I don't know if I can trust myself anymore. I can't risk the Alchemists finding out about you and me. I can't risk exposing Jill to what we'd do together. They'll send another Alchemist to look after her, and hopefully Stanton will take precautions against the Warriors."

"Jill knows I can't put my life on hold."

"You should," I snapped.

Now he *was* angry. "Well, you'd know all about that since you're an expert in denying yourself the things you want. And now you're going to leave the country to make sure you can deprive yourself even more."

"Yes, exactly." I walked over to the callistana and spoke the incantation that turned him back into his inert form. I put the crystal into my purse and summoned all my will to give Adrian the coldest look I could manage. It must have been a powerful one because he looked as though I'd slapped him. Seeing that pain on his face made my heart break. I didn't want to hurt him. I didn't want to leave him! But what choice did I have? There was too much at stake.

"This is done. I've made my choice, Adrian," I said. "I'm leaving this weekend, so please don't make it any more difficult than it has to be. I'd like us to be friends." The way I spoke made it sound like we were closing a business arrangement.

I walked toward the door, and Adrian hurried after me. I couldn't bear to face the agony in his eyes, and it took all my resolve not to avert my gaze. "Sydney, don't do this. You know it's wrong. Deep inside, you know it is."

I didn't answer. I couldn't answer. I walked away, forcing myself not to look back. I was too afraid my resolve would falter—and that was exactly why I needed to leave Palm Springs. I wasn't safe around him anymore. No one could be allowed to have that kind of power over me.

All I wanted to do after that was hide in my room and cry. For a week. But there was never any rest for me. It was always about others, with my feelings and dreams shoved off to the side. Consequently, I wasn't in the best position to give Eddie romantic advice when we met up that night. Fortunately, he was too caught up in his own emotions to notice mine.

"I should never have gotten involved with Angeline," he told me. We were at a coffee shop across town that was called Bean There, Done That. He'd ordered hot chocolate and had been stirring it for almost an hour.

"You didn't know," I said. It was hard maintaining my half of the conversation when I kept seeing the pain in Adrian's eyes. "You couldn't have known—especially with her. She's unpredictable."

"And that's *why* I shouldn't have done it." He finally set the spoon down on the table. "Relationships are dangerous enough without getting involved with someone like her. And I don't have time for that kind of distraction! I'm here for Jill, not me. I should never have let myself get caught up in this."

"There's nothing wrong with wanting to be with someone," I said diplomatically. *Unless that person turns your world upside down and makes you lose all self-control.*

"Maybe when I've retired, I'll have the time." I couldn't tell if he was serious or not. "But not right now. Jill's my priority."

I had no business playing matchmaker, but I had to try. "Have you ever thought about seriously being with Jill? I know you used to like her." And I was absolutely certain he still did.

"That's out of the question," he said fiercely. "And you know it. I can't think of her like that."

"She thinks about you like that." The words slipped out before I could stop them. After my own romantic disaster today, a part of me longed for at least someone to be happy. I didn't want anyone else hurting the way I did.

He froze. "She . . . no. There's no way."

"She does."

A whole range of emotions played through Eddie's eyes. Disbelief. Hope. Joy. And then . . . resignation. He picked up the spoon again and returned to his compulsive stirring.

"Sydney, you know I can't. You of all people know what it's like to have to focus on your work." This was the second time today someone had said "you of all people" to me. I guess everyone had a preconceived idea of who I was.

"You should at least think about it," I said. "Watch her the next time you're together. See how she reacts."

He looked as though he might consider it, which I took as a small victory. Suddenly, alarm flashed on his face. "Whatever happened with you and Marcus? The St. Louis trip? Did you find out anything about Jill?"

I chose my next words very carefully, both because I didn't want to alarm him and because I didn't want him taking some drastic action that could accidentally reveal my dealings with Marcus. "We found some evidence that the Warriors have talked to the Alchemists, but nothing that shows they're working together or have actual plans for her. I've also taken some steps to make sure she's protected."

I hadn't heard anything from Stanton today and wasn't sure if that last part would actually pan out. Eddie looked relieved, though, and I couldn't bear to stress him out any further today. His gaze shifted to something behind me, and he pushed the untouched hot chocolate away. "Time for us to go."

I looked back at a clock and saw he was right. We still had a comfortable window before curfew, but I didn't want to push it. I finished off the last of my coffee and followed him out. The sun was sinking into the horizon, coloring the sky red and purple. The temperature had finally cooled off to normal levels, but it still didn't feel like winter to me. There'd been a bunch of badly parked cars in the front of the lot, so I'd parked Latte in the back in case some careless person opened a door too fast.

"Thanks for the moral support," Eddie told me. "Sometimes it feels like you really are a sister—"

That was when my car exploded. Sort of.

I have to admit Eddie's response time was amazing. He threw me to the ground, shielding my body with his. The boom had been deafening, and I cried out as some sort of foam landed on the side of my face.

Foam?

Cautiously, Eddie rose, and I followed. My car hadn't exploded in flames or anything like that. Instead, it was filled with some sort of white substance that had blasted out with such force that it had blown the doors off and broken the windows. We both approached the mess, and behind us, I heard people coming out of the coffee shop.

"What the hell?" asked Eddie.

I touched some of the foam on my face and rubbed my fingertips together. "It's sort of like the stuff you'd find in a fire extinguisher," I said.

"How did it get in your car?" he asked. "And how did it get there so fast? I glanced over at it when we first walked out. You're the chemical expert. Could some reaction have happened that fast?"

"Maybe," I admitted. At the moment, I was too shocked to really run any formulas. I rested a hand against Latte's hood and wanted to burst into tears. My emotions were at a breaking point. "My poor car. First Adrian's, now mine. Why do people do stuff like this?"

"Vandals don't care," said a voice beside me. I glanced over and saw one of the baristas, an older man who I believed was the owner. "I've seen stuff like this before. Damn kids. I'll call the police for you." He took out his cell phone and backed away.

"I don't know if we'll make curfew now," I told Eddie.

He gave me a sympathetic pat on the back. "I think if you show a police report at the dorm, they'll be lenient with you."

"Yeah, I hope that—ugh. The police." I hurried over to the passenger side and stared bleakly at the wall of foam.

"What's wrong?" Eddie asked. "I mean, aside from the obvious."

"I have to get to the glove compartment." I lowered my voice. "There's a gun in there."

He did a double take. "A what?"

I said no more, and he helped me dig through the foam. Both of us ended up covered in it by the time I reached the compartment. Making sure no one was behind us, I quickly retrieved the gun and slipped it into my messenger bag. I was about to shut the lid when something shiny caught my eye.

"That's impossible," I said.

It was my cross, the gold one I'd lost. I grabbed it and then immediately dropped it, yelping in pain. The metal had burned me. Considering the foamy substance was cool, it didn't seem likely it had heated up the cross. I wrapped my sleeve around my hand and gingerly picked up the cross again.

Eddie peered over my shoulder. "You wear that all the time."

I nodded and continued staring at the cross. A terrible feeling began to spread over me. I found a tissue in my purse and wrapped the cross up before adding it to the bag. Then I retrieved my cell phone and dialed Ms. Terwilliger. Voice mail. I hung up without leaving a message.

"What's going on?" asked Eddie.

"I'm not sure," I said. "But I think it's bad."

I hadn't yet developed the ability to sense magical residue, but I was almost certain something had been done to the cross, something that had resulted in Latte's foamy demise. Alicia hadn't been able to find the cross. Had Veronica doubled back and taken it? If so, how had she located me? I knew personal items could be used to track back to a person, though the most common ones were hair and nails. As advanced as Veronica was, it was very likely an object—like this cross—would serve just as well.

Veronica might very well have found me. But if so, why vandalize my car instead of sucking out my life?

The police came soon thereafter and took our statements. They were followed by a tow truck. I could tell from the driver's face that it wasn't looking good for Latte. He hauled my poor car away, and then one of the officers was nice enough to return Eddie and me to Amberwood. Against all odds, we made it back just in time.

As soon as I got to my room, I tried Ms. Terwilliger again. Still no answer.

I emptied out my bag onto my bed and found it had gathered a number of items today. One of them was a donut I'd picked up at the coffee shop. I put it and the quartz crystal into the aquarium and summoned the callistana. He immediately went after the donut.

I found the cross and discovered it was now cool. Whatever spell it had been used in was gone. The gun was near it, and I quickly hid that back in the bag. That left Ms. Terwilliger's envelope, which I'd neglected all day. Maybe if I hadn't been so distracted by personal matters, I could have saved Latte.

I pulled the latest spell book out of the envelope and heard something jangle. I removed the book and then saw another, smaller envelope inside. I pulled it out and read a message Ms. Terwilliger had written on the side: *Here's another charm to mask your magical ability, just in case. It's one of the most powerful out there and took a lot of work, so be careful with it.*

That same guilt I always felt about her helping me returned. I opened the small envelope and found a silver star pendant set with peridots. I gasped.

I had seen this charm before, this powerful and painstakingly made charm that could allegedly hide strong magical ability.

I had seen it around Alicia's neck.

CHAPTER 23

FOR A MOMENT, I THOUGHT it had to be a coincidence. After all, what was so special about a peridot star? For all I knew, Alicia might have been born in August and was just sporting her birthstone among that mess of necklaces she always wore. And yet, if there was one thing I believed more than ever, it was Sonya's adage that there were no coincidences in the world of the supernatural.

I sank to the floor and tried to reason my way through things. If the charm Alicia had worn was like this one, then it meant she too was a strong magic user trying to mask her abilities. Did she know about Veronica? Was Alicia trying to protect herself? If so, then it seemed like she wouldn't have been so casual about Veronica staying at the inn. So, that meant either Alicia didn't know about Veronica's true nature—again, a suspicious coincidence—or that Alicia was covering for Veronica.

Could Alicia be in league with Veronica?

That seemed the likeliest answer to me. Although Veronica apparently sought out young, powerful magic users, it was totally possible that she'd seen the advantage of having one as an assistant. And, as we'd observed, Veronica had plenty of other victims to choose from. Alicia could therefore help and cover up Veronica's nefarious plans—like when a curious couple came asking questions.

I groaned. Alicia had been playing us from the beginning. From the instant we'd stepped through her door with stories about our anniversary and "friend" Veronica, she'd known we were lying. She'd known we weren't actually friends with Veronica, and she might have been strong enough to fight Adrian's compulsion a little. She'd gone along with everything—even being so helpful as to call me when Veronica had shown up again. I had no idea now what was true, if Veronica had ever left in the first place or returned from being gone. I did, however, have a sinking suspicion that my car wasn't the only one she'd incapacitated.

I could understand if she'd used the cross to find me, but how had she initially located the Mustang? I racked my brain for any identifying information. Adrian's spirit magic should have muddled our appearances, covering up any connection to us. Then I knew. Alicia had walked us out and admired the Mustang. A clever person—someone who was already on high alert because of our visit—could've made note of the license plate and used it to track down where Adrian lived.

But why slash the tires? *To delay us*, I realized. That was the night Lynne had been attacked. And we had arrived too late to warn her.

The more I began to sift through the events of the last few

weeks, the more I began to think we had been very, very careless. We'd thought we were being so cautious about concealing ourselves from Veronica. No one, not even Ms. Terwilliger, had considered that she might have an accomplice we also had to watch out for. And the dreams . . . those had started the day Adrian and I had been on the velvet bed. The day my garnet had slipped and had possibly been enough for Alicia to sense a magic user in the inn.

Which brought me back to the present. Ms. Terwilliger. I had to tell her what I'd found. I called for a third time. Still no answer. Although I often had images of Ms. Terwilliger conducting late-night rituals, it was entirely reasonable that she'd be in bed right now. Was this the kind of thing that could wait until morning?

No, I decided on the spot. No, it wasn't. We were dealing with dangerous, violent magic users—and my car had just been attacked. Something might be happening as I stood there, trying to decide. I would have to wake her up . . . provided I could get to her.

It took only a moment to make my next decision. I called Adrian.

He answered on the first ring but sounded wary, which I couldn't blame him for after what I'd done earlier. "Hello?"

I prayed he was the noble guy I thought he was. "Adrian, I know things are bad between us, and maybe I have no right to ask, but I need a favor. It's about Veronica."

There was no hesitation. "What do you need?"

"Can you come over to Amberwood? I need you to help me break curfew and escape my dorm."

There were a few moments of silence. "Sage, I've been

waiting two months to hear you say those words. You want me to bring a ladder?"

The plan was already unfolding in my head. The security guards that patrolled at night would have eyes on the student parking lot, but the back property would be relatively unguarded.

"I'll get myself out of the building. If you come up the main road that leads to Amberwood and then go past the driveway, you'll see a little service road that runs up a hill and goes behind my dorm. Park there near the utility shed, and I'll meet you as soon as I get out."

When he spoke again, his earlier levity was gone. "I'd really like to believe this is some awesome midnight adventure, but it's not, is it? Something's gone really wrong."

"Very wrong," I agreed. "I'll explain in the car."

I quickly changed into clean jeans and a T-shirt, adding a light suede jacket against the evening chill. To be safe, I also decided to pack my bag with a few supplies and bring it along. If all went well, I'd simply be warning Ms. Terwilliger tonight. But with the way things had been going lately, I couldn't presume anything would be simple. Bringing the suitcase this time would be unwieldy, so I had to make a few quick decisions about chemicals and magical components. I tossed some in the bag and stuffed others in my jeans and coat pockets.

Once I was ready, I headed down to Julia and Kristin's room. They were dressed for bed but not asleep yet. When Julia saw me with my coat and bag, her eyes went wide.

"Sweet," she said.

"I know you've gotten out before," I said. "How'd you do it?"

Julia's many dates often occurred outside of sanctioned

school hours, and both she and Kristin had bragged about Julia's exploits in the past. I'd hoped perhaps Julia knew about a secret tunnel out of the school and that I wouldn't have to attempt some crazy feat of acrobatics. Unfortunately, that was exactly what I had to do. She and Kristin walked me to their window and pointed at a large tree growing outside it.

"This room has a view and easy access," said Kristin proudly.

I eyed the gnarled tree warily. "That's easy?"

"Half the dorm's used it," she said. "So can you."

"We should be charging people," mused Julia. She flashed me a smile. "Don't worry. We'll give you a freebie tonight. Just start on that big limb there, swing over there, and then use those branches for handholds."

I found it amazing that someone who'd claimed badminton in PE was too "dangerous" would have no qualms about scaling a tree from her third-floor room. Of course, Marcus's apartment had been on the fourth floor, and that fire escape had been a million times more unsafe than this tree. Thoughts of Alicia and Ms. Terwilliger snapped me back to the importance of my mission, and I gave Julia and Kristin a decisive nod.

"Let's do this," I said.

Julia cheered and opened the window for me. Kristin watched just as eagerly. "Please tell me you're running off to meet some breathtakingly handsome guy," she said.

I paused, just as I was about to climb out. "Yes, actually. But not in the way you're thinking."

Once I made it to the limb Julia had indicated, I discovered she was right. It was pretty simple—so simple, in fact, that I was surprised no school official had noticed this easy access escape route and chopped it down. Well, so much the better for those of us with late-night errands. I made it to the ground and waved goodbye to my watching friends.

The dorm's back property had some lights on it, exactly for the reason of deterring wayward students like me. It was also along the patrol route of one of the security guards but wasn't a spot he stayed regularly stationed at. He wasn't in sight, so I crossed my fingers that he was busy with another part of his beat. There were enough shadows on the lawn that I was able to stay within them the whole way—until I reached the back fence. It was lit up pretty well, and really, the only assets I had were that I was a fast climber and that the guard hadn't surfaced yet. Falling back on that hope that the universe owed me some favors—especially after tricking me about Alicia—I gulped and scrambled over. No one shouted at me when I landed on the other side, and I breathed a sigh of relief. I'd made it out. Getting back in would be harder, but that was a problem for later, hopefully one Ms. Terwilliger could help out with.

I found Adrian waiting for me in the Mustang, exactly where I'd indicated. He gave me a sidelong glance as he drove us away. "No black catsuit?"

"It's in the laundry."

He smiled. "Of course it is. Now, where are we going, and what's going on?"

"We're going to Ms. Terwilliger's," I said. "And what's going on is that we've been walking around in front of the enemy this entire time without even realizing it."

I watched Adrian as I related my revelations and saw his face go from disbelieving to dismayed the more I spoke. "Her aura was too perfect," he said once I finished. "Perfectly neutral, perfectly average. No one's is like that. I brushed it off, though. Figured maybe it was just a weird human one."

"Can someone influence how their aura looks?" I asked.

"Not to that extent," he said. "I don't know enough about these charms you guys use, but I'm guessing it was one of those that skewed the way her colors looked."

I slumped into the seat, still angry at not having figured this out sooner. "On the bright side, she doesn't know we're on to her and Veronica. That could give us an advantage."

When we reached Ms. Terwilliger's house, we found all the lights on, which was a surprise. I'd assumed she was in bed, though this certainly wouldn't be the first time she'd missed a phone call. Only, when we reached the house and knocked on the door, there was no answer. Adrian and I exchanged looks.

"Maybe she had to leave abruptly," he said. The tone of his voice conveyed what his words didn't. What if Ms. Terwilliger had already found out what we had and had taken off to fight Alicia and Veronica? I had no idea how powerful Alicia was, but the odds didn't seem promising.

When no answer came from my second knock, I nearly kicked the door in frustration. "Now what?"

Adrian turned the doorknob, and the door opened right up. "How about we wait for her?" he suggested.

I grimaced. "I don't know if I'm comfortable breaking into her place."

"She left the door unlocked. She's practically inviting us in." He pushed the door open farther and looked at me expectantly.

I didn't want to go back to Amberwood without speaking to her tonight, nor did I want to sit on her doorstep. Hoping she wouldn't mind us making ourselves at home, I gave a nod of resignation and followed Adrian inside. Her house was the same as ever, cluttered and redolent with the scent of incense. Suddenly, I came to a standstill.

"Wait. Something's different." It took me a moment to figure it out, and when I did, I couldn't believe I hadn't realized it immediately. "The cats are gone."

"Holy shit," said Adrian. "You're right."

At least one of them always came to greet visitors, and others were usually visible on furniture, under tables, or simply occupying the middle of the floor. But now, there were no cats in sight.

I stared around in disbelief. "What in the world could—"

An earsplitting shriek made me jump. I looked down toward my hip and found the dragon sticking his head out of my satchel and trying to claw his way up my side. Belatedly, I realized I'd forgotten to cover the aquarium. He'd apparently slipped inside the bag back in my room. The sound he was making now was similar to his hunger cry—except even more annoying. Then, impossibly, he nipped my leg. I bent over and tried to pull him off me.

"I don't have any pie! What are you trying to—ahh!"

Something zoomed over my head and smashed into the wall behind me with a loud splat. A couple wet drops of something landed on my cheek and began to burn. It was a wonder I didn't hear a sizzling sound.

"Sydney!" Adrian cried.

I turned toward where he was looking and saw Alicia standing in the doorway between the living room and the kitchen. Her palm was raised toward us, a shimmery and gooey substance cupped in it. Presumably it was the same substance that currently seared my skin. I almost wiped it away but feared I'd simply be spreading it to my fingers. I winced and tried to ignore it.

"Sydney," said Alicia pleasantly. "Or should I say, Taylor? I figured I'd be seeing you two again. Just not so soon. I guess your car trouble didn't delay you tonight."

"We know everything," I told her, keeping on an eye on that goo. "We know you're working for Veronica."

The smug look on her face momentarily shifted, overcome by surprise. "Working *for her*? I got rid of her ages ago."

"Got rid of. . . ." For a few seconds, I was at a loss. Then the rest of the puzzle pieces fell together. "*You're* the one who's been absorbing those girls. And that witch in San Diego. And . . . Veronica Terwilliger."

I'd been able to track Veronica back to the inn with the scrying spell. When Ms. Terwilliger had attempted a different locating spell, she'd come up blank. She'd assumed it was because Veronica had some sort of shielding. But the truth, I was suddenly certain, was that Veronica was already comatose. There was no active mind for Ms. Terwilliger to reach because Alicia had consumed Veronica.

Ms. Terwilliger . . .

"You're here for her," I said. "Ms. Terwilliger. Not me."

"The untrained do make easy targets," conceded Alicia. "But they don't have the same power as full-fledged witches, who can be just as easy to absorb if you break them down first. I don't need the youth like Veronica did, just the power. Once she showed me how the spell works, I was able to catch her in a weak moment. That other college girl tided me over until I wore down Alana Kale." Where had I heard that name? Alana . . . she was Ms. Terwilliger's comatose coven sister. "And finally I can take out the big hit: Jaclyn Terwilliger. I actually wasn't sure if I'd be able to break her, but it turns out she's done an awesome job of wearing herself out these last few weeks, all in the service of protecting her sweet little apprentice."

"I'm not her . . ." I couldn't finish. I'd been about to say I wasn't her apprentice, and yet . . . wasn't I? I wasn't just dabbling in magic anymore. I had joined the ranks. And now, I had to protect my mentor, just as she'd protected me. If it wasn't too late.

"Where is she?" I demanded.

"She's around," said Alicia, clearly delighting in having the upper hand here. "I wish you hadn't found out about all this. You would've made a good hit, once you'd learned a little bit more. You're just a small spark to Jaclyn's flame right now. She's the big score tonight."

"Tell us where she is," ordered Adrian, a powerful note in his voice that I recognized.

Alicia's gaze flicked from me to him. "Oh, please," she scoffed. "Stop wasting my time with your vampire compulsion. I realized what was going on after that first visit, when I kept having trouble remembering your faces." From her jumble of necklaces, she showed us a jade circle. "I acquired this afterward. Makes me impervious to your 'charms.'"

Something that resisted vampire magic? That would be a useful item to have in my bag of tricks. I'd have to look into it . . . provided I survived tonight.

I saw Alicia tense to throw again, and I managed to jump out of the way, pulling Adrian with me toward the living room. More of that goo splattered behind us with a hiss. I produced a dried thistle blossom and crumpled it toward Alicia, shouting a Greek incantation that would blind her. She made a small wave with her left hand and sneered at me.

"Really?" she asked. "That remedial blindness spell? Maybe you aren't a prodigy after all."

Adrian suddenly flipped open a small panel in the wall beside us. I hadn't even noticed it, largely because I'd been too distracted about having my face melted off. I saw a flurry of motion from his hand, and suddenly, we were plunged into darkness.

"Now *this* is remedial blindness," he muttered.

Alicia swore. I froze, immobilized by the blackness around me. As much as I appreciated any attempts to slow Alicia down, I was kind of at a loss myself.

I felt Adrian's hand grab hold of mine, and without a word, he tugged me farther into the living room. I followed quickly, relying on his superior vampire eyesight to guide us. I could already hear Alicia chanting and was sure some light-giving spell was coming soon. Either that or something that would magically fix a fuse box.

"Careful," Adrian murmured. "Stairs."

Sure enough, I felt my foot hit a wooden step. He and I hurried down as quietly and as quickly as we could, descending into a basement. My eyes still hadn't adjusted to the darkness, and I wondered if I'd just entered some secret dungeon. Yet as he wound us through stacks of boxes, I realized the basement was just used for ordinary storage. There was a lot of junk down here. After seeing Ms. Terwilliger's already messy house, I wondered what more she could possibly own.

Adrian finally stopped when we were in a far corner behind

some oblong boxes stacked nearly as high as me. He pulled me to him, keeping me in his arms so that he could speak softly in my ear. My head lay against his chest, and I could hear his rapid heartbeat, a mirror for my own.

"That was a good idea," I said in as low a voice as I could manage. "But now we're trapped down here. It would've been better if we could go outside."

"I know," he whispered back. "But she was too close to the door, and I didn't have time to mess with a window."

Above us, I could hear the floor creaking as Alicia walked through the house. "It's just a matter of time," I said.

"I was hoping it'd give you a chance to think of something to get us out of here. Can't you use that fireball? You were pretty good at it."

"Not inside. Especially not in a basement. I'd burn this place down around us. And we don't know where Ms. Terwilliger is yet." I racked my brain. The house was small enough that there weren't that many places Alicia could have stashed Ms. Terwilliger. And I had to assume she *was* stashed somewhere, if she hadn't come to our aid already. Alicia's language made it sound like she hadn't sucked away Ms. Terwilliger's power yet, so hopefully she was just incapacitated.

"You must be able to do something," said Adrian, tightening his hold on me. "You're brilliant, and you've been reading all those spell books."

It was true. I'd consumed tons of material these last couple of months—material I wasn't even supposed to have learned—but somehow, in this one terrified moment, my mind couldn't focus on any of it. "I've forgotten everything."

"No, you haven't." His voice in the darkness was calm and

reassuring. He smoothed back my hair and pressed one of those half kisses to my forehead. "Just relax and focus. Sooner or later, she'll be coming down those stairs after us. We need to take her out or at least slow her down so that we can escape."

His reasonable words centered me and allowed the gears of logic that ran my life to take over again. A little light was coming through from the basement's small, high windows, allowing my eyes to finally adjust and make out some of the dark shapes in the basement. I could still hear Alicia moving around upstairs, so I crept away from Adrian and walked over to the staircase. With a few graceful hand arcs, I chanted a spell over the steps and then hurried back to my corner with Adrian, slipping back under the shelter of his arm.

"Okay," I said. "I think I've got a minor delay ready."

"What is it?" he asked.

Just then, we heard the door at the top of the stairs open. Light spilled down, though we still remained in the shadows. "You're out of options," I heard Alicia say. "No place left to—ahh!"

There was a loud *thump-thump-thump-thump* as she went sliding down the stairs and hit the bottom with a crack.

"Invisible ice on the stairs," I told Adrian.

"I know I'm not supposed to say this," he said. "But I think I love you more than ever."

I took his hand and tried not to think about how happy his words made me, even in this life-or-death situation. "Come on."

We left our hiding spot and found Alicia sprawled ungracefully on the floor, trying to get to her feet. A silver orb of light hovered in the air near her, bobbing along faithfully with her movements. Seeing us, she snarled and waved her hands to cast at us. I'd anticipated this and had an amulet ready. I swung it on its silken cord and said a few quick words as we passed her. A brief, shimmering shield flared between us and her, just barely absorbing the small glowing darts she hurled our way. The shield was similar to the one Ms. Terwilliger had used at the park but had to be summoned on the spot and didn't last long.

I didn't know what Alicia planned on doing next, but obviously, something bad was coming. I cast a preemptive spell I'd never used before, one of the ones that Ms. Terwilliger had told me not to bother with. It took a lot of energy and was powerful if used correctly, yet was deceptively simple and elegant in its effects. I merely blasted Alicia across the room with a wave of power just as she was about to stand. She flew backward, into a stack of Christmas items. A box of ornaments fell down, shattering near her on the hard floor.

Casting the spell left me dizzy, but I managed to keep moving. I summoned a fireball when we reached the stairs but held it in my hand, keeping it low as though I were going to roll a Skee-Ball—though my Intent was simply to carry it. I prayed it would melt the ice, and after my first few steps, I knew I was right. "Careful," I warned Adrian. "They're wet."

We made it to the top, but Alicia had already scrambled after us. From the bottom of the stairs, she used the same spell on me that I'd used on her, throwing a wave of invisible energy at Adrian and me that knocked us to the floor. I'd been holding on to the fireball, despite Ms. Terwilliger's warnings about how doing so would drain my own power. When Alicia knocked me down, the fireball flew from my hand and landed on Ms. Terwilliger's couch. Considering it looked as though it was covered in some cheap fabric from the 1970s, I wasn't entirely surprised that it lit up so fast.

On the bright side, the fire solved our darkness problem. On the downside, it meant the house was likely going to burn down around us after all. The callistana, who hadn't been fast enough to keep up with us when we'd gone downstairs, came scurrying over to my side. I had only half a heartbeat to make a decision.

"Go look in the rest of the house for Ms. Terwilliger," I told Adrian. "I'll stop Alicia."

The growing fire created weird shadows on his face, highlighting his anguish at this. "Sydney."

"This is one of those times you have to trust me without question," I said. "Hurry! Find her and get her out."

I saw a thousand emotions flash through his eyes before he obeyed and ran off toward the other wing of the house. The fire was spreading rapidly throughout the living room, in a way that had to be magical. The increasing smoke gave me an idea, and I cast a spell that enhanced it, creating a hazy wall at the entrance to the basement stairs. It allowed the dragon and me to make a short retreat before Alicia appeared, parting the smoke as cleanly as though she were opening curtains.

"That," she declared. "Hurt."

I cast a spell that should've encased her in spiderwebs, but they fell away before they even reached her. It was infuriating. I'd memorized so much, but these "remedial" spells weren't working. I understood now why Ms. Terwilliger's main strategy had been for me to lie low and hide my ability. How would I have ever been able to take on Veronica? True, Alicia had taken her out, but only after probably weakening her as she had Ms.

Terwilliger. I even understood now why Ms. Terwilliger had told me to get a gun—which, I realized now, I'd left in the car.

The ice spell had worked because Alicia hadn't seen it coming. The only other spell that had worked on her was the blast of power, an advanced one that had still left me weak. It was going to take another one of those, I realized. I had no idea if I had the ability to do a second one, but trying was the only chance I had of—

I screamed as what felt like a thousand volts of electricity shot through me. Alicia's hand movement had been so subtle, and she hadn't even spoken. I fell down again, writhing in pain as Alicia strode toward me, her face triumphant. The dragon bravely put himself between the two of us, and she simply kicked him aside. I heard him yelp as he skittered across the floor.

"Maybe I should absorb you," said Alicia. The shocks abated, and I could only sit there and gasp for breath. "You could be my fifth. I can come back for Jaclyn in a few years. You've turned out to be a lot more powerful than I thought—and annoyingly resourceful. You even made a good effort tonight."

"Who says I'm done?" I managed to say.

I cast the first of the advanced spells that came to mind. Maybe it was inspired by the broken Christmas ornaments, but suddenly, I had broken shards on the brain. The spell required no words or physical components and only the slightest of hand movements. The rest was taken from me—a draining of energy and power that hurt almost as much as the electrifying spell Alicia had just used.

But oh, the results were breathtaking.

On Ms. Terwilliger's coffee table (which was now on fire) sat a set of five perpetual motion balls. I used a transmutation spell on them, forcing them out of their spherical shape and breaking them apart into thin, sharp razor blades. They broke free of their strings and came at my command. That was the easy part.

The hard part was, as Ms. Terwilliger had told me, actually attacking someone. And not just making them slip and fall. That wasn't so bad. But an actual physical attack, one you knew would cause direct and terrible damage, was an entirely different issue. It didn't matter how terrible Alicia was, that she'd tried to kill me and wanted to victimize Ms. Terwilliger and countless others. Alicia was still a living person, and it was not in my nature to show violence or try to take another's life.

It was, however, in my nature to save my own life and those of my loved ones.

I braced myself and ordered the razors forward. They slammed into her face. She screamed and frantically tried to pull them out but in doing so lost her balance and went back down the stairs. I heard her shriek as she fell into the basement. Although I couldn't see her, her magical lantern orb merrily followed her all the way down.

My triumph was short-lived. I was more than dizzy. I was on the verge of passing out. The heat and light from the fire were overwhelming, yet my vision was going dark from the exhaustion of casting a spell I was in no way ready for. I suddenly just wanted to curl up there on the floor and close my eyes where it was comfortable and warm. . . .

"Sydney!"

Adrian's voice jolted me out of my haze, and I managed to peer up at him through heavy eyelids. He slipped an arm around me to help me up. When my legs didn't work, he simply scooped me up altogether and carried me. The dragon, who'd suffered no permanent damage from the kick, clung to my shirt and scurried into the bag that was still draped over my shoulder.

"Where . . . Ms. Terwilliger. . . ."

"Not here," Adrian said, heading swiftly toward the front door. The fire was spreading over the walls and ceiling now. Although it hadn't quite made it to the front of the house yet, our way was still thick with smoke and ash. We both were coughing, and tears ran out of my eyes. Adrian reached the door and turn the knob, yelping at how hot it was. Then he managed to kick the door open with his foot, and we were free, out into the clean night air.

Neighbors had gathered outside, and I could hear sirens in the distance. Some of the spectators watched us curiously, but most were transfixed by the inferno that was Ms. Terwilliger's bungalow. Adrian carried me over to his car and gently set me down so that I could lean against it, though he still kept an arm around me. We both stared in awe at the fire.

"I really did look, Sydney," he said. "I couldn't find Jackie in the house. Maybe she escaped." I prayed he was right. Otherwise, we had just abandoned my history teacher to a fiery death. "What happened to Alicia?"

"Last I saw, she was in the basement." A sickening feeling twisted in my stomach. "I don't know if she'll get out. Adrian, what have I just done?"

"You defended yourself. And me. And hopefully Jackie." His arm tightened around me. "Alicia was evil. Look what she did to those other witches—what she wanted to do to you guys."

"I never saw it coming," I said bleakly. "I thought I was so smart. And each time I talked to her, I dismissed her as some dumb, scattered girl. Meanwhile, she was laughing and countering my moves every step of the way. It's humbling. I don't meet many people like that."

"The Moriarty to your Holmes?" he suggested.

"Adrian," I said. It was all I needed to say.

He suddenly did a double take, noticing my attire for the first time tonight now that the jacket had come open. "You're wearing your AYE shirt?"

"Yeah, I never wage magical battles without—"

A small mewling noise suddenly caught my attention. I searched around until I spotted two green eyes peering at me from under a bush across the street. I managed to straighten up and found that my legs, though weak, could support my weight again. I took a few halting steps toward the bush, and Adrian immediately ran to my side.

"What are you doing? You need help," he said.

I pointed. "We have to follow that cat."

"Sydney—"

"Help me," I pleaded.

He couldn't resist. Supporting me with his arm again, he helped me walk across the street toward the cat. It ran ahead between two bushes, then glanced back at us.

"It wants us to follow," I told him.

So we did, cutting through houses and streets until when we were about four blocks from the bungalow, the cat dashed off into a park. Whatever energy I'd had when I started after the cat was long gone. I was panting and dizzy again and fighting hard to resist asking Adrian to carry me. Something in the center of the park caught my attention and gave me one last burst of adrenaline to run forward.

There, lying on the grass, was Ms. Terwilliger.

She was awake, thankfully, but looked nearly as exhausted as I felt. Tears and smudges suggested she'd been through quite an ordeal. She had managed to escape Alicia, but not without a fight. That was why we hadn't been able to find her in the house. Seeing me, she blinked in surprise.

"You're okay," she said. "And you found me."

"The cats led us," I said, pointing. All thirteen of them were sitting around in the park, surrounding their owner—making sure she was okay.

She glanced around at them and managed a weary smile. "See? I told you cats are useful."

"Callistanas aren't so bad either," I said, looking down at my satchel. "That 'pain in the ass' screeching saved me from a face full of acid."

Adrian put his hand to his heart in mock horror. "Sage, did you just swear?"

Glancing over, Ms. Terwilliger noticed him for the first time. "And you're here too? I'm so sorry you had to get dragged into this mess. I know you didn't ask for any of this trouble."

"It doesn't matter," said Adrian, smiling. He rested a hand on my shoulder. "Some things are worth the trouble."

CHAPTER 24

I FELT PRETTY BAD about burning down my teacher's house.

Ms. Terwilliger, for obvious reasons, seemed to think that was the least of her problems. She wasn't sure if her insurance would cover the damage, but her company was pretty speedy in sending someone out to investigate the cause. We were still waiting to hear their verdict on coverage, but one thing they didn't report finding was any sign of human remains. Part of me was relieved that I hadn't actually killed anyone. Another part of me feared we hadn't seen the last of Alicia. What silly comparison had Adrian made? *The Moriarty to your Holmes.* I had to imagine that being hit in the face with razor blades and then left in a burning building would make anyone hold a grudge.

A little investigation eventually turned up Veronica at a Los Angeles hospital, checked in as Jane Doe. Visiting her comatose sister became the greatest of Ms. Terwilliger's priorities, and she harbored hopes of possibly finding a way to undo the spell. Despite how busy she now was, my teacher still managed to urge me to meet her coven, and I agreed for a few different reasons. One was that it was kind of impossible for me to act like I didn't want to wield magic anymore.

The other reason was that I didn't plan on being around.

I was still resolved to go with Marcus to Mexico, and the week flew by. Winter finals were a breeze, and before I knew it, it was Friday, the day before our trip to Mexico. I took a risk by telling my friends goodbye. The safest thing would've been to disappear without a trace, but I trusted them all—even Angeline—to keep my secret and feign ignorance once the Alchemists discovered they had a runaway. I told Trey as well. No matter what had gone down between us, he was still my friend, and I would miss him.

As the day wore on, the dorm grew quieter and quieter—aside from unending Christmas music playing in the lobby. Not wanting to exclude other religions, Mrs. Weathers had also set out a menorah and "Happy Kwanzaa" banner. Tomorrow was officially the last day before everyone had to be out, and a number of people had already left for winter break. I'd finished my own packing, which was light. I didn't want to be burdened down with excess luggage since I really had no idea what to expect in Mexico.

I still had two people I needed to say goodbye to: Adrian and Jill. I'd avoided them both for very different reasons, but time was running out. I knew Jill was just a flight of stairs away, but Adrian was more difficult. We'd been in touch a couple times after the fire, simply to sort out some details, but he'd soon gone silent. No calls, no texts, no dreams. Maybe I should've been glad. Maybe I should've welcomed the chance to leave without any painful goodbyes . . . but I couldn't. My chest ached with the thought of not seeing him again. Even though he was the reason I was leaving, I still felt like I needed some closure.

It's not about closure, Sydney. You want to see him. You need to see him. And that's exactly why you have to leave.

Finally, I took the plunge and called him. It took me so long to work up the nerve that I could hardly believe it when he didn't answer. I resisted the urge to immediately try again. No. I could wait. There would still be time tomorrow, and surely . . . surely he wasn't avoiding me?

I decided to hold off on talking to Jill until the next day. Telling her goodbye was just as difficult—and not just because of what she saw through the bond. I knew she'd think I was abandoning her. In truth, if I stayed and ended up with Adrian, I'd possibly be caught and never be able to help her at all. At least if I was away and free, I could try to help her from the outside. I hoped she'd understand.

Waiting on her gave me the opportunity to take care of an unwelcome errand: returning Malachi Wolfe's gun. I'd never gone to his home without Adrian, and even though I knew I had nothing to fear from Wolfe, there was still something a little unsettling about going to the compound alone.

To my complete and utter astonishment, Wolfe let me into the house when I arrived. All was quiet. "Where are the dogs?" I asked.

"At training," he said. "I have a friend who's an expert dog trainer, and he's giving them some stealth lessons. He used to work for a local K-9 unit."

I didn't think it was in the Chihuahua genetic code to ever be stealthy. I kept that to myself and instead stared around in amazement at Wolfe's kitchen. I'd expected something like a ship's galley. Instead, I found an astonishingly cheery room, with blue-checkered wallpaper and a squirrel cookie jar. If someone had asked me to describe the most unlikely Wolfe kitchen out there, it would've looked something like this. No—wait. On the refrigerator, he had some magnets that looked like ninja throwing stars. That, at least, was in character.

Adrian's going to flip out when I tell him. Then I remembered I might not see Adrian for a very long time. That realization killed whatever amusement I'd just felt.

"So what do you need?" asked Wolfe. Peering at him, I suddenly had a strange feeling the eye patch really was on a different eye from last time. I should've paid more attention. "Another gun?"

I returned to the task at hand. "No, sir. I didn't even need the first one, but thanks for lending it to me." I removed it from the bag and handed it to him.

He gave the gun a once-over and then set it inside a drawer. "Fixed your problem? You can still hang on to it if you want."

"I'm leaving the country. Bringing it over the border might cause me some trouble."

"Fair enough," he said. He grabbed the cookie jar and took off the lid, leaning it toward me. An amazing scent drifted out. "Want one? I just made them."

I was really regretting not being able to tell Adrian about this. "No thanks, sir. I've had more than enough sugar these last few weeks." I felt like I should have a frequent customer card for Pies and Stuff.

"I thought you looked better. Not all skin and bones anymore." He nodded in approval, which felt really weird and slightly creepy. "So where are you two kids going?"

"Mexi—oh, Adrian's not going with me. I'm going with someone else."

"Really?" He slid the squirrel back across the counter. "I'm surprised. I always figured when you two left here, you went home and had your own private 'training sessions.'"

I felt myself turning bright red. "No! It's not like—I mean, we're just friends, sir."

"I had a friend like that once. Silver Tooth Sally." He got that faraway expression that always came on when he had an anecdote to share.

"I'm sorry, did you say—"

"Never met a woman like Sally," he interrupted. "We fought our way across Switzerland together, always watching each other's backs. We finally got out alive—just barely—and she wanted to come back to the States and settle down. Not me. I had dreams, you see. I was a young man then, drawn to danger and glory. I left her and went off to live with an Orcadian shaman. It took two years and a lot of vision quests to realize my mistake, but when I got back, I couldn't find her. When I close my eye at night, I can still see that tooth sparkle like a star. It haunts me, girl. It haunts me."

I frowned. "I don't think the Orcadians have vision quests, sir. Or shamans."

Wolfe leaned forward and shook a finger at me, his eye wide. "Learn from my mistakes, girl. Don't go to the Orkneys. You don't need some mystical vision to see what's in front of you, you hear me?"

I gulped. "Yes, sir."

I hurried out after that, thinking that being in a different country from Malachi Wolfe might be a good thing.

The next morning, I prepared to tell Jill goodbye, but she beat me to it and showed up at my door. It was the first time we'd truly spoken since the morning after that last dream with Adrian.

She walked into my room and frowned when she saw the suitcase. "You're really going?"

"Yes. And I'm sure you know why."

She crossed her arms and looked me straight in the eye, without any of the reservation she'd shown last time. I had trouble holding that stare. "Sydney, don't leave Adrian because of me."

"It's more complicated than that," I said automatically.

"It's really not," she said. "From everything I've seen and heard, you're just afraid. You've always controlled every detail of your life. When you couldn't—like with the Alchemists—you found a way to seize back that control."

"There's nothing wrong with wanting control," I snapped.

"Except that we can't always have it, and sometimes that's a good thing. A great thing, even," she added. "And that's how it is with Adrian. No matter how hard you try, you aren't going to be able to control your feelings for him. You can't help loving him, and so you're running away. I'm just an excuse."

Who was she to lecture me like this? "You think I'm lying about how awkward it is for you to see everything that happens between us? Every intimate detail is on display. I can't do that. I can't live like that."

"Adrian's learned to."

"Well, he's had to."

"Exactly." Some of her fierceness mellowed. "Sydney, he brought me back from the dead. It's the greatest thing anyone can or will do for me. I can't pay him back, but I can let him live his life the way he wants to. I don't expect him to shelter me because of the bond, and I'm not going to judge him—or you. Someday, he and I will learn to block each other."

"Someday," I reiterated.

"Yes. And until then, we do the best we can. All you're doing by leaving is making three people miserable."

"Three?" I frowned. "I'm helping you."

"Do you really think I'm happy when he's miserable? Do you think I like the darkness that crawls over him?" When I said nothing, she pushed forward. "Look, I don't have the same physical reaction to you that he does, but when he's with you, he's so full of joy . . . it radiates through to me, and it's one of the greatest experiences I've ever had. I've never been in love like you guys are."

"I'm not—" I couldn't say it, and she gave me a knowing look. I tried a different tactic. "Staying here is dangerous, especially with him. The Alchemists might find out about everything—him, my tattoo, Ms. Terwilliger, and God knows what else."

"And if they don't find out, look at what you get. Adrian. The rest of us. Magic. The chance to uncover their secrets. I know you love this life. Why would you give it up? You're too smart to get caught. We'll help you. Do you really think Marcus and his Merry Men can do that much fighting when they're always on the run?"

I shook my head. "They're like me. They understand me."

She was obstinate. "They aren't like you at all. They talk. You act."

It was so surprising to see her like this, so confident and so much wiser than her years. It was also a little irritating. If

she was so wise, w ....
at stake?

"Jill, staying is a bi ....

"Of course it is!" s ...... exclaimed ....
anger. "Any life worth livin .... going to ....
Mexico, you'll regret it—an ....

My phone rang, cutting of ....
He rarely called, and panic seize ....

"What's wrong?" I demanded. ....

He sounded mystified. "I wouldn't .... just
surprising. Is Jill with you? You guys s........ ...ally come down.
We're outside"

He hung up, and I was left totally confused. "What's up?"
asked Jill.

"Something surprising, apparently."

She and I went down to the lobby, with no more mention of
Adrian. When we stepped outside, we found Eddie and Angeline
pointedly avoiding eye contact with each other. Standing near
them was a tall, good-looking guy with neatly trimmed black
hair and bright blue eyes. He wore a stern, serious expression
and was scanning the area.

"He's a dhampir," Jill murmured to me.

His eyes locked onto us at our approach, and that fierce
look relaxed.

"Jill, Sydney," said Eddie. "This is Neil Raymond. He's going
to be joining us here."

Neil swept Jill a bow so low, it was a wonder he didn't hit
the ground. "Princess Jillian," he said in a deep voice. "It's an
honor to serve you, and I'll do so to the best of my abilities, even
if it means sacrificing my own life."

her eyes wide as she took him in.

back and forth between them, a small frown on his face. "Neil's been sent as backup. I guess you some complaint about Jill not having enough protection?" That was to me, and unless I was mistaken, there was an accusatory note in his voice.

"No—I. Oh. I guess I kind of did." When I'd been trying to do damage control with Stanton, one of my grievances had been that I never felt Jill was safe. I guess this was Stanton's response. It was surprising, just as Eddie had said, but more eyes on her couldn't hurt. From the way she was sizing Neil up, she certainly didn't seem to mind either.

I shook his hand. "Nice to have you around, Neil. Are they passing you off as another cousin?"

"Just a new student," he said. That was probably just as well. Our "family" was in danger of taking over Amberwood.

I would've liked to learn a little more about him, but my time was up. Marcus was picking me up soon to go to the train station, seeing as Latte had been declared totaled. I guess that was a different sort of closure, albeit a sad kind.

I told them all goodbye as I left to get my suitcase, acting as though I just had to run an errand. Eddie, Angeline, and Jill knew the truth, and I could see the hurt and regret in their eyes—especially Jill. I prayed they'd be okay without me. When I came back downstairs, I found Jill was the only one still there.

"I forgot to give you this," she said, handing over a small envelope. My name was on the outside, and I recognized the writing.

"I've been trying to get a hold of him and thought he might be avoiding me. This is his goodbye, huh?" I felt disappointed that I wouldn't be able to see Adrian in person one last time. Maybe a letter was better than nothing, but I wished I could have left with those beautiful eyes fresh in my mind. "Is he . . . is he really upset?" I couldn't stand the thought of him hurting.

"Read the letter," she said mysteriously. "And remember, Sydney. This isn't about me. This is about you guys. You can control everything else, but not this. Let go, and accept how you feel."

We left on that note, and I went outside to sit on the curb and wait for Marcus. I stared at the envelope, looking at the way Adrian had written my name. Three times I nearly opened it . . . but chickened out each time. Finally, I saw Marcus drive in, and the envelope disappeared into my purse.

As soon as he picked me up, he began talking excitedly about the big plans ahead. I barely heard. All I kept thinking about was Adrian and how empty my life was going to seem without him. Marcus and I were meeting Wade and Amelia at the train station, but I couldn't picture any of them understanding me like Adrian—even if they were human and shared the same background. None of them would have his dry wit or uncanny insight. And simmering beneath all those emotions were the more heated memories . . . the way we'd kissed, the way it had felt to be wrapped up in him. . . .

"Sydney? Are you even paying attention?"

I blinked and glanced over at Marcus. I think it was another of those moments where he couldn't believe someone wasn't hanging on to his every word. "Sorry," I said. "My mind's somewhere else."

He grinned. "Well, shift it to beaches and margaritas because your life's about to change."

It was always beaches and margaritas with him. "You left out the part about us sealing the tattoo. Unless your tattooist is also a bartender."

"There you go again, funny and beautiful." He laughed. "We're going to have a great time."

"How long will we be down there?"

"Well, we'll take care of the tattoos first. That's the most important thing." I was relieved to see him taking that seriously. "Then we'll lie low, enjoy the sights for a few weeks. After that, we'll come back and follow some leads on other dissatisfied Alchemists."

"And then you'll repeat the process?" I asked. In the rearview mirror, I could see the Palm Springs skyline disappearing as we drove north. I felt a pang of longing in my chest. "Get others to retrieve critical information and then free them?"

"Exactly."

We drove in silence for another minute as I processed his words. "Marcus, what do you do with that information you gather? I mean, what are you going to do about Master Jameson?"

"Keep finding more evidence," he said promptly. "This is the biggest lead we've ever had. Now we can really push forward in finding out more."

"It's more than a lead. Why not leak it to the Moroi?"

"The Alchemists would deny it. Besides, we don't want to be hasty."

"So what if they do deny it?" I demanded. "At least the Moroi will have a heads-up."

He glanced over at me with a look that reminded me of a parent trying to be patient with a child. Ahead of us, I saw a sign for the train station. "Sydney, I know you're eager, but trust me. This is the way we've always done things."

"I don't know that it's the right way, though."

"You have a lot of ideas for someone who just joined up." He chuckled. I wished he'd stop doing that. "Just wait, and then you'll understand."

I didn't like his condescending attitude. "I think I already understand. And you know what? I don't think you guys do anything. I mean, you've uncovered some amazing information . . . but then what? You keep waiting. You run away and skulk around. How is this really helping? Your intentions are good . . . but that's all they are." I could almost hear Jill's voice: *They talk. You act.*

Ironically, Marcus was speechless.

"You could do so much," I continued. "When I first found out about you, you seemed to hold all the potential in the world. Technically, you still do. But it's being wasted." He pulled into the train station's parking lot, still looking utterly stunned.

"Where the hell is this coming from?" he asked at last.

"Me," I said. "Because I'm not like you guys. I can't do nothing. I can't run away. And . . . I can't go with you."

It felt good to say that . . . and it also felt right. All week, my brain had been telling me the right thing to do was to walk away before things with Adrian and the Alchemists blew up. And yes, that probably was the smart thing. My heart had never entirely been on board, but I'd tried to ignore it. It wasn't until I'd listened to both Jill and Marcus that I realized just this once, my brain might have to opt for the less logical solution.

I had to give Marcus credit. He actually looked concerned and wasn't just put out at not getting his way. "Sydney, I know how attached you are to this place and these people, but it's not safe for you here. It's not safe for you anywhere, not as long as the Alchemists are watching. Not as long as your tattoo is vulnerable."

"Someone told me any life worth living has risks," I said, unable to hide a smile. I never thought I'd be quoting Jill.

Marcus slammed his fist against the dashboard. "That's sentimental bullshit! It sounds good in theory, but the reality is completely different."

"What kind of reality could you have created if you'd stayed with the Alchemists?" I asked. "How much could you have uncovered?"

"Nothing if I was caught," he said flatly. "And no matter how useless you think we are, I've freed dozens of Alchemists. I've helped Clarence and other Moroi."

"You aren't useless, Marcus. You do good work, but we're just not on the same path, that's all. I'm staying and doing things my way. Isn't that what you said when we first met? Helping the Moroi on our own terms? These are mine."

"You're wasting your time!"

"It's my time to waste," I said. Adrian had said exactly the same thing to me on the flight to the wedding, when I'd told him he couldn't keep loving me. I felt bad for Marcus. I really did, especially since he'd truly been counting on me to come with him.

He caught hold of my hand. "Sydney, please don't do this," he begged. "No matter how confident you feel, no matter how careful you think you are, things will spiral out of control."

"They already have," I said, opening the passenger door. "And I'm going to stop fighting them. Thank you for everything, Marcus. I mean it."

"Walt, Sydney," he called. "Just tell me one thing."

I glanced back and waited.

"Where did this come from? When you called me to tell me you were coming, you said you'd realized it was the smart thing to do. What made you change your mind?"

I gave him a smile that I hoped was as dazzling as one of his. "I realized I'm in love."

Marcus, startled, looked around as though he expected to see my *objet d'amour* in the car with us. "And you just realized that? Did you just have some sort of vision?"

"Didn't need to," I said, thinking of Wolfe's ill-fated trip to the Orkneys. "It's always been right in front of me."

CHAPTER 25

ONCE MARCUS FINALLY ACCEPTED that I wasn't going, he wished me well, though he still wore that stunned expression. He'd planned on abandoning the car at the station but handed the keys over to me as a parting gift. I watched him walk away and wondered if I'd made a mistake. Then I thought of green, green eyes and all the work Adrian and I had to do together. This was the right choice . . . I just hoped I wasn't too late.

He still wasn't answering my calls. Did he hate me? Or was he holed up somewhere, depressed and drinking away his sorrows? I fished his note out of my purse, wondering what I'd find. Knowing Adrian, I'd expected some long, flowery expression of love. Instead, all I found was a long series of numbers.

The numbers meant nothing to me. I studied them for a while in the car, applying a few common codes I knew. No answer appeared, though I wasn't entirely surprised. Codes and complex mathematics weren't exactly Adrian's style. But then, why had he left the note? Obviously, he assumed I could decipher it.

I held the note far away from me, hoping something visual would reveal itself. It did. As I looked at the numbers again, I saw a natural break in the middle of them, in a format that looked familiar. I entered the two sets of numbers into the latitude and longitude screen of my GPS. A moment later, it turned up an address in Malibu. Southern California. Was that a coincidence?

Without even thinking twice, I pulled out of the train station's parking lot and headed toward the coast. It was entirely possible I was about to waste two and a half hours (five, if you counted the round trip), but I didn't think so. *There are no coincidences.*

It felt like the longest drive of my life. My hands tightly clenched the wheel the entire time. I was eager yet terrified. When I was only a few miles from the address, I began to see signs for the Getty Villa. For a few seconds, I was confused. The Getty Center was a very famous museum, but it was closer to Los Angeles. I didn't understand the connection or why I had ended up in Malibu. Nonetheless, I dutifully followed the directions and ended up in the Villa's guest parking lot.

When I reached the entrance, I received my answers. The Villa was a sister museum to the Getty Center, one that specialized in ancient Greek and Roman art. In fact, a good part of the Getty Villa was set up like some ancient temple, complete with pillars surrounding courtyards filled with gardens, fountains, and statues. Admission was free but required a reservation. Things were slow today, and I quickly rectified the problem by making an online reservation on my phone.

When I stepped inside, I nearly forgot why I was there—but only for a heartbeat. The museum was a dream come true for a lover of classics like me. Room after room focusing on the ancient world. Jewelry, statues, clothes . . . it was as if I'd entered a time machine. The scholar in me longed to study and read about each exhibit in detail. The rest of me, with a racing heart and barely contained excitement, only briefly stopped in each room, just long enough to search and move on.

After looking in almost all the interior areas, I stepped into the outer peristyle. My breath caught. It was a huge outdoor garden built around a pool that had to be at least two hundred feet long. Statues and fountains dotted the pool's surface, and the whole space was surrounded in gorgeously manicured trees and other plants. The sun, warm despite the December day, shone down on everything, and the air hummed with birdsong, splashing water, and soft conversation. Tourists milled around, stopping to admire the sights or take pictures. None of them mattered, though—not when I finally found the person I was looking for.

He sat at the opposite end of the garden from where I'd entered, on the pool's far edge. His back was to me, but I would have known him anywhere. I approached with trepidation, still churning with that odd mix of fear and eagerness. The closer I got, the more detailed his features became. The tall, lean body. The chestnut glints that the sun brought out in his dark hair. When I finally reached the pool's end, I came to a stop just behind him, not daring to go farther.

"Sage," he said, without looking up. "Figured you'd be south of the border by now."

"No, you didn't," I said. "You never would've given me the

note or come all the way out here. You knew I wouldn't leave."

He looked up at me at last, squinting in the bright sun. "I was pretty sure you wouldn't leave. I *hoped* you wouldn't leave. Jill and I debated it forever. What'd you think of my sweet use of latitude and longitude? Pretty brilliant, huh?"

"Genius," I said, trying to hold back my smile. Some of my fear faded. We were back in familiar, easy territory again. Just Adrian and me. "You took a risk I'd know what those numbers meant. You could've been sitting out here all day."

"Nah." Adrian stood up and took a step toward me. "You're a smart girl. I knew you'd figure it out."

"Not that smart." The closer he came, the more my heart began to race again. "It took me a long time to figure some things out." I gestured around us. "And how is it possible that you knew this place existed, but I didn't?"

His fingertips traced the edge of my cheek, and suddenly, the warmth of the sunshine felt like nothing compared to the heat of that touch. "It was easy," he said, holding me in his gaze. "I had to start my search somewhere, so I typed 'ancient Rome' and 'California' into my phone. This was like the first hit."

"What search?" I asked.

He smiled. "The search for some place more romantic than Pies and Stuff."

Adrian tipped my face up toward his and kissed me. Like always, the world around me stopped moving. No, the world became Adrian, only Adrian. Kissing him was as mind-blowing as ever, full of that same passion and need I had never believed I'd feel. But today, there was even more to it. I no longer had any doubt about whether this was wrong or right. It was a culmination of a long journey . . . or maybe the beginning of one.

I wrapped my arms around his neck and pulled him closer. I didn't care that we were out in public. I didn't care that he was Moroi. All that mattered was that he was Adrian, my Adrian. My match. My partner in crime, in the long battle I'd just signed on for to right the wrongs in the Alchemist and Moroi worlds. Maybe Marcus was right that I'd also signed myself up for disaster, but I didn't care. In that moment, it seemed that as long as Adrian and I were together, there was no challenge too great for us.

I don't know how long we stood there kissing. Like I said, the world around me was gone. Time had stopped. I was awash in the feel of Adrian's body against mine, in his scent, and in the taste of his lips. That was all that mattered right now, and I found myself thinking of our unfinished business in the dream.

When we finally broke the kiss—much too soon, as far as I was concerned—we still stayed locked in an embrace. The sound of giggling caused me to glance to the side, where two small children were laughing and pointing at us. Seeing me watching them, they scurried away. I turned back to Adrian, wanting to melt away with happiness as I looked up into his eyes.

"This is a lot better than loving from afar," I told him.

He brushed some hair from my face and gazed into my eyes. "What changed your mind? I mean, I knew you'd never be able to stay away from me, but I won't lie . . . you had me scared there for a little while."

I leaned against his chest. "It was a combination of things, really. Some surprisingly good advice from Jill. One of Wolfe's charming anecdotes—I have to tell you about his kitchen, by the way. Plus, I kept thinking about when we were on the table."

Adrian shifted just enough so that we could look at each

other again. It was one of those rare moments where he was completely floored. "Let me get this straight. The future of our relationship hinged on advice from a fifteen-year old girl, a probably untrue story from a one-eyed Chihuahua trainer, and me unromantically—yet skillfully—kissing you on top of silverware and china?"

"Yup," I said after a few moments of thought.

"That's all it took, huh? And here I thought winning you over was going to be hard." He grew serious again and pressed a light kiss to my forehead. "What happens now?"

"Now we check out this awesome museum you've lured me to. You're going to *love* Etruscan art."

That roguish smile I adored returned. "I'm sure I will. But what about the future? What are we going to do about us—about this?"

I caught hold of his hands, still keeping him close. "Since when are you worried about consequences or the future?"

"Me? Never." He considered. "Well, that is, as long as you're with me, I'm not worried. But I know *you* like to worry about those kinds of things."

"I wouldn't say I 'like' to," I corrected. A soft breeze ruffled his hair, and I resisted the urge to brush it back into place. If I did, I was pretty sure we'd start kissing again, and I supposed I should first be responsible and answer his questions.

"Are we going to run off to the Keepers?" he suggested.

"Of course not," I scoffed. "That'd be cowardly and immature. And you'd never survive without hair gel—though you might like their moonshine."

"Then what are we going to do?"

"We're going to keep all of this secret."

He chuckled. "That's not cowardly?"

"It's exciting and daring," I said. "Manly and brave, even. I figured you'd be into that."

"Sage." He laughed. "I'm into anything, so long as you're with me. But is it going to be enough? I'm not completely oblivious to consequences, you know. I get how dangerous this is for you, especially if you keep questioning the Alchemists. And I also know you're still worried about Jill watching us."

Right. Jill. Jill, who was probably witnessing all of this right now, whether she wanted to or not. Was she happy for his happiness? Was she filled with the joy of our love? Or was this excruciatingly uncomfortable for her?

"The three of us will find a way to cope," I said at last. I couldn't think much more about it right now or I probably would start freaking out. "And as for the Alchemists . . . we'll just have to be careful. They don't follow me everywhere, and like you said, I'm with you half the time anyway." I just hoped that was enough. It *had* to be.

And then the kissing started again. There was no avoiding it, not when we were together like this, far away from the real world of our normal lives. The setting was too perfect. He was too perfect, despite being one of the most imperfect people I knew. And honestly, we'd wasted far too much time with doubts and games. The one thing you learn from constantly having your life in danger is that you'd better not waste it. Even Marcus had admitted that in the arcade.

Adrian and I spent the rest of the day at the Villa, most of it kissing in the gardens, though I did convince him to check out some of the artifacts inside. Maybe I was in love, but I was still me, after all. When things finally closed down for the evening, we had dinner at a beachside fondue restaurant and lingered there for a long time afterward, keeping close to each other and watching the waxing moon shine on the ocean.

I was caught up in watching the crashing waves when I felt Adrian's lips brush my cheek. "Whatever happened to the dragon?"

I mustered my primmest tone. "He has a name, you know."

Adrian pulled back and gave me a curious look. "I didn't know, actually. What'd you decide on?"

"Hopper." When Adrian laughed, I added, "Best rabbit ever. He'd be proud to know his name is being passed on."

"Yes, I'm sure he would. Did you name the Mustang too?"

"I think you mean the Ivashkinator."

He stared at me in wonder. "I told you I loved you, right?"

"Yes," I assured him. "Many times."

"Good." Adrian pulled me closer. "Just making sure, Miss 'I'm a Quick Study.'"

I groaned. "I'm never going to live that down, am I?"

"Live it down? Hell, I'm going to hold you to it."

I suspected Marcus's car was stolen, so we left it in Malibu. Adrian drove me back to the dorm and kissed me goodbye, promising to call me first thing in the morning. It was hard to let him go, even though I knew I was being silly to think I couldn't go without him for twelve hours. I walked into my dorm like I was dancing on air, my lips still burning from his kisses.

It was crazy, I knew, attempting to have a relationship with him. Scratch that. It was going to be perilous—enough so that some of my euphoria dimmed as that realization hit me. I'd talked a good game with him, trying to ease his fears, but I knew the truth. Trying to figure out secrets within the Alchemists was going to be difficult enough, and my tattoo still wasn't secure. What I had going on with Adrian had raised the stakes exponentially, but that was one of those risks I gladly accepted.

"Miss Melrose."

Mrs. Weathers's cool voice snapped me back to reality with a jolt. I came to a halt in the middle of the dorm's lobby and looked over at her. She stood up from her desk and strolled over.

"Yes, ma'am?"

"It's midnight."

I looked at a clock, surprised to see she was right. "Yes, ma'am."

"Even though winter break is here, you're still registered in the dorm until tomorrow, which means you're still subject to the rules. It's after curfew."

The only thing I could manage was stating the obvious. "Yes, it is, ma'am."

Mrs. Weathers waited, as though she were hoping I'd say more. "Were you . . . doing another assignment for Ms. Terwilliger?" There was an almost comically desperate look on her face. "I didn't receive notification, but surely she can retroactively fix things."

I realized then that Mrs. Weathers didn't want me to be in trouble. She was hoping I had some reason for breaking the rules, some reason that I could avoid punishment. I knew I could've lied and said I'd been helping Ms. Terwilliger. I knew Ms. Terwilliger would even back me up. But I couldn't do it. It seemed wrong to taint my day with Adrian with a lie. And really, I *had* broken the rules.

"No," I told Mrs. Weathers. "I wasn't with her. I was just . . . out."

Mrs. Weathers waited a few moments more and then bit her lip with resignation. "Very well then. You know the rules. You'll have to serve a detention—once classes start again."

I nodded solemnly. "Yes, ma'am. I understand."

She looked as though she was still hoping I'd correct the situation. I had nothing to offer her and turned to walk away. "Oh, I nearly forgot!" she called. "I was too astonished by this . . . transgression." She turned back into the efficient dorm matron I knew. "Please let me know if your cousin will be staying with you in your room or if she needs her own."

I blinked in confusion. "Why would Angeline be staying with me?"

"Not her. Your *other* cousin."

I started to say I didn't have another cousin, but some warning voice inside me told me to neither deny nor confirm her words. I had no idea what was going on, but all my alarms were saying that *something* was definitely about to happen. Whatever it was, I needed to keep my options open.

"She had all the appropriate paperwork," explained Mrs. Weathers. "So I just let her into your room since it's only for the night."

I swallowed. "I see. Can I, um, let you know after break?"

"Certainly." After a moment's hesitation, she added, "And we'll discuss your detention then too."

"Yes, ma'am," I said.

I went upstairs, a feeling of dread in the pit of my stomach.

Who was waiting in my room? Who in the world was part of my imaginary family now?

As it turned out, it was someone from my real family.

When I unlocked the door, I found Zoe sitting on my bed.

Her face lit up when she saw me, and she sprang forward to grab me in a fierce embrace.

"Sydney!" she exclaimed. "I was so worried you weren't coming back tonight."

"Of course I was," I said stiffly. I was so shocked that I could barely return her hug. "What are you doing here?"

She pulled back and looked up at me with a big grin. There was no anger in her, not even the wariness she'd had in St. Louis. She was full of joy, truly happy to see me. I didn't know why she was here, but hope began to blossom within me that we'd finally get our reconciliation.

Until she spoke.

"They gave me a field position! I'm assigned here." She turned her face, showing me a golden lily tattoo on her cheek. My heart nearly stopped. "I'm officially an Alchemist now. Well, a junior one. I've got a lot to learn, so they thought it'd be best if I was with you."

"I see," I said. The room was spinning. Zoe. Zoe was here— and she was an Alchemist, one who would be staying with me.

Her exuberant expression became a little perplexed. "And I guess you were telling Stanton something about needing Alchemist backup? That it was really hard being around so many Moroi by yourself?"

I tried to smile but couldn't. "Something like that." I'd urged Stanton to take action, and she had. It just wasn't the kind I'd expected.

Zoe's enthusiasm returned. "Well, you aren't alone now. I'm here for you, not that you probably even need me. You don't ever get into any trouble."

No, I just had a romance going on with a vampire, was on

the verge of joining a coven, and was investigating secrets no one wanted me to know about. No trouble at all.

How in the world was I going to hide all that from her?

Zoe hugged me again. "Oh, Sydney! This is going to be great," she exclaimed. "We're going to be together all the time!"

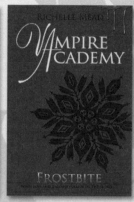

ROSE
OR
LISSA?

WHICH ARE YOU?

Take this fun quiz to see if you pack
a Dhampir punch or you'd be more
at home as Queen of the Moroi pack!

Your favourite outfit is:

a) combats and a tight tee – it's all about
the attitude!
b) always a skirt or dress – you like to
look pretty.

Your favourite film is:

a) *Kill Bill.*
b) *The Princess Diaries.*

Your perfect boy is:

a) dark, brooding and would protect you against
anything and everything.
b) cool, witty and totally gets you.

Given the choice for extra-curricular classes, which of these would you choose?

a) Self-defence Masterclass: how to
make eyes at your dreamy instructor
b) Magic and Wizardry: how to unlock
your true destiny

**You're on the dancefloor
with your best mates when
a boy grabs you and tries some
of his own sort of dance moves
– a complete lack of regard for
your personal space. You . . .**

a) punch him in the nose.
b) feel a little bit upset to begin with
but then turn around and walk away.
He isn't worth your attention.

Your favourite band is:

a) Linkin Park – although they were
better before everyone knew them.
b) Backstreet Boys
– swooooooooooooooooooon!

If you answered mostly As:
Dimitri is in for a lot of trouble with a Rose mark 2 on
his hands.
If you answered mostly Bs:
It sounds like you've got royal blood coursing through
your veins like Lissa.

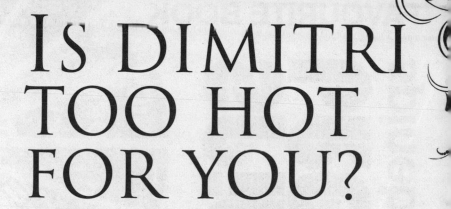